The Right Time

Dianne Blacklock

The Right Time

EPUB format: 9781925579680
Print on Demand format: 9781925579697

Cover design by Red Tally Studios

Publishing services provided by Critical Mass
www.critmassconsulting.com

Dianne Blacklock has been a teacher, trainer, counsellor, check-out chick, and even one of those annoying market researchers you avoid in shopping malls. Nowadays she tries not to annoy anyone by staying home and writing.

Also by Dianne Blacklock

Call Waiting
Wife for Hire
Almost Perfect
False Advertising
Crossing Paths
Three's a Crowd
The Secret Ingredient
The Best Man

To my family

Ellen

'Oh not just yet, thanks, I'm waiting for my sisters,' Ellen told the waitress who had come to take her order.

It occurred to Ellen that she had spent a good deal of her life waiting for her sisters. As the eldest she supposed that was her lot in life. Waiting for them to be born, waiting for them to start walking, talking, *relating*. Waiting for them to start school . . .

Then waiting for them to get ready for school every morning. By the time Evie started, Eddie was on his way, so the task of getting the girls ready and out the door fell squarely onto Ellen. Emma was the worst, preening herself in the bathroom for ages, even in primary school. And Liz was just perennially disorganised. She could never find her hockey stick, her flute, her debating notes . . . She did so many extracurricular activities their mum was always threatening to make her quit something. Only that was never going to happen. Liz was far too bright for their ordinary little public school, but their parents didn't believe in private or selective schooling, so the best way to deal with their prodigy was to keep her busy.

It wasn't so bad being the eldest though. Ellen knew people who complained about being the so-called test case for their parents – they were harder on the eldest, the younger ones got to do things sooner, you had to pave the way. But Ellen didn't mind all that. Her parents hadn't been so hard on her, and she was well aware of the privileges that came with her position. Not only was she held in her parents' confidence, she enjoyed a level of rapport with them that the younger ones were not likely to experience, and there had never been any shortage of attention. Even after her siblings had come along vying for their share, Ellen had always been the first to do everything. She'd always had the most photos taken, always had both her parents there in the audience on presentation day at primary school, right through to graduation day at uni. By the time Liz had started scooping the prize pool, Ellen hadn't felt any rivalry at all; in fact, from her lofty position she'd even been generous with praise. Her sister's considerable achievements hadn't detracted from the fact Ellen had still been racking up firsts – graduating from high school, attending her formal (which, incidentally, was the first thing to get Emma's attention), and starting university.

She had also been the first to get married and have a baby, though unfortunately not in the customary order. Ellen had not graduated before the wedding, and while the ceremony did come first chronologically, five months later she had presented her parents with their first granddaughter, and a couple of years later, their first grandson.

Emma was still waiting for Blake to propose, but Ellen certainly wasn't holding her breath. Liz was patiently waiting for the ever elusive day when Andrew would leave his wife, but Ellen wouldn't hold her breath for that either. So it was Evie who had been next to follow Ellen down the aisle, marrying her childhood sweetheart when she was barely out of childhood herself. And although she started popping out babies straightaway, it still meant that Ellen's two didn't have cousins until they were in primary school.

The mere thought of her children now brought back the pain. She hadn't expected it to be so physical, it felt like she'd pulled a muscle in her chest. This week had been the hardest week of her life, Ellen was sure nothing came close. Not even when Kate had had her first bout of croup and Ellen had been convinced she was going to choke to death right there in her arms. Or when Sam had fallen through a glass door and needed sixteen stitches. Since they were born, Ellen's every waking moment had been about protecting them from harm, or sadness, or distress. Of course she'd learned pretty quickly that this was impossible, but at least she could buffer it. Being the cause of it was something she had never imagined possible.

Now Ellen had to break it to everyone else. Over and over. She thought she'd prepared herself, but in some ways telling people felt harder than actually going through with it. She wished she could just release a statement like a celebrity or a politician, and then leave everyone to gossip among themselves, construct their theories and form their own version of what happened. That's what they were going to do anyway, no matter what Ellen told them. But still she had to go through that process of telling them. Over and over.

So that was why, after her children, her sisters were going to be the first to hear the news. Whatever they thought in the privacy of their own minds, they'd still be her best advocates, they'd be on her side. Even Emma, in her own way.

Evie was first to arrive at the café, Ellen spotted her flushed but smiling face searching for her through the front window. While the other sisters had remained firmly anchored to the inner west suburbs of Sydney, Evie's husband, Craig, felt no such attachment. He was not about to live in a 'pokey old house', so after they married they had moved out past Parramatta to what had been a new subdivison at the time. So even though she had the furthest to come and three kids to organise, along with a husband who wasn't much better, Evie was on time. She would have been up at the crack of dawn, thrown on a load of washing, dropped Jayden to cricket and arranged for someone to bring him home, organised Tayla's activities – though, being January, Ellen supposed dance classes and the like were suspended, but for a ten year old that kid had a busier social life than most adults. That would leave only four-year-old Cody for Craig to 'look after'. Evie had probably made separate lunches for everyone the night before – something special, because she'd be feeling guilty about going out and leaving them all for a few hours on a weekend. She would have done her utmost to ensure nothing would be a hassle for Craig, and if she'd had any inkling that it was likely to be, she would have made arrangements for his mother to come over to 'help' or, in other words, take over for the day.

Evie's smile broadened when she caught sight of her sister, and she waved excitedly. Ellen watched her as she bustled through the door, pink-faced and breathless, and then proceeded to bustle in and around the tables and chairs towards her. Evie was a bustler – she never simply walked, she always kind of trotted everywhere, always on the go. Despite this she had never really lost her puppy fat, except for a brief period in her teens, the result of some crazy unsustainable diet, the kind that only self-loathing adolescents and supermodels would be desperate enough to undertake. That was around the time she started going out with Craig, from the nearby boys' school. They became engaged when Evie was in her final year of a childcare diploma at TAFE, and married six months later. Evie started eating again at the reception, and thus began her grand obsession with food. Her life was ruled by one overriding philosophical question – to eat or not to eat – and she spent her days counting calories, grams of fat or carbohydrates, or whatever was the unit of measurement du jour.

She bustled over to the table, squeezing past chairs, apologising profusely to anyone who made eye contact with her.

'Hi,' she beamed, lurching at Ellen to hug her. 'It's so good to see you! I was thinking the whole way here that we really don't see enough of each other,' she added, pulling back to look at her sister. 'I know we're all busy, and we don't live so close now, but we really ought to make an effort to get together more often.'

Ellen smiled. 'We should.'

They took their seats and Evie rooted around in her bag, finally retrieving her phone.

'Do you need to call home?' asked Ellen.

Evie shook her head as she glanced at the screen. 'No, just checking for messages. I don't need to call, Craig's mum's over for the day. I figured that way I don't have to worry. And she loves to do it.' She popped her phone back in her bag. 'Did you see the cakes as you walked in? They look absolutely delicious!' she squealed with delight. 'I know I shouldn't, but what the hell, I'm having lunch with my sisters, and that's a special occasion, so I'm going to treat myself. If I have a salad without any dressing, and maybe just a bit of lean chicken, it won't be so bad. And I'll only have something light for dinner tonight.'

Just then Emma came into view, gliding past the front window, her filmy scarf floating on the breeze behind her, big dark glasses shielding her eyes so you couldn't tell for sure if she was looking at her reflection in the glass. But Ellen knew she most likely was. She entered the café much as a celebrity might walk into a social function, posed, ready for the cameras. Ellen loved her sister, she loved all of her sisters, but sometimes it felt as though she and Emma had been raised in different families, even on different planets. The things that mattered so terribly to Emma were of little or no interest to Ellen, and Emma was well aware of it. Ellen did make an effort to take an interest, sometimes, when she could, but Emma always seemed to be on the defensive with her, and Ellen didn't know what she could do about that.

Evie jumped to her feet as Emma marched over to the table in a cloud of scent.

'Hi Em, isn't this great!' Evie exclaimed. 'I was just saying to Ellen that we don't see each –'

'So Liz hasn't turned up yet,' Emma interrupted, leaning her cheek in Evie's direction to receive her kiss while her eyes remained trained on Ellen. 'I've rushed the entire morning to make it here on time, and now we're going to have to wait around for Liz. As – per – usual.'

'I'm not sure if she had appointments this morning . . .' Ellen offered by way of excuse.

Emma shook her head as she sat down. 'I had appointments too, and I still managed to be on time.' She sighed theatrically. 'This had better be important, Ellen, Saturdays are my only day for catching up on everything. I had to be at the gym at five thirty so I could fit everything in. It was just as well I had my colour done last week so today was only a short appointment at the hairdressers, because my light therapy was scheduled for this morning and I simply cannot miss that. It's not an option.'

'Light therapy?' asked Evie, frowning. 'Are you depressed, Em?'

'No of course I'm not depressed, Evie. Why would you say that?'

'It's just that I've heard light therapy is used –'

'I'm talking about "photo-biostimulation".'

Evie blinked. 'Huh?'

'It's the very latest skin therapy,' Emma explained. 'And it's incredible. It's like a facelift, except it's totally painless and noninvasive. I'm telling you, it's better than plastic surgery.'

'How does it work?' Ellen was trying to sound interested, but she feared her inner cynic was showing.

'It's a machine,' Emma began, 'which uses different wavelengths of LED light to penetrate deep into the tissue of your skin.'

'What's LED?' asked Evie.

'We got some LED Christmas lights last year,' Ellen offered.

Emma ignored that. 'It stands for light-emitting . . . something.'

'Diodes,' said Ellen. 'I think that's the term,' she added apologetically when Emma looked annoyed.

Evie bit her lip. 'Is it safe? It's not like a sun bed, is it?'

'Sun beds are perfectly safe,' Emma dismissed. 'You shouldn't listen to all the scare-mongering, Evie.'

'People have died, Em,' Ellen pointed out.

'People have died driving cars, but no one's suggesting banning them.'

That was typical Emma logic.

'Honestly, we're living in such a nanny state these days,' she went on. 'We can't turn around without a regulation telling us in which direction. Adults should be left to make their own decisions about what they do to their own bodies.'

This from someone who made a living telling people exactly what to do with their bodies, their hair, clothes, makeup . . .

'Anyway, Evie,' Emma continued, 'light therapy isn't like a sun bed at all. It's not about getting a tan, it works from the inside out.'

'What's the point of that?' Evie frowned.

This'll be good.

'It stimulates natural cellular regeneration and repair.'

'Oh . . .' Evie looked more confused now. 'How does it do that?'

'I don't know, I'm not an expert,' said Emma. 'But the results speak for themselves, wouldn't you say?'

They both gazed blankly at her.

'My facial tissue and muscle tone have improved out of sight. See how fresh my skin looks?' Emma held her face up to them and they drew closer.

'Mm,' Evie murmured appreciatively, though Ellen knew she was only agreeing with Emma for the sake of it. Evie always tried so desperately to please.

'And fine lines, well, you can hardly see them anymore,' said Emma.

'You mean those ones around your eyes?' Evie asked guilelessly.

'But you have to look closely to even see them now, don't you?' Emma insisted.

'It's true, they're very faint.'

Emma nodded, sitting back. 'What did I tell you? Incredible. But the thing about it is you have to stick to the program for it to work. It's scientifically designed, and you can't fool science.'

But you can fool some of the people some of the time.

Emma glanced at her watch. 'I wonder how long we're going to have to wait for Liz? I really don't know why we had to do this today, Ellen. If it's about the anniversary party next weekend, you realise there is such a thing as email. Or even the phone. Besides, I thought we were pretty well organised, aren't we?'

'Well, I know I am,' Evie piped up. 'I've made five dozen mini quiches already, because they freeze really well. And I've planned my week for the rest. I'll start Wednesday with the spicy meatballs, and Thursday I can do the cheese puffs.'

'Evie, you do realise it's being catered?' Emma said. 'I wouldn't overdo it.'

'I won't, I'm only making my specialties. I've set aside the whole of Friday for the cake.'

'What cake?' asked Emma.

'You know,' she smiled coyly, '*the* cake.'

'You're not doing *the* cake, Evie. We discussed this.'

'I don't remember . . .' she faltered. 'What are you saying?'

'You're not doing *the* cake,' Emma repeated. 'Come on, Evie, this is not one of the kids' birthday parties.'

'No, it's Mum and Dad's anniversary,' said Ellen. 'And I think they would love one of Evie's cakes.'

Emma groaned. 'We discussed this.'

'I don't remember discussing it,' said Ellen. Evie was shaking her head in solidarity.

'We may not have discussed it in person,' Emma maintained, 'but I'll have it on file.'

Now Ellen groaned.

'I've been sending updates regularly, it's not my fault if you girls don't read your emails,' Emma said curtly. 'Anyway, it's a moot point, I've already paid a two hundred dollar deposit to the patisserie –'

'The *deposit* is two hundred dollars?' Ellen gasped. She felt sick. They had agreed to go ahead with all the arrangements and work out the money afterwards. She realised Emma didn't know how radically her circumstances were about to change, but Ellen should have known that Emma would overdo things. She should have suggested a budget.

'Oh chill, Ellen,' Emma was saying. 'The deposit was more than half, it's only another hundred and fifty.'

Evie looked stunned. 'The cake cost three hundred and fifty dollars?'

'Congratulations, you can add up,' said Emma. 'Look, would everyone just get over this? You obviously have no idea how much an "event" cake costs these days – and I got a sizeable discount. I've used this particular patisserie before, given them lots of publicity, they were bending over backwards for me. Wait till you see what they're going to do, it's sensational.'

'It'd want to be,' Ellen muttered. 'It'd want to have Ryan Gosling jumping out of it for that kind of money.'

Evie stifled a giggle.

'Oh, yeah right,' said Emma, rolling her eyes. 'Ryan Gosling is going to jump out of a cake for three hundred and fifty dollars.'

'Is he?' said Liz coming up behind them.

Evie jumped to her feet. 'Liz, we didn't see you come in!' she exclaimed, hugging her sister.

'Where have you been?' Emma accused darkly, as Liz bent to kiss her on the cheek. 'God, you look awful, have you just got out of bed?'

Liz gave Ellen a wink as she dropped into a chair. 'Yeah, I have actually,' she said. 'And I need caffeine desperately,' she added, looking around for a waiter.

'Well, that's just great,' said Emma. 'You've been home having a nice sleep-in while we all rushed around to make it here on time.'

'I was up all night at the hospital,' Liz said. 'I got home about seven this morning and thought I could fit in a few hours' sleep. Sorry, I forgot to set an alarm.'

'What kind of dermatological emergency has you at the hospital all night?' Emma sniffed.

'Skin cancer,' she said bluntly. 'A longstanding patient of mine. She's been in the care of an oncologist, of course, but her family called me last night. She died at three this morning. She was only thirty, had two little boys . . .'

'Oh,' Evie sighed, reaching over to touch her arm. 'Are you okay, Lizzie?'

She nodded. 'I will be once I get some caffeine.'

Ellen raised her hand to attract the attention of the waiter. Liz wouldn't want them all fussing over her. She probably wouldn't have mentioned it at all if not for Emma's carry-on. At least it had silenced her, for now.

When the waiter arrived at their table, it seemed practical to order their food as well. Ellen wasn't really hungry, her stomach felt like jelly, but she ordered a sandwich so as not to draw attention. She didn't know why. She was about to draw so much attention that what she ate was hardly going to be noticed.

The waiter left and Emma and Evie settled back in their seats, with a vague air of anticipation. Ellen met Liz's eyes. She knew. She'd known what had been going on for some time now, and while Ellen hadn't had the chance to talk to her recently, she could tell Liz knew what was coming. And she was glad for that.

'So, okay, what else about the party do we need to go over?' asked Emma.

'I'm a little worried about final numbers,' said Evie. 'There's been hardly any RSVPs.'

'Girls,' Ellen broke in suddenly. She couldn't stand it anymore. 'I didn't ask you here today to talk about the party.' She was surprised by the sense of foreboding in her own voice.

'What is it, Ellen?' Evie asked nervously.

She didn't know why this was so hard, they were her sisters. They loved her.

The problem was saying it out loud. This thing that had hung over her for years was finally going to be out in the open. It should have felt liberating, but in fact it felt a little terrifying.

'Ellen?' Emma prompted.

She stirred. She wondered how long she'd been sitting with her mouth slightly open, poised to speak.

She cleared her throat. 'I'm just going to say it, okay? Tim and I are separating.'

'What?'

That was Emma. Evie just looked baffled. Liz sat forward, slipping her hand over Ellen's.

'I don't understand,' said Evie.

'You're separating. You and Tim. You've got some issues you're working through, you're getting counselling,' Emma rattled off, as though she was going through a checklist of facts. 'This is one of those trial things.'

Ellen blinked. 'No . . . no, it's not a trial. It's for real.'

'So you're getting a divorce?'

Evie gasped audibly.

'No.'

'So you might get back together?' Emma persisted.

'We're not getting back together.'

'But you're not getting a divorce?'

'God, I don't know, Emma,' Ellen groaned. 'I haven't thought that far yet.'

'Well, I'm just saying, this seems to have come out of the blue, yet you're so certain it's for real, but at the same time you're saying no divorce.'

'I'm not saying anything, Emma,' Ellen almost snapped. 'Only that we've separated. Can we take one thing at a time?'

Emma shrugged. 'I'm just trying to make sense of it.'

'Then why don't you drop the inquisition and give her a chance to explain?' Liz suggested.

'Fine.' Emma sat back again, folding her arms.

'What happened, Lenny?' said Evie in a small voice, her eyes wide. 'Is there . . . is there someone else?'

'Come on,' Emma sniggered, 'we are talking about Tim.' Then her eyes narrowed. 'Or is it you . . . Are you having an affair, Ellen?'

'No,' she insisted. 'There's no one else involved. No one did anything wrong. We just . . . fell out of love.'

'What, just like that?' Evie asked, tears welling in her eyes. 'This is so sudden.'

'But that's the thing, Evie, it's not sudden at all,' Ellen started to explain. 'This has actually been coming for a long time.'

Evie was shaking her head, bewildered. 'I don't understand. You two have the most amazing, solid marriage.'

'Apparently not,' Emma muttered.

'You're like . . . the model couple.'

'Again – not so much.'

Liz looked at Emma. 'Do you think that's helpful?'

Emma shrugged. 'I don't know. I don't understand any of this.' She stared at Ellen. 'It seems to me that basically you've been putting on an act . . . for how long?'

Sam had said something like that. 'So our whole lives, it's all been a lie?' he'd asked. It had felt like a kick in the guts.

'It wasn't an act,' Ellen defended. 'We stayed together for the kids. Lots of people do that. But you can't tell everyone that's what you're doing, that would pretty much defeat the purpose. Besides, we were still a family, just because Tim and I were no longer a couple didn't mean we couldn't function as a family. We wanted to wait for the right time, when it would have the least impact on Sam and Kate.'

'And this is the right time?' said Emma, raising an eyebrow.

'Well, as close as we can get. Kate's finished her final exams now, and Sam's only just starting his senior years. I guess the most ideal time would have been to wait till he finished as well, but that's another two years away and we weren't prepared to do that.'

'Things were that bad?' said Evie.

'No, we don't hate each other or anything,' Ellen assured her. 'Actually, once we sorted out how we felt, and accepted the fact it wasn't going to last forever, we were quite civil to one another. We had nothing to fight about anymore –'

'You and Tim fight?' Evie exclaimed.

'Of course we do. Or we used to – when we had expectations of each other. When we stopped having those, we got on like polite housemates, courteous, respectful . . .'

'Were you having sex?' Emma asked.

'Emma!' said Liz.

'What?'

'I don't think that's any of our business.'

'I'm only trying to understand all this. She's saying they were like polite housemates. I don't know many polite housemates who share a bed.'

'We weren't having sex,' Ellen said bluntly.

Emma frowned. 'So how long has this been going on?'

'About five years,' said Ellen.

'You've gone five years without sex?'

There had been sex occasionally, when she'd had too much to drink, when she just wanted to be close to someone. But afterwards it always made her feel guilty, and even a little queasy, like over-indulging in junk food – all calories and artificial additives, no nutritional value.

'Five years ago was when we started counselling anyway,' Ellen explained.

'You had marriage counselling?' said Emma.

'Of course we did. Do you think we'd get to this point without doing everything we could?'

'How should I know? You got to this point shrouded in secrecy,' she retorted.

Ellen sighed. 'I told you, Em, it was for the sake of the kids.'

'Still, I don't understand how you could be going through all that and manage to keep it a secret. Didn't you need to talk about it to someone?'

Ellen and Liz exchanged a furtive glance.

'What?' said Emma, her eyes narrowing. 'You knew, didn't you, Liz?' she accused.

'Did you?' Evie blinked.

'Why did you tell Liz and not us?' Emma demanded.

'I didn't plan it,' said Ellen. 'It just came out one night, when we were having a few drinks.'

'It just came out?' Emma said dubiously.

'I was complaining about how the world is designed for couples,' Liz explained. 'And that you don't fit in if you're not part of a couple and that's why so many unhappy couples stay together . . . and . . .'

'. . . and, well,' said Ellen, taking up the story, because Emma was not giving any indication of letting them off the hook, 'it just came out. I told her that Tim and I were one of those unhappy couples, but we weren't going to stick it out forever.'

Emma frowned. 'How long ago was this?'

Ellen glanced at Liz. 'I don't know. Last year?'

Liz shrugged. 'Something like that.'

'So she's known all this time and you didn't think you could trust us with it?'

'It's not that,' said Ellen. 'I just felt that it wasn't right for too many people to know before Kate and Sam were told. What if something were to slip?'

'So you didn't trust us.'

'For Chrissakes, Emma!' Liz broke in. 'This isn't about you. Or me, for that matter. It's about Ellen. Are you going to withhold your support because she didn't tell you first?'

'Of course not.'

'Then can we talk about what's important here?' said Liz. 'Like how Ellen is coping, what she needs from us?'

Evie nodded. 'You're right, Liz. What can we do, Lenny? How can we help?'

'I'm okay, really,' she said. 'It's a completely amicable arrangement, and I've had a long time to get used to the idea.' She paused. 'I just wanted to tell you before I tell Mum and Dad.'

'So they don't know yet?' said Evie.

'No, you are the first to know, after Kate and Sam.'

'And Liz,' Emma muttered.

'Let it go, Emma!' Liz groaned.

The waiter arrived with their coffees and they sat in silent contemplation as she distributed them.

'So when do you plan to tell Mum and Dad?' Emma asked, stirring her coffee.

'I'm going round there tomorrow.'

She looked up abruptly. 'You're telling them before the party?'

'No, I'm telling them tomorrow,' Ellen reiterated. 'The party's next weekend.'

'I mean, you don't think you should leave it until *after* the party?' said Emma.

Oh, what now? 'Why do you say that, Emma?'

'This is their fortieth wedding anniversary. I think they deserve to celebrate it without the dark cloud of their daughter's broken marriage hanging over it.'

Liz sighed loudly. 'That's a little melodramatic, don't you think, Em?'

'No, I don't,' she said. 'I think it could ruin it for them.'

'Look,' said Ellen, 'I told you it's all completely amicable. We're not going to make it uncomfortable for everyone, so no one has to feel uncomfortable around us.'

'Tim's coming to the party?' asked Emma.

'Yes, he'll come.'

'Then who's going to know the difference?' she persisted.

Ellen hesitated. 'Well, what about the kids? Are they supposed to act like nothing's happened? Lie to their grandparents?'

'Why would they have to lie?' said Emma. 'It's not going to be a topic of discussion if you don't say anything beforehand. And Tim'll be there, so everything will be as normal. I think for the sake of Mum and Dad you could leave telling them till the week after.'

'Tim will call in to the party,' said Ellen, 'but he won't stay the whole time.'

'Why not?'

She shrugged. 'Because . . . that'd be weird.'

Emma groaned. 'That's what you think is weird?'

'Stop!'

Everyone turned to look at Evie. Her eyes were glassy and her face was flushed pink.

'This is a marriage we're talking about,' she said, her voice wavering. 'This is eighteen years and two children. It deserves some respect, not all this bickering.'

'Here we are, sorry for the delay,' the waiter chirped arriving at their table, her arms laden with plates.

Ellen sighed inwardly. Evie was right, she had hoped for compassion and understanding from her sisters, not sniping and bickering. No wonder she dreaded telling everyone else.

'I can't eat this salad,' said Evie with a sigh.

'Do you want to order something else?' Ellen asked her.

She cast a furtive glance around the table. 'Cake,' she said. 'I feel like a great big piece of chocolate fudge cake.'

'Evie,' Emma scolded.

'Actually,' said Liz, 'I feel like cake too.'

'Honestly . . .'

'Good idea, we'll all have cake,' said Ellen, beckoning the waiter.

Emma

Emma flatly refused to eat cake for lunch. The others indulged Evie, just as they always had. It was getting a little ridiculous now that she was a grown woman in her thirties.

The heels of Emma's designer shoes clicked on the footpath as she walked back to her car and opened the door, sliding elegantly into the driver's seat. As she settled back into the leather upholstery, she took a long, deep breath. Well, what do you know.

Emma had never expected this, not in a million years. Hadn't seen it coming at all, and she usually had a bit of a nose for these things. Ellen and Tim, the stable, 'model' married couple, with the 'model' children, now apparently embarking on the 'model' separation. Ellen's separation couldn't be like everyone else's – messy and nasty and painful. God, she had always been so tiresome, dolling out relationship advice to all of them, whether they asked for it or not.

'Well, Tim and I always talk *about these things, we think that it's vital to keep the lines of communication open.'*

So much for that.

'Tim's always helped around the house, without being asked. It's never been an issue.'

But clearly there were issues.

When Evie had had kids it had got even worse, Ellen became the final authority on child-rearing. Whether it was constipation, circumcision or sleeping habits, she knew the right way, and there was no other way. She was like a born-again Christian.

So of course now she was going to have the exemplary separation. Amicable. Ha! Emma would be interested to see just how amicable things were in a year's time, when money was tight and they were haggling over care of the kids, when Tim started seeing someone.

But he wouldn't, would he? Tim was just so . . . insubstantial. Emma had known him for twenty years, but she didn't *know* him. She couldn't say what he thought about anything, what his opinions were, if he even had any. He was just a pleasant, agreeable, accommodating man. A good father and 'provider', he had worked in a safe government job all his life; clearly he didn't have an ambitious bone in his body. He laughed at other people's jokes but rarely made any of his own, always showed polite interest in the conversations around him but never had anything of note to contribute. He did whatever Ellen told him to do without fuss. Had he simply bored her to death in the end?

No, according to Ellen this was mutual – they'd come to the decision together, neither was to blame, she wasn't kicking him out and he wasn't leaving her. They had just grown apart. True to form, Ellen intended to conceal the cracks even while her marriage was publicly collapsing. It was exactly like when she fell pregnant in her first year at uni. Somehow she managed to spin it so there wasn't the faintest whiff of indiscretion about it. She and Tim had already talked about getting married, and when they did marry they wanted to start a family as soon as possible, she'd maintained. So this was just a little ahead of schedule.

Hmm, ahead of a wedding, a place to live, a job that could support them. But Ellen didn't make mistakes. Occasionally she might get the timing wrong, but she never *did* anything wrong, and she certainly never failed.

Well, her marriage had failed. Like it or lump it. Whether the separation was going to be amicable or otherwise, Ellen's marriage had failed.

No wonder she'd been so secretive. Though of course she'd told Liz. And what were they doing having drinks together anyway? Emma didn't remember being asked out for drinks any time and not being available to join them. So that meant they hadn't asked her. Of course if she'd said that out loud, Liz would have made another 'It's not about you' crack. All right when you're on the inside. Liz seemed to be everybody's confidante. She was the only one Eddie would talk to about anything. Evie probably went to her as well. Though she couldn't imagine Evie had any deep dark secrets. But Emma had always had her suspicions about Ellen. She always sounded . . . rehearsed or something. Everything couldn't have been as perfect as she'd made out. And clearly it hadn't been.

Emma wondered how their parents would take the news. She couldn't help but see this as yet another episode that would place Ellen firmly on the centre stage as they rallied their support around her.

Of course Ellen needed their support, Emma wasn't begrudging her that. But here in the privacy of her car, all alone, she felt the familiar stirrings of jealousy and resentment. Sandwiched between the eldest and the freakishly intelligent, Emma had done nothing to distinguish herself in the eyes of her family. Evie had never done anything particularly distinguishing but she was the baby – at least until Eddie came along more than five years later – so she didn't have to. Throughout her childhood Emma tried to explore her talents and her strengths, just as her parents encouraged, but her mother wasn't interested in the same things, and her father barely even noticed her, beyond that she was pretty. It was little wonder she didn't score prominent roles in any of her dance concerts. Her mother never offered to work on the costumes, or help backstage for the actual performance; she rarely even made it to regular classes. Emma used to watch all the other mothers, lined up along the wooden bench at the back of the church hall, tapping their feet in time with their daughters, humming the tunes, knowing the routines off by heart.

'And how many of those mothers have five children?' her mother would respond whenever Emma mentioned it.

But somehow she managed to make it to Ellen's debating competitions – 'They're Friday nights' – and Liz's rowing training – 'That's at five in the morning, I'm there and back before anyone's even out of bed.'

Despite the excuses, Emma knew her particular talents were just not valued by her family. Her eye for fashion, her flair with makeup and hair, her innate sense of style, were all considered trivial. And even though those skills had eventually got her to where she was today – a highly sought-after stylist and image consultant – her parents still didn't take her seriously. She had tried to get them to come along to magazine shoots in the past, thinking they might be impressed once they saw the kind of power she wielded, but they always maintained they'd only be in the way. They'd nod and smile when she'd show them the resultant fashion spreads, or drop names of the celebrities she'd worked with, but Emma knew they thought it was essentially trivial. She'd even taken on a couple of politicians as clients, but that only seemed to make them uncomfortable.

The only aspect of her life they did seem to take an interest in was when Blake was going to 'do the right thing' and marry her. Like it was all up to him! Emma would insist it wasn't a priority right now, they were both just too busy. They would come back with, 'Your sisters have both managed to get married.'

'Liz hasn't.'

'Liz is a *specialist*!' one of them would always respond, as though that was an excuse for everything. Whenever Liz was late, or forgot it was someone's birthday, or even forgot to show up at all, they would nod in that knowing, smug, frankly infuriating way, and say, 'She is a *specialist*, after all.'

'Eddie's not married,' Emma tried on occasion.

'Eddie is only in his twenties. He's still sowing his wild oats.'

For parents who claimed they were not conservative, Emma found their obsession with her tying the knot a little out of character. And she said as much.

'It's only because we know how important it is to you, Emma,' her mother had insisted. 'You've been planning your wedding since you were a little girl, it was all you ever talked about for a while there. You used to drive us mad.'

It was true. Everybody was well aware of Emma's obsession with weddings, it wasn't like she kept it to herself, although now she wished she had. Her very first job was working for a wedding planner, it was like putting a kid in a candy store.

She started collecting swatches of fabric, and samples of stationery, and brochures of venues, caterers, car hire places, anything and everything related to weddings, until she had accumulated several bulging folders. But she was a starry-eyed eighteen year old at the time. Nonetheless, she still adored doing wedding issues for magazines, though she kept that fact to herself these days. When Blake hadn't proposed after a few years, she'd had to start acting as though she didn't care any more. Not that anyone had fallen for it.

'Now you and Blake have bought a place together,' her mother continued, 'and you *seem* so settled, it just begs the question, why *won't* he marry you?'

The whole thing was demeaning. Did they think Blake actually didn't want to marry her, that he was just holding off till someone better came along? It wasn't as if Emma hadn't thought of any of that herself, but Blake always insisted it was no such thing. They'd probably marry one day, maybe if they had kids, though that was another sizeable 'if'. He just felt there were far better things to spend all that money on, not to mention the time and effort. And the hassle – he wasn't even all that close to his family, so why invite a whole bunch of people he didn't like to witness them taking part in an outdated convention he didn't believe in?

'We're happy as we are, aren't we?' was Blake's frequent mantra. 'What difference is a piece of paper going to make?'

Well, thought Emma, it might just make all the difference in the world right now.

*

Blake was in the shower when Emma let herself into the apartment, she could hear the water running. He had probably been for a run, or maybe it was racquetball today. She tossed her keys into the bowl on the hall table and walked through the living room, pausing to take in the view of Sydney Harbour. They had bought their Pyrmont apartment off the plan before the area had really taken off. Blake was in property development, so it had given them an inside edge. Now of course everyone wanted to live here.

The apartment had been superbly fitted out, with stainless steel European appliances in the kitchen, green glass splashbacks, parquetry flooring. But Emma had turned it into the showpiece it was today. The sweeping, custom-made modular sofa in burnt orange suede, the designer coffee table, the Philippe Starck clear perspex dining chairs surrounding the Nicholas Dattner table – a daring combination, but she was a stylist, after all. There were a few carefully selected investment art pieces – paintings on the walls, a sculpture – but she hadn't overdone it, Emma wasn't into showing off. This was her home, her sanctuary, she chose to surround herself with objects that gave her pleasure. The fact that *Vogue Living* had begged her to feature it in their magazine was merely a testament to her personal taste.

She walked into the bedroom and stepped out of her shoes as she heard the shower stop.

'Hey, I'm home,' she sung out with a light tap on the bathroom door. A muffled acknowledgement came back in reply. Emma had taken a shower at the gym this morning, but she'd need another before they went out tonight. She removed her jewellery as she wandered into the walk-in robe. She already knew what she was going to wear. Whenever they accepted an invitation Emma automatically assembled her outfit in her head, right down to accessories, taking into account what else she had on that week, what she had worn the previous time they were out with the same people, and any other relevant factors. It was a hazard of the profession, Emma's mind just worked that way. She had even developed a code that she entered into her iPhone at the same time she added the event to her calendar. Emma never had to waste time fretting in front of the mirror, trying out combinations, stressing about what she was going to wear. It was a useful skill and she was proud of it.

She tapped on the bathroom door again and opened it. Blake was standing in front of the mirror, a towel tucked around his hips, frowning at his reflection as he smoothed one hand over the light bristle shading his jaw and chin.

'What do you think?' he asked her. 'Should I shave, or does this qualify as designer stubble?'

She brought her arms around him from behind and ran the back of her hand against his cheek. 'I think you should leave it. You look very sexy, very . . . Chris Hemsworth.'

'Why thank you,' he said, turning his head to give her a light kiss on the lips. 'How was your lunch?'

Emma leaned her head on his shoulder, watching his reflection in the mirror as he squeezed moisturiser into his hand.

'Actually, it was quite eventful,' she said.

'Oh?' he murmured, smoothing the lotion over his face.

'*Quite* eventful,' she repeated for effect. 'In fact, I don't think you're going to believe it.'

He lifted an eyebrow, meeting her gaze in the mirror. 'Don't tell me Andrew finally left his wife for Liz?'

'Hm, that would be pretty unbelievable.' Emma turned around, propping herself against the vanity cabinet. 'No . . . it's Ellen and Tim. They've separated.'

Blake stopped then and looked at her. 'Seriously?'

She nodded. And then, unexpectedly, she felt a pang of sadness.

'Wow,' he said thoughtfully, leaning his hip against the cabinet and folding his arms. 'Didn't see that coming. They were one of those couples that just seemed . . . I don't know, carved in stone. It was like they'd always been together and always would be.'

'I know.'

'So you had no idea?'

Emma shook her head. 'She's been a total dark horse about it . . . all for the sake of the kids, apparently.'

Blake frowned. 'Is there someone else involved?'

'According to Ellen there's no third party, no indiscretions, no fault. They just grew apart.'

He shrugged. 'Marriage'll do that to you.'

She wished he hadn't said that. 'She's going to tell Mum and Dad before the anniversary party. I think it's really bad form, don't you? Bloody selfish if you ask me.'

'Does that surprise you?' Blake picked up a bottle of cologne and turned to face the mirror again. 'Ellen's always been about Ellen. She'll work it to get the most mileage out of this.'

'Blake, don't say that.'

'Why? You know it's true.'

'She's my sister.'

He leaned across to give her a peck on the cheek. 'You'd have said it if I didn't.'

'It's all right for me to say it.'

He smiled faintly as he dabbed the cologne on his neck and chest. Emma watched him.

'I don't know how Mum and Dad are going to take it.'

'Oh, they're pretty savvy, they'll take it in their stride.'

'But it's their fortieth wedding anniversary,' said Emma. 'You don't want news that the marriage of one of your kids has just fallen apart. It's like one of your children dying, it's not supposed to happen before you.'

'I don't think I'm following you,' said Blake. 'According to that logic parents are supposed to get divorced before any of their kids do.'

Emma sighed. 'Oh, you know what I mean. I just think it should be a time for good news. For celebrating the future.'

'It's more a celebration of the past, isn't it? The forty years they've spent together?'

'It's more than that,' she insisted. 'It's a celebration of their life together, of everything they've achieved, their family, all going back forty years to the day they stood in front of each other and made that commitment. That should be the focus of the day.'

'What are you proposing?' he asked. 'Do you want to have them renew their vows or something?'

She grinned then. 'Did you say something about proposing?'

Blake frowned, she could tell he was mentally backtracking through the conversation. Then he rolled his eyes. 'Oh come on, are you seriously going to tell me that's the first thing that came to mind?'

It generally was.

But she just said, 'Why, what's wrong with that?'

'Your sister's marriage has just collapsed and that makes you want to get married? I would have thought it was the last thing you'd be thinking of right now.'

'But we're nothing like Ellen and Tim. They were kids who got pregnant, so they got married. You and I have chosen to be together, and stay together, for a long time. We're established financially and in our careers. We know what we want, we wouldn't be doing this on a whim, we've had years to think about it.' She paused, waiting for some kind of response. 'You're always saying "one day", so why not now, when it would bring some happiness into the family – a sense of hope?'

Blake raised a cynical eyebrow as he walked past her and out into the bedroom. Emma followed him.

'Oh, I was supposed to tell you,' he said, 'Gordie and Sal want to meet a little earlier and have a drink first.'

'You're changing the subject,' Emma said, folding her arms.

'Just relaying a message, my sweet.' He gave her a sugary smile and disappeared into the walk-in robe.

Emma fell onto the bed on her stomach. She propped herself up on her elbows. 'You're never going to marry me, are you?' she said glumly.

'Never say never,' he muttered from inside the wardrobe.

'Yeah, well just so you know, I won't wait around forever, Blake. I'm not going to be a middle-aged bride, older women look ridiculous in all the white regalia. You have to tone it down, but I don't want to tone it down. Not that I wouldn't be elegant, of course, you know me. But I want to be a proper bride.'

'Okay.'

Emma dropped her head onto the mattress and groaned. 'You're not even listening to me!'

He appeared above her a few moments later, staring down at her as he buttoned his shirt.

'I was listening,' he said. 'But I don't think you were. I said okay.'

'Okay about what?' she pouted.

'Okay,' he paused, 'maybe it is time we did this.'

Emma frowned, lifting her head slowly and then sitting all the way up. 'What are you talking about?'

He perched on the edge of the bed, still buttoning his shirt. 'It's funny, we were talking about this at work the other day. Mitch had this theory that the married guys move up ahead of the rest of us. They get more opportunities, the biggest contracts, the important clients. And being given so many chances to perform, they ultimately get the promotions. I said he was crazy, he'd been watching too much *Mad Men*. That kind of attitude was from another generation. No one cares anymore if you're married or not, in fact sometimes they're happier if you don't have a family. They like ambitious, unattached young turks who'll work long hours and take off at a moment's notice. So Mitch bet me, and we went through the entire section, and it was uncanny. I don't know if it's just coincidence, but –'

Emma was not actually listening anymore, she hadn't been for some time. The only words that had sunk in, the last words she'd really heard, were 'maybe it is time we did this'.

'Blake!' she said, interrupting him and grabbing him by the scruff of the collar.

'Hey, careful,' he protested. 'You'll crease my shirt.'

'Did you say "maybe it's time we did this"?' she said urgently.

'Well, I've just been thinking lately that –'

'Blake, is that what you said?' she cut him off. 'More importantly, did you mean it? You can't kid around about something like this, not with me, not after all this time. It would be cruel. And I've never known you to be cruel, Blake. So you have to tell me, did you really say it's time we got married, and did you mean it?'

Emma's voice had risen considerably and she was breathing hard, glaring at him, waiting for an answer. He just smiled back at her.

'What?' she said.

'This really matters to you, doesn't it?'

'Blake, are you serious? Have you even been listening to me for the past . . . I don't know how long?'

She was still clenching his collar as she brought her face close to his.

'Em, the shirt!'

'Screw the shirt!' she said. 'But don't screw around about this, Blake.'

'Okay, okay,' he said, gently unfastening her hands from his collar and holding them in his. 'Let's do it, let's get married.'

Emma whooped, lurching at him with such force they both slid right off the bed and landed on the floor. She kissed him soundly on the mouth and then sat up, straddling him. 'Hold on, are you only marrying me because it'll look good at work?'

'No, not only that,' he said with a wry grin, drawing her down to kiss her again. 'I am quite fond of you as well.'

Emma realised she didn't actually care. Well, of course she did, but she knew Blake loved her, and that they were a good match, an ideal match in fact. More than Ellen and Tim had ever been, despite appearances. So if the work thing had made him finally come around, Emma really didn't care. She broke away and sat up again.

'Okay, we have so much to do and not much time,' she said, climbing off him. 'First things first, you have to propose, obviously.'

Blake frowned up at her. 'Didn't I just do that?'

'You can't call that a proposal, Blake,' Emma chided. 'We have to do this right. Unless you have some other scenario in mind, a restaurant is best. A little conventional, but it's all about location, location, location. Nothing under two hats, are we clear about that, Blake? And preferably three. And we'll never get in anywhere next weekend, so it'll have to be through the week, but not lunch, okay? It has to be dinner. I have contacts, I'll give you some names, and once you tell them what you're planning, they'll find you a table this week, I guarantee.'

'Why the hurry?' he asked. 'You think I'm going to renege?'

'Not if you value your testicles,' she shot back. 'No, we have to do it this week if we want to announce it at the anniversary party, which is the whole point. This is the perfect, elegant solution to defuse Ellen's bombshell, move it right to the back of everyone's minds so this can be a real celebration.'

Blake was listening thoughtfully. 'You wondered if I was doing this to score points at work.' He lifted himself up on one elbow. 'I'm beginning to think you're doing this to score points over your sister.'

'Not at all, I'm doing it for Mum and Dad!' she insisted. 'Blake, honey, I can finally be the one doing the right thing, give them something to be happy about, to celebrate. They might even be proud of me for once. Are you onside?'

He linked his fingers through hers and drew her closer. 'I am,' he said, kissing her.

Emma responded briefly before breaking away again and jumping to her feet. 'So first thing Monday, you're going to have to see about the ring.'

'You expect to get the ring this week as well?'

'It's not worth doing if you don't have the ring, dummy!' she chided. 'It's all about the ring.'

'Honey, I hate to say this,' he said, standing up, 'but you are a little . . . particular.'

'A little?'

'Exactly. How am I going to find a ring you'll be happy with inside a week?'

She smiled. 'Don't you worry about that, I know exactly the ring I want, and where you can get it. I'll show you online, and then you just have to take my size into Tiffany's.'

He pulled a face. 'Doesn't sound very romantic.'

'Are you kidding me? What could be more romantic than an engagement ring from Tiffany's?'

'That you picked out yourself.'

'Blake, this is what girls do.'

'Is it?'

She nodded. 'No matter what you've seen in the movies, no girl wants to be surprised by the ring. I know you have wonderful taste, Blake, and you'd probably get it right, but why take the risk?' she said, walking towards the bathroom.

'If you say so.' He turned to inspect himself in the mirror. 'Emma, look what you did to my shirt!'

She came back over to check the damage, smoothing his collar out with her hands. 'Wear another one, you have at least half-a-dozen white shirts.'

'But I wanted to wear this one,' he grizzled.

'Then I'll iron it for you,' she said, heading back to the bathroom again. She turned suddenly at the doorway. 'Oh, and you realise you have to come up with something a little inventive for the ring.'

'Huh?'

'You know, pop it in a glass of champagne, or on an oyster in the shell, or in the dessert. They'll give you ideas at the restaurant.'

Blake was frowning.

'You're not still upset about your shirt, are you?' she sighed. 'I said I'd iron it.'

'No, it's not the shirt.'

'Then what?' she asked, leaning against the door frame.

He took a breath. 'You don't find this all a bit . . . staged?' he suggested carefully.

Emma came over to him, pressing up against him and looping her arms around his neck. 'It's about setting the scene, Blake, about creating a story we can tell our grandchildren. You're not going to begrudge me that, are you?'

She brought her lips up to meet his, engaging the full strength of her persuasive powers. Emma felt him relax into her, and . . . oh, hold on just a minute, she couldn't have him getting all aroused or they'd never get out of here.

She pulled back abruptly and darted across to the bathroom. 'We're going to be late if I don't get a move on!' she declared, glancing back at him. Blake was just watching her, a little glazed-eyed.

'Oh, and not a word to Gordie and Sal, or anyone else tonight for that matter. Okay?' she added over her shoulder. 'I don't want anything to spoil the surprise before next Sunday.'

Elizabeth

Liz hitched the grocery bag up on her hip and unlocked the door of her apartment. As it swung open she stepped back out of the way.

Ellen gave her a plaintive look. 'Are you sure about this? You've hardly had any sleep.'

'How many times are you going to ask me the same question?' said Liz. 'Would you just get inside before I drop this bag?'

Liz had learned over the years that subtlety did not work with Ellen. She would have been feeling crushed by the way things had played out today, but she'd never admit it. She was the eldest, she didn't ask for help, and she didn't accept it easily either. So Liz had resolved not to let her go home alone this evening, and not to take no for an answer.

Emma had no sooner finished her lunch than she'd checked her watch and said she had to 'dash'. She always had to dash off somewhere. She wore her busy schedule like a badge of honour, always making it clear that she had somewhere more important to be.

Evie had stayed a little longer, but her anxiety had mounted visibly with every tick of the clock. Ellen had finally given her a pass out, and Evie had left, bustling out of the café, much as she'd arrived, pink-faced and breathless.

Once it was just the two of them, Liz had looked across the table at Ellen. 'So what now?'

Ellen had shrugged. 'Well, like I said, I'm staying in the house and Tim's moving into a flat, as we speak, actually.'

'No,' said Liz, 'I mean what *now*. Where are the kids going to be tonight?'

Ellen gave a small sigh of resignation. 'They're staying with their father at his new place. We thought it was important that they were involved in the process of unpacking and settling in. We really want them to feel like it's as much their place.'

'So what are you going to do?' Liz persisted.

'Oh, I guess I'll go home and straighten up, move things around, fill in the gaps he's left,' she said with a half-hearted laugh.

'Well, you're not doing that,' Liz said plainly. 'You're coming home with me.'

'Thanks, Liz, but I have to face this sometime.'

'Don't be so stoic,' she scoffed. 'There'll be plenty of time for you to face being alone, I guarantee you. Avoid it whenever you're offered an alternative.'

She had finally got Ellen to agree to follow her home, they'd just have to make a quick stop on the way. Liz had no idea what was in her fridge, but she doubted there was anything particularly appealing. She'd given up buying much in the way of groceries, or fresh fruit and vegetables, because she always ended up throwing most of it out. She could never see much point in cooking just for herself. So they called in to Liz's favourite deli, which just happened to be conveniently located next door to a bottle shop.

As they started to unpack the supplies, Ellen suddenly turned to look at her. 'What if Andrew wants to come over?'

Liz shrugged. 'I don't drop everything for Andrew.'

Ellen raised an eyebrow.

'I don't!' she insisted. 'Besides, he would have called by now. And I rarely get to see him on weekends anyway. If he's called into the hospital he can sometimes pop in on his way home, say he's been held up with a complicated surgery, or an emergency, that kind of thing. But the weekends are for family.'

Ellen was shaking her head. 'I don't know how you handle it.'

'You get used to it,' she dismissed. Then she gave Ellen a wry smile. 'Sometimes I wonder what I'd do with him if he was here all the time.'

Though more often she wondered if anyone actually believed her when she made offhand remarks like that, or if quietly they just felt sorry for her. Liz wanted to say, don't feel sorry for me, I have a relationship – such as it is – with a wonderful man who's intelligent, and passionate, and who makes me laugh. I'd rather spend a little time with him than a lot of time with almost anyone else I know. Unfortunately, he was married long before we met; we're victims of bad timing and there's nothing we can do about that, except be glad that we found each other at all. We could have spent the rest of our lives never knowing this feeling.

Liz comforted herself in the knowledge that he wasn't choosing his wife over her anyway, not that she'd feel at all comfortable breaking up a marriage. Theirs was an unusual situation; it was not about his wife – according to Andrew they didn't even sleep together anymore. It was about his son. Danny was autistic – he needed continuity, he couldn't cope with even the slightest change to his routine or his surroundings. His father was one of the few people he responded to. His mother was loving, but not exactly emotionally robust. That was how Andrew put it. Liz secretly thought she was hopeless. She was always falling apart at the slightest thing, needing Andrew to take over. She would not be able to handle caring for Danny on her own.

So the universe had conspired to make it impossible for them to be together, at least for the time being. Andrew always spoke of a future when they would be free to be together. They'd hoped things were heading that way after Danny started high school, but then puberty hit. He grew a head taller than his mother, and she was no longer physically able to manage his outbursts. Andrew said that once Danny settled down again, and matured a little, he was sure the boy would gain a lot more independence, and there would come a time when he wouldn't need both parents around constantly, when he would be able to cope with his father living somewhere else, with someone else.

Liz mentally counted the years that would take, fully aware that her chances of having a family of her own were diminishing by the month. And yet that was all she'd ever wanted. When she'd finished school everyone had had an opinion about what she should do, mostly the same opinion – of course she had to do medicine. She couldn't give up an opportunity like that. It would be almost irresponsible. So Liz had accepted a place in medicine, and she'd liked it well enough. In due course she'd become an intern at a large teaching hospital, where she met Andrew. He was not quite thirty at the time – a typically overworked surgical registrar in crumpled scrubs, with ruffled hair, eyes that were perennially tired, but vivid blue nonetheless, and always a ready smile. Most surgeons were a bit full of themselves, it came with the territory, but Andrew was different. He had an inherent sweetness, and deep, genuine compassion for his patients. He handled everything in the same calm, reassuring manner – emergencies, frayed tempers, other doctors' considerable egos, and students' predictable ineptness – and Liz promptly developed a crush, even though she'd never been one to develop crushes easily.

And then one night, after too many beers at the staff watering hole, Andrew chose her shoulder to cry on. Danny had just been diagnosed. Liz took him back to her place and the inevitable happened, but when he woke up at daybreak and realised where he was and what he'd done, he freaked. Not at her, he was sweet to her, and terribly apologetic. He blamed himself, berated himself. He did the same when he arranged to meet her for coffee a few days later. He wanted to apologise again; it was unforgivable, he'd never done anything like that before, it was just the pressure since Danny . . . and it all came tumbling out again, a little more coherently this time. His marriage was fraying at the edges, his wife was not coping with the diagnosis, much less the child himself, and there was another child as well, a daughter, Samantha, who needed attention and reassurance. It was not unusual for Andrew to work sixty-hour weeks, then he had to come home to a family in crisis. Sometimes he wondered if he should give up medicine, go into something with regular hours, not so much pressure. But his wife wouldn't hear of it. She couldn't go out to work because of Danny, so they needed Andrew's income to cover all the expenses involved in getting their boy the best treatment and therapies available. Andrew didn't know what to do. And Liz said she didn't know what to say. He told her she didn't have to say anything, just having somebody listen was enough. He didn't have anyone else. They didn't sleep together again for six months, but they did become best friends. They'd been each other's best friend ever since.

*

Liz and Ellen sat out on the balcony, working their way through their first glass of red and a wedge of brie. Liz would never have bought an apartment without a balcony, that was almost her only criteria. She needed some space out of doors. In truth she would have loved to buy a house, but houses were for children and pets, it seemed greedy to have a house all to herself. The apartment was convenient, close to work, easy to maintain. But it didn't feel like a home. They'd grown up here in Annandale, only a few blocks away, in a big sprawling house with a yard. Liz suspected the family home remained home until you had your own family. Which was something of a bummer considering her situation.

'Do you know anything about light therapy?' Ellen asked her.

'For depression?'

'No, for skin.'

Liz nodded. 'Why, are you thinking of trying it?'

'Yeah, right,' Ellen pulled a face. 'No, Emma was talking about it, she's on a course of treatment.'

Liz smiled faintly. 'Of course she is, it's the latest thing. A client asked me about it only the other day.' She shook her head. 'I'm a dermatologist, a doctor of medicine, and yet I seem to spend all my time fielding queries about Botox and anti-wrinkle creams. Emma once said I was nothing but a glorified beautician. She's probably right.'

Ellen was quiet for a bit, sipping her wine. 'Do you think Emma was right about not telling Mum and Dad before the party?'

Liz looked at her. 'Do you?'

'I don't know, I'm asking you.'

'I think you should do what feels right for you.'

Ellen frowned. 'Is that a thinly veiled way of saying that you don't think it's right?'

Liz laughed. 'No, but that's a hefty dose of not so thinly veiled paranoia you've got going there.' She shook her head. 'What I'm trying to do is give you unconditional support to do what feels right for you. I can't tell you what that is, because I'm not you. You know how to handle Mum and Dad better than any of us. If you're really not sure, we can talk about that, but if you're not sure because of something Emma said, well, that's not a good enough reason.'

Ellen smiled. 'You're very wise.'

'Aren't I? Especially after a glass of wine. Give me anyone else's problems . . . sorted!' Liz said, raising her glass. 'Uh-oh, running on empty.'

She picked up the bottle and Ellen held her glass out for a refill.

'One thing I do know is that Emma will be having a field day with this,' said Ellen. 'She and Blake are probably celebrating my downfall as we speak.'

'I don't think she'd actually celebrate it,' said Liz. 'But don't worry about her. She can be smug if she ever gets Blake to marry her. Now, what shall we drink to?'

'God, I don't know,' Ellen sighed. 'Doesn't feel like I have anything to drink to right now.'

'What are you talking about?' Liz chided. 'You have a whole new future ahead of you.'

Ellen pulled a face. 'As a middle-aged single woman?'

'Well, thanks for that,' said Liz. 'Should I just end it all now?'

'Sorry, I didn't mean . . .'

'And we're not middle-aged!'

'You're not.'

'I'm four years younger than you, Len, we're in the same boat. Except you've got kids along for the ride.'

'Which makes me a single mother,' she shuddered. 'I've always hated the sound of that.'

'Oh cripes, Lenny,' said Liz. 'Don't you realise how lucky you are? You know, I can handle only being with Andrew part-time, and the secrecy, even though it makes me look like the most pathetic dateless woman in the country. But I made my bed and I'll lie in it willingly. The hardest part is that I probably won't have kids now.'

'Liz . . .'

'No, it's true. It's still going to be a few years before Andrew can leave Danny, and by then it'll be too late.'

'Then why are you sticking it out?'

Liz gave her a sidelong glance. 'Because I love him.'

'But –'

'Ellen, are you going to say anything you haven't said to me before?' she asked plainly. '*Several* times?'

'Probably not,' Ellen admitted.

'So let's drop it. And anyway, we're not talking about me, we're talking about you. And the point I was making is that no matter what else happens from here on in, you have two wonderful children and no one can take that away from you.'

Ellen nodded slowly. 'I hate that I'm doing this to them.'

Liz gave her arm a squeeze. 'How are they coping?'

'Hard to say . . .'

'Must have been awful telling them.'

'Mm . . . Sam was in shock, he obviously didn't have the slightest clue.'

'He's a male,' Liz said automatically, before smacking herself on the forehead. 'God, that's a terrible thing to say. It just comes out, without thinking. You can't get away with saying something like that about a woman anymore, not even as a joke.' She looked at Ellen. 'Please continue . . . of course the poor kid was in shock.'

'I went to check on him afterwards, and he asked me if our whole lives had been a lie. Actually, he said "bullshit".'

'Ouch. What did you say?'

'I told him that just because Tim and I didn't feel the same way about each other, that didn't change the way we felt about them, or our family as a unit. That we couldn't have stayed together so long if we hadn't enjoyed our family life.'

'Did he buy that?'

'It's the truth!' Ellen exclaimed. 'As a family, we worked. Just not as a couple.'

'What about Kate?' asked Liz. 'How's she taking it?'

'You know what she's like, she's gone quiet, observing from arm's length. Though she did say she'd suspected things weren't right for a while.'

'Yeah, well, kids are smart, it's hard to pull the wool over their eyes for long.'

Ellen blinked. 'Is that what you think we were doing?'

'I didn't mean –'

'I really don't want people to think we set out to deceive them, the way Emma seems to think.'

'You really have to stop worrying about what Emma thinks.'

'I can't help it. She was suspicious and she's my sister. What are other people going to think?'

'It doesn't matter what they think.'

'I wish that were true. I know it's really no one else's business, and no one can know what it was like between me and Tim, but people will still judge, have their opinions.' Ellen paused. 'I wish there was some way to do this without all the fuss.'

'We should have contracts for marriage, just like anything else.'

'Marriage is a contract,' Ellen reminded her.

'Yes, but it's not like any other contract. I mean, really, imagine going into a contract where death was the only way out.'

'I guess that's true, especially with everyone living so much longer now. You used to get married when you were a teenager, and you were lucky to live another twenty years. Now a marriage can last three times that long.'

'Exactly. So what if you just signed up for ten or twenty years?'

'Then when the term was served, you would have the option to renew, but no obligation.'

'Wow,' Liz said. 'What would happen to all the lawyers and therapists if divorce didn't exist any more?'

'No more guilt or angst, no stigma for kids from broken homes.'

'There would be no "broken" homes, only expired ones.'

Ellen smiled. 'You could have a partner to suit every phase of your life.'

'Yeah, I've heard of that idea,' said Liz. 'One for sex, one for children, and then one who's your soul mate.'

'Is the soul mate the one who'll nurse you when you're old?' Ellen asked. 'That's what I worry about . . . who's going to be there for me then?'

'Your kids, your sisters, your brother,' Liz pointed out. 'I've actually had this fantasy for years that Eddie will be left to care for all of us in our dotage. I've told him more than once – we had to change his nappies and wipe his dribble, it'll be his turn then.'

Ellen laughed. 'What does he say to that?'

'He said the first sign of dementia in any of us and he's leaving the country with no forwarding address.' She grinned. 'Anyway, you'll find someone else, Ellen.'

'Maybe. Eventually. It's not exactly high on my agenda though.'

'Really? After all those years without sex, I thought you'd be champing at the bit.'

'The idea of getting naked in front of a man whose babies I didn't bear . . .' She shuddered.

'You do realise that's every other man on the planet, bar Tim?'

'Tim was there to see how the damage was done, and there'd be a lot of things he wouldn't have even noticed. You know how it is, you're not aware of changes when you're around them every day. Whereas a stranger has nothing to prepare him for the shock.'

'Oh for godsakes, Ellen, you're not exactly Frankenstein.'

'Look, I know I'll probably have to face it one day, but I'll worry about it then. It's hard enough to adjust to the idea of being single. I mean I know this has been coming for a long time, but now that it's here, it feels . . . surreal, I guess. All my adult life I've been a married person. I'm not sure I know how to be anything else.'

'You're still the same person, Len,' said Liz. 'And you've done something very brave that most people don't have the courage to do.'

Saying that out loud caused an involuntary twinge in her chest. Liz knew Andrew's situation was more complicated than most, but occasionally she couldn't help but wonder if he was simply not brave enough to end his marriage and deal with the consequences. Was it easier, safer, to maintain the status quo? Liz shuddered, she really didn't want to explore that train of thought.

'The thing is, Len, whatever is ahead of you, at least you're not going to waste away in a dead marriage. How many people do you know who are really happy in their marriages long-term?'

'Mum and Dad,' said Ellen plainly.

'Yeah, they've got a lot to answer for, those two,' Liz sighed. 'Making us believe a happy marriage was the norm.'

'Do you think that's why Evie puts up with Craig?'

Liz looked at her.

'They've got such a strange little 1950s marriage, don't you think?'

'I don't know, I don't get the attraction, but Evie seems happy.'

'Do you really think she is, though?'

'You don't?'

'I don't know. Sometimes I feel like I don't really know Evie. She's buried in there somewhere, but it's like she's too afraid to be herself, stand up for herself.'

'Well, that's not surprising with the three of us as big sisters, she was outnumbered into submission. Maybe that's why she ended up with someone like Craig – Evie was born to serve and to please.'

'God, I could think of nothing worse.'

'Of course you couldn't. You're the eldest, you were born to rule.'

'Ha,' said Ellen. 'So where's my empire?'

'You lorded it over all of us,' said Liz, 'which is why Emma's got that massive chip on her shoulder, and why she'll grab any opportunity to stick the knife in, like today. You shouldn't take it personally, Len, it's her own stuff.'

Ellen seemed to be thinking that over. 'And what about you?' she said finally.

'Oh, don't you know? I'm the poor misunderstood middle child,' said Liz. 'Quietly going her own way, not bothering anyone, but always kind, and wise, and incredibly insightful . . .'

Ellen laughed. 'And just a little blind to her own shortcomings.'

'What shortcomings?'

Evie

'Honey, can I ask you a question?'

Craig grunted in response but his gaze didn't shift from the TV. Evie snuggled in closer to his side. All the way home she had kept thinking about how lucky she was. She was the most ordinary of all the sisters, yet clearly she was the happiest. Poor Emma would be such a beautiful bride, but Evie couldn't ever see Blake going through with it. And Liz, the smartest of the lot, stuck in this pointless affair with a married man. And now Ellen and Tim, the model couple, over, just like that. Evie started to think it was fine to be ordinary, to have ordinary hopes and dreams – it was a lot easier to be happy that way.

Then she had been overtaken by a sense of dread. What if Craig wasn't happy? Evie hadn't been able to tell there was anything wrong between Ellen and Tim, they had seemed like the perfect couple. What had started the decline? This? Sitting at home on a Saturday night watching TV, not talking to each other? Not really knowing what the other was thinking?

Ellen said they had fallen out of love. The idea that you could just fall out of love was bewildering to Evie. She loved Craig the same way, well maybe not the *same* way, but she loved Craig like she loved her children, her parents, her sisters. You couldn't just fall out of love with any of them. That was impossible. Wasn't it?

So she'd resolved to make a special effort tonight. She had stopped off on the way home and bought all of Craig's favourites – the pricey beer with the gold label that they only had on special occasions, a couple of handfuls of king prawns – just for Craig. Evie wouldn't have any, they were too expensive and she couldn't stretch the budget that far. She bought steak and mushrooms and potatoes for baking – Craig loved his baked potatoes – and she'd smother it all in gravy. She wouldn't even bother with vegetables so he didn't have to push them around on his plate and take a half-hearted couple of bites.

She'd bought some wine for herself – a bottle of sweet sparkling. Craig loved it when she drank. He said it made her more uninhibited, which meant he could probably talk her into giving him oral sex. And Evie had to be at least a bit tipsy for that.

Once she was home she'd rounded up the children and organised their baths. Then she'd rinsed the prawns and put them in a nice bowl, and spooned some cocktail sauce into a dish, and laid it all out on the coffee table in the good lounge room, where the kids wouldn't bother Craig. Then she'd called him in from the backyard where he'd fled with a beer as soon as she'd arrived home.

He walked up to the back door and held it open. 'What?'

Evie held up one of the special beers. 'Why don't you go and watch the sports roundup in the good lounge room?'

'S'not on yet,' he said, glancing at his watch. 'It's just news now.'

'Then go and play your Wii for a while,' she said, coming towards him and handing him the beer. 'I left a treat in there for you.'

He looked at the bottle. 'Sweet. What's all this in aid of?' he said before taking a long swig.

Evie hadn't told him about Ellen and Tim yet. She would, later, once the kids were in bed. She realised she was a little apprehensive about telling him, she didn't want to put ideas into his head. That was silly probably, but she couldn't help it.

'Well, I got to have a special day out,' she said, 'while you've been stuck minding the kids. So I wanted to do something special for you.'

He shrugged. 'Mum was here.'

'Still . . .'

'Yeah,' he said, throwing an arm around her shoulders. 'Sometimes she's more of a hindrance. Yackedy yacking in my ear all day long.'

Evie smiled up at him. 'Then you go in and relax now,' she said, propelling him into the hall. 'And I'll get on with dinner.'

She heard him whoop a few moments later. 'Prawns! Bloody unreal, hun.'

She prepared their meal while the kids ate their fish fingers and chips, and after they were finished she sent them in – '*Quietly!*' – to say goodnight to their father. And then she marched them off to bed.

'Why did Daddy got pornth and we didn't?' Cody asked. He was her baby, though at four, not so much a baby anymore. But he was so adorable, Evie could just eat him up.

'You don't like prawns, remember, sweetheart?' Evie said.

'But I do!' cried Jayden as he made a running dive for his bed.

'Jayden, please settle down.' Evie seemed to spend her life telling Jayden to settle down. She tried to recall if he'd ever been sweet like Cody, but when he was four she only remembered chasing him around shopping centres, out of trees, down off fences.

'You have to be quiet now,' she said, trying to be stern. 'Daddy needs a break, he's been looking after you all day.'

'No he hasn't,' Tayla refuted, appearing in the doorway. 'Nanna looked after us. Dad said he had to go see a man about a dog.'

'Are we getting a dog?' Jayden whooped.

'I don't think so, honey,' Evie said vaguely.

'He was gone for hours and hours,' Tayla added, gazing accusingly at her mother, her arms crossed. Evie was a little intimidated by her daughter, and she was only ten years old. Heaven forbid when she hit her teens.

'We're getting a dog! We're getting a dog!' Jayden chanted, bouncing on his knees on the mattress.

Cody clapped his hands. 'Are we really getting a dog, Mummy?'

'It's just an expression,' she said.

'What kind of dog isth that?'

'Can we please forget about the dog right now? I don't know anything about it, you'll have to ask your father tomorrow,' she said, passing the buck to where it belonged. 'Now, listen up, we're going to have a competition.'

'Can I win the compition, Mummy?' Cody asked wide-eyed.

'No way, you stupid dumbhead!' Jayden taunted.

'Am not.'

'Are too. You're only four. You can't win a competition 'gainst us!'

'Can't I win, Mummy?'

'You can all win,' Evie reassured him.

'Then it's not a competition, Mother,' said Tayla, leaning against the doorjamb with a dramatic sigh.

'It is, but you have to work together, like a team,' she said, thinking on her feet. 'It's not like *Australian Idol* or *MasterChef*, this is more like . . . soccer. Like your team has to work together at soccer, Jayden.'

'I hate soccer,' Tayla curled her lip in disgust.

'I'm not asking you to actually play soccer,' said Evie. 'Only that everyone has to work together or no one gets a prize.' Tayla's eyes narrowed. 'What's the prize?'

'Well, the prize is . . .' She hadn't thought that far. 'That tomorrow I'll take you to McDonald's for lunch.'

'Yay!' Jayden and Cody chorused.

'I hate McDonald's,' said Tayla.

'You didn't hate it when we had it last week,' Evie reminded her.

'Yes, but now I'm a vegetarian.'

Evie sighed. 'No you're not. You're too young to be a vegetarian.'

'Am not,' she insisted. 'Madison's a vegetarian.'

'Fine, if you want to be a vegetarian, you don't have to come to McDonald's with us tomorrow.'

'Hehe, suck eggs!' said Jayden.

'Well, obviously I can't suck eggs, Jayden,' Tayla sniffed. 'They come from chickens. But I can have a salad, and I can have fries.'

'Can we get on with the rules of the competition?' said Evie.

'What do we have to do?'

'Okay, listen carefully,' she said solemnly. 'You all have to be especially quiet, and I mean not a peep. No one's allowed to come out of their room, not even once, not to ask for a drink or to go to the toilet or anything else, or you all lose. Remember, you're a team.'

Cody looked worried. 'But what if I'm bery firthty, Mummy?'

'Sweetheart, you know you're not allowed to have a drink after bedtime.'

'But what if I get bery frytinned?'

'It's okay, matey,' Jayden reassured him, 'I'll be here, and I'll protect you with my laser sword.'

Funny how Jayden became the protective big brother when there was something in it for him.

But it had worked: they hadn't heard a sound from the kids all night. Evie served dinner on the coffee table so they could watch TV while they ate, which she didn't like to do normally, but Craig loved it. She even encouraged him to watch *Die Hard* 2 or maybe it was 3, or 5, or 11, for all Evie knew, they all looked the same to her.

'Craig,' she repeated tentatively. 'I want to ask you something.'

'Can't it wait till the ad?' he asked, not looking at her. 'The good bit's coming up.'

He must have seen it a dozen times, but Evie bit her tongue until the ad break, and then she picked up the remote and muted the sound.

'What are you doing?' he protested.

'I said I wanted to ask you a question. And it's only the ads.'

He groaned. 'Okay, but make it quick before it starts up again.'

Now Evie groaned. 'You have seen this before, Craig.'

'So?' he said. 'What are we watching it for if we're not going to watch it?'

'All right,' she said, shifting around to face him. 'I just want to know . . .' She paused, biting her lip.

'Spit it out, love. Clock's ticking.'

'Well, I want to know . . . are you happy, honey?'

He frowned. 'I will be if I can get to see the rest of this movie.'

'Craig,' she chided.

'Okay, I'm happy, now can we turn the sound back on?'

'You don't understand,' she said. 'Something happened today.'

Now she'd got his attention. He turned to face her. 'Did you do something to the car? Did you have a prang?'

'No!' she insisted. 'The car's fine.'

'You had me worried there for a minute.' He breathed out, reaching for the remote, but Evie grabbed his arm.

'Wait, I have to tell you something, and it's important.'

He frowned. 'You're not pregnant again, are you?'

'Of course I'm not pregnant, Craig, I had my tubes tied, remember?'

'Yeah, I do, so I'd be pretty bloody suspicious if you were.'

Evie frowned, that didn't even make sense. 'Craig, the thing is, Ellen and Tim have split up.'

He looked at her blankly.

'It's true,' she nodded. 'They've separated. Ellen and Tim. Can you believe it?'

He shrugged. 'So what? They had a fight and she spent the night at your mum's. They'll sort it out.'

'No, that's not what happened. This is for real, Tim's moved out into a flat.'

'Fuck me.'

'Craig,' Evie admonished.

'So bloody Tim's gone and got himself a piece of arse,' he said, shaking his head. 'Didn't think he had it in him.'

'No, that's not what happened either,' said Evie. 'They just . . .' She didn't want to say it. 'They just fell out of love. Apparently.'

Craig shrugged, his eyes wandering back to the TV. 'Well, they have been married for, like, forever.'

'Craig!'

'What? It's true. And they had to get married, maybe they never really loved each other.'

'What a thing to say,' Evie declared. 'They've been together for eighteen years, they definitely loved each other.'

'Well, looks like they don't anymore,' he said.

'So are you saying you'll just fall out of love with me in a few years?' she blurted, wishing she hadn't said that out loud.

'Ah, come on, darl,' he said, patting her knee. 'We're not the same as them.'

'You don't think so?' she said in a small voice.

'Of course we're not.' He leaned over and gave her a kiss. 'Chalk and cheese. I never did get Tim, he doesn't even like sports. Do you know I was talking about the State of Origin one time and he asked me who was playing? What a moron!' He chuckled, scratching his stomach.

Evie didn't know what that had to do with anything.

'So,' said Craig, picking up the remote, 'can I go back to the movie now?'

She snatched it out of his hand. 'I'll record your damn movie!' she snapped, fumbling with the buttons.

'Okay, okay,' said Craig, holding up his hands. 'I thought we were finished talking. I didn't realise it was so important.'

'Craig!' she cried. 'Ellen is my sister! And her marriage is over! Of course it's important.'

'All right, love,' he said, putting his arm around her. 'No reason to get so upset.'

'Of course it's a reason to get upset.' You moron, she said to herself.

'I mean you don't have to get upset about us,' he said, giving her a squeeze. 'We're good. You're my puddin', you know that.'

Evie breathed out, leaning her head on his shoulder. 'It's just that we never talk about us, Craig. And we should. Obviously people can fall out of love and they don't even see it coming.'

'I don't reckon they broke up because they didn't talk,' he said. 'I reckon Ellen probably did enough talking for the both of them.'

Evie looked up at him. 'What do you mean by that?'

'She's never short of an opinion, your sister.'

'You think that's why they broke up?' She pulled a face.

'I dunno why they broke up,' he said. 'Whad'she tell you?'

'Like I said, that they fell out of love.'

'So they stopped having sex.'

'Craig, it's not necessarily the same thing,' she insisted. 'People might stop having sex once they fall out of love with each other.'

'Maybe they fall out of love because they stop having sex, did you think of that?'

Was he trying to say something here? 'Don't you think we have enough sex?'

'Of course I don't! I'm a red-blooded male, love, I could have sex all day, every day,' he laughed, scratching his stomach again. He looked at her fraught expression. 'Don't worry, I know we can't, with the kids and everything.'

'Well, apart from quantity, are you happy with our sex life? Is there anything you want that you're not getting?' she asked warily.

Evie had heard that anal sex was the latest thing; she hoped Craig didn't want to try that. It sounded gross.

'Ah, nuh,' he shrugged. 'Not really.'

Evie sat bolt upright. That didn't exactly sound reassuring. 'What do you mean, "not really"?'

'Nothing,' he said. 'I mean, there are things, but I don't reckon you'd be into them.'

Oh no, he did mean anal sex. But if this was really important to him, she'd have to try it. But surely it must hurt? She wondered if there was a way to make it . . . easier. She could google it. God, what was she thinking? She couldn't even imagine what might come up if she googled 'anal sex'.

'What's the matter, hun?' asked Craig. 'You look pale.'

Evie took a deep breath. She looked straight at Craig, and then she realised she couldn't look at him while she said this. She closed her eyes and blurted, 'Do you want it anally?'

'What?' he exclaimed.

Evie opened her eyes, relieved to see the shock on his face.

'You think I'm a bloody poofter?'

'No!' she assured him quickly. 'I've heard it's what some men like . . . with women.'

He grimaced. 'Still pretty gay if you ask me.'

She breathed out, putting a hand to her chest. 'Oh, I'm so relieved,' she said, collapsing against him.

He put his arm around her. 'You funny little puddin'. Where are you getting ideas like that?'

She shrugged. 'I don't know. I think I might have seen it on *Sex and the City* once.'

'They showed them doing that on *Sex and the City*?'

'No, they didn't show it,' she said. 'They just talked about it.'

He laughed. 'Yeah, that's all those women did on that bloody show – talk about it.'

Evie cuddled into her husband and the warm glow she had felt on her drive home today resurfaced. She was so lucky. She wasn't going to end up like poor Ellen. What was her sister's life going to be like now? Would she be able to find someone else, someone like Craig, who loved her despite the fact she'd gained a little weight over the years and he was still trim. Well, he had a bit of a beer belly, but what man of his age didn't? The thing was, he could easily attract a slim woman, if he wanted to. But he didn't and he hadn't. He had stayed faithful to Evie, called her his puddin'. Oh, he had a bit of a dig sometimes, but it was only for her own good – like when she went to have a second helping of dessert, or if they were out and she was about to head back to the buffet table one too many times. But despite all that, or even because of it, Evie knew Craig loved her, and that they'd always be together, no matter what.

'You know, you've got me thinking though,' said Craig after a while.

'Mm?' she murmured, her head on his chest, feeling the beat of his heart . . . that she noticed had just speeded up a little.

He shifted, turning to face her. Evie looked up at him.

'What is it?'

'Well, I was just thinking, if you were prepared to consider doing that . . .'

Ruby Weddings

Edward and Evelyn Beckett (nee Turner): Married 23rd January, forty years ago, at St Swinbourne's. With all our love and best wishes for another forty years together, Ellen and Tim, Kate and Sam, Emma, Elizabeth, Evie and Craig, Tayla, Jayden and Cody, and Eddie.

'Did you see the announcement in the paper?' Emma demanded of Evie, hands on hips.

They had arrived at the house at almost the same time, and Evie was ushering the kids out of the car when Emma marched up to her.

'Hi Aunty Emma!' Tayla cried, throwing her arms around Emma's waist and burying her face in the folds of her dress.

Tayla idolised her Aunty Emma, thought she was so stylish, so beautiful, so much more *everything* than her mother.

'Tayla, darling,' Emma said, patting her niece gingerly on the head. 'Careful of Aunty Emma's dress, sweetie, it's silk and it's very expensive. Look, there's Uncle Blake, why don't you go say hi.'

She removed herself from the child's clutches before grabbing Evie's arm and yanking her aside.

'So, did you see the announcement?'

'Um, I think, yes,' Evie said, flustered, turning back in time to witness Jayden shove Cody so he fell onto the grass. 'Jayden!'

'I got it, love,' said Craig, scooping Cody up into his arms as he took Jayden by the scruff of the neck. 'C'mon, you little ratbag.'

'Ow, Dad!'

'Oh, I better –'

'Craig's handling it,' Emma snapped, holding firmly onto Evie's arm. 'Bloody Ellen, you saw what she wrote? What she put in the *newspaper*!'

'Um . . .'

'"Ellen and Tim", "Evie and Craig" . . . "Emma, *Elizabeth*"!' she exclaimed. 'What the hell? What's Blake? Swiss cheese? For heaven's sake, he's my . . . he's my *partner*. And she and Tim are separated! She was the one who bloody insisted on telling Mum and Dad before today. So why didn't she leave *him* off the announcement?'

She paused, looking closer at Evie. 'Are you all right?'

Evie nodded vaguely.

'You don't look so well. You're a bit pale and your eyes are all glassy. Are you coming down with something?'

'I'm . . . I'm just feeling stressed, I have to get all this food inside.'

'Okay, settle down,' said Emma, giving her arm a rub. 'Come on, I'll help you.'

They walked around to the back of Evie's car and she lifted the hatch to reveal stacks of Tupperware containers, filling the entire space.

'Whoa Evie,' Emma exclaimed. 'You know we have caterers?'

'It's just what I promised,' she said quietly.

'Well, I'll ruin my dress carting all this in,' Emma declared. 'Let me pop in and get one of the caterers to help you.'

'Wait,' Evie gasped, clutching her sister's arm.

'It's okay, Evie, you really need to calm down,' said Emma. 'The caterers are paid to do this.'

'It's not that.' She gave her sister a plaintive look. 'Can I ask you something?'

Emma glanced towards the house. Blake and Craig were standing to one side of the front door, nodding and smiling as guests trickled past them. She could see Blake's irritation from here, especially when he glanced across at her with a look that plainly said, 'Don't leave me alone with this idiot.'

'We really should be going in, Evie.'

'I'll be quick,' she said urgently. 'I promise.'

Emma sighed. 'Fine, what is it?'

Evie composed herself, clearing her throat and looking straight at her sister. 'Have you . . . Don't think I'm strange, okay?'

'Okay,' said Emma, growing impatient.

She took a breath. 'Have you ever done it with anyone else?'

Emma frowned. 'What on earth?'

'Please just answer the question, it's really important. I'll explain later.'

'Well, of course I have,' she said. 'Sorry to shock you, Evie, but I wasn't a virgin when I met Blake, and neither was he.'

'No no, I'm not explaining myself properly,' she shook her head. 'I mean, *since* Blake.'

'What? No, of course not, we're completely faithful to each other,' she declared indignantly. 'God, you don't take us seriously either, because we're not married. You're just like Ellen –'

'No, sorry, of course I take you seriously,' Evie insisted. 'I just . . .'

'Hey, you two.'

They turned to see Liz strolling across the grass towards them.

'Mum and Dad are wondering what's happened to you,' she said, drawing closer. 'You've got to get inside. Tim's here, and the menfolk are all standing around shuffling their feet; they don't know what to say to each other. It's getting awkward.'

'Come on, Evie,' said Emma, taking her sister's arm and leading her towards the house. 'We'll talk about it later.'

'What are you talking about?' said Liz.

'Never mind,' Evie said weakly.

*

Ellen looked relieved to see her sisters walking down the hallway. 'Here they are,' she announced.

Edward and Evelyn appeared just as relieved, rushing forward to break away from the group of disparate sons-in-law.

'Hello, darling,' said Edward as he gave Emma a hug. 'You look like a million dollars.'

'You're probably not far off there,' said Evelyn. 'Honestly, Em, it's just family and our old friends, no one to impress here.' She laughed. 'Are you okay, Evie? You don't look so well.'

'I'm fine. Happy anniversary, Mum,' said Evie, returning her hug.

'Liz, take a look at your sister,' Evelyn persisted. 'Don't you think she's pale?'

'Liz is a dermatologist, Mum,' Emma sighed.

'Darling, she had to become a regular doctor first, how do you think she got to be a *specialist*?'

'Ah, and here's Eddie!'

'Eddie!' the girls all chorused.

They adored their baby brother, who was, of course, not a baby any more, but a tall, handsome twenty-six-year-old man who didn't actually need five mothers fussing over him. But they couldn't help themselves. They had doted on him since he was a baby, fiercely protected him once he started school, and never stopped bossing him around and telling him how to live his life since. Then he'd started bringing the odd girl home. Well, they were all odd, as far as the Beckett sisters were concerned. It seemed that no one was good enough for their Eddie, so there was only one way for Eddie to deal with that. He stopped bringing dates home at all. Then the girls started to worry that he wasn't seeing anyone, that perhaps he was . . .

'Not that there's anything wrong with that,' Ellen had stated clearly for the record at the time.

'But Mum and Dad will be so disappointed,' Evie lamented.

'Why?' Emma wanted to know.

'Well, because you know, he is the only son, carrying on the family name and all that.'

'Evie, we're not all as old-fashioned as you,' said Emma. 'I'll be keeping my name when Blake and I get married.'

'You two are talking about marriage already?' Ellen raised an eyebrow. 'You've only been going out a couple of months.'

'Yes, but I know he's the one,' Emma said airily. 'I expect him to propose before the year is out.'

'But what surname will you give the kids?' Ellen persisted. 'Won't Blake want to have his?'

She shrugged. 'Maybe we'll hyphenate.'

'But his name's already hyphenated,' Liz remarked. 'It'd be Chamberlain-Smith-Beckett. Or Beckett-Chamberlain-Smith.'

'Either way it's a mouthful,' Ellen muttered.

'I don't know,' Emma sniffed. 'All I'm saying is that there are other ways to pass on the family name, it's not all on Eddie's shoulders. And we better get used to the idea, because I think there's a good chance he's gay. I've got a bit of a nose for these things.'

'Eddie is not gay,' Liz said flatly.

'Just because you don't want him to be –'

'I wouldn't care if he was, but he's not, okay?'

Emma narrowed her gaze. 'You're saying that like you have inside information.'

'He goes out with girls all the time,' said Liz. 'One even lasted six months, we nearly got to meet her.'

'How do you know all this?' asked Ellen.

'Oh, we were having drinks one night, it just came out,' she said vaguely.

'Why is he keeping it from us?' Emma was indignant.

Ellen sighed then. 'Why do you think? We've only got ourselves to blame.'

The sisters had vowed then and there to back off the next time Eddie brought a girl home, but they hadn't had the chance.

'So are you seeing anyone we should know about, Eddie?' Emma asked him now.

'Nope,' he said simply.

'Your mistake was in the wording, Em,' Ellen winked. 'Are you seeing anyone, Eddie?'

He shook his head with a wry smile. Emma scooped her arm through his and drew him aside.

'Did you see the announcement in the paper?' she asked him.

'Um, yeah.'

'No comment?'

He shrugged. 'It was nice?'

'Didn't you notice? Blake wasn't included. Don't you think that's rude?'

'Maybe it was just family.'

'Blake's not considered family, then? Is that what you're saying?'

'I'm not saying anything, Em, I didn't write the announcement.'

'No, Ellen did,' said Emma. 'So of course Tim was included.'

'Well, he's still family, he is the father of the kids.'

'And Blake is my partner.'

Eddie looked at her. 'I know, and he should have been included, Em. I just don't think Ellen's thinking straight right now. Maybe we should cut her a bit of slack.'

Emma felt like she was being chastised, like she was the one in the wrong. So Ellen was going to get away with murder because of the separation, and everyone was going to have to pussyfoot around her? Emma certainly hoped there was some kind of statute of limitations on that.

'I better go say hi to Tim,' said Eddie. I haven't seen him since . . . you know.'

*

Ellen came out of the kitchen and noticed Eddie talking to Tim in a corner of the living room. Bless him. She was grateful everyone was making such an effort. She didn't mind that Tim had come, and she realised it was probably polite to stay for the speeches and cake, but Ellen would actually be relieved when he finally left. The whole point of being separated was to lead separate lives, but trying to keep things amicable was going to blur those lines quite a bit. She hoped Tim understood he really had to make a life of his own. She worried about him; he wasn't the most socially adept person, he'd always piggy-backed onto her life, her family, and he didn't seem to have any independent friends or interests. She really didn't want to think of him sitting alone in his flat, waiting for his weekends with the kids to come around.

'Excuse me, Ellen.' It was Evie, behind her, holding two trays of mini quiches.

'Evie, what are you doing?' said Ellen, relieving her of one of the trays. 'The caterers can do this.'

She shrugged. 'Oh, I don't mind. Helps get me around to everyone to say hi.'

'Well, I'll take this one,' Ellen insisted, keeping the tray. 'You should take it easy, Ev, you really don't look so well.'

*

Evie wished everyone would stop asking her if she was all right. She'd finally gone to check her face in the bathroom and she did look washed out, but she hadn't got much sleep in the past week. And every time Craig brushed past her, or smiled at her across the room, she thought she was going to be physically sick.

Everything had changed. The world as she knew it had been turned on its head. She wandered around the room with her tray of mini quiches, amongst all these long-married couples, people she'd known all her life. But what were they really like, behind closed doors? Were they happy, or were they living separate lives, like Ellen and Tim had been all this time? Were they having affairs, leading double lives . . . getting up to things Evie would never even have imagined until now. She watched her mother approach her father and touch his arm in that familiar way, as she had probably done every day for the past forty years. He turned to her, leaning in to listen to what she wanted to tell him. And then he smiled at her, covering her hand with his own, his eyes connecting with hers . . . They were probably talking about when to serve dessert or something, but the love between them was always so real, so tangible. Evie thought she and Craig were going to be like that. They would be together forever, their love would deepen over time. She used to imagine them as two old people, holding hands, Craig still calling her his puddin' . . . She couldn't see it anymore. Evie couldn't see forever. She could barely even see next week.

*

Liz meandered over next to Emma. 'Look at Evie, staring into space. Something's not right with her today. What was she talking to you about earlier, outside?'

'It was weird,' said Emma, shaking her head. 'She wanted to know if Blake or I had done it with anyone else – since we've been together.'

Liz frowned. 'Seriously? That's an odd thing to ask.'

'You're telling me,' she agreed. 'I don't know, I think she's been really shaken up by Ellen's news. Maybe it's made her suspicious of Craig.'

They both automatically searched out Craig. He was standing in a circle with their dad and a couple of their dad's old colleagues, beer in hand, scratching his belly and looking way out of his depth.

'I don't think she's got anything to worry about there,' Liz muttered.

Her gaze drifted across to Tim, and Liz wondered if there had been anything going on ... Nah. Not Tim. He was too much the solid family type, not the womaniser type, or even the type with something to hide. She wondered if people ever suspected Andrew ... probably not. He was a solid family type as well. She missed having him at things like this. She often fantasised about it, imagined herself sidling up to him as he stood in a group, slipping her arm into his. Her dad would love him, they were quite similar in a lot of ways. He'd appreciate being able to have a real, muscular conversation; his other sons-in-law left a lot to be desired in that respect. One day ...

'Tim's still hanging around,' Emma observed. 'I thought he wasn't staying for the whole thing?'

'I guess he's probably waiting for the speeches, to be polite.'

'Who's giving the toast, by the way?'

Liz shrugged, just as their father tapped his glass with a fork to get everybody's attention. 'I'd say we're about to find out,' she said.

'Evelyn and I couldn't be happier that you're all here to celebrate this momentous occasion with us.' He turned to gaze down at his wife. 'Forty years with this amazing woman. The love of my life who I was lucky enough to meet before I did anything stupid, like marry someone else.'

*

Emma listened as her father launched into his standard speech. Oh, he'd change it around a bit, mix up the anecdotes, but it was basically the same speech every time. At least he was an entertaining speaker; all those years as a teacher, then a principal, had honed his public speaking skills. He was recounting how they had met, which certainly bore repeating on this occasion. It was at teachers' college . . .

'Of course, I spotted her straight away, all the boys did, but she didn't notice any of us.'

Her mother was shaking her head and giving him a nudge, though there was a coy smile playing around her lips. The fact was she had been quite the looker in her day; she was still a very attractive woman, but she'd got lost somewhere in the sixties and had a touch of the old hippie about her. Her hair was shoulder-length and grey right through, though it did suit her, and she was fond of kaftan-type dresses and tops, scarves and beads and big dangly earrings, in orange, purple and emerald. Emma would have loved to rein her in, she could be so elegant if she only refined her look a little.

'So I had to rely on sheer wit to get her attention,' her dad was saying, and fortunately, that was something he had in spades. He was also a very handsome man, certainly he had aged well. The two of them had remained blissfully in love for forty years. It was the real thing. Emma wondered if people could see that in her and Blake.

'We can't talk about the success of our marriage without talking about our children,' Edward continued.

Ah, he'd decided to go in reverse order this time, starting with the joke about Eddie being their favourite son.

'. . . I can get away with saying that because he's our one and only.'

Now he would move onto Evie, what a sweet girl she had always been, what a beautiful wife and mother she had become.

'Evie and Craig are the very picture of good old-fashioned domestic bliss . . .'

Evie was crying, which wasn't unusual in itself, she was always emotional at times like this. But she was actually sobbing. Craig put his arm around her, and then Emma witnessed something she had never seen before – Evie shrugged him off. What on earth was going on with those two?

'Which brings us to Elizabeth. Now, have I mentioned our Liz is a doctor?'

Oh, here we go. His line got the intended laugh, with one guest calling out in response, 'Once or twice.'

There followed a homage to Liz ... her extraordinary intelligence, ability, compassion . . . Emma stifled a yawn.

'And just look at our beautiful Emma, standing over there. Always so immaculate, so poised, never a hair out of place.'

Was that the best they could ever say about her? The highest compliment? That she was pretty? Praising your children's good looks was a bit self-congratulatory, it seemed to Emma. She actually resembled her mother most strongly, that's why her dad was always making such a fuss about her looks. But she had been born with this face, and while she did work hard at looking her best, Emma didn't see that as an accomplishment, it was just good grooming. Her parents never talked about what she did, her achievements, her successful career; she doubted they even thought of it as a career.

'And finally we come to Ellen, our eldest, the girl who made parents out of us in the first place. I don't think a day has gone by that she hasn't made us proud. A career teacher in the public school system, she has the kind of integrity and commitment and values that have resulted in the two exemplary individuals we are proud to call our beautiful grandchildren, Kate and Sam. And now you'll be pleased, and no doubt relieved, that I'm going to shut up and hand the proceedings over to Ellen, who is going to propose the toast for us.'

Ellen had been standing over to one side, and she moved in closer beside her parents. 'I met Mum and Dad in the usual way,' she began. 'I was quite young, inexperienced in the ways of the world. So I thought I'd better hook up with some people who knew what they were doing . . .'

'Ellen always gets asked to speak,' Emma muttered aside to Blake, who had come to stand behind her as the speeches began. 'I give presentations to hundreds of people all the time, but am I ever asked?'

He just squeezed her shoulder reassuringly. It didn't matter anyway. Emma slipped her hand into her clutch purse and felt for her engagement ring. She hadn't worn it here, of course, or she would have spoiled the surprise. She had planned the precise moment to make the announcement, just after the toast, as her parents prepared to cut the cake. Once the cake was cut everyone would disperse, and she didn't want their announcement to seem like an afterthought. They were going to step up to the front, and Emma was going to say, 'Actually, before we go on, Blake and I have some news.' The buzz would be immediate, everyone would be guessing babies, weddings . . . Emma had pictured herself, one hand in Blake's, while her parents held her free hand in both of theirs, their eyes shining, bursting with anticipation.

But as she stepped forward, her arm linked in Blake's, and the words came out of her mouth, she saw the expression on her mother's face, her lips set in a grim line, her eyes with that look she used to get whenever they had visitors and one of the children went to take a piece of cake before the guests. Her eyes were saying, *Don't you dare*, but barely perceptibly; only her children could read that look.

Emma froze.

'What the news, darling?' her father prompted.

She stirred, glancing around at all the eyes on her, though avoiding her mother's. 'Um, well,' Emma swallowed. She took a breath. She could do this, she was going to do this. She had every right.

'Blake and I are engaged.'

She didn't really hear the happy cry and burst of applause, she only saw her mother's forced smile as she lifted her glass with everyone else.

'Well, let me be the first to say it's about time, because I'm sure I'm not going to be the last,' her dad declared, but he said it with a twinkle in his eye. 'To Blake and Emma.'

'Blake and Emma.'

'Well, we'd best get this cake cut,' her mother said briskly.

The guests swarmed around Emma and Blake, congratulating them, but it was all a blur. As soon as she was able, Emma extracted herself from the throng and darted towards the kitchen. As she went through the door, she felt a firm hand on her arm. Emma turned and her mother propelled her into the kitchen, bringing her face close. 'Honestly Emma, how could you?'

'What?'

'Don't play innocent,' she said, her voice low. 'All these years, no word of getting married, and then you decide to spring it on us today. How could you do that to your sister, with everything she's going through?'

Emma could feel tears stinging her eyes. 'I don't know what you mean.'

'Of course you do, you knew exactly what you were doing,' she said, releasing her arm. 'Rubbing your poor sister's face in it. I hope you're happy.'

Emma turned away and rushed to the back door as she heard her name called. But she didn't stop, she pushed on the door and disappeared outside.

*

'Mum, what did you say to her?'

Evelyn turned to see both Ellen and Liz looking expectantly at her.

'Say to whom?'

'Mum!' Ellen groaned. 'Cut it out. What did you say to Emma?'

'Nothing . . .'

Her daughters just stared at her.

'I only said, or *suggested*, that maybe this wasn't the best time to make her announcement.'

'Why not?'

'It didn't seem very sensitive to me, in light of recent developments.'

'Mum . . .' Ellen sighed, pressing her fingers to the bridge of her nose.

'I'll go,' said Liz as she headed for the back door. She pushed it open and walked through, and as the door swung back behind her with a familiar thwack, Liz was overcome by a wave of nostalgia. Summer holidays, the heat, the cicadas, the smell in the air, same as it ever was, she thought now, breathing it in. The backyard had been their playground, their own private world when they were little. It was huge, a developer's dream, you could probably fit half-a-dozen townhouses back here. Thank God her parents would rather be carried out in their respective boxes than see a developer get their hands on the place.

Liz slipped off her shoes and left them on the back verandah. She wanted to feel the cool, spongy grass under her feet as she wandered down into the depths of the yard towards the ancient jacaranda, where she could just see the back of Emma's head through the foliage.

'Hey Em,' she announced, so she wouldn't startle her.

Emma didn't respond, didn't turn around. Liz circled the tree and came to stand in front of her. Emma was perched on a lowlying bough, her back straight, her legs crossed elegantly, dabbing at her cheeks with a white lace handkerchief.

'Are you all right?' Liz asked her.

She sniffed. 'Sure. Why wouldn't I be? I'm engaged,' she said flatly.

'Congratulations,' Liz offered.

'She hates me. My own mother despises me.'

'She doesn't hate you,' Liz sighed, leaning against a higher bough. 'You know Mum, she just worries about everyone's feelings.'

'Well, she wasn't too worried about mine just then.'

'It's okay, Len is putting her back in her box right now.'

Emma barely nodded, staring down at the grass at her feet.

'So show me the ring,' Liz tried next.

She folded her arms, tucking her hands out of sight. 'What makes you think I have a ring already?'

'Because I was nearly blinded a moment ago when you had your hand up to your face.'

Liz detected a hint of a smile as Emma lifted her hand and held it out for her sister.

'Oh my God, that is a ring,' Liz declared.

It had to be close to a couple of carats but it was dead classy, a simple, brilliant-cut whopper set in platinum.

'I know, isn't it beautiful?' Emma sighed. 'It's Tiffany, exactly the ring I've wanted for as long as I can remember.'

'So you picked it out together?'

'No,' she denied. 'Blake surprised me. The whole thing came totally out of the blue.'

'So how did he know what ring to get you?' asked Liz.

Emma waved her hand dismissively. 'This is *the* Tiffany setting. It's all I've ever wanted. Blake knew that.'

Just then Ellen appeared around the perimeter of the tree and walked over to join them. 'I'm really sorry about that, Emma.'

She shrugged. 'It wasn't your fault.'

'Mum was just trying to protect me,' Ellen explained. 'You know what she's like. But I told her she was being ridiculous, it's not like I'm anti-love and marriage all of a sudden. Good news is good news, there's barely enough of it to go around without playing it down.'

Emma lifted her eyes then to meet Ellen's. 'I wasn't trying to –'

'I know, and I told Mum that,' Ellen assured her. 'I'm really happy for you, Em.'

She gave her a small smile. 'Thank you.'

'So can I see the ring, please?'

Her face broke into a proper smile then, as she held her hand out and Ellen took it. Ellen gave a low whistle. 'Oh my God.'

'Let me see, let me see.' It was Evie, trotting down the yard towards them, breathless as ever.

'It's all right, Evie, take your time, we're not going anywhere,' Liz assured her.

She gasped when she laid eyes on the ring. 'Oh, Emma, it's so beautiful, it's the most beautiful ring I've ever seen!'

'Isn't it?' Emma said proudly. 'It's exactly the one I've always wanted.'

'So how long have you been planning this?' asked Ellen.

'I didn't plan a thing,' she declared. 'It came as a total surprise, I was just telling Liz. I mean, let's not be coy here, everyone knows how much I wanted this, and apparently Blake noticed how many people at work were getting married, and it suddenly occurred to him that he didn't know what we were waiting for. And that if it meant so much to me, we should just do it.'

'That's sweet,' Evie cooed. 'Is that what he said when he proposed?'

'Oh, no, that all came out afterwards.' She sighed dreamily. 'It was the most romantic proposal ever.'

'So tell us!' Evie insisted, with a little jump.

Ellen and Liz glanced at each other. It was the happiest they'd seen her all day.

'Well, okay . . .' Emma took a breath, looking around at her sisters as though she was about to tell them a story. 'First I knew of anything Blake rang me at work on Wednesday. "How about we eat out tonight?" he said. I replied sure, I could meet him straight after I finished up at the office.

'But he said, "No, go home, get dressed up, let's do something nice,"' Emma added, becoming animated.

'I said, "What's going on?" I suppose I should have twigged, but I didn't. Blake just fobbed me off anyway. "You get all dressed up for everyone else," he said, "how about you get dressed up for me this time?"

'Then, when I was at home, a text message arrived,' Emma went on. 'Blake was sending a cab for me. Well, I told him not to be silly, I could get a cab myself. But he insisted it was already on its way.'

'And you still didn't wonder what was going on?' Ellen asked.

'No,' Emma shook her head, holding her hands up with an innocent shrug. 'I said, "Where will I tell the driver to take me?" And he said, "Don't worry, he knows where to go."'

Evie let out a little cry and clapped her hands together. 'It's so exciting!'

'So the taxi drives through the city streets, towards the harbour, and pulls up outside the Park Hyatt. Blake was standing there, waiting for me.' Emma sighed, as though she was seeing him again now. 'He was dressed in a *tux*. Have you ever seen Blake in a tux? He wears it so well,' she swooned.

Liz's stomach was starting to turn ever so slightly.

'I said to him, "What's going on?" I still hadn't twigged. Honestly after all this time, I never suspected what was coming, it didn't even cross my mind.'

Liz was beginning to find that hard to believe.

'I thought maybe he got a promotion,' Emma went on, 'or a big bonus, that he was going to surprise me with tickets for some exotic overseas holiday. Anyway, he took me up to a *suite* – it was gorgeous, three rooms, three balconies with views across the harbour to the Opera House. He really surpassed all my expectations.'

'But you said you weren't expecting it,' said Ellen.

'Well, no, of course, but you know what I mean,' she dismissed, and went on with her story. 'There was champagne chilling in a bucket and Blake poured us both a glass. By then I was so excited, I just had to say, "What are we toasting to?"' Emma took a breath. 'And he said, "To our future."

'And right at that precise moment, a waiter walked in carrying a tray covered with a sterling silver dome. I'm almost certain it was Georg Jensen.'

'Who, the waiter?'

'No, Evie,' Emma smiled. 'The silver. Anyway, the waiter passed it to Blake and then he disappeared. I said, "What's this?" And Blake said, "Something special to start with." And he lifted the lid . . .'

Evie squealed.

'And there, on the tray, was a blue Tiffany box!'

'What did you do?' Evie gasped.

'My eyes filled with tears as Blake picked up the box and opened it to reveal my engagement ring.' She paused to gaze at it now. 'And then he said – let me remember this right – "Emma, you're my best friend, my partner, and now I wonder if you'll take the next step and consent to be my wife."'

That did it for Evie, she burst into tears.

'That's beautiful, Em,' said Liz, though she thought it was a bit prosaic after all the build-up.

Evie was wailing now. 'Evie, are you okay?' Ellen asked her, giving her back a gentle rub.

'Yes, yes,' she sobbed, 'it's just all the emotion. It's been a very emotional day,' she added, her voice barely a squeak.

'Does this have anything to do with what you wanted to talk about before?' asked Emma.

But that just set her off again.

'Hey guys.' It was Eddie coming around the perimeter of the tree. 'What's wrong with Evie?'

'Nothing, she'll be fine,' Liz assured him, her arm firmly around her sister.

'Okay, well, people are starting to leave and Mum and Dad were wondering where you all got to.'

*

The house was finally empty of guests, the caterers had packed up and left, but Edward and Evelyn had asked the family to stay back a while longer. They put Sam and Kate in charge of the littlies and had sent them all to the lounge room to watch a DVD. The adults were gathered around the dining room table.

'Dad and I have something important we need to tell you.'

'What is it?' Evie looked fearful. 'You're not sick?'

'Of course not, darling, we're fine. This is nothing bad, okay? In fact, it's good news. We're actually pretty excited about it and we hope you will be too.' Evelyn glanced at her husband. 'We wanted to let you know that we're selling the house.'

The announcement was met with complete silence as the shock reverberated around the table.

'What?' Evie said weakly after a while.

Ellen felt shattered. 'Why?'

'For the same reasons anyone does it at our age,' said Edward. 'The house is too big for us to maintain –'

'We can help,' Liz volunteered. 'We all should be helping out more anyway. We can work out a roster –'

Her father was shaking his head. 'It's not just that, Liz. There's the expense involved in keeping a big house . . . The rates alone –'

'If it's a matter of money,' she persisted, 'you know I can help there too.'

Evelyn covered her daughter's hand. 'That's very generous, darling, but it's not what we want.'

'But surely you can't *want* to sell the house?' said Ellen.

'Yes, actually, we do,' Evelyn nodded, with another glance at her husband.

'It's time, girls,' he said. 'This house has been a wonderful family home, and we'll miss it. But it's time for us to move on, for the house to take its place as part of our family's history.'

'Not if some developer gets hold of it,' Liz declared, 'and demolishes it.'

Blake shifted uncomfortably in his chair as Evie gasped, her eyes filling with tears again. 'Oh no, could that actually happen?'

'Things change, girls,' Edward reassured them. 'And that's okay. Come on, you're all adults, you've all moved on with your own lives, you have to let your mother and I do the same thing. You can't expect us to stay put, be some kind of caretakers of your childhood memories.'

'But why now?' said Ellen. 'Aren't we going through enough change right now? Couldn't this wait?'

'Not everything's about you, Ellen,' said Emma.

'I'm not just talking about me.'

'Well, who else is going through a big change?'

'You are,' she countered. 'You're getting married.'

'So what?' said Emma. 'This doesn't affect my wedding plans.'

'Not everything's about you, either,' Ellen threw her words back at her.

'I don't think this has anything to do with any of us,' Emma said archly. 'It's Mum and Dad's house, it's their life, and therefore their decision. And I for one am right behind them.'

Ellen folded her arms. 'Well I just think it's terribly sudden. Don't you think you should take more time to make such a huge decision as selling up the family home? I mean, it's such a big move.'

'Absolutely,' Evie sniffed.

'And now that it's out in the open we can all help you decide,' agreed Liz.

'We can discuss all the alternatives,' Ellen added.

'It's not our decision,' Emma maintained.

'I think your parents are old enough to know what they want.'

'Whose side are you on?' Evie glared at Craig.

The discussion, such as it was, rapidly descended into squabbling, with no one actually listening to what anyone else was saying, and Edward and Evelyn sitting dumbfounded at the end of the table.

A loud thump sounded from the other end of the table. All heads turned to look at Eddie.

'Now that I have your attention,' he said. 'The house is already listed with the realtor. The signs go up on Monday.'

'How do you know that?' Ellen asked him accusingly. 'Did he put you up to this?' she added, turning back to her parents.

'No, we actually approached Eddie,' said Edward.

'Why didn't you come to us as well?'

'If you want to know the truth, we were trying to avoid this very scene,' said Evelyn.

'So much for that plan,' said Liz.

'And what does Eddie know about all this?' Ellen said indignantly. 'He's just a kid.'

'Girls,' Eddie interrupted, 'I might be the baby of the family, but I'm not a kid any more. And I do have some experience, and contacts.'

'Come on, Eddie,' Ellen rolled her eyes. 'What experience do you have in real estate? You still live in a rented share house.'

'Not real estate, but finances,' he explained. 'I have been running a successful business for several years now, in case you forgot.'

'You teach people to hang-glide,' Ellen said drolly.

Maybe it was being surrounded by so many nurturers that had made Eddie a tearaway from the time he took his first steps. He climbed trees and made billycarts, before progressing to dirt bikes and skateboards. He was attracted to anything that had an element of danger. When he discovered hang-gliding, he found his true calling.

Ellen turned back to her parents. 'He takes risks for a living and he's who you go to for financial advice?'

Eddie managed to keep his cool. 'I have made a lot of contacts, Lenny, people who could give Mum and Dad the kind of advice they were looking for. They didn't need a realtor, they needed to secure their future. And we've figured things out so that they can live comfortably till they're a hundred and fifty.'

'Well, what's the point of that?' said Ellen.

Her parents looked taken aback.

'I mean, no offence, Mum and Dad,' she added quickly, 'but you're not going to live that long, much as I wish you could.'

'Me too,' Evie croaked.

'The point is,' Eddie resumed, 'we've worked out an investment portfolio that gives them a comfortable lifestyle, with security to cover all contingencies. They can travel –'

'You want to travel?' asked Liz.

'Of course.'

'First I've heard of it,' Ellen muttered.

'We've talked about travelling all of our lives,' Evelyn insisted.

'Yeah,' said Liz, 'but that's just like everyone talks about it.'

'No,' said Edward, 'we *really* want to travel, we always have, but it's a little hard to do with five kids,' he added rather bluntly.

'On our existing government super we could have done a little travelling,' said Evelyn, 'but we have so much equity tied up in this house, we were shocked when we realised how much, and what we could do with that money.'

'Remember when we bought this house?' Edward said, squeezing his wife's hand and looking fondly at her. 'Our parents thought we were mad for buying in Annandale. It was little better than a slum back then. Of course, there were still some very grand houses around, but we weren't in the market for any of those. We bought the worst house in the worst street, according to our parents. But we couldn't afford anything else.'

'Don't you see, girls,' said Evelyn, 'we won't have to worry about money for the first time in our lives, and we'll have the freedom to go wherever we want for as long as we want.'

'We're going to live like kings,' added their father.

'But *where* will you live?' asked Liz.

'We've been looking at studio apartments in the city,' said Evelyn.

'What?' said Ellen. 'But they're tiny.'

Evelyn shrugged. 'Down the track we might buy something more substantial, maybe up or down the coast, or in the mountains, we don't know yet. But for now, we only need a base, somewhere we can lock up and leave when we're gone.'

Who are you people and what have you done with my parents? Ellen felt like saying. 'So where are the grandchildren supposed to stay when they come to visit?' she put to them.

'We'll visit them instead,' Evelyn smiled.

'And family dinners?'

'You kids already take turns,' said Edward.

'Well, that's it,' Liz declared with a loud sigh. 'Call the realtor tomorrow, Eddie, tell them not to bother with the signs. I'm going to buy the place.'

Now Eddie sighed, rubbing his forehead as if he was getting a headache. 'Liz, we are going to get full market value for this house. I know you earn good money, but it's a very valuable piece of property.'

'Of course I'll pay market value,' Liz said. 'You think I'd rip off Mum and Dad?'

'But you wouldn't get finance, Liz,' Blake chimed in. 'A developer is going to pay premium because they'll earn on the investment.'

'I knew it!' Liz declared. 'You're selling out to developers. You can't think that's okay, Mum? Dad?'

'We're not the devil incarnate,' Blake muttered.

'Look, cards on the table,' said Edward. 'We were approached sometime back by a developer. A proposal to rezone the street was about to be put to council, which would allow low-density development of large blocks. The offer they made, well, your mother and I have never seen that kind of money. And that wasn't the last offer we got. Don't you see, it's an opportunity too good not to take up.'

He looked around the table at the stunned faces of his daughters. 'What exactly is it that you're so worried about, girls?'

'That they'll pull the house down!' Ellen said plainly.

Evie looked like she was in shock.

'Some of the proposals we've been shown have them keeping the house and incorporating sympathetically designed town-houses into the backyard. Council around here is pretty strict about preserving the streetscape.'

'But you can't guarantee that,' said Liz.

'If we sold to a private buyer we couldn't guarantee they wouldn't turn around and sell it either,' Evelyn pointed out.

'Surely you didn't expect us to stay here forever?' said Edward. 'And once it's sold, it's out of our hands.'

'And we lose our family home,' said Ellen. 'The place where we grew up, our history.'

'But we can't lose our history, Ellen. You of all people should know that, you teach the subject,' said Edward. 'History is not in bricks and mortar, and leadlight windows, it's in our memories, in our hearts. Tearing down the house can't destroy that.'

He looked around the table. 'You're all in the process of creating your own histories, with your own families, in the work that you do. People move on, and life goes on. Mum and I have got a little more history we want to create ourselves. It's our time.'

Autumn

Evie dropped down on one knee to retie her laces. She'd put her runners on in a hurry this morning and her left foot felt sloppy inside her shoe. She pulled the laces in firmly; that was better. She stood up again, positioning the earphones of Tayla's iPod into her ears. Tayla would have a holy fit if she knew her mother was using it, but Evie always had it back in place before she was home from school, so what she didn't know . . .

Evie did a quick survey of her surroundings. She hadn't walked here before. It was a bush reserve with a level walking track that bordered a creek for part of the way. She had discovered all sorts of places over the last month or so, courtesy of Google Maps. She liked going out of the area a bit, she was less likely to bump into anyone she knew that way. It made her feel anonymous, and free. At first she hadn't cared where she walked. She just had to walk. It was better than wandering aimlessly around the house, wondering how her life had got to this point, what had happened to the man she had married.

She took off along the path, her shoes pounding on the concrete, quickly establishing a rhythm in time with the music piping into her ears. The day after that dreadful night Evie had functioned on autopilot. She had sent Craig off to do whatever he wanted for the day, in truth because she could barely stand to look at him. She had taken the kids to McDonald's as she had promised and ordered herself a large burger meal with every extra available, and a thickshake instead of Coke. Once they had sat down and she had organised everyone with their meals, laid out Cody's burger and emptied his chips into the box the way he liked, Evie had opened hers and the look of it had made her feel suddenly queasy. Even the smell was nauseating. She'd been feeling sick to the stomach since the previous night.

'So, there are these places, for adults, you know,' Craig had said. 'Where adults can get together.'

She'd frowned. 'What, like a club?'

'Yeah, they are like clubs. That's exactly right. You can have a drink, and there's music, and you get to meet people.'

Evie didn't know what this had to do with their sex life. She'd heard some couples liked to go to dance classes. Her friend, Wendy, had only recently decided to take up dance classes with her husband, to spice things up a little, she'd told the girls one morning at playgroup. Everyone had oohed and aahed, and giggled and asked questions. Evie had wondered how dance classes could spice things up – Craig would hate it. She was glad they didn't need to spice things up.

Or so she had thought.

'Is there dancing?' she asked him.

'I reckon there's probably some dancing.'

'But you hate to dance.'

'I don't think you have to dance.'

'So you're not talking about dance lessons?'

Craig had laughed a big belly laugh then.

'I don't get what you're talking about,' Evie said, becoming a little frustrated. 'I thought you were going to tell me something you wanted . . . *sexually*,' she added, lowering her voice.

He seemed a little nervous. 'Well, I am.'

She frowned. 'What's going to a club and meeting people got to do with . . .' And then she stopped suddenly, her mouth hanging open, her heart dropping like a stone.

'There's these clubs,' Craig went on carefully, 'and they're all above board, they're only for married couples. Well, maybe you don't have to be married, but they're for couples anyway. Swingers' clubs.'

'What?' she said, her voice barely making it out of her throat.

'It's all really safe, and clean, and respectable.'

'*Respectable?*' she squeaked. 'Married couples . . . swapping with each other? You call that *respectable?*'

'Look, you were the one who wanted to talk about this,' he said defensively. 'This goes on everywhere, you've got no idea, Ev. In regular neighbourhoods, with normal people. Probably someone you know is doing it.'

'I doubt it,' she grimaced.

'How would you know? You think anyone's going to tell you? You're so narrow-minded.'

'I'm not narrow-minded . . . it's just a shock.'

'You're shocked, yet you were prepared to take it up the arse?'

'Craig!'

'You said it, not me,' he taunted. 'I wouldn't ask you to do something so disgusting.'

'But you want me to . . . *be* with someone else's husband, and you don't think there's anything wrong with that?'

'Not between consenting adults, no. And anyway, you don't even have to do anything if you don't want to.'

'What, I'm just expected to sit and watch?' she cried.

He groaned. 'I knew you wouldn't be into it. I dunno why you asked if you weren't going to have an open mind.' He stood up. 'You were the one who said you don't want to end up like Tim and Ellen.'

She looked up at him. 'You think partner swapping is going to keep our marriage together?'

'Think about it, Evie, we've never even had sex with anyone else,' he glared down at her. 'How long do you think it'll be before curiosity kills the cat? Don't you reckon it might be better to at least try it, in a safe place, with both of us involved, giving our blessing?'

How could she ever give her blessing to that?

'*Mother!*' Tayla cried. 'Aren't you going to *do* something?'

Evie had been jolted out of her reverie in time to see Fanta streaming across the table and Cody in tears while Jayden laughed hysterically.

'It's going everywhere,' Tayla squealed, jumping clear of the table and clutching her packet of fries to her chest.

'Jayden! What did you do?' Evie demanded, grabbing the cup, though there was nothing left to save.

'I didn't do nothin!' Jayden protested. 'He did it himself, the stupid dumbhead!'

Cody wailed as Evie attempted to stem the flood with flimsy paper napkins. People were staring. A young boy in uniform appeared with a mop and bucket.

'It's all right, ma'am,' he said. 'I'll clean it up.'

'My frieth are all wet, Mummy,' Cody sobbed.

'It's okay, darling, I'll get you some more.'

'Go up to the counter, ma'am,' said the boy, 'they'll replace his drink for you.'

'Oh, no, it's okay,' said Evie, trying to wipe Cody off with the sodden napkins. 'It was my fault.'

'It's all right, ma'am, part of the service,' he said. 'Hey matey, you can get another drink, okay?'

'Can I get another drink too?' Jayden piped in.

'Shoosh, Jayden,' said Evie, gathering up their things.

'How come he gets everything just because he's so stupid?'

'I not thtupid, Jayden!'

'Are too!'

'Be quiet!' Evie hissed, ushering them out of the young man's way. 'Thank you so much.'

Evie had herded the children over to the counter and bought them whatever they asked for. More fries, drinks, sundaes, whatever. She paid for it all, she didn't care, she just wanted to get out of there.

'But where are we going to eat all this, Mother?' Tayla wanted to know as Evie bustled them out the door.

'We'll go to the park,' she said.

She'd sat on the park bench, watching the kids, her head still buzzing. Cody stayed snuggled in beside her, eating his sundae, out of harm's – and his brother's – way.

Craig had stormed off to bed that first night, his back turned away from her when she came into the room. She thought about talking to him, coaxing him, offering sex. But she really didn't feel like it, she was too upset. She climbed into bed and stayed over on her side, but she couldn't get to sleep for ages.

When she woke in the morning Craig was already up. He was sitting out at the breakfast table, reading the paper, totally ignoring the mayhem the boys were creating around him trying to make their own breakfast.

'Why don't you go and have the day to yourself?' Evie had suggested wanly.

'Fine with me,' he'd returned, slapping the paper down on the table and walking out of the room.

Evie leaned against the railing now, breathing hard, her legs rippling as oxygen pumped through her veins. She'd been surprised by that sensation at first, even a little startled, but now she loved it. It made her feel like she was alive.

The next week had gone by in a blur. Evie had thrown herself into making the food for the anniversary party, back-to-school shopping and end-of-holiday outings and play dates for the children. She'd filled in every minute of every day, had said yes to every request from the kids all week, which had meant that although she'd been run ragged, she hadn't had time to think.

Craig had been morose, but Evie had managed to stay out of his way for the most part. Gradually, though, things had begun to thaw between them. Frostiness had melted into begrudging politeness, until, on the night before the anniversary party, he had called her Pud with some affection.

When she had come downstairs that evening after putting the kids to bed, Craig was sitting at the table rather than in front of the telly. He obviously wanted to talk.

Evie took a seat at the table opposite him.

'I don't want things to be like this, Craig,' she said first.

'Me either,' he said, putting his hand over hers. 'I knew you'd come around.'

Her stomach lurched. She'd hoped he would say let's just drop it, pretend it never came up. But she knew in her heart that wouldn't work either. It would be the elephant in the room from now on. Evie knew what her husband wanted, and if she didn't go along with it, he might go ahead and do it without her. Curiosity would one day kill the cat, he'd said so himself. There was no getting out of this.

'I'd just like a little time to get used to the idea,' Evie said in a small voice.

He'd picked up her hand then and kissed it. 'Take all the time you need, Puddin'.'

So now it was hanging over her like clouds on washing day, threatening to ruin everything. She could think of little else, but she couldn't talk to anyone about it. How could she? She'd foolishly tried to bring it up the next day with Emma, but it had just come out, she desperately needed to hear someone say that it was sick, or weird, or just plain wrong, so that she didn't have to feel like there was something wrong with her. Maybe Craig was right, normal people were doing it on their very street, but she had her doubts. And if they really were doing it, then she had her doubts they were normal.

A few days later, she had finally found herself alone in the empty house. She had taken the kids to school, and Cody to preschool, and returned home to get on with her chores. But the house felt strange and quiet, and her thoughts were too loud, echoing off the walls of her skull, replaying Craig's words over and over. She decided she just had to face this head-on, see what she was up against. She googled 'clubs for swingers', and then clicked on the first thing that came up without looking too closely. A page opened, purple and black with blinking lights. She scanned the page, her eyes taking in random words and phrases – no prostitution, no single guys . . . adult play . . . fantasy . . . orgy room. Evie gasped. Her eyes drifted to photos down the side panel. At first glance they looked like those awful pictures from the holocaust, limbs and bodies all thrown together in a heap. She blinked, looking more closely.

Evie's heart had leapt out of her chest as she fumbled with the mouse to close the page. She felt sick. What if one of the kids stumbled across this? She knew there was a way to delete the history, so she searched through the menu until she found it. It went back day by day for a week, but something compelled her to click on 'Show All History'. Evie sat stunned as pages of porn sites came up, all mixed in with the kids' Google searches and fan sites, and her email. The proximity alarmed her: surely it wasn't that difficult for any of the kids to come across this? Jayden was far more cluey on the computer than she was, and she'd found it easily enough. Evie felt the walls closing in around her, making it hard to breathe. She had to delete all of this, obviously, but then Craig would know she'd seen it, wouldn't he? But she couldn't just leave it here. Well, so what, what was he going to say to her? How could he defend this?

With a trembling hand Evie clicked on Clear History and it was all gone. Just like that. Now she had to get out of here. She grabbed her keys and ran out the door in the clothes she was wearing – a skirt, T-shirt, and thongs on her feet. She hadn't walked very far before her feet started to hurt, and her thighs began rubbing together uncomfortably. But she couldn't stop, and she couldn't go back to the house, not yet. She walked and walked, till her thighs were chafed and the balls of her feet were burning, all the way to the local coffee shop. She ordered her usual skinny cappuccino, and a rich chocolate and caramel slice. But when it was placed in front of her, Evie had the same queasy feeling as she'd had that day at McDonald's. Well, she had to get over this. Food was her comfort, her solace; nothing made her feel better than food. She took a tentative bite, then another, but as she swallowed it down, it felt slimy, like eating liver, leaving a sickly aftertaste. She pushed the plate aside and finished her coffee, blinking back tears. When she paid at the counter, she bought a bottle of water and began the long, painful walk home.

The next day when the walls began to crowd in on her again, Evie changed into a pair of comfortable three-quarter length pants and put on socks and sneakers. It was a vast improvement on the day before, but the sneakers had thin soles, so her already tender feet were burning again before long. As were her nose and cheeks under the blazing late summer sun. So she went out shopping that afternoon and bought herself some proper runners – not expensive ones, they were only from Kmart – and a pair of stretchy gym pants. When she tried them on at home they looked hideous, she could almost see the cellulite on her thighs and backside through the fabric. But she could cover up most of that with a long T-shirt, and anyway, she didn't care how she looked, she just wanted to be comfortable.

Craig never mentioned that his porn sites had been deleted, however, that was the least of Evie's problems. He had taken to showing her articles, even testimonials, about these so-called swingers' clubs that were supposedly frequented by normal couples.

Evie was beginning to wonder if she was naive, perhaps even frigid. But she didn't really believe that; she was no more frigid than any of her girlfriends. When they got into bed at night they desired nothing more than an unbroken night's sleep. Most admitted that once they got going, it wasn't too bad, and Evie felt the same. It was just the getting going. She was sure she wasn't frigid, in fact she knew women who simply refused to give oral sex, no matter how much their husbands begged for it. Craig should realise how lucky he was.

But clearly he didn't think he was lucky at all. Clearly Evie was not enough.

The only thing that helped was to walk. She couldn't eat; food didn't comfort her anymore. Anything she ate just sat in her stomach, setting like a lump of concrete. But walking felt good. And the longer she walked, the better she felt. Sometimes she wished she could just keep walking and walking, like Forrest Gump, till she was far away, out of reach.

But Evie could never leave her children. This was her life, like it or not. But why did it have to be this? She was a good wife, a compliant wife, a willing wife. If Craig wanted to try sailing, she would have overcome her fear of deep water; if he'd wanted to start playing tennis, she would have taken lessons. She didn't know how on earth she was supposed to prepare herself for this, and her time was running out.

Wednesday

'Do we need to know this, miss?'

Ellen sighed inwardly.

Education, in fact knowledge itself, apparently only had value these days if it was going to be in an exam. It drove Ellen nuts.

'What do you mean, do you *need* to know it?' she said, launching into her usual homily. 'Why does anyone need to know anything?'

She saw a few eyes roll. They'd heard it before.

'If people only bothered to find out about anything because they were going to have an exam on it, where do you think we'd be today as a society?'

It occurred to her that this would make an excellent assignment: choose a great discovery and imagine what the world would be like without it. But she couldn't set something like that, because it wasn't in the syllabus, or the exam. She was hamstrung by the very establishment she was trying to defend.

The bell sounded, signalling the end of the period. Ellen was relieved she had a free next. And it was a proper free period, because the Year 12s had Maths now so she wasn't going to be bothered by any earnest, or anxious, or otherwise needy students.

The staffroom was empty. Ellen logged onto her computer and checked her emails.

From: Emma Beckett
To: Cara, Ellen, Evie, Liz
Subject: Crunch Time!

Well ladies, it's down to the cinnamon or the pewter. I adore them both, and I don't need to tell you that the final choice is going to affect everything – the flowers, the decorations, the entire theme, really. So I have to get it right. I wish I could have two weddings, I just can't choose!

The only way is to line everyone up and compare the colours against all the skin types. So I'm calling a meeting for a week from Thursday, in the evening, of course. That should give you all plenty of notice, so you really have to let me know straight away if you can't make it so that I can reschedule. But I would like to get this settled before Easter.

Looking forward to it!

xx Emma

Ellen groaned, picking up the phone and dialling Liz's office on the off-chance she might catch her between patients. She was in luck, her receptionist put her through.

'Did you get the latest email?' she asked Liz.

'Of course,' Liz said down the phone line. 'It's almost fun seeing what's going to come next.'

'You think?'

'I said "almost".'

The last few months could have been made into a reality series entitled 'Crazy Emma, the Bride from Hell', the kind of reality show that Ellen would never watch. In reality, Ellen didn't watch reality shows. Ever. And yet she was being dragged into this one, whether she liked it or not. And she definitely did not. They were constantly being notified, updated, or 'consulted' (ha!) on every minute detail. And it was going to keep up this way right until the big day – Emma had already sent out a schedule of dress fittings and cake tastings and floral viewings, hair and makeup practice sessions and an alarming number of what she called 'progress meetings'. She had just lately decided that she was accumulating so much information she needed to set up her own blog, so that everyone involved could simply subscribe and keep up to date. Fabric swatches had been dispatched physically – by courier, no less – because Emma could not ensure the colours would be reproduced faithfully on the computer screen. But apart from that, she had been so thrilled with the blog concept that she had decided to link a blog to the wedding invitations when the time came – a one-stop spot where her guests could find helpful gift suggestions, maps and directions to the venue, a tantalising glimpse of the menu, and even 'what to wear' guidelines.

'It's the *exhaustive* detail,' groaned Ellen. 'Don't you find it . . . well, *exhausting*?'

'What did you expect?' said Liz. 'Emma's been planning this since she was, what? Six?'

'Yeah, I know. I just don't understand why we all have to be involved in every little detail. I'd be happy just to show up on the day.'

'That's okay for you to say,' said Liz, 'you're not a bridesmaid.'

That had been Emma's first major announcement. She loved *all* her sisters, wished she could have them *all* in the bridal party, but that was just not going to work. Blake didn't have any brothers, so of course his best friend, Gordie, would be the best man. Liz was the perfect partner for him: complementary height, colouring, age. Of course she had to include Blake's family, and they were both closer to his younger sister, Cara. Eddie was the obvious choice for her partner; again, they were physically a good match. Blake had no other significant male friends to pair with her remaining sisters, so Emma instead suggested a 'representative' from each of their families. Kate was to be the representative for Ellen's family, as she would make the perfect partner for Blake's eldest sister's son. Emma would never have chosen Melinda herself; she was older and, frankly, she had let herself go since the divorce, Emma had confided. But she was sure her son, Chris, would clean up quite nicely with a decent haircut and shave, and a well-cut suit. Lastly she had to include Evie's family, so Tayla was to be paired with Blake's second cousin . . . or his second cousin's son . . . Ellen was not sure of the genealogy. Tayla was beside herself, and Evie was so thrilled for her daughter it never occurred to her why she had not been considered.

The brutal truth was that Emma had applied the same styling principles to her bridal party as she would to a magazine spread. Ellen was simply too plain and mumsy for Emma's line-up. Kate was slim, honey blonde, and would be barely nineteen by the wedding. Kate could wear anything. Plump little Evie, on the other hand, could not. She would spoil the entire effect.

So Emma would have her picture-perfect wedding. And Ellen found herself resenting the whole thing. She didn't care how much time, energy and money Emma was prepared to waste, but she couldn't expect the same commitment from everyone else. With each fresh email or blog post, the costs ratcheted up another notch, while Emma kept insisting this was a massive bargain, or that was an unbelievably generous discount. She really did live on another planet. Sure, she had a contact who was going to be able to get their shoes half-price, but they were shoes that retailed for eight hundred dollars. Ellen had never spent anything like four hundred dollars on a pair of shoes for herself, let alone her teenage daughter.

'I told Tim if it kept on like this he was going to have to help out,' she said to Liz. 'He said he had enough expenses without having to pander to Emma's extravagance, and that I should just talk to her and tell her how it is. Like it was that easy! Easy for Tim, he can sit back and be the nice guy, and never have to confront anyone, just like he did right throughout our marriage –'

'Sorry Ellen,' Liz broke in. 'I'm going to have to go, I have a client in a few minutes.'

'No, I'm sorry for carrying on,' she said. 'It just gets to me, you know, every single thing is a negotiation. It's exhausting. Like the other day Sam brought home a note about the Year 11 camp, which costs a bomb, and so naturally I approached Tim about it. He said, "Doesn't that come out of child support?" Well, I said that child support or no child support, as a sole parent I simply can't afford extras like this, which means Sam would have to miss out. Then Tim tried to argue that I'm not a sole parent if I'm getting child support, but I think he's missing the point, don't you?'

'Um, yeah, maybe . . . Look, I can't really get into this now, Len,' Liz apologised. 'I do have a client.'

'Sorry, sorry, talk to you later, bye,' she said quickly, hanging up.

Ellen cringed when she heard that tone – the awkward, 'I really don't want to listen to this' tone. She didn't mean to put Tim down, she was only getting stuff off her chest. But she couldn't help feeling that no one wanted to hear about her woes; that, as this was her choice, she should just get on with it and stop complaining. But it was hard sometimes, and she did have valid grounds for complaint. Keeping the separation amicable was for the kids' sake; didn't she have a right to have a whinge occasionally to the people closest to her?

Sometimes Ellen felt terribly alone.

*

Liz put down the receiver, feeling a twinge of guilt for cutting off her sister like that. Ellen may complain about Emma, but she was just as hard work at the moment. Liz wished she could hear herself sometimes, the way she sounded when she started ranting about Tim . . . Liz understood, she really did – Tim could definitely be a thickhead at times – but Ellen didn't do herself any favours harping about it. Liz wondered if she should say something to her . . .

Oh, sure, like she could ever do that. Liz loved her dearly, but Ellen was not accustomed to being told, something to do with being the eldest probably.

She brought up her appointment schedule on the computer screen, then clicked on the patient file. Her heart sank.

New referral, female, thirty-nine years of age. Condition undisclosed. Requests dermatological assessment and consultation.

In other words, most likely confronting a midlife crisis and here to find out about Botox and other age-defying options.

Liz was feeling increasingly frustrated with her profession of late – Emma was right, she had turned into little more than a 'glorified beautician' – and she was getting tired of it. She'd never had a burning desire to specialise in dermatology, she doubted anyone did. It was emergency and surgery that appealed to Liz more than anything – the adrenalin, the life and death nature of the work, the fact that you were actually doing something, on the spot, often to save a life. But she was also a pragmatist; she knew there was no way she could be a surgeon or a trauma specialist if she was going to have a family one day. So she'd chosen dermatology for its regular hours and relative lack of stress.

But she had also needed to get right away from surgery, back then. It was around the time – or one of the times – that she and Andrew had attempted to call it quits. He was being eaten up by guilt, and as for Liz's part, she had hardly planned on being the 'other woman'. But she knew she couldn't be around him and not be with him, so she moved specialities, and hospitals, and far out of his reach. It worked for about six months but something always drew them back together. Occasionally it was some work-related event, more often than not Andrew would contact her during a tough time with Danny.

So here she was, a fully-fledged dermatologist with her own private practice. A thousand diseases, two creams – or so the standing joke went. It was a little more complicated than that. There were genuine and serious skin diseases that she was trained to diagnose and treat, but more and more of her time was being taken up by women who wanted their fears about ageing to be taken with equal gravity, and to be treated scientifically. They had moved on from the beautician and were prepared to pay for a specialist and wait weeks for an appointment to demonstrate the serious medical nature of their condition.

Liz would try to tell them that ageing was an inevitable process, and that Australians were particularly susceptible, being a largely Caucasian race living in a country suited to people with much higher melanin levels in their skin.

But *she* had good skin, they would invariably remark, what did *she* use on her skin? Ever since Liz had gone into dermatology and learned just what was in the goop in those overpriced jars, she'd given up using anything at all on her face. But people didn't want to hear that, they wanted a magical potion. So she simply told them 'sunscreen'.

Of course that wasn't good enough either, what they were really after was Botox. Liz was quite horrified by the rapid take-up of the procedure; it was becoming as common as having your hair streaked or your legs waxed. So she told her clients exactly what 'bo-tox' was – 'botulinum toxin', a *toxin* derived from the same bacteria that grows on decaying meat. They would in fact be injecting botulism into their skin. Then she would hammer home the gory details – it was the most acutely toxic substance known to man, a mere ninety nanograms could kill an average ninety kilogram person. Possible side effects included headaches, muscle weakness, flu-like symptoms and allergic reactions. Paralysis of the wrong muscle group could result in a drooping eyelid, an uneven smile, or loss of the ability to close the eyes, chew solid food or even swallow. Worse, Botox had been known to spread to other parts of the body causing pneumonia, speech disorders and breathing problems. Although these were extreme and rare, why would anyone take the risk for a nonessential procedure that offered nil health benefits?

Of course Liz wanted to shock them, except she was the one who usually ended up shocked – she even had one woman respond that the inability to swallow or chew solid foods wouldn't be so bad, it might help her lose some weight!

Liz was a doctor, she was supposed to heal people, not enhance them. So she refused to administer Botox or anything else for purely cosmetic reasons. And lately she was wondering more and more if she shouldn't try to get into a surgery program again. Her income would take a substantial dive, but that didn't bother her. She earned far more than she knew what to do with anyway. She wasn't built for the high life. She had a reliable but standard car, a comfortable but ordinary apartment – without harbour views, a gym, swimming pool or concierge. She didn't spend a lot of money on clothes, and almost nothing on cosmetics.

Her accountant was always pleading with her to lease a luxury car, take more overseas junkets, buy an investment property he could negatively gear, *do* something with her money . . .

'Why?' Liz had asked him.

'So that I can minimise your tax burden.'

What a concept. 'Tell me, have you been inside a public hospital lately?'

'Ah . . . can't say that I have.'

'Well, if you had, perhaps you'd understand why I'm happy to pay my fair share of tax.'

So it wasn't the drop in income that was stopping Liz from applying to join a surgical program. However, she suspected that a thirtysomething woman who had practised what was considered 'soft' medicine for nearly a decade was not going to be high on any list of candidates.

There was a light knock and then Michelle stuck her head around the door. 'Is everything all right?' she asked Liz. 'Your next appointment's waiting, and it's ten minutes past, and you have a full schedule this afternoon.'

Liz smiled to herself. That was something she'd miss, having an assistant to keep her on track. 'Sorry, Michelle. I'll be right there.'

Pyrmont

Ellen swung around the corner again on her third lap of the block; parking around Emma's place was always a nightmare.

'Someone's coming out up there, Mum,' Kate said, pointing further up the street.

'Well spotted.' Ellen accelerated, pulling up behind a four-wheel drive manoeuvring its way out of the space. It would leave plenty of room for her modest hatchback. She positioned herself for a reverse park, but as she started to back in, the car stalled.

'Damn,' she said under her breath. She started the ignition again and the engine rattled back to life. 'I don't know what's wrong with this car, it's running so rough,' she said, backing into the spot. 'I'm going to have to book it in for a service and get it checked out.'

Ellen sighed inwardly, mentally counting the likely cost. Everything seemed to be breaking down lately. An element had blown on the stove, and she hadn't had the chance to replace it; besides, she figured they could do without it for a while. Same with the microwave that had decided to die the following week. But when the washing machine refused to drain water, she had no choice. She rang up the local repairer and was shocked to discover it would cost ninety dollars just to get him in the door. She felt like asking him to do a tap dance on the threshold for that kind of money. Three hundred and eighty-five dollars and a new pump later, her washing machine was working again, and then the toilet sprung a leak, necessitating an emergency callout from a plumber, and the resultant extortion. Ellen mentioned it to Tim when he was picking up Sam one Friday afternoon.

'Mm,' he murmured disinterestedly. 'I just got my first electricity bill. Bit of a shock. Airconditioning must be expensive to run.'

'Well, I wouldn't know, we don't have airconditioning, remember?' Ellen said tightly. 'Which is just as well, because with my luck it would break down. But then again, being a *luxury*, I'd just do without it, like I'm doing without a whole lot of things these days.'

'We knew this wasn't going to be cheap, Ellen,' was all he had to say to that.

'Yes, I know,' she returned. 'But you're renting, Tim, you don't have to worry about maintenance costs.'

'Well, I do actually, I pay maintenance for the kids. That's calculated to cover a share of all that.'

She hated this, hated the constant negotiations, the forced politeness. She no longer had any right, apparently, to tell Tim that something needed to be done, or paid for, and he seemed to be deriving a certain amount of pleasure from her diminished power. He didn't seem to understand, or care, that she wasn't asking for anything for herself; Ellen was doing without, across the board. Everything was for the kids, or for the house, and as the kids lived in the house most of the time, really, it was all for the kids.

But Tim had changed. Almost overnight he'd become quite profoundly self-centred – he had his own life now and everything and everyone else came second, or so it seemed. Ellen had never expected that. The preceding years had not been happy ones, for either of them. Sticking it out in a loveless marriage was not for the fainthearted. At times it had been positively gruelling, to say the least. But Ellen hadn't been able to bring herself to make the break any sooner because of the kids. She'd been blessed with the happiest of childhoods; she had witnessed real, abiding love between her parents, and had grown up with the kind of security that provides. She had always hoped to give her children the same.

So when she fell pregnant at nineteen, there was no choice but to marry Tim. Not that she didn't want to at the time – in truth, she didn't think about it all that much. She was pregnant, he was prepared to marry her, so that's what they did. She loved him as any nineteen year old loved her boyfriend, without any real perspective of life, the future, even of herself.

Babies took up all their focus for those first few years, and Tim was a good father, it had to be said. He changed nappies, got up in the middle of the night, whatever was required. Ellen thought she'd hit the jackpot, and she boasted as much to her friends who complained that their husbands never did anything, except pester them for sex at the end of a long, tiring day caring for small children. Ellen was glad Tim didn't pester her, but she didn't boast about that. It took quite some years, once the kids had started school and their life settled down into a more predictable routine, for Ellen to realise that Tim wasn't really present. He was operating on some kind of autopilot, reacting or responding automatically to his surroundings without really being engaged. And their sex life didn't pick up, despite the fact the kids went to bed at a civilised hour and slept right through the night.

Ellen began to think there was something wrong. She got hold of some books on the subject and they confirmed her fears. One of the major sources of conflict for married couples was a mismatched desire for sex – men almost exclusively wanted more than their wives did. Men who didn't want sex were barely mentioned in the literature. Ellen began to doubt herself, her attractiveness, whether Tim even loved her anymore. Was it her fault, had she put him off too many times when the kids were babies? Maybe she wasn't any good at it. How would she know? Ellen didn't even know if she liked sex that much, she felt she hadn't really had a chance to try it out enough to see.

It came to a head when finally, on their tenth wedding anniversary, they had their first weekend away alone, ever. The kids went to stay with their grandparents and she and Tim went to stay in a flash hotel in Terrigal. They checked in late morning, and though the room was luxurious and inviting, Tim was keen to get out and enjoy the day. Ellen was okay with that; sex in daylight hours might be a bit of a leap at this stage.

So they enjoyed a pleasant couple of hours on the beach, and then lunched in an overpriced café, the kind they would never have stepped foot in with the kids in tow. Tim had a light beer and

Ellen indulged in a glass of champagne. They were both definitely unwinding, and Ellen started to feel hopeful about the evening ahead. When Tim announced he could do with a nap, Ellen harboured the small hope that he was making a veiled suggestion – which was dashed when they returned to their hotel room and he promptly fell asleep. She consoled herself that it was difficult to break the habits and routine of years; certainly their entire married life had not allowed for spontaneous sex in the middle of the afternoon. She just had to be patient.

They went out to dinner and talked about the kids and work and the food, all very amiable but not very romantic. Ellen wanted to lead the conversation into more intimate territory, but realised she had no idea what to say. You don't just blurt out in the middle of your entree, 'Are you satisfied with our marriage? Are you satisfied in bed? Do you love me?'

Back in their room, with a few glasses of wine under her belt, Ellen picked up the nightgown she had bought specially for the occasion, and headed for the bathroom. When she slipped the slinky nightie over her head, she sighed, lamenting the shape of her body. It didn't sit right under the unforgiving fabric, with no underwear to smooth things out and keep things in. And hold things up – her breasts just sagged. She adjusted them into place and tightened the straps. That was a little better, at least she had a cleavage now instead of a chasm. She pulled a brush through her hair and fluffed it out a bit, squirted some perfume in strategic locations, sucked in her stomach and opened the bathroom door.

Tim was sitting in the one single armchair in the room, staring fixedly at the telly, clutching the remote.

'Hi,' she said, hoping he'd only turned it on to fill in time.

'Hey, I've always wanted to see this movie,' he returned without so much as a glance in her direction. 'How lucky that it's on here!'

Ellen's heart dropped in line with her breasts. She couldn't demand he switch off the TV and ravish her, that was hardly the point. Maybe she had to give him more time, not put the pressure on. She got herself a mini bottle of wine from the fridge and poured the contents into a glass, before draping herself across the bed. Little or no conversation passed between them at all for the next hour and a half, except for Tim making the occasional remark about the amusing regional ads. Meanwhile Ellen made her way through half the contents of the minibar, eventually even succumbing to a chocolate that she didn't really want, and which probably cost what ten of the same would in a supermarket. But she didn't care, she was becoming quite thoroughly pissed off with the whole scenario. Finally the interminable film ended and Tim got up from the chair. 'Do you want me to turn it off?' he asked.

'Yes,' she said, through gritted teeth, 'I want you to turn it off.'

He didn't seem to notice. He walked into the bathroom and presently she heard the toilet flush, the water running in the sink, the brushing of teeth. He reappeared and went around the room turning off all the lights. Then he changed in the near dark and made his way to the bed, slipping in under the covers. Ellen gave him the benefit of the doubt that, in the dark, he hadn't realised she was still lying on top of the covers. She got up and threw them back, startling him, before dropping down onto the mattress beside him.

'Happy anniversary,' she said, lurching across to kiss him.

Thank God he responded or Ellen didn't know what she would have done. But the sex that followed was perfunctory at best. Not a great deal of foreplay, just enough to get the motor running, and it was all over in about ten minutes. He rolled off her and lay flat on his back. Ellen turned on her side and nestled her head on his chest. 'I love you,' she said.

'Love you too,' he replied.

They lay that way for a while longer, until she heard his breathing settle into a steady rhythm. He made a couple of grunting noises and shifted, bringing his arm up and over her. She shrunk out of his way and he rolled straight over, his back to her. Ellen lay in the dark, as tears slowly filled her eyes, brimming over to slide down her cheeks. This couldn't be right, this couldn't be normal.

She slept fitfully, and when she woke in the morning, feeling groggy and washed out, Tim wasn't in the bed beside her. She could hear the shower running. She'd had enough, they had to find a way to connect, they would be home with the kids again in just a few hours and the opportunity would be lost.

Ellen got up out of bed and walked across to the bathroom door to open it. But it was locked. *What?* She knocked.

'Can I come in?' Ellen said through the door.

'Nearly finished,' he called back.

She felt like she'd been kicked in the stomach. What was going on? This was not the way a couple behaved on their tenth anniversary weekend away, or any weekend alone together for that matter.

Ellen was sitting composed at the end of the bed when Tim emerged from the bathroom, fully dressed. He'd obviously taken his clothes in there with him.

'Why did you lock the door?' she accused.

He just shrugged. 'Force of habit, I guess.'

Maybe that was fair enough, they did tend to lock the door now that the kids were older.

'Well,' Ellen continued, 'then why didn't you open it when I asked if I could come in?'

'I was all covered in soap,' he declared.

'So?' Ellen countered. 'I could have helped you rinse it off.'

He looked a little uncomfortable at that idea.

'Is there anything wrong?' she asked, trying to soften her tone.

He turned away, tossing his toiletries bag into the suitcase.

'Tim, I asked you a question.'

He didn't look at her. 'Nothing's wrong.'

'I don't understand what's going on here.'

He turned around. 'Nothing's going on.'

'Exactly.'

He frowned. 'What are you getting at?'

'Tim,' she said, standing up, 'we're away for a weekend alone and you lock yourself up in the bathroom. That's not normal.'

'I didn't "lock myself up", you're making it sound weird. Locking the bathroom is completely normal at home.'

'But we're not *at* home,' she persisted, her voice rising. 'We're staying in a beautiful hotel, we don't have to check out till eleven. What's your hurry?'

He shrugged. 'I just wanted to make the most of the day.'

'And you don't think lying in together might have been making the most of our time?'

'I can't sleep in late like you.'

She groaned. 'I'm not talking about sleeping!'

Now he looked outright embarrassed.

'Well?' she persisted.

'Jeez, Ellen,' he said. 'We had sex last night, and we never have sex in the morning. How am I supposed to know that's what you wanted all of a sudden?'

It was no use. She didn't have it in her to keep arguing the point while he kept evading it. She waited a few days and brought it up again. When she said she couldn't go on like this, Tim was mystified.

'You're making such a big deal about this,' he said. 'If I'd known it was so important to you, I would have had sex with you that morning.'

'That's not the point, Tim.'

'Then what is the point?'

'We hardly ever have sex!' she declared.

'You don't seem interested,' was his comeback.

Ellen blinked. 'How would you know? Have you suddenly become a mind reader? I mean, you don't touch me, you don't come near me, you're not affectionate. You hardly ever initiate sex.'

'You don't either,' he accused.

She felt like screaming. But instead she just said, 'Fine, then don't you think we need to do something about it?'

She suggested counselling, but Tim was reluctant, refusing to acknowledge the problem, or at least that it was such a big deal. But it had been said out loud now, and Ellen wasn't going to let them settle back into the same rut. She gave him an ultimatum, and he was eventually persuaded that he didn't have a choice.

That was the beginning of the end. Tim was noncommunicative in the counselling sessions at first, but thankfully they had an excellent counsellor who was eventually able to get him to open up.

Ellen was well aware that Tim's family was cold and distant and not given to open displays of affection. But she'd never realised just how deeply he had been affected. He said he couldn't ever remember being told he was loved. He recounted cruel punishments, dispassionately administered, which would be considered abuse in anyone's language these days. Slowly Ellen watched her husband open up, admitting how much it had hurt, how much it hurt still, and finally in the middle of a counselling session he broke down sobbing.

Ellen saw it as a major breakthrough, but before their next session Tim sat her down and told her he was through with counselling, he didn't want to deal with all that, he couldn't, it was too hard. He begged her not to make him. He was like a child. And Ellen feared that's exactly where he was stuck, emotionally.

So they stopped the counselling, and things deteriorated from there. They couldn't go back to where they were before, but Tim didn't have either the will or the skills to work on their relationship. The sex, or lack of it, was only a symptom. There was no genuine intimacy, no real connection between them. Eventually the writing on the wall was as plain to him as it was to Ellen. Their marriage was surviving on life support, but there was no hope for the long-term, and eventually someone was going to have to pull the plug.

*

Ellen locked the car and tucked her arm through Kate's as they walked up the street. 'So, this should be fun,' she said brightly, not really believing it herself, but she didn't want Kate to realise that. 'Are you excited?'

Kate shrugged. Nothing much seemed to excite her daughter these days. She had settled into uni without any apparent drama, but she didn't tell Ellen much anymore. They used to talk about everything, share everything, but Kate had become a bit of a closed book lately. She was particularly spiky whenever mention of her father was made, even though Ellen went to great pains to make sure she didn't say anything negative.

'He's fine, he seems okay' was about as much as Ellen could get out of her when she asked after Tim. And Sam wasn't any better. If she had any questions about a weekend with his dad, he seemed reluctant to divulge details. Ellen didn't know why everyone had suddenly got all cagey on her. This was an amicable, mutual separation. She sincerely hoped Tim was holding up his end and wasn't putting her down when she wasn't around to defend herself.

But she seriously didn't think he would do that. What Ellen feared was that, despite all her efforts, her family was falling apart in front of her eyes.

They arrived at Emma's building and caught the lift up to her apartment.

'You're the first to arrive,' Emma declared happily, when she opened the door. 'Look at you, Kate, you get more gorgeous every time I see you.'

Kate shrugged her shoulders, clutching at her arms self-consciously. 'No I don't.'

'Oh, you just don't realise how beautiful you are,' Emma gushed, scooping her arm around her niece and drawing her inside. 'Wait till we have you all gussied up for the wedding, you'll see. I really think the cinnamon is going to be your colour, Kate, with those highlights in your hair.'

'I don't have any highlights,' said Kate.

'Oh, I'm sure I've noticed highlights in your hair in the sun,' she scoffed. 'And if not, my hairdresser will give you some,' she added with a manic laugh.

They entered the vast living room, where three long racks of plastic-shrouded dresses were lined up against the wall. One was all in tones of grey and silver – the 'pewter' Ellen assumed – and the next appeared to be the 'cinnamon' shades. The third rack held a range of jewel colours.

'You have actual dresses?' said Ellen. 'I thought you were just going to try the girls up against the fabrics?'

'I know,' said Emma with a cat-that-got-the-cream look. 'But I realised we wouldn't get the full effect. I was able to scrounge these from various designers, they were only too happy to help. The wedding's likely to get at least some press, so they're not about to knock back a little free publicity. Besides, this way we can kill two birds with one stone and get some idea of a style that will suit each of the girls. I've already decided I'm not dressing them identically.'

'Oh?' Ellen remarked. 'The bridesmaids won't be wearing the same style dress?'

'It's so passé, Ellen.' Then she winced. 'Of course it was fine in your day,' she added quickly.

Her day? There were only two years between them! Though, Ellen had to admit begrudgingly, there would be nearly twenty years between their wedding dates.

'So, what do you think, Kate, aren't these cinnamon shades divine?' Emma drew Kate over closer to the rack, holding a dress up against her. 'I can see you in this, I really can. But then Cara is so dark, with that porcelain skin, and I'm sure the pewter is going to suit her best. Thus my dilemma!' she declared, dropping the dress so it swung back into line. 'But, never fear, we'll sort it out tonight. That's why we're here.'

She stepped backwards with a sweep of her hand, like a game-show hostess. 'Over here I've gathered up a few samples in stronger, complementary colours as well. Just between us, I'm a little worried about Tayla. Unfortunately she's got her mother's pasty colouring, and I'm not sure she can pull off the cinnamon or the pewter. Emeralds and sapphires and rubies could all work in contrast, but what with different styles of dresses, I don't want things to start looking hotchpotch, as though a few stray guests have wandered amongst the bridal party.' She laughed that same manic laugh as before.

The intercom buzzed. 'Oh wonderful, more arrivals! You two go ahead and browse away.'

Ellen and Kate glanced at each other as she swanned off.

'Is she on drugs?' asked Kate. 'She's so wired, she's hardly stopped to take a breath.'

Ellen grinned. 'She's just very excited. Your Aunty Em has waited a long time for this.'

'I don't know why she's bothering,' Kate muttered. 'Such a waste of time.'

'At least this is better than being dragged around shopping all day.'

'No, I mean the whole thing, the wedding. It's just a big waste of time, money and effort.'

'You don't have to do it on such a grand scale.'

'I won't be doing it at all.'

Ellen looked at her. 'How can you be so sure?'

'Because I'm never getting married,' Kate said flatly.

'Why do you say that?'

She pulled a face. 'Why do you think?'

Ellen opened her mouth to say something, but Kate turned away, running her hand along the rows of dresses as she walked the length of the racks. Ellen sighed. This was exactly the type of thing that had weighed on her – that the kids would get the wrong idea about marriage and commitment if their parents broke up. Well, what did she expect? Still, Ellen wanted them to be able to recognise that she and Tim didn't have regrets, and that there had been good times. That sometimes in life you have to dive in, hoping for the best. But if it doesn't work out the way you plan, you have to be flexible, even courageous enough to move on. She wanted her children to regard marriage as a positive thing, a challenge but not a trap.

God, that was so convoluted she was making her own head hurt.

She peered closer at the tags on the dresses. Anthea Crawford . . . Lisa Ho . . . Colette Dinnigan . . . Cripes, how was she going to be able to afford this? And if the 'press' was going to be involved, Ellen knew her sister would be pulling out all the stops. No expense would be spared, which was fine for Emma, but Ellen didn't want to have to take out a loan so Kate could be part of the bridal party.

Evie arrived with Tayla, who made up for her so-called pastiness with unbridled enthusiasm for everything she laid her eyes on.

'Oh, Aunty Emma,' she gushed, 'they're all so beautiful.'

Ellen kissed Evie hello. 'You look –'

'You've lost weight, haven't you?' Emma broke in.

Evie shrugged, her head down. 'Maybe, a little.'

'Well, you look great,' Ellen said reassuringly. Though she noticed her younger sister's eyes were sunken and dull. She hoped she wasn't on one of those crazy diets.

The intercom buzzed again and Blake's sister was next to arrive. 'You've all met Cara,' Emma announced, escorting her into the living room.

Cara refrained from kissing anyone, she just nodded her head at the assembled group. Sloe-eyed and slender, with sleek black hair cropped close to her head, she oozed a languid kind of glamour; she looked like the girlfriend of a rich gangster in the thirties.

'I think it's time to open the champagne!' Emma declared. 'We're still waiting on Liz, but who knows how long she'll be?'

'I'll be out on the balcony,' said Cara in a tone that suggested she was already bored, 'having a cigarette.'

Liz actually turned up not long after the champagne was popped, and by the time Emma refreshed their glasses, everyone was beginning to loosen up, even Cara.

'I'm sorry, Emma,' she said, 'but I don't wear brown.'

'It's *cinnamon*,' Emma corrected her, keeping her tone upbeat. 'I actually think it might look stunning against your complexion, Cara. But nothing's been decided yet. That's why we're here.'

'I'll try the grey Wayne Cooper.'

'Pewter,' Emma stressed, as Cara plucked a hanger from the rack and slithered off towards the bedroom. 'Well then, why doesn't everyone try the pewter first and we'll see how we go?'

Emma busied herself checking sizes and passing out dresses. By the time Ellen followed Kate to the bedroom, Cara had already changed into hers, a slinky backless number with a fishtail hem. She looked breathtaking as she passed them coming out the door. 'Room's all yours.'

Kate coyly ducked into the bathroom to change as Liz, Evie and Tayla all filed into the room. Evie plonked down to sit on the bed with a sigh. 'Okay, come here, sweetie, let's get you changed.'

Tayla screwed up her face. 'I don't like this dress, it's just grey. I want something pretty, like the red one out there, or the purple!'

'This is Aunty Emma's wedding,' said Evie, her voice strained. 'You'll get to wear whatever colour you want at your own wedding, Tayla.'

'Don't be crazy, Mother, at my own wedding I'll be wearing white. Don't you know anything?'

Ellen couldn't stand to hear Tayla speaking to her mother that way, but she bit her tongue, Evie looked miserable enough as it was.

'Is everything okay, Evie?' she asked.

She shrugged. 'I'm just tired.'

'You are eating properly?' Liz added, coming to stand beside Ellen and folding her arms as she gazed down at Evie.

'Of course,' she dismissed, lifting the dress over Tayla's head and pulling it down carefully into place.

Just then Kate stepped out of the bathroom. Her dress was incredibly simple, with shoestring straps and a filmy overlay, but it was so well cut, it fell beautifully over her tall frame.

'My dress isn't as nice as Kate's,' Tayla pouted.

'Oh nonsense,' said Kate, 'you look very sophisticated.'

'Do I?' Tayla was impressed, though clearly she didn't have a clue what that meant.

'Yes you do, so come on, let's go show Aunty Emma.' Kate held out her hand and Tayla rushed forward to take it. Evie stood up wearily and followed in their wake.

Ellen flopped down on the bed, leaning back on her elbows. 'Do you think Evie's all right?' she asked Liz.

'No,' Liz said, pulling her top up over her head. 'She's probably on one of those ridiculous diets, starving herself half to death.' She slipped off her skirt and picked up the hanger, examining the dress. 'Here goes nothing.' She lifted the dress up over her head and started to wriggle into it.

'Should we say something?' Ellen wondered.

Liz adjusted the dress into place. 'No, she's a grown woman. Besides, you know it won't last,' she added, turning around. 'Can you zip me up?'

'Sure.' Ellen sat up and felt for the end of the zip. It was sewn right into the seam, making it virtually invisible. 'They really are gorgeous dresses,' she sighed. 'I just don't know how I'm going to be able to afford all this.'

'So tell Emma.'

'I can't,' she said, sliding the zip up. 'You know how she is with me, she'll take it as a criticism.'

'Then don't worry about it, I'll pay for Kate's dress.'

'I can't ask you to do that.'

'You didn't,' she said simply, turning around to face the mirror. The dress was a slim-fitting silk sheath with beaded detailing on the bodice.

'Wow,' said Ellen, shaking her head in admiration, 'you look amazing. How is it that your figure hasn't changed since you were in high school?'

Liz raised an eyebrow. 'Oh, it's changed. You haven't seen me starkers. And don't forget I haven't had kids.'

*

As the evening wore on, the girls tried on virtually every dress, and every combination. Cara even relented and tried on one in cinnamon, but she'd been right all along, it didn't suit her colouring. But the pewter didn't do a great deal for Kate either, and it was simply drab on Tayla, despite the addition of various jewel-coloured sashes. And putting her in a different colour dress altogether did look a bit hotchpotch.

'Oh, dear, I think I'm going to have to go back to the drawing board,' Emma frowned, biting her lip. She eventually decided the only thing to do for now was to take photos of each of the girls and consult with some of her favourite designers.

This was going to be a long process.

Cara left as soon as her photo was taken, and straight after Liz excused herself to the balcony when her phone beeped to signal an sms message. When she came back inside she announced she had to get going.

'Andrew, I assume?' Emma said stiffly.

Liz glanced warily at her young nieces. 'There's nothing else we can do now, is there? And Cara is already gone.'

Emma shrugged. 'I just thought we'd have a drink together . . .'

'It's a school night,' said Evie. 'I really have to get Tayla home.'

'School night for me too,' added Ellen.

'And I've got a class at nine,' said Kate.

Of course. Emma saw them all off at once. She shouldn't have been surprised by their lack of interest, she hadn't even been able to get their mother to come along tonight. Evelyn told her daughter it really didn't have anything to do with her, and she was so busy getting the house ready for the auction. Besides, she said, it would be fun to get a surprise like everyone else, which made it crystal clear to Emma that she was not intending to be involved with the wedding preparations at all.

Emma sighed heavily as she went around the room, picking up discarded dresses and returning them to the racks. So much for bonding. She had put such a lot of energy into trying to make tonight fun, but all everyone had done was turn up to fulfil their duty and then hotfoot it out of here as soon as they had the chance. She brushed away a tear from the corner of her eye, feeling stupid, and disappointed, and hurt, yes, hurt, as she hung up the last dress and looked around the empty apartment.

Whenever it came up around other women that she had three sisters, they would carry on about how wonderful that must be – especially those who didn't have sisters. It must be like having built-in best friends, they would say. But it wasn't like that at all. Best friends would still be sitting here with her now, having a drink, as excited as she was about her wedding plans. But Emma wasn't going to let it get to her. Blake was her best friend, her partner, now her fiancé. Ellen's marriage was over; Liz was stuck on a man she could never have, and Evie was stuck with a man no one else would want. She wasn't alone in the world. She was being silly. She picked up her phone and dialled Blake's mobile.

'Hi,' she said when he answered. 'The coast is clear, you can come home.'

'Oh, already?' he said. 'We're actually in the middle of something here, Em, I might be a while yet.'

Emma could hear noise in the background, the clinking of glasses, voices, faint music. 'Where are you?'

'We were hungry so we decided to continue the meeting over dinner.'

'Oh.'

'Well, I knew there was no hurry.'

'No, of course, it's fine.'

'So I'll see you later, don't wait up though.'

Emma hung up the phone and slowly walked along the racks, lightly touching the dresses as she passed. She noticed the champagne bottle on the coffee table. Picking it up, she realised there was still some left. She dropped into the sofa and drank straight from the bottle.

*

When Liz let herself in through the door of her flat, Andrew had already made himself a drink and was sitting out on the balcony.

He jumped up when he heard her and slid open the glass doors. 'Stay there, I'll grab a drink and join you,' said Liz.

But he had already closed the door behind him. 'I don't have much time,' he said, coming towards her and taking her in his arms. 'I only hope Jen hasn't decided to wait up for me.'

Liz always bristled slightly when he mentioned his wife, especially when he used the diminutive. It seemed too familiar, even intimate. But Andrew was kissing her now and thoughts of his wife rapidly faded into the background. She felt his hands sliding up under her top.

'Whoa boy, can you give me a minute to catch my breath?' she said.

'I'd rather not,' he murmured, nuzzling into her neck. 'Breathless is good. Breathless is sexy.'

'Andrew . . .'

'Sorry,' he said, lifting his head to look at her, a glint in his eyes. 'I just miss you, it feels like ages.'

'It's only been a week.'

'Eight days, actually,' he corrected her. 'Which is at least seven days too long,' he added, leaning in to kiss her again.

And who's fault was that? She didn't know where that thought had come from. It wasn't his fault, she knew that, she knew all the reasons, all the restrictions on his time . . . She was just feeling cranky tonight. She'd started to feel cranky at Emma's. She hadn't wanted to go; Andrew had phoned before she'd left the office to let her know he'd been called into emergency surgery and he'd already told Jennifer that he couldn't say how long he'd be, thus giving them a window of opportunity. Immediately Liz was pissed off that she had to be somewhere else. But moments later she was equally pissed off at the idea of hanging around at home waiting for him. But when she arrived at Emma's and she was pouring champagne and running around manically, Liz couldn't help resenting being there. She resented that Emma was getting married, and that she would be the last sister left on the shelf.

Which was all very childish of her. She hadn't been left on the shelf, she had the love of a wonderful man who was currently guiding her, gently but persistently, towards the bedroom, while he removed each piece of her clothing, and ran his lips over her bare skin, and made her forget, for now, what had made her feel so pissed off in the first place.

*

All too soon Andrew was sitting up on the side of the bed, buttoning his shirt.

'Stay,' Liz said impulsively.

'What?' he said, turning around to look at her.

'Stay the night, say that the surgery had complications, it took longer, that you were too tired to drive home, that you slept at the hospital.'

Andrew breathed out, leaning over to kiss her lightly on the lips. 'You know I wish I could.'

'Why can't you?'

He frowned. 'What's going on?'

'Nothing.'

He shifted around fully to face her, planting a hand either side of her. 'Lizzie, don't do this. This is not what we do.'

'No, we just have sex and then you go home.'

He sighed. 'What's the matter?'

Tears were stinging her eyes. She blinked, she didn't want to cry in front of him.

'Nothing,' she repeated, turning away from him.

Andrew curled in behind her, drawing his arms around her and holding her tight. 'Talk to me,' he said, close to her ear.

Liz swallowed down the lump in her throat. She didn't behave like this; they both knew how things stood, she didn't get petulant and needy. And she didn't like herself when she did.

She cleared her throat. 'It's nothing, really. I must be premenstrual.'

'This isn't like you,' he said. 'Where were you tonight?'

She sighed then, shifting around to look at him. 'I was at Emma's, for the bridesmaids' dress fitting.'

He stroked his hand across her forehead, moving her hair away. Then he kissed her. 'I'm sorry,' he said.

That was the thing about Andrew, he knew exactly how she was feeling without her having to spell it out. And Liz had not a doubt he felt as badly as she did right now. They were so good together, so perfectly in sync that it made her ache inside. It was incredibly unfair that he couldn't be hers, completely, all the time . . . Circumstances were to blame here, bad luck, bad timing. She knew he would be hers, completely, if he could. Liz didn't doubt that for a moment. It was all that held her together.

'No, I'm sorry,' she said, kissing him. 'I love you so much.' 'I love you too.' He held her for a while longer, then he got up and dressed, and inevitably, he left the apartment to go home to his own particular challenges. They were far worse than anything Liz had to face, she consoled herself as she turned around to the empty flat.

A week later

Evie peered out of the car window up at the house. It looked ordinary enough. In fact it looked like every other house on the street. Maybe Craig was right, there were houses like this all throughout the suburbs, that lots of people were into it, that it was just a lifestyle choice between consenting adults.

So why did she feel sick in the stomach, not just now but all the time? She had barely been able to eat for months and she'd lost twelve kilos. Evie had never been on such an effective diet in her whole life. But even the weight loss wasn't giving her any joy. She didn't care what she looked like; in fact, she would have preferred to look less attractive tonight, if anything.

But here they were, and Evie was wearing her best dress, the one she hadn't been able to fit into for the anniversary party. Craig's mother had made such a fuss when Evie had walked down the hall this evening.

'Oh, Evie, you look gorgeous, darl!' she'd exclaimed. 'When was the last time you even fitted into that dress?'

Evie had just given her a weak smile.

'I'm so thrilled you're having a night out, just the two of you,' she went on. 'You never get to do that! And for no special reason! That son of mine is a hidden treasure, so romantic. Don't know where he gets it from, certainly not his father.'

'Evie?'

She stirred, Craig was watching her expectantly from the driver's seat. 'Are you ready?'

No, she wasn't ready, she would never be ready for this. But she had no choice. She just had to get through tonight. If she made the effort at least, then surely that would make him happy, and maybe he'd get it out of his system. Maybe he wouldn't even like it very much.

But the spring in his step, his sweaty palm in hers as they crossed the road, made her doubt that very much.

It was a woman who opened the door to them. Evie instantly disliked her, and then hated herself for it. She didn't instantly dislike anyone. It took her a long time to dislike people, and they usually had to do a lot to make her dislike them. But all this woman had done was open the door, give them a sugary smile and say, 'Here for the party?'

Evie let Craig do the talking, she had nothing to say anyway. The woman 'Crystal' – like that was her real name – offered to give them a tour of the house, and Craig jumped at it with an eagerness that turned Evie's stomach even more. Crystal relieved them of their cooler bag – you had to bring your own to this shindig: selling or even supplying liquor without a licence was illegal. Evie found it ironic that they were so concerned with legalities. However, they did provide a cheery barman, who took the cooler bag from Crystal and promised a drink would be waiting on their return.

'So through here . . .'

She led them into a large living room with a massive flat screen on the wall playing porn, predictably. A curved leather modular lounge took up most of two other walls, where several people lolled about and there was some kissing and fondling going on. It reminded Evie of the parties she'd been to as a teenager, except for the porn. Crystal ushered them across the room and opened the sliding doors to outside, where a steamy spa was crammed with eight people, all naked. Well, Evie assumed they were; the women's bare breasts were bobbing away on the surface like melons floating on water.

'Hey,' Craig said to her, 'maybe we can have a go in there later?'

'I didn't bring my swimmers,' Evie said flatly.

Crystal laughed. 'You don't need your swimmers, love.'

Evie tuned out after that, as Crystal continued the tour upstairs to the bedrooms. She remained resolutely in the hall while Craig happily followed Crystal into rooms that were . . . in use, so to speak. 'If you leave the door open,' Crystal explained, 'that means you're happy for others to join in, or you can close it if you're happy as you are.'

The place smelled heavily, and sickeningly, of scented candles, sweaty bodies and something chemical. Then it occurred to Evie it was probably lubricant. Yuck.

They went back downstairs where their drinks were waiting on the bar.

'Well, have fun!' Crystal said. 'That's why you're here, remember,' she added, with a rather pointed look at Evie.

Evie slid onto a stool at the end of the bar and quickly gulped down a few mouthfuls of her wine. Maybe she should just get really drunk and then she might not care. But they hadn't brought enough wine with them for that.

Craig perched himself on the stool next to her, turning immediately towards a couple sitting further along.

'Hey, I'm Craig,' he said, 'and this is my wife, Evie.'

They introduced themselves as Cheryl and Steve, and then the three of them rearranged their stools so that they could all face each other. Evie stayed where she was, leaning heavily on the bar. Cheryl immediately commandeered Craig's attention, yabbering away in an annoying, tinny voice. Evie could feel Steve watching her. She gulped down some more wine.

'First time?' he asked.

'Is it that obvious?'

He smiled kindly. 'You get used to it.'

'I don't want to get used to it.'

'So it was all his idea?'

She nodded glumly.

'Well, we all seem to be getting along,' Cheryl chirped. 'Shall we go find a room where we can relax a bit, have some privacy?'

'No!' Evie cried.

They all looked a little taken aback by her outburst.

'Come on, hun,' Craig cajoled. 'You said you'd give it a go.'

'I'm here, aren't I?' she hissed. She turned away from the other two. 'For godsakes, Craig, we've been here barely fifteen minutes.'

'You just need more time then?' he asked hopefully.

'You said I didn't have to do anything.'

'I'll stay here with her,' Steve offered. 'Why don't you two go along?'

'Is that all right with you, hun?' Craig asked.

No it wasn't, of course it wasn't! What kind of a buffoon had she married? One that would leave his wife sitting with a strange man and go into a room alone with another woman and do God knows what. Evie felt her heart breaking; she wanted to cry, she wanted to scream, she wanted to beg him not to go. But here she was, in a stranger's house, with all of these 'consenting adults' who were so open and mature and comfortable within themselves. Evie had never felt so uncomfortable, less of an adult, more powerless. But she had agreed to come . . .

So she said, because she felt she had no choice, 'Go ahead.'

Craig reacted like a giddy schoolboy who'd been given permission to raid the lolly jar. That's what she gleaned from his voice anyway, because she couldn't look at him. He leaned over to kiss her, but she turned her cheek, and he went ahead and planted an exuberant kiss, oblivious to her distress. Evie kept her eyes downcast as he walked away, she presumed arm in arm with Cheryl.

'Are you okay?' Steve asked after a while.

Evie breathed out. 'Look, if you think you've got a chance with me, you're wasting your time. It's not you . . . really, you should go and talk to someone else.'

She heard a deep chuckle and looked across at him.

'You think I don't know you're not interested?' he said. 'I'm not going to try and come on to you, Evie. I'm happy just to sit and talk, if you don't mind.'

Evie lifted her gaze to meet his. His eyes seemed genuine.

'Would you like another drink?' he asked.

She nodded.

He gestured to the barman. 'Could we have top-ups here, please?'

After their glasses had been refilled, Steve turned to her. 'Your husband shouldn't have forced you to come.'

'He didn't force me,' she returned. 'I came of my own free will.'

'But you'd rather be anywhere else but here?'

She glanced around. 'Surely there are a lot of women who come along reluctantly.'

He nodded. 'My wife for one.'

'Who, Cheryl?'

'Yep.'

'Well, she seems to have got over it.'

'Yes, she has, admirably.'

'So this was your idea, but you're happy just to sit and talk?'

'You have to understand, we've been coming for a long time,' Steve explained. 'The novelty's worn off a little.'

Evie was intrigued. She wasn't sure whether to believe him or not. Maybe this was some sort of come-on line, to lull her into a false sense of security so she'd trust him. 'Why would you keep on coming if the novelty's worn off?'

'It hasn't worn off for Cheryl,' he said. 'Not one bit. Funny, I had to talk her into it, and she was reluctant the first time. Maybe not quite as reluctant as you, there was a tiny bit of curiosity there that helped her get over the starting line.'

'Whereas me? No curiosity at all,' said Evie, sipping her wine.

'No kidding.' He grinned.

She looked at him. 'I suppose you think I'm frigid or something.'

'Of course I don't,' he scoffed. 'A lot of people wouldn't be into this, they can't all be frigid.'

That was nice of him to say. It made her feel normal in a completely abnormal situation. 'So what was your first time like?' she asked.

'Like I said, it was my idea, so I was champing at the bit,' he said. 'But I had to restrain myself, give Cheryl a chance to get used to it. Surprisingly, for both of us, she enjoyed herself. We hardly did anything, mind you, just a bit of kissing and touching . . .'

Evie suddenly got a mental picture of Craig and Cheryl and she recoiled.

'. . . she was less reluctant the next time, and by the time after that she was beginning to get enthusiastic. It used to excite me. For the first year –'

First *year*? How long had they been coming?

'– I was on an absolute high,' he said, somewhat wistfully. 'But then when you're coming month after month, sometimes more often, a funny thing starts to happen. You start to lose interest in sex on tap, or at least I did. That's weird for a guy, right?'

'I don't know,' Evie shrugged. 'Doesn't sound all that weird to me.'

'Maybe. Most people who become regulars, I reckon they must get addicted to it.'

'But you didn't?'

He shook his head. 'It was there for the taking, all the time, whenever I wanted it. There was no chase, no emotion, no excitement anymore, nothing. Just sex.' He paused, taking a drink. 'But Cheryl couldn't get enough.'

Evie didn't know what to say.

He shrugged. 'Ah, but I've got no one to blame but myself. I couldn't very well insist she give it up when I was the one who suggested it in the first place. I just had to let her get it out of her system.'

'So how long have you been coming?'

'Five years last summer.'

Five years and his wife still hadn't got it out of her system? Is that what Evie could expect?

'You should be really clear with your husband before it becomes a habit too hard to break.'

Evie sat for a while, sipping her wine. She didn't know how much more of this she could take.

'Listen,' said Steve, taking out his wallet. 'I'll give you my card, in case you ever want to talk.'

'Oh no,' Evie shook her head, holding her hand up to stop him. 'I couldn't.'

'Evie, I swear to you I'm not trying to come on to you,' he insisted. 'But how many people can you talk to about this?'

He was right. She couldn't talk to anyone, not her sisters, not her friends. That's why she'd been going so crazy.

She took the card. 'Thanks.'

'Hey you two,' said Craig, coming up behind them. 'What's going on here?'

'Nothing much,' said Evie, crossing her arms and hiding the card.

'Where's Cheryl?' Steve asked him.

'Oh, she met someone she knew . . .' Craig shrugged. He looked awkward and disappointed at once.

Steve nodded, almost as if he expected as much.

'So, you wanna get going?' Craig asked Evie.

'Really?' she said, relieved. 'You've had enough?'

'Oh, yeah, for now.'

Evie jumped off the barstool, she was so grateful to be getting out of here. 'Nice to meet you, Steve,' she said. 'Thanks for keeping me company.'

'My pleasure.'

*

As they drove off, Evie rested her head back, feeling the tension that had built up over days, and much longer, glide away. She knew it wasn't over yet, but at least it was for now.

'So what was that Steve giving you when I came back?' Craig asked after a while. 'It looked like a business card.'

'It was.'

'What'd he give you that for?'

'Just if I ever want to talk . . .'

'Why would you want to talk to him?'

'I don't know, I probably won't anyway,' she said, gazing out the window.

'Okay, then toss it.'

She glanced back at him. 'What?'

'Get rid of his card.'

'No, why should I?'

'Well, because, you're a married woman and you've got another guy's phone number in case you want to "talk". It's weird.'

'You think that's weird?' said Evie, sitting up. 'We just went to a swingers' club and you went off to a room with some other guy's wife.'

'We didn't do anything.'

'Oh, really?'

'We didn't, just a bit of canoodling, and then some other guy came in –'

'Stop!' she said loudly, holding her hands to her ears. 'I don't want to know. And you don't need to know anything I get up to.'

'That's not how this is supposed to work,' he said.

'Well, you should have thought about that before you opened this can of worms, Craig,' said Evie, feeling emboldened. 'Because now you're going to have to be prepared for whatever crawls out.'

Friday

Ellen reversed out of her parking space and steered the car towards the gates of the school. She was so glad to get out of here. It had been a hell of a day, a hell of a week for that matter. But it was Friday afternoon of her weekend with the kids, and that always made the preceding week bearable. She loathed the weeks leading up to Tim's weekend. She mulled over it the whole time, dreading the coming weekend, often becoming irritable, even picking on the kids, she'd noticed. Suddenly she couldn't stand Sam's perennially untidy room, his dirty socks strewn around the house, Kate cluttering up the bathroom with empty shampoo bottles and old razors and always leaving her hair straightener turned on. It was as though Ellen had to make herself glad to see the back of them. But she never was.

Ellen especially hated Friday nights on her own. Their regular treat of ordering pizza and watching a movie held no attraction solo. She'd end up drinking too much and sobbing over some soppy film on Netflix, then collapsing into bed in the small hours of the morning and waking up with a hangover. Weekends without the kids were something to be endured. She realised that all her energies before the separation had been focused on the kids, and how they would cope. She hadn't prepared herself at all.

She pulled up at a red light. Ellen didn't like leaving work this late, she only wasted time sitting in traffic, bumper to bumper, almost the entire way home. She glanced at her watch; she was late,

Sam would be finished football training by now, and she was still fifteen minutes away.

The lights turned green and Ellen put the car into gear, accelerating gently. But nothing happened. She applied more pressure to the pedal but it was as though someone had cut the cable, the car wasn't responding at all. She heard a horn sound and she raised her hand to indicate to the car behind her that she wasn't daydreaming. Flustered, she put the gear back into neutral, and then into first, accelerating again, but still the car didn't respond. More horns started beeping impatiently. Was the engine even running? She tried the ignition; nothing. She hadn't felt the car stall.

She wound down her window and waved the cars around as she flicked on the hazard lights, watching helplessly as the lights turned orange and a cacophony of horns sounded in response. What did they think, that she was doing this on purpose to annoy them? The lights had turned red now. Okay, she had time. She breathed deeply, in and out, then calmly tried the engine again. Nothing happened. She checked the temperature gauge. It was normal. What the hell was wrong? Her heart started beating faster. This was ridiculous. There had been no indication, no warning; the car hadn't rattled to a stall, it hadn't overheated, there was nothing ominous like smoke coming from the engine. Ellen had no clue what was wrong.

The lights turned green and the horns started up again. Car engines revved aggressively as their drivers pulled out and around her, still sounding their horns, and worse, shouting abuse from the windows. She had to do something. She was stuck in a lane in the middle of a main road; she couldn't move the car out of the way if she couldn't even get the damn thing to start. She couldn't even get out and open the hood, it was too dangerous with cars whizzing by her in both directions. The lights turned red again, and in her rear-view mirror she could see the cars barrelling up behind her, screeching to a halt and inevitably blaring their horns. Ellen could feel her throat tightening, her eyes beginning to sting. Get a grip. What to do . . . what to do . . . Of course, she had to call road service. She fumbled for her phone in her bag, but once she found it and flipped it open, her fingers instinctively scrolled for

Tim's number. She pressed it automatically. She knew he couldn't do anything about her immediate predicament, but she could get him to pick up Sam at least, and that would be one less thing she'd have to worry about. And besides, she always called Tim first, somehow sharing the problem would make it easier to deal with.

He picked up. 'Hello?'

'It's me, Ellen,' she snapped. Didn't he even look at the screen first?

'Oh, hi.'

'I've broken down. I'm in the middle of that big intersection on Burwood Road, and the car just died.'

'What's wrong with it?'

'How the hell should I know?'

'Did it overheat?'

'No, nothing happened, it just refuses to start.'

'Do you think it could be a flat battery?'

'How the hell should I know?' she repeated.

There was silence for a moment. 'Well, I don't know what I can do –'

'Can you go pick up Sam, please? He's waiting for me, and God knows how long this is going to take. I'll have to ring road service.'

'Yeah, you should ring them right away,' he said. 'But I can't pick up Sam, you better call him as soon as you get on to road service.'

The lights had turned green again, and the horns started up. What was wrong with these people? Couldn't they see her hazard lights flashing? 'What do you mean you can't pick up Sam?'

'I just can't . . . I'm not in the area.'

'Well, neither am I, obviously. You've got your car, haven't you?'

'Yeah, but . . . I'm way over at the northern beaches, it'd take me an hour at least to get back there. And I can't really leave anyway.'

'Why, what are you doing?'

There was a pause. 'I'm just out, okay? I'm with . . . friends. It's not my weekend, Ellen, I'm not on call.'

What the fuck?

'Tim, this is an emergency, I'm stranded, and so is your son right now.'

'I get that, Ellen,' he said tightly. 'But there's nothing I can do, I'm too far away. If you want, I'll call Sam and tell him what's happening, and that he should make his own way home.'

'Oh, don't put yourself out for us,' she sneered, and she snapped her phone shut. Bastard. What was he doing that was so friggin' important that he couldn't leave it to pick up his son? Is this how things were going to be now? *Jesus Christ!* She was trembling, and once again the lights were turning green and cars were trundling up her backside, sounding their horns.

She fumbled in her wallet for her road service card and plucked it out. She punched in the number on her phone and an operator answered, demanding all the basic information before Ellen could get a word in. Finally, after she had her membership and registration, the operator asked her what the problem was.

'I have no idea. My car has stopped dead in the middle of an intersection and I'm holding up traffic and I can't move, I can't even get out. Someone has to come right away!'

'Of course, ma'am,' the operator replied. 'You can't start the car?'

'No, that's what I said!'

'And you're on your own?'

'Yes.' In every way imaginable.

'It's okay, I'll put you on top priority, just tell me exactly where you are.'

Ellen wanted to cry, someone was finally taking her predicament seriously. The operator took the details and reassured her that a patrolman would be there asap. And though it took only ten minutes, it felt like she spent another hour waving traffic past her while the horns sounded louder and angrier.

So where the hell was Tim? They didn't know anyone over on the northern beaches. Who were these 'friends'? How come he suddenly had a life? She used to have to virtually put a bomb under him to get him to do anything on the weekends, and now his social life was so busy he couldn't take time out to pick up his son?

Oh, bugger, she hadn't called Sam yet. She flicked open her phone and scrolled for his number. Please have your phone on! He picked up straight away.

'Hi Mum, where are you?'

'Sorry, Sam, the car's broken down, I'm stranded.'

'Bummer.'

'I'm waiting for roadside service, they promised they'd be quick but I don't know how long it's going to take once they get here. I called your father to come get you, but apparently he's too busy.'

'S'okay Mum, I can get myself home.'

'But do you even know what bus you have to catch?'

'I'll figure it out. I'm sixteen, Mum.'

'I don't understand what's going on with your father. What's so important that he couldn't leave –'

'I better go, I don't want to miss the next bus.'

'Okay, just keep in touch, let me know if you get stuck somewhere, if you're going to have to wait a long time.'

'What are you going to be able to do about it?'

'I don't know, maybe I'll be on my way by then. Just keep in touch, okay? And please message me as soon as you get home if you haven't heard from me already.'

Finally Ellen spotted the road service van pulling up behind her, all flashing lights and fluoro stripes. Thank God. Maybe the horns would stop now. The patrolman emerged from the driver's door and edged up to her window, keeping close to the side of the car.

'Hi there, you're in a spot of bother, love. What seems to be the problem?'

Ellen promptly burst into tears.

'Hey, come on now, it's okay, we'll get you out of this.'

He managed to get a blubbering account from Ellen of what had happened, and then he asked her to open the hood. She flicked the lever under the seat and he walked around to the front of the car, lifting the hood and disappearing from view. Ellen wiped her eyes with a tissue and blew her nose. She was mortified. She wasn't one of those women who fell apart, crying to total strangers. What was happening to her?

She was feeling abandoned and alone, and she just wanted someone to fix it up and make it all better. She was sick of having to be strong, and responsible, and resilient. It was hard and it was tiring and she'd had enough. She wanted someone to look after her for a change.

The repairman got her to try the engine a couple of times, and although it sputtered into life once, it didn't sustain it. He came back to her window.

'Listen love, I have to get you off this intersection,' he said. 'So I'm going to have to rope tow you around the corner and into that parking lot. See it, over there?' he asked, pointing down the cross-street.

Ellen nodded. 'But I'm not sure how . . .'

'It's okay, we'll take it nice and easy,' he reassured her. 'You just have to make sure you brake whenever I do.'

'But I have power brakes. They won't work without the engine, will they?'

'You'll have to use your handbrake.'

'Seriously?' she said in a weak voice.

'It'll be all right, I'll take it very gradually. Your steering'll also be heavy, but you'll manage. It's only one wide sweep and we'll be around the corner. You can do it.'

It took some time as he waited for a sufficient break in the traffic so that he could manoeuvre the van around her car, and then reverse in front of her, and finally attach the winch. He came to her window and went over the procedure again, before returning to the van. Then they waited for the next light change.

Ellen's heart was in her mouth as he advanced slowly through the intersection, pulling the hatchback along behind him. She kept her hand on the handbrake, but she was shaking, barely breathing, terrified. She willed herself to focus. She had to have both hands on the steering wheel as they turned, it was so stiff and heavy. But they made it into the parking lot safely, and he came to a slow, gentle stop, giving her ample time to ease on the handbrake.

He jumped out of his van and came over to open her door. 'See, that wasn't so hard, was it? You did great! Why don't you get out now and stretch your legs, I'll take it from here.'

Ellen stepped away from the car and left him to it. She didn't know anything about cars, there was no point hovering anxiously over his shoulder. She realised she hadn't heard from Sam so she gave him a call.

'I'm just getting off the bus now, Mum, it's all good,' he reported.

'Have you got your key? I think your sister has late classes.'

'Yeah, I've got my key. When will you be home?'

'Your guess is as good as mine, mate. The repairman doesn't seem to be having much luck, I'm afraid.'

'Jeez, what's going to happen?'

'I don't know, but don't worry, I'll be all right. I'll let you know as soon as I know something.'

She hung up as the man approached her, wiping his hands on a rag.

'It's not looking good, Ms . . . ah . . .'

'Cosgrove, actually it's Ellen.'

'Ray,' he said with a nod. 'I don't know what's up, Ellen. It's behaving like it's overheated, but the radiator's full. There could be a blockage further along in the pipes, but even if I could get it started, I wouldn't want you driving it, you'll risk blowing the gasket.'

Ellen rubbed her forehead. 'So it'll have to be towed?' she said with a resigned sigh.

''Fraid so,' he confirmed. 'Where's your regular mechanic?'

'Down in Sydenham, we live in Petersham.'

He stroked his beard, thinking.

'Is that too far to tow it?' she asked.

'Oh no, it still should be inside the free tow zone. But this time of day,' he shook his head, 'it's gunna take a while. Can you give him a call?'

'Oh, um, well I don't have his number on me,' said Ellen. 'God, I can't even think what the name of the place is.'

'Don't worry, as long as you can direct the tow-truck driver, and even if it's closed, you can still have it towed there,' he assured her. 'Just lock it up, then take the key around tomorrow and explain the whole deal.'

Ellen wondered how she was going to do that without a car.

'Or look, there is an approved repairer not far from here, just up in Five Dock on the other side of Parramatta Road. He's a good bloke, he'll sort it out, and you can still have it towed back to your mechanic after you get his quote if you want.' He glanced at his watch. 'I've got his number, I can give him a call so he waits around, and I can explain everything to him as well.'

That sounded preferable to Ellen, so the calls were made and Ray bid her goodbye and good luck. She sat it out in the car, waiting for the tow-truck driver, fielding calls from Sam about what there was to eat –

'I don't know, Sam, look in the fridge.'

'I am.'

'Well then, you can see better than me. Figure it out.'

– and Kate when she arrived home –

'What's going on? When will you be home?'

'I don't know. I'm waiting for a tow.'

'I was hoping to use the car tonight. Sarah and I were going to the movies.'

'Well, that's not going to happen.'

'What am I supposed to do?'

'Figure it out.'

– and finally a text from Tim –

What's happening? Is everything ok?

Ellen was tempted to reply 'Fuck you', but decided against it. She sat for a moment, thinking about how to answer. Then she decided, screw it, he could call if he was that concerned.

The tow truck turned up eventually, and the driver promptly hoisted the car up ready to go. Ellen took a seat in the cabin and made awkward small talk for the short drive.

'Finn's a good bloke,' he told her. 'He'll get you sorted.'

'Who's Finn?'

'The mechanic I'm taking you to,' he said. 'Top bloke. You're in good hands.'

When they arrived at the garage, Ellen got out of the truck and out of the way, while the driver and the mechanic – 'Finn', she assumed – proceeded with the complicated manoeuvres to unload the car into position. She walked across to the small office and waited at the door. This was not one of the big chain service stations – there were a couple of petrol pumps, but set back as it was in an industrial area, petrol was obviously not his main trade. This was an old-school garage, which Ellen hoped was a good thing.

Finally the tow-truck driver gave her a wave and jumped into his truck. The mechanic strolled over to where Ellen was standing.

'Not a great start to the weekend for you,' he remarked.

'Do you know what's wrong with it?' she asked.

He smiled, scratching his head. 'Ah, no, not without looking at it.' He indicated for her to walk through into the office ahead of him. 'Let me get your details.'

Ellen stepped into the office, which was surprisingly neat. He walked around the counter and flipped open an appointment book.

'I'll get your number, and I'll give you a call on Monday or Tuesday, let you know what's what.'

'I beg your pardon?'

He looked up.

'Monday or Tuesday?' she said. 'But it's Friday.'

'Exactly.' He picked up a half-empty bottle of beer on the counter and took a swig. 'I'm already completely booked up tomorrow, and I don't open Sundays. I'll do my best Monday –'

'I can't do without a car all weekend,' said Ellen.

He lifted one eyebrow slightly. 'You don't have another car?'

'No. Why would you assume that?' she said curtly.

He shrugged. 'I don't know. It's not unusual for a family to have a second car.'

She was about to say, well, I'm separated, the second car is AWOL somewhere over on the northern beaches. But she didn't.

'Well we don't. And I can't get through a weekend without a car, and I have to get to work next week. What am I supposed to do?'

'Listen, Ms . . .'

'Cosgrove.' She wasn't going to give him her first name – best to keep it professional.

'. . . Ms Cosgrove, from what Ray told me on the phone, this isn't going to be a quick fix. Even if I could get to it tomorrow to see what's wrong, I wouldn't be able to start on it till next week anyway. You're going to have to make alternative arrangements.'

She bristled. Easy for him to say. Bloody tradesmen.

'Fine, but I'd appreciate if you could make it a priority.'

If Ellen wasn't mistaken, he was doing a pretty poor job of trying to suppress a grin. Bloody *bloody* tradesmen.

'I'll do my best,' he said solemnly.

'Well, if you can't, you should just say so, and I'll arrange to have it towed back to my regular mechanic.'

He breathed out. 'I will do my best,' he repeated evenly. 'What's the best number to contact you?'

He wrote down her details as she dictated them, and then he gave her his card. He picked up his beer again. 'Is someone coming to pick you up?'

She looked blankly at him.

'Do you need a lift home?' he said.

Ellen glanced at the beer in his hand. As if she was going to get into a car with him.

'No, thank you, I'm fine.'

He shrugged. 'Okay. I'll be in touch.'

Ellen walked out of the office and into the evening. It was getting dark, and a little chilly. She pulled her light cardigan around her as she crossed the tarmac of the service station to the street. How the hell was she going to get home from here? She paused, looking up and down the road. It was all light industry, and everything was closed at this time of the evening. She glanced back at the service station; the office was clearly illuminated in the gathering dark, and the man, Finn, she assumed, appeared to be watching her. Ellen turned around again quickly and started up the street in the direction of Parramatta Road, where she hoped she had a chance of finding a taxi.

Saturday night

Liz waved when she saw Eddie walk into the bar. He spotted her and smiled, weaving his way through the tables till he got to hers. Liz stood up and they hugged.

'Hello brother.'

'Hello sister.'

'What do you want to drink?'

'I'll get it,' said Eddie. 'What are you having?'

'I'm still on this one,' Liz said, indicating her glass.

'Okay. I won't be a minute,' he said, heading for the bar. He returned to the table with a glass of red, and slipped off his jacket before taking a seat. 'So how've you been, sis?'

'I'm not too bad,' she replied. 'Can't complain.'

He lifted his glass. 'To siblings,' he toasted.

'Eye contact!' they said in unison. It was their silly standing joke. Eddie had heard somewhere that you had to make eye contact when you clinked glasses in a toast, or else it was seven years of bad sex. They weren't superstitious, but neither were they prepared to risk that.

'We haven't done this in a while,' said Eddie.

'Because you're always too busy for me,' she lamented.

'Hoh,' he scoffed. 'How many times have you put me off because Dr McDreamy has called?'

'I don't know anyone called Dr McDreamy,' Liz said airily.

Eddie took a sip of his wine. 'How is the magnificent medico anyway?'

'Magnificent,' she quipped.

'Left his wife yet?'

'Don't be smart.'

'I'm not the smart one,' he returned. 'You're supposed to be the smart one, aren't you?'

Liz set her glass back down on the table and looked at him. 'So, have you brought me here for a lecture, little brother?'

'Nah,' he said with a grin. 'I just keep hoping that one day you'll tell me he's done it . . . or that you have.'

'Done what?'

'Dropped him and moved on.'

Liz sighed. 'This is beginning to sound like a lecture.'

'Just wishful thinking out loud,' said Eddie. He sat forward. 'Are you okay, Liz? Are you happy?'

'Of course I am,' she dismissed.

'Okay then, we'll drink to that.'

'Eye contact!' they both repeated, glaring at each other.

'So anyway,' said Liz, 'what about you? Who is she?'

He feigned ignorance. 'Who is who?'

'Oh, knock it off. It always has something to do with a girl whenever you want to get together for a drink.'

Eddie shook his head. 'And here I was thinking I was a man of mystery.'

Liz laughed. 'You might get away with that with everyone else, but not with me. And truth is, you don't want to. I'm like your confessor.'

Eddie reached across the table and squeezed her hand. 'It's good to see you, Liz, it's been too long.'

'I know,' she agreed. 'I haven't even had the chance to tell you off for talking Mum and Dad into selling up.'

The house had been snapped up immediately for a record price for the area, with at least a couple of developers bidding for it even before the auction. Their parents were going to be very comfortable indeed.

'I didn't talk them into anything,' Eddie denied. 'They came to me. Because you're all too bossy.'

'I'm not bossy!'

He raised an eyebrow.

'I totally am not bossy.'

'Okay,' he allowed, 'you're not as bossy as Ellen and Emma, but you're bossier than Evie.'

'Everyone's bossier than Evie. You even bossed her around and she was five years older than you.'

'I know,' he said wistfully. 'Poor Evie, she's such a pushover.' He took a mouthful of wine and set his glass down on the table again. 'So, back to Mum and Dad. They're like two pigs in mud right now. They've started collecting travel pamphlets, and they're so funny, every time I talk to them they've added a new country to their itinerary.' He paused. 'They said they haven't seen you in a while.'

Liz shrugged. 'I've just been so busy, I haven't had a chance . . .'

Truth was, she had been avoiding the house. It felt so sad these days. They had packed a lot of stuff out of the way before the auction, and the one time Liz had been since, it had nearly broken her heart. There were half-filled boxes all over the place, paintings stacked against walls; they'd even packed a lot of the family photos away. They seemed so enthusiastic about moving on. She wished they could have given it some time before they started dismantling their whole past. But if she said any of that to Eddie, he'd be all sensible and tell her to snap out of it, that she was being selfish, she should be happy their parents were getting to go off and live their lives. And he was right, but she didn't need to hear it. It was better to change the subject.

'So you haven't told me her name yet,' said Liz.

Eddie gave her a sheepish smile. 'You're not going to believe this.'

'Why, is it someone we know?' she frowned.

He shook his head. 'No, it's not that. It's her actual name.' He took a breath. 'It's Eliza.'

Liz blinked 'You're kidding me? Another E?'

'I know,' he said. 'Maybe it means she's a keeper?'

'What was it with Mum and Dad? No wonder they could never get our names straight.'

'I think they were being romantic, in a way.'

'How is it romantic to give all your kids the same initials as your own?' Liz pulled a face.

'Maybe I meant sentimental,' said Eddie. 'Anyway, you shouldn't complain. At least you got your own name. Mum and Dad just recycled theirs when they got to me and Evie. And you get to call yourself Liz.'

That prompted a thought. 'Please tell me your Eliza doesn't shorten hers to Liz?'

'No, and if she did, I wouldn't call her that, for obvious reasons,' Eddie assured his sister. 'She gets Ellie sometimes, but I don't call her that either, too close to Ellen.'

'But Ellen never gets Ellie,' said Liz.

'Still too close for comfort.' He shuddered. 'How is Ellen anyway? I keep meaning to call her.'

Liz sighed. 'I'd avoid it if I were you.'

'Why?'

She shook her head. 'Forget it, I shouldn't have said that, it's mean. I'm a bad sister.'

'You're not a bad sister,' said Eddie.

'You should call her, we all should call her, often, and then maybe she'd get it all off her chest a lot sooner.'

Eddie looked at her. 'So she's a bit stuck?'

'A bit,' Liz repeated wryly. 'She's like a broken record. Worse thing is she's just so bitter.'

'I thought the whole thing was supposed to be amicable?'

'It is,' said Liz. 'That doesn't make it easy, though.'

'I guess not.'

'It's so hard to listen to her. I know she has to talk it through, but I don't think it's doing her any good to go on and on about it, ad nauseam.' Liz sighed. 'But then, poor thing, if I don't listen to her, who's she got?'

'She's got all of us. I'll give her a call.' Eddie took out his iPhone and began to type in a reminder.

'Boys and their toys,' Liz shook her head. 'What would you do if you lost that?'

He gasped. 'Don't even suggest it! This is like my own personal hard drive, it's my whole life backed up. I'd be lost without it.'

Eddie finished his memo and put the phone back in his pocket. 'There, done. And you'll get in touch with Mum and Dad?'

'Sure.'

'Promise?' he persisted. 'They've mentioned it a few times.'

'Okay, I promise,' said Liz. 'Now, can we finally get back to Eliza, the subject of which we seem to keep going off track.'

'Did you just call her a witch?'

'Ha ha, did you say she was a keeper?'

'Did I say that out loud?'

'Yes, you did,' said Liz. 'So, out with it. I want all the details.'

Monday

'I'm thinking champagne.'

'Oh, it's a bit early in the day for me.'

'No, Emma, darling,' Isabelle said with a smile. 'Champagne will be your *colour*.'

This was her first dress consultation with her dream designer. The fact that Isabelle Mohavy had made room to see Emma personally was enough cause for celebration, to shout from the rooftops, in fact. It was such a huge deal Emma should have made a party of it. But here she was alone. Not one of her sisters was able to make it. Liz, maid of honour no less, apparently couldn't move a few appointments around. Ellen sited work as well – she couldn't possibly, she was on class – which made Emma wonder why they even had relief teachers if you could never take a day off. And Evie . . . well, once the other two couldn't make it Emma hadn't bothered to ask Evie. She could be a bit much one on one, and she'd been such a misery guts lately. Besides, they had very different taste – which was the nicest way of saying that Evie didn't have much in the way of taste at all.

Emma had talked herself into believing that it was better if she did this on her own. Her sisters were not interested, so how much use could they be anyway? And she didn't really have a *best* friend, as such. She had lots of friends, of course, dozens of women friends, in fact. They were always bumping into each other at parties and functions and shows. People in the industry, minor celebrities, Emma was friends with them all, which was why the guest list for the wedding was currently climbing over two hundred. But she would never have asked one of those women to come with her today, they didn't have that kind of relationship.

Blake was her best friend. But already he seemed bored with the wedding. Emma had to be careful about how much she said in front of him, she didn't want him to get so thoroughly sick of it that he might . . .

What was she thinking? Might what? It wasn't as though Blake would pull out of it, or put his foot down. As long as his life could hum along relatively unimpeded, he would go along with whatever Emma wanted to do. He just didn't need to hear about every little detail. Besides, letting him in on too much was like letting him watch her get ready for a date. As much as possible, Emma still tried to keep a little mystery. They lived together, so of course he'd seen her without her makeup, but she was very careful to make sure she always looked presentable. On her wedding day, of all days, she wanted to absolutely blow Blake's mind . . . so he wouldn't have a moment's doubt that he'd made the right choice.

But she had to admit, this thing she'd been waiting for her whole life didn't feel like it was supposed to. Somehow it was hollow if no one else was involved, or even the least bit interested. Like that saying about a tree falling in the forest – really, what was the point of making a big noise if no one was around to hear it?

'You have been going about this totally the wrong way, Emma,' Isabelle was saying. 'You're not used to being the star, are you?'

Hmm, that was an understatement.

'You know what the problem is here,' she went on, 'Your job is to worry about how other people look, to put them at their best. I've seen you in action and you're absolutely brilliant at it. Now you need to turn the spotlight on yourself for a change.'

She was right, that was so true.

'Imagine for a moment that you're an image consultant for yourself on your wedding day,' said Isabelle. 'If Emma was your primary client, would you be making such a fuss about the attendants? I don't think so. You would only be concerned with doing everything to enhance Emma.'

Emma liked the sound of that.

'You see, your skin tone requires something in the ivory range. Not cream, but creamy. I know you were quite taken with the pewter, but you would have to dress in pure white against pewter, and pure whites have a blue undertone, which is just not right for you. And as for the cinnamon, no.' She sniffed distastefully, 'I don't like it, it's too strong, it will overpower the bride. And everything must work to enhance the bride.'

'But what if it doesn't suit the girls?' asked Emma.

'Uh uh.' Isabelle wagged her finger. 'This is not about the girls. This is about Emma. So what if they don't look their best, *you* will . . . In ivory, offset by champagne, you will look striking, my dear.'

Yes, she would. She really would.

'Then everything else falls into place,' Isabelle assured her. 'The flowers – do you have any idea all the tones of cream roses, pale golds, or you could go to gardenias, even lilies, with the slightest hint of green. Gorgeous!'

Emma could hear the trees falling in the forest. She was going to be *gorgeous* on her wedding day. She would focus on herself for a change. She had been going about this the wrong way, worrying about everyone else. Well, enough of that.

Tuesday

'No . . . I said I'd call you.'

Ellen looked blankly at . . . Mr Finn– . . . oh God, what was his name? Was it Finnegan? Or maybe Finnian? Or Flynn? She glanced around the desk for a hint, but the place was called Southside Auto Care, so that was no help. Well, she wasn't going to call him Finn, she didn't want to be that familiar. She needed to maintain a professional distance if she expected him to behave professionally.

'Ms Cosgrove?' he prompted. 'I was going to call you, remember?'

'No,' she said. 'I don't remember that. I'm sure you said you'd look at it no later than Monday. I assumed the car would be ready for me to pick up today. I mean you have had it since Friday.'

Did he just clench his jaw for a second?

'Friday doesn't really count, Ms Cosgrove, it was towed here after hours. And I said I wouldn't get the chance to look at it Saturday, and that I'd do my best to check it out and call you Monday or Tuesday.'

'No, you said it would be ready Monday or Tuesday,' Ellen said in her best teacher's voice, the one she used to interrogate students when they were making excuses about why they were late with an assignment. 'And so when I heard nothing yesterday I assumed, by a process of elimination, that the car would have to be ready by today.'

And when she had mentioned it to Zoe at work, and she had said she was going to pass this way this very afternoon, Ellen had grabbed the opportunity of a lift. She hadn't had his card with her or she would have called first, of course. But she was absolutely sure he said it would be ready . . .

'Well, the car's not ready,' he said plainly. 'It's nowhere near ready. In fact I was just about to call you.' He paused to take a breath. 'I'm afraid it's not good news.'

Ellen's heart sank. The weekend had been impossible without a car. She'd called Tim about borrowing his, but he'd refused. Point blank. He had 'plans', apparently.

'So?' she'd said. 'Can't you find an alternative?'

'Can't you?'

'I have the children,' she reminded him.

'They're not *children*, Len,' said Tim. 'They're old enough to make their own way about. You run around after them too much.'

'Excuse me?'

'They're old enough to use public transport,' he restated. 'Or else let them make alternative plans.'

Obviously she wasn't going to win this argument putting the kids first, Tim clearly didn't give a damn.

'Well, what about me?' said Ellen. 'I have . . . errands . . . grocery shopping . . . I need a car.'

'So do I,' said Tim. 'I have things I have to do as well. Why is it any easier for me to do without a car than it is for you?'

She gritted her teeth. 'If the kids were with you, and for some reason you didn't have your car, I would let you use mine.'

'Well, that's all very well, but it's hypothetical.'

Ellen was incensed. 'So you think I'm just saying that?'

'That's not what I meant.'

'That's what you're implying.'

'I didn't imply anything,' he sighed. 'I'm just saying that I would have as much trouble doing without my car as you're having doing without yours.'

'Since when did it become "your" car and "my" car anyway?' she said. 'They're *our* cars, so this is *our* problem.'

'Listen, I have to go,' Tim had said suddenly. 'Obviously if this drags on then we'll have to negotiate something.'

God she was beginning to hate that word.

'. . . so I flushed out the radiator –' The mechanic had launched into a lengthy explanation of what was wrong with the car, '– though it's relatively new, maybe six months old, I'm estimating. But the hoses weren't replaced at the same time. Maybe they weren't as old as the previous radiator, but they still should have been changed, it's standard practice. So I checked all the hoses for leaks and the clamps for corrosion, then I tested the coolant reservoir for cracks, because that can cause all kinds of headaches. See if you get combustion gas in the coolant –'

'I don't need a lecture in engine maintenance,' Ellen interrupted with mounting frustration. 'Can you just tell me what's wrong with my car, and how much it's going to cost?'

He took a breath. 'Basically, the entire cooling system is stuffed. Whoever's been servicing your car has been ripping you off. When they replaced your radiator they should have checked the whole system and started a schedule of repair before it got to this. But that didn't happen, and the engine's suffered major damage as a result. It's probably going to cost in the vicinity of a couple of thousand to fix it.'

Ellen gasped. 'What? But it didn't even overheat! It just stopped.'

'Exactly, the engine more or less seized because it was running dry. You're lucky you didn't crack the head, or blow a gasket.'

'Lucky?' she almost shrieked. 'You call this lucky? *Winning* a couple of thousand dollars might be considered lucky. Having to shell it out for something I can't even see is definitely *not* lucky. And now you're telling me it should have been fixed by my original mechanic? Well, fine, I'll just have to take it back to him and tell him it's his problem.'

'You can try,' said Finn, Flynn, Flip, whatever his name was. 'But he can just argue it's normal wear and tear, which it is. If he'd charged you for any of the repairs I mentioned, then you'd have a case. But unfortunately you can't get him on neglect, or oversight, or just plain incompetence, which is what this is.'

'But you don't understand!' Ellen cried. 'I don't know how I'm going to pay for this. Seriously. It's been one thing after another lately – first the stove, then the microwave, the washing machine, they've all conspired to break down one after the other, ever since my husband and I separated. Yeah, that's right, I'm separated, that's why I don't have another car to use, and I've got two kids and I live on a teacher's salary. Four years at university and I bet I don't earn as much as you. And don't go telling me I get all those holidays because holidays don't pay the bills, even though I work through most of them, and I don't get paid any overtime. What am I supposed to do?'

She was breathing hard, tears stinging her eyes as she stared at this man she barely knew, who was staring back at her, obviously a little stunned by her outburst. Bugger.

'Can I get you some water?' he asked carefully.

Ellen swallowed. Her throat was dry. 'No, it's okay,' she croaked.

'I'll get you some water,' he said, crossing to the fridge and grabbing a bottle. He put it on the counter in front of her. 'Go on, it's on the house.'

Ellen reached for the bottle, her hand shaking. 'Thank you,' she said in a small voice, not looking at him. The phone rang and she breathed out as he turned away to answer it. Get a grip, you crazy woman. She took a couple of sips of the water and breathed steadily, calming herself. This was excruciating. She'd never carried on like this in front of a complete stranger.

Apparently she did now.

When he hung up the phone he turned around to face her.

'Are you okay?'

She nodded. 'I'm sorry about that.'

'No worries.'

'It's just a difficult time right now,' she said, regaining her composure. 'I'm going to have to discuss this with my hus- . . . my ex-husband.'

'Sure,' he said. 'Have you still got my card? Get him to give me a call and I'll go over it with him if he wants.'

That wasn't going to do any good, Tim wouldn't have a clue. He was absolutely hopeless with cars. Ellen had had suspicions about their mechanic for some time. The car never felt any different after services, and more than once they'd had to take it back when he'd missed something. But Tim was too coy, or too lazy, to take it to someone else. Well then, he was going to have to wear this as well. It was *their* car, *their* joint responsibility. He couldn't play the child support card this time.

'Just give me a sec,' the mechanic was saying, 'and I'll give you a lift home.'

Ellen stiffened. 'No, you don't have to do that.'

'It's part of the service,' he said with a shrug.

'Really, it won't be necessary,' said Ellen. 'I'll let you know what we've decided as soon as possible.'

She turned and walked quickly out of the office, picking up her pace as she crossed the tarmac to the road. She didn't know how she was going to get home, she probably should walk in the direction of Parramatta Road again, grab a taxi. Not that she could afford one. For now she just needed to walk. Clear her head. Calm down.

She was actually feeling mortified. She didn't know whether she could even go back to this mechanic now. Maybe she could get Tim to deal with it? Fat chance. He didn't give a flying fig about her problems anymore.

Ellen crossed at the lights and started along the path in the direction of home, which had to be more than an hour away on foot. She would not be able to walk the distance, not in these shoes. She should have checked, should have rung first. But she hadn't been able to find the card in her purse, she must have left it at home; she vaguely remembered slipping it under a magnet on the fridge. And then when it occurred to her that she hadn't heard from the mechanic today, the simplest solution seemed to be to accept the lift from Zoe and get over here in person. It was stupid and short-sighted, she realised that now. Ellen was usually much more organised and rational. She planned, she didn't do things on impulse. In fact Ellen had been the responsible one all her life, among her siblings, at work, in the marriage.

Apparently not anymore. Now she was someone capable of flying off the handle at a complete stranger, embarrassing them both in the process. It was so unlike her. She had never even lost her temper with her students – no matter how atrociously they were behaving, Ellen always kept in control. Maybe she was finally cracking under the strain.

She was startled then by a car horn close behind her. She turned to see a green ute creeping along the road beside her. The mechanic dipped his head to look at her from the driver's seat.

'Can I give you a ride?'

Ellen bristled. 'I told you that wouldn't be necessary.'

'Look, Ms Cosgrove, you can't walk the whole way.'

'Yes, I can, it's not that far.' That was a lie.

'It will be in those shoes.'

She looked down at her feet, trying to think of a response, while he stopped the engine and got out. He walked around in front of the ute.

'Ms Cosgrove, we always give customers a lift home,' he said, 'or to the train station, or even to work, whatever's most convenient for them. It's part of the service, I'm not doing you any special favours. Didn't your original mechanic ever give you a ride home?'

'But I live over in Petersham,' she said. 'It's not really in your area.'

'All the more reason you need a lift, I reckon.' He opened the passenger door for her and was standing patiently, watching her. This was starting to get ridiculous; that is, her stand-off was starting to get ridiculous, particularly as a follow-up act to her outburst earlier. She should just accept the lift graciously and show this man she wasn't a complete lunatic.

'Okay, thank you,' she said, walking towards the open door. She got in and he closed the door for her. She was about to tell him that she could do it, but she had a feeling that might sound petulant, and she had been petulant enough for one day.

He returned to the driver's seat and pulled out into the traffic. 'So where to?' he asked.

Ellen gave him her address, then settled back and tried to relax. She wasn't the best of passengers. She put it down to the fact that Tim was not the best of drivers – he was absentminded and easily distracted, and Ellen felt as though she had to be constantly vigilant when he was behind the wheel. Fortunately, this man seemed to be an alert, competent driver, not surprising considering his line of work, she supposed. And he wasn't speeding, Ellen hated speeding.

'Listen, Ms Cosgrove,' he said after a while. 'I want to assure you that I'll do everything I can to keep costs under control.

I'll reuse parts where possible, and as for the more major parts, I should be able to get good, reconditioned alternatives in most cases. It just might take a bit longer.'

She groaned inwardly. 'That really is very kind of you,' she said. 'But I can't expect you to do that. This isn't your problem.'

'It is if you can't pay,' he said, glancing across at her with a grin.

Ellen felt embarrassed. 'Look, I don't want you to worry about getting paid. Of course you'll be paid. I'm not someone who doesn't pay her bills.'

'I didn't mean to imply that,' he said. 'It was just a joke.'

She really needed to 'chill', as Sam would put it. She took a breath.

'The thing is, I just don't think I can do without a car for very long.'

'Okay . . .' He seemed to be mulling that over. 'Well, if it's any help, I can probably organise a loaner for you, say, by the end of the week.'

Ellen looked at him. 'A loaner?'

He nodded. 'I have an arrangement with a local smash repairer. They have a couple of old cars on hand to lend to customers when jobs go over a week. They're nothing fancy, but they're roadworthy.'

'Won't they need them?'

'If I put dibs on one, it should be all right,' he said. 'I'll call them when I get back to the garage.'

Ellen bit her lip. 'That's very kind, again, but how much is that going to cost me?' she asked meekly.

'Part of the service.'

She breathed out then, shaking her head. 'I've never had service like this from a . . .' She was about to say 'tradesman', but she worried that might sound like a slight.

But he was just grinning that grin of his. 'I know mechanics can't be trusted half the time. I used to work for some right bas –' he stopped short, glancing sideways at her, '– not very honourable people. They'd just clean up parts instead of replacing them, and then charge for new parts, that kind of thing. And they'd always inflate the labour costs. I vowed when I had my own business I wasn't going to get into any of that. It's worked out all right for me so far.'

Ellen wondered if he was spinning her a line. But what choice did she have save to believe him?

'Well, like I said, I'll have to call my hus- . . . my ex-husband,' she corrected herself, again, 'to discuss it.'

They pulled up at lights. They weren't far from her place now.

'So you haven't been separated long?' he asked.

She turned her head sharply to look at him.

'Just that you don't seem used to calling him your ex,' he said. 'Sorry, it's none of my business.'

Ellen looked straight ahead again. She was tempted to say, you're right, it is none of your business. But she just said, 'It's the next one on the left.'

'Okay.'

He turned the ute into her street.

'Just up there behind the red car will be fine,' said Ellen. 'Thanks.'

He pulled up where she'd indicated. 'So I'll wait to hear from you,' he said, the engine idling. 'And I'll find out about the loaner in the meantime.'

She opened the car door and put one foot out onto the road. 'Thank you,' she said, looking back at him. 'Mr . . . I'm so sorry, I've forgotten your name.'

'It's Finn,' he said.

'Okay Mr Finn . . .'

'No,' he smiled. 'Finn's short for Finlayson.'

'Okay, Mr Finlayson.'

He winced. 'Really, everyone calls me Finn.'

'Well, everyone calls me Ms Cosgrove,' she said, then she realised how that probably sounded. 'I mean, you know, because I'm a teacher,' she added quickly.

He nodded. 'Okay, Ms Cosgrove.'

She took a breath. She was going to have to talk to this man at least a few more times, she was being obtuse for no good reason, and she'd better snap herself out of it.

'It's Ellen,' she said. 'And I really do appreciate the lift . . . and everything . . . *Finn.*'

He nodded again. 'No worries.'

She stepped away from the car and closed the door.

'Hey Ellen,' he said as she started across the road to her house.

She turned to look back at him.

'I know this sucks and it's not fair,' he said, 'but just remember, nobody died.'

So a cutesy little aphorism was supposed to make this all okay?

Ellen was beginning to stun herself – when had she become such a hard bitch? He was grinning that grin of his, but he wasn't teasing her, there was a warmth in his eyes that she found oddly comforting.

So she said 'Thank you' graciously, before turning again and continuing across the road.

He tooted the horn and lifted his hand in a wave. Ellen raised her hand in return as he drove out of sight around the corner.

The following week

Evie got back to her car and switched on the ignition to check the time. Oh blast! She was going to be late picking up the kids. She would have to go straight to the school in her walking gear. She fumbled with the iPod, untangling the earphone cords from around her neck and under her T-shirt. She shoved it right down into her handbag, out of sight so Tayla wouldn't see it. She'd have to distract her once they were home so she could sneak it back into her drawer.

She drove through the suburbs, her anxiety building with each red traffic light. She glanced at the time on the dashboard and took a breath, calming herself. Really, she wasn't going to be late, as such, it was just that the kids were used to her being there early, already waiting as they walked out of their classrooms. She liked to get there early because that way she always got a park nice and close to the gate. But it's not as though they were going to be stranded in an empty playground or anything.

Although from the look on Tayla's face when Evie made it to the school, you'd think she'd been stranded on a desert island for a year.

'Where have you been?' she scowled, arms folded, tapping her foot impatiently.

'I was slightly held up,' said Evie.

'Doing what?' she demanded. 'And what are you wearing, Mother, you're so embarrassing.'

Evie decided to ignore that. 'Where's your brother?' His bag was tossed next to Tayla's, but he was nowhere to be seen.

'How should I know?' Tayla retorted. 'He's not *my* responsibility. You should have been here on time.'

'Tayla,' said Evie, 'I heard the bell go as I was walking up the street. You've been waiting a minute or two. Get over it.'

She sniffed. Evie picked up Jayden's backpack. 'Come on, we better go find your brother or we'll be late for Cody.'

Jayden was where Evie thought he would be, down on the grass oval kicking a ball around with some friends. He left under duress and they eventually made it to Cody's preschool, just on time. His teacher reported he'd been a bit out of sorts today, which was unusual for Cody, so they both wondered if he might be coming down with something. Evie carried him out to the car and saw Tayla through the window, waving her iPod manically, her face a picture of indignation.

'How could you take my stuff like that without even asking?' she accused shrilly as Evie opened the back door to deposit Cody in his car seat.

'I'm sorry I didn't ask,' said Evie, buckling him up. 'But you looked in my bag without asking, so I guess that makes us even.'

'Hoh!' Tayla cried. 'It's not the same. I just needed a tissue, and I didn't take something very special of yours –'

Evie closed the back door and walked round to the driver's side and opened the door. Tayla was still ranting, but now Cody was whimpering as well.

'What's the matter, honey?' she asked, looking over her shoulder.

'Jayden poked my tummy and it did hurt.'

'Dibberdobber dibberdobber,' Jayden chanted.

'Be quiet, Jayden,' said Evie. 'Cody's not feeling well, leave him alone.'

Just as well it was only five minutes to home, because Jayden kept up the 'dibberdobber' mantra the whole way, Cody whined in protest and Tayla would not let up about the iPod.

'You're the one who made the rule about respecting each other's stuff,' she threw at her mother. 'Wait till I tell Daddy, he's going to be so mad at you.'

Evie did her best to switch off. She pictured herself out walking, less than an hour ago. She could hear the birds, smell the eucalypts, feel the blood rippling through her limbs.

'Why are you smiling?' Tayla wanted to know. 'You're not even taking me seriously. You're such a horrible mother, I hate you so much.'

Evie despised the hate word, but decided to let it pass: she wasn't up to going several rounds of the table with her daughter right now. She pulled up in the driveway and turned off the engine.

'I feel thick, Mummy,' Cody whimpered from the back seat.

'It's okay, darling,' she soothed. 'Mummy will get you inside and you can lie down with a cool facewasher.'

Evie carried Cody inside, the other two trailing behind her. He did feel quite hot against her, she'd better give him something to bring down the fever. She popped him on the kitchen island bench and turned to the cupboard where she kept the medicine box.

'Mummy . . .'

Evie turned around as Cody projectile vomited, the height of the bench giving it some momentum as it hit the floor, just as Jayden and Tayla walked into the kitchen.

'Awesome spew, Codes!' Jayden whooped.

Tayla was shrieking. 'It's disgusting! Clean it up! Yuck!'

Evie had quickly grabbed a bowl and was holding it in front of Cody as she comforted the poor kid, who was understandably distressed.

'Both of you go to your rooms while I clean up.'

This was met with more howls of protest.

'Why are we getting punished?' Tayla cried.

'Would you rather stay and help?' Evie suggested. That got them moving. 'Change out of your uniforms while you're up there,' she called after them.

Evie stripped Cody off and popped him in the laundry tub in lukewarm soapy water, while she quickly cleaned up the mess on the floor. She'd have to mop it again later, but it would do for now. She wrapped Cody in a towel and carried him upstairs to his room. Jayden was playing on the floor with his action figures and he sprung up. 'Eew, why do you have to bring him in here?'

'Because it's his room too, Jayden.'

'But I don't want to get sick,' he said, backing himself against the wall.

'Fine, then go downstairs and play on your Wii.'

She'd barely said the words before he'd shot out the door. She had dressed Cody in a pair of boxers and was settling him into bed when Tayla came to the door.

'How come Jayden gets to leave his room and I don't?'

'Fine,' Evie sighed. 'Go and do what you want, but please keep it down, and don't fight with your brother.'

Evie sat holding a cool facewasher to Cody's forehead, until he drifted off to sleep. She hoped the other two wouldn't catch this bug as well, though they usually did. Evie never seemed to get sick, neither did Craig, but he baulked at cleaning up vomit, or changing dirty nappies, or at anything gross for that matter. What, did he think she enjoyed it? She certainly wasn't enjoying the idea of three kids home for the next few days, taking turns throwing up. When would she get a chance to walk? She gazed down at Cody and lifted the facewasher off his forehead. He was sleeping peacefully now, but she'd have to keep him home from preschool tomorrow regardless, even if he rallied this evening. So she wouldn't be walking again this week anyhow. That depressed her more than anything.

She went downstairs to check on the others. Jayden didn't even acknowledge when she asked if he wanted some afternoon tea, he was so absorbed in his game. She found Tayla out on the back deck.

'What are you doing out here?' Evie asked her.

'It absolutely stinks in there, Mother, you have to do something about it.'

'I'm about to, Tayla,' she said. 'I had to look after Cody first, what did you expect me to do?'

Tayla just sniffed. 'Well, I've got homework to do, so I hope it won't take long.'

Evie opened every window to air out the place, and mopped the floor with disinfectant. She made them each a plate of afternoon tea and called them to the kitchen. 'I think it's safe to come in now.'

'Are you sure?' Tayla asked suspiciously.

'Try it for yourself.'

She sauntered inside. 'I guess it's okay, but it smells like chemicals now.'

'Well, which would you rather?'

Jayden didn't seem to notice, wolfing down his food before racing back to his game. Evie was about to call after him to ask if he had any homework, but as he'd probably need her help, not least her supervision, she'd put that off for a little longer. She was desperate for a cup of tea and for a moment to sit down.

'Do you need any help with your homework?' she asked Tayla while she waited for the kettle to boil.

Tayla gave her a pained look. 'It's Maths. You can't even do Maths.'

She was about to argue with that, till she remembered it was quite true. Maths had never been a strength, but why did Tayla have to be so nasty all the time? Where did she get that from? Evie had been assured by other mums that prepubescent girls were a bit of a handful, but sometimes Evie suspected that Tayla was on a whole other level. She seemed to despise her. Evie had adored her mother when she was that age, she thought she was beautiful and clever and wonderful. Tayla seemed to think her mother was an idiot.

After quickly popping upstairs again to check on Cody, Evie made herself a cup of tea and carried it into the study, turning on the computer. She might as well check her emails while she sat here in the quiet, sipping her tea. There was one from Emma, cc'd to all the bridal party.

Dear all

Bridesmaid dress fittings will be held Saturday afternoon, the 28th, at the salon in Surry Hills.

Please check the attached schedule of appointments and confirm as soon as possible. As I'm giving you plenty of notice, I trust everyone will be able to prioritise half an hour. You will not be required for longer.

Emma

God, what was with everybody today? Maybe she could see where Tayla got her snippiness from after all.

Evie sat back in the chair and threw her head back. She felt like she had when she was a kid getting picked on. She wanted to cry out, *everyone just leave me alone!*

She looked around for her handbag and took out her wallet, sliding out the card she had tucked behind her driver's licence. Evie sat there staring at it, gradually becoming aware that her heart was beating faster. That was just silly. She didn't need to feel anxious, and she certainly had nothing to feel guilty about. Steve was barely an acquaintance really, but still he was the only person she knew at the moment who she could be totally honest with. Which was weird, considering she didn't even know his surname until now, reading it from his card – *Steven Walsh, Principal, Swan Financial Services* – or that he was an accountant.

Well, what was she waiting for? She picked up the phone and dialled the number.

'Steve Walsh,' he answered on the first ring.

What was she doing, what was she going to say? Maybe she should just hang up.

'Hello, is anyone there?'

She took a deep breath. 'Hi, Steve, my name is Evie, we met the other night . . .'

'Of course,' he said warmly. 'Hi, Evie, how are you?'

'Oh, fine thanks,' she said absently. She wasn't fine at all.

'I'm glad you decided to call,' he said. 'How have you been feeling since . . .?'

'I don't know, confused mostly.'

'Have you managed to talk to your husband about how you feel?'

'No,' she said after a pause.

It was strange, she and Craig had been acting almost like it had never happened. They didn't talk about it – Craig didn't refer to it, and she certainly wasn't going to bring it up. He looked at her warily sometimes, maybe he was a bit ashamed. She could only hope. More likely he was waiting for her to bring it up. And that was not going to happen.

'Do you want to talk about it?' Steve prompted.

'Oh, I can't really talk right now,' she said. Then why'd you call and bother him in the first place, you doofus? 'It's just that the kids are home, it's not a good time. I shouldn't have called. I shouldn't have bothered you.'

'Hey, wait on,' he said. 'Why did you call, Evie? You must have had a reason.'

She sighed heavily. 'I don't know. Impulse, I suppose. I've just been having a bad day.'

'Well, look, maybe we could meet for coffee or something, then we could talk freely –'

'I don't think so ...' It was an automatic response, but something inside her was hoping he'd persist, talk her into it.

'Listen, it's only coffee, in a public place,' said Steve. 'There's nothing untoward about it, nothing wrong with it. You need someone you can talk to, Evie.'

'Mm.'

'Do you have time through the week when you can get away?'

'Not really,' she said. 'My son has come down with some kind of bug. I think I'll be confined to quarters this week.'

'All right, then let's mark out a time next week, early ... how's Monday?'

'Well, I usually go for a walk.'

'Great, I can use the exercise. Where would you like to meet?'

Wednesday

'God, animal farm's exhausting.'

'You're doing *Animal Farm* with that lot?' Zoe frowned.

'Of course not. I don't mean the book, I mean them, 9G, *they're* the animal farm.' Ellen sighed, dumping a stack of books onto her desk. 'I'm getting too old for this.'

'Aren't we all,' Zoe murmured, clicking her mouse and staring absently at the screen of her computer.

Ellen didn't know what Zoe was on about, she'd only just turned thirty. And she was trim and attractive – they'd never had so many boys enrolling for Drama since she'd come to the school to teach it.

'I just feel so tired all the time lately,' said Ellen.

'Maybe you're not getting enough iron,' Zoe suggested.

'Maybe I'm not getting enough sleep,' Ellen countered. 'There's only one of me now, but there's still two mouths waiting to be fed when I get home, two lots of clothes needing washing . . .'

'You should have the kids doing some of that for themselves.'

'Good one.' Ellen gave a dismissive laugh but Zoe swivelled in her chair to face her.

'I'm serious,' she insisted. 'How old is Kate now?'

Of course Kate was old enough to help out, but Ellen hadn't asked her. She didn't want her place to be all about chores and homework, while Dad's place was all about takeaway food and staying up late . . . and whatever else they got up to over there.

'She has her studies.' Ellen shrugged. 'I want her to focus on them.'

'And what were you doing while you were studying?' Zoe persisted. 'You had both kids by then, didn't you?'

'Not when I first started.'

'Oh yeah, that's right, when you first started you were dealing with morning sickness.'

Ellen looked at her. 'I've told you way too much about myself, haven't I?'

Zoe grinned. 'Christmas staff parties, a bottle of wine, can't shut you up.'

'Well, anyway, the kids are going to have to fend for themselves some nights, because it looks like I'm going to have to look for work after school.'

'What kind of work after school? Not Macca's I hope?'

Ellen pulled a face. 'No, I was thinking maybe tutoring.'

'I could think of nothing worse,' Zoe groaned. 'Crowd control by day, and one on one by night. Why would you want to put yourself through that?'

'How else am I going to pay all these bills? I'm not managing on a teacher's salary alone, even with Tim's "incredibly generous" child support.'

'You could go work in a private school.'

Ellen shuddered. 'No I couldn't.'

'Why not?'

'I don't know, it's against my principles, I suppose.'

'We're public school teachers, of course it's against our principles,' said Zoe. 'But principles don't pay the bills unfortunately.'

'No, it's more than that. It's a family institution. Dad and Mum were both schoolteachers, and my dad's father was a schoolteacher as well. You know my sister, the doctor? She could have got a scholarship to go anywhere, and she did get into selective school, but they still made her go to the local high school. They said if everyone went to their local public school, there wouldn't be any bad schools.'

'We all know that argument,' said Zoe. 'And I agree in theory. But it's not the way things are turning out in reality, is it?'

'Yeah, I know,' Ellen sighed. 'But my parents are so proud that I've stuck with it. I don't know if they'd ever forgive me if I sold out.'

'So they're going to cover your bills?'

Ellen looked at her.

'Listen, you know who I bumped into the other day?' said Zoe, not waiting for an answer. 'Jodie Cartwright. Remember her? She did a maternity leave block here a couple of years ago?'

'Vaguely,' said Ellen. 'Pretty girl, young? Not long out of college?'

'That's the one. She looked amazing, perfect hair, makeup, immaculate suit.'

'So she gave up teaching?'

'No, this was straight after school.'

Ellen blinked. 'I look like I've been through the wringer straight after school.'

'We all do, here in the trenches. But she's working at the Privileged Ladies Club.'

They had barely disguised pseudonyms for all the private schools.

'She told me she has twenty to a class, *max*, no special needs, double the non-teaching periods, and she can call in guest speakers as often as she likes. They go to the theatre regularly, literary festivals, trips overseas. And she's on nearly fifty percent more pay than us, even though she only has half as many years' experience.'

Ellen sighed. 'So what are you waiting for?'

Zoe frowned. 'No thanks, I don't want to teach kids with a better credit rating than me.' She got to her feet, picking up the mug off her desk. 'Besides, you're the one looking for extra work. I've still got a husband at home to help pay the bills. I knew he was good for something. Want anything while I'm up?'

'No, thanks.'

Ellen's phone started to vibrate in her pocket. She took it out and looked at the screen.

'Speak of the devil,' she muttered to herself. 'Hello,' she said in the key of weary.

'Hi,' Tim replied, in the key of chirpy. 'Haven't caught you on class, have I?'

'I wouldn't be answering my phone if I was on class, Tim.'

He laughed a nervous laugh. Which made Ellen nervous.

'So how did everything turn out with the car?'

Now he was interested. Their last conversation regarding the car had been strained to say the least. She'd called him after Finn had dropped her home that day.

'Well,' he'd said when she'd explained the situation, 'I'm not sure what you want me to say. It's really up to you, it's your decision.'

'What exactly do you mean by that?'

'Well, it's your car –'

'No, Tim, it's *our* car,' she said evenly. 'It says so on the rego. And these rather major problems it's experiencing obviously started while we were still together.'

'Look, Ellen, we decided when we split who got what car, you can't renege on that now because yours has broken down. We could never allow for every possible contingency, but the arrangement we came up with at the time was fair and equitable.'

Ellen had lost it then. 'Fair? You want to talk about fair? If you think this is even vaguely fair, then let's imagine swapping the entire scenario. I'll go live in a flat and have the kids every second weekend, and I'll pay you child support, which will be less because I earn less than you do, or have you forgotten that? So, once I pay my "fair" share, I'll only have to cover their food and incidentals when they're with me, while you get to pay for everything else, fees and books and clothes and all their food and basic needs, plus maintain the house, deal with a dud car and only get three days a fortnight to yourself. What do you think?'

That had shut him up. He'd mumbled a promise to give her some money towards the repairs.

When she'd called Finn to give him the go-ahead, he had outlined her payment options. As long as she paid for the parts straight up, she could pay off the labour costs over time. Although she tried to argue with him, he assured her, once again, that it was part of the service. But he left it up to her, it was merely an option, he said. And the loaner was available for her any time she wanted to pick it up.

Ellen didn't know why her immediate reaction was to baulk at all this. She should have been thrilled to find such a terrific mechanic, and she was, on one level. But she also felt . . . beholden, as though she was going to owe him . . . and Ellen didn't like being in that position.

'So you'll be right for a car this weekend then?' Tim was saying, after she told him about the loaner. 'Because I probably could have arranged for you to have my car.'

She would have liked to correct 'my' car, but she couldn't be bothered arguing with him. 'No, I'm all set.'

'So,' he said, obviously cutting to the chase and the reason he was calling, 'I was just checking to see if it was okay if I popped round to the house and grabbed the camping gear?'

'Oh.' Ellen wasn't expecting that. 'Sure. You're going to take Sam camping? That's a great idea. I don't know how you talked him into tearing himself away from the computer, but it'll do him good, get him out into the fresh air. It'll be good for the both of you. Male bonding and all that.'

She was met with deafening silence.

'Oh, well, yeah, that is a great idea,' Tim finally spoke. 'And I'll do that, I'll organise to go camping with Sam real soon. But I need the gear for this weekend, and you know, I don't have the kids this weekend.'

'No, that's right,' Ellen replied. 'So where are you going?'

Another silence. Or was it hesitation?

'Just to a jazz festival, up the coast.'

'Jazz? You never liked jazz.'

'I don't mind it,' he said defensively. 'Depends on who's playing it.'

Hm. 'So who are you going with?'

There was that hesitation again.

'Just friends, I'm going with friends,' he stammered. 'No one you know,' he added quickly.

Ellen shrugged. 'Well, fine, of course you're welcome to the camping gear. I'm not sure where everything is. It's been ages since we used it.'

'I'll find it. Is it okay to go to the house when you're not there?'

'Sure, but I'm never home much later than five, so I should be there anyway.'

'I'll probably go round tomorrow during the day.'

'Oh?'

'Taking a few days off work, might as well make a real break of it,' he said with an awkward laugh. 'Better get going, bye then.'

Zoe plonked down in her chair, and Ellen stirred, dropping her phone on the desk.

'He doesn't even like jazz.'

'Huh?' said Zoe, jiggling a tea bag in her mug.

'He doesn't like jazz, and he never takes days off work.'

Zoe frowned. 'Is this some kind of riddle?'

Ellen turned to look at her. 'That was Tim,' she explained, indicating the phone. 'He wants to borrow the camping gear to go to a jazz festival. And he's taking a few days off work.'

'Okay . . .' said Zoe, waiting for the significance of that piece of information to be illuminated.

'The thing is, Tim never takes time off. I mean *never*. He works for the local council, for godsakes, and okay, he is senior, but he acts as though the whole place will grind to a halt if he's not there. He wouldn't even take rostered days off to come to the kids' school functions.' She shook her head. 'Something's going on.'

'So, he's trying new things,' Zoe said, 'reinventing himself. Trying to be cool. It'll be the red sports car next.'

'I don't know.' Ellen shook her head. 'He gets this weird tone in his voice when he's awkward and he's trying to hide something – he sounds like a teenage boy whose voice is breaking.'

'What would he be trying to hide?' asked Zoe. 'That he's seeing someone?'

Ellen pulled a face. 'I can't imagine it.' She paused, trying to do just that before wincing and shaking her head. 'I really can't imagine it.'

'Does it bother you that much?'

'No,' she scoffed, waving her hand. 'Why should it? We're separated. And we were separated a long time before it was official.'

'Then what is it?'

'I genuinely just cannot imagine it,' she said. 'I mean, you'd hardly call Tim a ladies' man . . . he'd be so awkward!'

'The voice-breaking thing would be a feature?'

'Absolutely.' Ellen snorted a laugh. 'Anyway, if he is seeing someone, I don't know why he'd keep it secret.'

Zoe shrugged. 'Maybe it's not serious, so there's no need to mention it.'

'That's true.' Ellen nodded with some relief. 'You're right, if he is trying to hide it, that means he's obviously not planning on involving the kids. We haven't really discussed how we'll handle dating, you know, with them. So this is good,' she decided. 'I don't care what he does in his own time.'

Annandale

Liz walked up the three steps to the front door. She gave the old brass doorbell a turn, before opening the door herself. She loved that they still had the kind of handle you could open from the outside if it wasn't locked. It didn't feel right somehow having to knock on the door of your own home, the place where you'd grown up . . . Oh no, she was getting maudlin already.

As she stepped inside, Emma and her dad were coming from the other end of the hall. 'Oh, hi Em, you're here,' said Liz.

'Just leaving,' she chirped, snapping open her handbag and taking out her keys.

'Not on my account, I hope?'

Emma smiled. 'Don't be silly. No, I have to dash and make myself beautiful. Blake has a dinner with important clients, and I'm the eye candy for the night.' She leaned forward to touch cheeks with her sister and kiss the air somewhere near her ear. 'I can expect you on Saturday?'

'Of course. I did confirm.'

Emma turned to her father. 'Just a tick or a cross, okay, Dad?'

'Whatever you say, love,' he said, giving her a kiss on the cheek and a quick hug.

'Must run,' she said, and then she was gone, her heels clacking on the tessellated tiles as she hurried down the front path.

'Lizzie, this is a lovely surprise,' her father said, taking her by the shoulders. 'Now, you look all right, you haven't been bedridden with a terrible debilitating disease? Or perhaps held hostage in your apartment, unable to leave?'

'Very subtle, Dad,' she chided, giving him a kiss.

'Really? That's funny, I didn't think I was being subtle at all.'

They started back down the hall, arm in arm. 'What was that about?' Liz asked. 'The ticks and the crosses?'

Her father had a chuckle, shaking his head. 'Your sister, I love her dearly, but she's a force of nature.'

'She certainly is.'

'She brought over a selection of the finger food she's thinking about having at the wedding. She wants your mother and me to try them, tell her what we think.' He grinned. 'What would we know?'

'Well, you know what you like, Dad.'

They arrived at the kitchen. 'Yes, but come and have a gander at this.' He crossed to the bench and opened a matt black cardboard box, like a cake box but not as deep, and almost as wide as the benchtop. Inside, arranged in a grid, with neat cardboard separators, were row upon row of delicate canapés, each one apparently different to the next.

'Wow,' Liz murmured.

'Wow is right. I said I don't know what they are, love, how will I be able to tell you which ones I liked? So then, look at what she did,' he said, 'just now, while she was here.'

He produced a piece of A4 paper, on which Emma had ruled a grid and written a code in each square, which Liz assumed corresponded to the contents in the box.

'Do you know what each code stands for?'

'No,' he dismissed. 'She said, don't worry about what they are, she knows what the code means, so just give them a tick or a cross. I said to her, what if I don't love it or hate it? She thought I was having a dig, but I wasn't, it's a genuine conundrum.'

Liz smiled, imagining Emma trying to keep her cool.

'Then she rattled off some nonsense about me being a Pisces and not being able to make up my mind, while she's a decisive Virgo and a perfectionist, so would I please just do as she asked.' He shrugged, holding up his hands. 'So that's what I'll do. Wanna help?'

'Shouldn't we wait for Mum?'

'She'll be along, she's been lunching with her old school crowd. But I say let's get started before she comes home and tells me they're bad for me, and that I'm not allowed to have any more.' He glanced at the clock on the wall, which Liz was glad to see was still where it had always been. For now. It was probably one of the last things left on the wall in the entire house.

'It's after five,' he said, a mischievous twinkle in his eye. 'We need to have a glass of wine with these, don't we?'

'Absolutely,' said Liz. 'We won't get the right sensation otherwise.'

'I like your thinking!'

They moved everything to the breakfast table where there was a view out to the garden, and began to sample the appetisers.

'Now, see,' her father said, with a slight grimace, 'this one has anchovies, and I'm not keen on anchovies.'

'Oh, which one is that?' asked Liz. 'I love anchovies.'

'This is where the system breaks down,' he said. 'I don't like anchovies, doesn't mean other people won't. Should I make a note of that?'

'Just do what she asked, Dad.'

He patted her hand. 'It's good to see you, Lizzie. Your mother will be so pleased when she gets home. We've missed you.'

'What can I say, it's eczema season, busy, busy.' She looked out the window at the garden. 'It's so beautiful in the autumn,' she murmured. She had toyed with the idea of setting up camp out in the backyard till the very last day, so she could enjoy it to the very end. But it was too sad knowing it was going to be bulldozed. 'I have to say it, Dad, it breaks my heart that this will all be gone. Aren't you going to miss it?'

'Of course I will, I love this yard, though I can't say I'll miss mowing it. You know, if I calculated the number of hours I've spent looking after that grass alone.' He shuddered. 'It doesn't bear thinking about. The books I could have read, for one thing . . .'

'I told you we could have got a gardener in, Dad.'

He gave her a sideways look.

'All right, all right,' she said. 'I know it's too late, it's done. Get over it, Liz.'

'Is this why you haven't been coming to see us?'

'No,' she denied, but he gazed at her steadily. 'Maybe a little . . . Okay, yeah.'

'Elizabeth,' he chided gently, giving her hand a squeeze. 'Now you're breaking my heart. Does this mean you won't come and see us at all after we move?'

'Of course it doesn't mean that. It's coming to the house that's hard, Dad, not seeing you and Mum. Don't ever think that.' She paused. 'I can't imagine it won't be ours anymore. I always dreamed I'd get married in this backyard.'

He cleared his throat. 'You didn't expect us to wait around for that, did you?'

'Cheeky!' she declared, giving him a nudge. 'It's just, this feels like the only home I've got, Dad. I don't even like my apartment. It's a place to sleep and store my stuff. It doesn't feel like a home.'

'Well, it's about time you made it into a home, Lizzie.'

She shook her head. 'You can't make an apartment into a home. At least I can't. A home has a front door facing the street, and a yard, and probably a dog.'

'Well, why don't you sell the apartment and buy a home? You can afford it.'

Liz shrugged, screwing up her face. 'It doesn't feel right without a husband and kids.'

Her father shook his head as he finished off another canapé and ticked the appropriate box. 'Dear oh dear, Lizzie, seems to me you're going to have to stop waiting around for someone to give you a life, and get on with what makes you happy.'

'I know. Sometimes I find it hard to believe that I've planned my whole life around an imaginary husband and children that have never materialised.'

'They will one day.'

'That's the problem growing up in a not-broken home, you know, Dad,' she said. 'You end up believing in true love, and then you plan for it, expect it. But just because you and Mum were happy, doesn't guarantee I'll find conjugal bliss. In fact, all evidence is pointing rather indisputably to the contrary,' she lamented. 'Now, if I'd had an absent father, an alcoholic mother, *some* kind of dysfunction, I could pin it on that.'

'Sorry we let you down,' he said. 'If I polish off the rest of this bottle and give your mother a backhander when she gets home, will that help?'

Liz just laughed.

'You've got to move on, Lizzie,' he said. 'Like your mother and me. This house is a good example. You stick with something for so long, you want to hang on to it because you've invested so much into it, somehow it feels all that time is a waste if you leave. But it's not a waste, it's all life experience.'

Liz was frowning. He was getting a bit close to the bone, but her parents had never known about Andrew, and never would. Well, not until they could be together openly.

'So, how are you going with the taste test?' she said, deciding that it was safer to change the subject. 'Have you left any for Mum to try?'

The next week

Evie arrived at Parramatta Park before Steve, and parked in the carpark near the stadium, as arranged. He worked in Parramatta, so he'd suggested walking here, and Evie didn't mind, she didn't want to meet him too close to home. She got out of the car and went to wait in the prearranged spot. She was feeling antsy, she hadn't been out walking for five days. Cody had stayed home for the remainder of the week, but fortunately his bug hadn't spread any further through the family, so the other two had gone off to school, leaving her and Cody home alone. It was nice to spend time with him, but she missed walking. She'd tried to talk him into letting her take him out in his old stroller, but he flatly refused. He wasn't a baby any more, he'd insisted.

So now that he was back at preschool, Evie couldn't get out of the house fast enough this morning. She was glad she had told Steve nine thirty, that had given her just enough time to drop the kids off and drive straight here. Which meant she'd had to wear her walking gear, and that hadn't gone down at all well with Tayla.

'Don't take us into school looking like *that*,' she'd insisted. 'Just drop us off at the gate.'

But Evie didn't mind the way she looked in her walking gear these days, since she'd lost so much weight. She'd had to buy new clothes, and she didn't have to wear a big loose T-shirt to cover herself up anymore. Now that it was getting chillier, she'd bought a black hoodie, but under that she wore a selection of coloured, fitted

T-shirts, and in her most positive moments she thought she looked quite smart, despite what her daughter thought.

She noticed a car pull into a parking spot not far from where she was standing. She didn't know it was Steve who stepped out of the car a moment later, until he waved and started coming towards her. She might not have recognised him otherwise – he looked different in the daylight. He was wearing tracksuit pants and a T-shirt, and dark glasses shielded his eyes. Very different to the other night, though to be honest, she hadn't really taken in much then. As he drew closer she noticed his hair was thinning a little, but he seemed to be in good shape for whatever age he was, maybe a bit older than Craig? He didn't have a beer gut like Craig, anyway.

'Hi,' he said as he walked up to her. 'Nice day for it.'

Evie nodded, feeling quite self-conscious all of a sudden. 'Well, shall we head off?' she said.

They walked for a while making small talk; he asked her if she had walked here before, where she usually went walking, how often, how long she'd been walking for exercise. He told her he didn't get as much exercise as he should, it was hard to get away from the office, he knew he made excuses. Eventually they exhausted the topic of walking and exercise.

'So,' Steve said, 'how are things at home?'

Evie felt herself reddening. 'I don't know. We haven't talked. I don't really want to bring it up. Hoping he'll forget about it, I suppose.'

'If I can be honest with you, I don't think that's likely to happen,' said Steve.

They walked on in silence.

'Do you mind if I ask you something?' Evie said after a while.

'Fire away.'

'How have you coped for so long? You said that you lost interest a while ago, how do you keep going for five years?'

'It hasn't been easy. I got pretty down about it for a while there, and at one point I gave Cheryl an ultimatum. I said it had to stop or we were over.'

'What did she say to that?'

'Well, she didn't like it,' he admitted. 'She reminded me that I'd started it, that she never would have suggested it herself, and now I wanted to change the rules. I couldn't really argue with that.'

No, he couldn't, Evie supposed.

'I'd made my own bed, so to speak, and she was going to lie in it,' he said with a weak smile.

'So, she didn't . . .' Evie had to be sensitive how she put this. 'She didn't care about how you felt?'

Steve glanced at her. 'No, she did. I told her I was worried that I wasn't enough for her anymore, that I couldn't fulfil her needs. But she assured me that she was happy with me, that she felt going to the club enhanced our marriage. She went to a lot of trouble to prove that to me. The sex was good, still is. I can't complain . . . until the third Saturday comes around every month.'

'But doesn't that change everything else?' said Evie.

'What do you mean?'

She stared out ahead. 'I used to be so happy, I thought I had it all – a husband who loved me and who I was certain would stay with me forever, three beautiful kids, a nice house. A future. Craig reckons we can afford to put a pool in next year, and he said we might manage a trip to Bali when Cody's a bit older. I mean, I always felt like I was living the dream. Now all of that stuff means nothing – I don't mean the kids, of course. But I can't look at Craig the same way. Everything's changed.'

They came to a bridge and walked across, pausing to lean on the railing and look down at the river.

'It's like when my mum started wearing glasses,' Evie said. 'We'd been hounding her for ages, her arms weren't long enough to hold the paper out to read it anymore. And so she finally got glasses, and then she was amazed at everything she'd been missing. Some of it was good, like being able to read more easily, but mostly she was alarmed – by her own wrinkles, the dirty windows and mirrors around the house, smudges on all the furniture, dust. She was horrified. That's how I feel now. I can see the smudges and the dirt and the flaws.'

'So you think it was better when you couldn't see them?' Steve asked.

'No, maybe not. It just makes me realise how short-sighted I've been. And now that I have seen them, I can't ignore them. I have to do something about them.'

Southside Auto Care

Ellen pulled into the service station and parked against the side fence, where her poor broken car had been unloaded from the tow truck a few weeks ago. She could see it inside the garage, facing out, ready to drive away. It looked all new and shiny, but that was probably just in comparison to the car she'd been driving. She had been a little embarrassed when she'd first come to pick it up, with its panels in different colours, some only undercoated. But beggars could hardly be choosers, and she was most certainly the beggar in this scenario, so she put up with the sniggers and jibes from the kids at school. Besides, she had to admit it had been reliable, which was all that mattered; she never would have survived this long without a car.

When she walked into the office, Finn was sitting behind the counter, his crossed feet resting on the desk, the phone wedged under his chin. It was Friday afternoon, so he was holding his customary beer, which he raised to her as she came to stand at the other side of the counter. He hung up the phone and looked up at her with a wide smile.

'Well, ma'am, your chariot awaits.'

'Thank you,' said Ellen. 'I saw it sitting out there, it looks brand new.'

He rose to his feet. 'I took it around to the smash repairers earlier and had them detail it for you.'

Ellen's eyes widened.

'No extra cost,' he assured her quickly. 'It's part of the –'

'– service,' she finished for him. 'I swear I've never had service like this before.'

'It's just all part of my plan to keep you coming back,' he said.

Ellen felt herself blush, which was faintly ridiculous. He was talking about keeping her as a customer, of course. What else would he be talking about?

She cleared her throat. 'So you lavish your customers with free extras to make sure they stay your customers? Isn't that a rather expensive form of marketing?'

'Oh but see, once I've lulled them into a false sense of security, then I start ripping them off. So it all works out in the end.'

Ellen smiled, shaking her head. 'Well, before we go down that path, I would like to show my appreciation.'

He frowned as she lifted a six-pack of beer up onto the counter.

'Aw, you didn't have to do that,' he said, and she wondered now if he was blushing just a little. 'You even got the right beer.'

'It's nothing,' she dismissed. 'Please, it really is nothing, just a small token. You've been so decent, after I was a raving lunatic.'

'That's going a bit far,' said Finn. 'I never thought you were a lunatic.'

'Just raving, eh?' She smiled. 'Well, I wanted you to know that's not what I'm like normally. I really don't go on like that. I can't stand people who do, it's so rude. I mean, it wasn't your fault that my car broke down, or that it was going to cost so much, so taking it out on you was not . . . Anyway, the thing is, I haven't been given too many breaks lately, so I really do appreciate everything you've done for me.'

He looked a little coy. 'What can I say, I'm a sucker for a damsel in distress.'

That wasn't very PC, but she'd let it pass, this time.

'So,' said Finn, reaching for the six-pack, 'you realise now that you're going to have to have one of these with me?'

'Oh no, really . . .' Ellen held up her hands. 'I have to get going.'

'Ah, come on,' he cajoled. 'Just one?'

She gave him an apologetic smile. 'To be honest, I don't even like beer.'

'I could put some lemonade in it for you, make it a shandy?' he offered. 'My mum used to like a shandy.'

'Thanks, but really, I should be getting home.'

He looked at her for a beat longer. 'All right, whatever you say.' He went to the desk and shuffled through some papers, returning with two sheets stapled together, which he placed on the counter in front of her. 'Here's your schedule of payment . . .'

Ellen winced. 'I don't know, Finn.'

He looked at her. 'What? We talked about this.'

'I know, but . . .'

'But what? You pay the cost of the parts, I'm not out of pocket. You pay the rest of it off in the next couple of months, that keeps my cash flow healthy.'

She bit her lip. 'Are you sure?'

'It's an option I offer any customer with a bill this size,' he said. 'It doesn't bother me either way, but if it bothers you, then fine, I'll take all your money now.'

'Okay, okay,' she relented. 'Thank you, I'll take the payment option.'

'All right then. So hand over your credit card,' he said with a grin. 'You're not getting your keys till I get the first instalment.'

He processed the payment and Ellen signed the receipt.

'And here,' he said, plucking keys from a row of hooks on the wall, 'are your keys.'

'Thank you,' she said as she took them from his outstretched hand. 'For everything.'

He met her eyes directly. 'It has been my pleasure.'

*

'Hi!' said Ellen, holding up a bottle of wine as Liz opened the door to her flat. Then she noticed the expression on her sister's face. 'Oh God, Andrew's here, isn't he?'

'No,' Liz assured her. 'Not yet.'

'I'm sorry.' Ellen winced. 'I should have called, I'll go.' She leaned forward to kiss Liz on the cheek.

'No, come on in,' she said, taking her by the arm. 'You're here now, we'll have a drink. He won't be here for a while anyway.'

'Are you sure?' Ellen said, hesitating on the threshold.

Liz drew her inside. 'I'm sure.'

Ellen walked into the flat, trying to hide her disappointment. She'd had it all planned in her head. After she'd left Finn's, she couldn't face the idea of going home to the empty house. Liz had been right when she'd said she should try to avoid it whenever possible. They had the bridesmaid dress fitting tomorrow, so she knew Liz would offer for her to stay the night once they'd had a few drinks. Then in the morning they could swing by her place on the way so she could change. Kate was at her dad's for the weekend, so she was going to meet them at the bridal place.

Ellen should have called first; this new streak of impulsiveness wasn't really working for her. But maybe it was just as well. If she'd known Liz's was not an option, she may well have accepted Finn's offer of a drink, and she suspected that was an impulse best left unexplored.

'So how was your day?' Liz asked Ellen when they were sitting on the sofa with a glass of wine each.

'Not too bad, actually,' she said. 'I finally picked up my car.'

'Here's cheers to that,' said Liz, clinking her glass against Ellen's. 'How's it going?'

'Great,' she said. 'It's running smoother than it ever has, and it's all clean and shiny – they had it detailed.'

'Wow, sounds like some mechanic,' said Liz. 'I might have to get his number.'

'Absolutely,' said Ellen. 'I couldn't recommend him highly enough. It's the best service I've ever had from a mechanic, or any tradesman for that matter. He went to a lot of trouble to keep the costs down, and he arranged the loan of a car for me. And . . . well, he's just really decent. I trust him. He's a really nice guy, easy to deal with.' She gave an awkward laugh. 'He even asked me to have a beer with him this afternoon.'

'Who?'

'The mechanic.'

'He asked you to have a drink with him and you refer to him as "the mechanic"?'

'You wouldn't have known who I was talking about if I used his name.'

'So you do know his name?'

'Of course,' Ellen said indignantly. 'At least, I know his surname, because he calls himself Finn, which is short for Finlayson. I don't know his first name, everyone seems to call him Finn. That's the only name I know him by.'

Liz was watching her with some amusement. 'You're getting all flushed talking about him.'

'I am not!'

'Yes, you are,' Liz taunted. 'Have you got a little thing for the mechanic?'

'No, he's just . . . my mechanic.'

'Ellen, you are a snob.'

'I am not.'

'Did you have a beer with him?'

'No.'

'I rest my case.'

'He only offered to be polite because I bought him a six-pack to say thank you.'

'And you're buying him gifts?'

'It was a token –'

'A *lurrve* token?'

Ellen's mouth dropped open, and Liz couldn't keep a straight face any longer.

'I was just revving you up.' She grinned, nudging her. 'Ha, get it? I was "revving" you up about the "mechanic".'

'That's terrible,' Ellen grimaced.

'So he doesn't blow your horn?'

'*Liz* . . .'

'Get your motor running?'

'Stop it,' Ellen insisted, 'you're hurting my brain.'

Liz chuckled happily. 'Okay. So if not the mechanic, is there anyone else on the horizon? Refrigerator repairman . . . plumber . . .?'

'Don't be ridiculous.'

'You're being a snob again,' Liz said. 'Okay, any white-collar contenders?'

'Of course not.'

'Why "of course not"?'

Ellen shrugged. 'I don't have time for any of that.'

'What do you mean you don't have time? You're free tonight, aren't you?'

'What? You expect me to walk into a bar on my own?'

'I suppose not,' said Liz. 'You could have had a drink with Finn the mechanic though.'

'Stop it,' she chided. 'Oh, I just hate Friday nights now. I used to love them. Getting home at the end of the working week and vegging out with a glass of wine, pizza, a movie. Bliss.'

'There's nothing stopping you doing any of that.'

'It just doesn't seem the same on my own. It feels a bit pathetic.'

'Welcome to my world,' Liz muttered.

'Sorry. I didn't mean . . .'

'It's okay. But really, Len, you will adjust in time. It's not that weird, lots of people live alone, go to the movies alone, order pizza for one, all kinds of stuff. If you can't handle that, you're going to have to stop being so fussy about who you have a drink with.'

'I wish I'd never mentioned that,' said Ellen. 'He's just my mechanic.'

'Sounds like he wants to do more than tinker under your hood.'

'Elizabeth!' Ellen exclaimed. 'What is it with these dreadful puns?'

'I don't know,' she said. 'I can't seem to help myself.'

Ellen stood up. 'Well, do you mind if I help myself to another glass of wine?' Then she hesitated. 'Oh, but Andrew . . .'

'He'll message when he's on his way,' Liz assured her, holding up her own glass. 'I'll have a top-up while you're there.' She turned around and rested her arms along the back of the sofa, watching Ellen in the kitchen. 'So does Tim know about the mechanic?'

Ellen rolled her eyes. 'There's nothing to know about the mechanic, Liz. But actually, while we're on the subject, I have a feeling Tim might be seeing someone.'

'Seriously?'

She nodded, pouring the wine. 'He borrowed the camping gear this weekend, he was going to a *jazz* festival.'

Liz gave her a blank look.

'Tim doesn't like jazz,' Ellen said meaningfully.

'And that's what makes you think he's seeing someone?'

She shrugged, walking back around the kitchen bench. 'It's a lot of little things. He always seems to be out whenever I call him.'

'That's probably better than hanging around on his own at home,' Liz pointed out, taking her glass from Ellen.

'But he was always so . . . not *un*sociable, I guess,' she mused, sitting down again. 'Maybe *a*sociable, if there is such a word. He was happy to stay home, weekend in, weekend out, when we were together. Now he's taking time off work, going to jazz festivals . . .'

'So it bothers you? The idea that he's seeing someone, getting out there?'

'No,' she denied. 'Really, I don't care what Tim does in his own time, it's only when it starts to impact on the kids.' She paused. 'And we haven't had *that* talk yet.'

'What talk is that?'

'The one about how we'll deal with either of us dating.'

'You're both consenting adults, isn't who you date your own business?'

'Yes, of course. I'm just talking about how we handle it with the kids. There has to be some ground rules, boundaries . . .'

'Such as?'

Ellen thought about it. 'Well, for starters, when should they meet, do you even bring the kids into it if it's only casual? But then if it progresses, well, is a "sleepover" acceptable when the kids are with you, that kind of thing.'

Liz was shaking her head.

'What?' Ellen asked.

'It just seems to me that you're adults, you're separated, do you really have to answer to each other anymore?'

'When there's kids involved you do,' Ellen said squarely. 'You can't just do whatever you want when you're a parent. Every action and decision you make affects them. And I think your first responsibility always has to be to the children.'

*

Ellen's words were going round in Liz's head, long after she left the apartment. There was no escaping it: Andrew's first responsibility was always going to be to his kids, his own happiness came second. Consequently Liz's happiness had to come second to his kids as well. And she didn't even know them.

She finished her glass of wine waiting for him to arrive, and she began to realise why drinking alone wasn't recommended. Her mind was going off on all kinds of tangents. Like, what if he had left his wife years ago? What if Liz had got to know the kids, if she'd worked hard and Danny had eventually responded to her? What if they had tried to build a life together like thousands of people do in second marriages?

Oh God, why was she having these thoughts? She looked at the glass in her hand. 'It's all your fault,' she muttered.

Just then a couple of light knocks sounded at the door – Andrew announcing himself – and Liz dragged herself up off the sofa as he let himself in with his key.

'Hi,' she said, coming towards him.

He opened his arms wide and then folded them around her, holding her close. 'You smell good,' he murmured, 'and you feel good.' He lifted his head then to face her. 'And you look good.'

'So I scored the trifecta.'

'No, I did,' he said, bringing his lips down onto hers, at the same time as he started to slide his hands up under her top.

'Andrew, slow down,' Liz protested mildly. 'Are you in a hurry? How much time have we got?'

'I said I'd be late, not to wait up.'

'Then sit, have a drink. Let's talk.'

'Okay,' he said with a resigned sigh, which Liz decided to overlook. He fell back onto the sofa as she traipsed over to the kitchen and brought back the wine bottle and a glass for him. Once she poured them both a drink, she clinked her glass against his. 'Hi.'

'Hi,' he said.

'So, how was your night?'

'Nothing special, just an appendix.'

'Tell me about it,' she said, shifting sideways to face him and drawing her feet up underneath her.

'You want to hear about an appendectomy?' he said dubiously.

'Why not?'

'Because it's boring,' he said. 'It's routine, why would you want to hear about that?'

'It couldn't have been all that routine if it was an emergency.'

'Well, no, it was infected, it had to come out,' he allowed. 'But come on, Liz, there's nothing very exciting about an appendectomy.'

'It's more exciting than what I got up to today.'

'Then,' he said, putting his glass down on the coffee table, 'why don't we leave our work behind and get up to something much more exciting.' He went to take her glass out of her hand but Liz pulled back.

'Don't, Andrew.'

He slumped back against the sofa. 'What's the matter?'

She paused, looking at him. Did she really want to do this now? She might spoil their whole night.

'What is it, Lizzie?' he asked with a bit more tenderness.

She took a breath. 'We don't seem to have a relationship anymore.'

'What's that supposed to mean?'

'We used to talk and talk all night.'

'I just don't want to talk about work,' he protested. 'It's been a long day and I want a break.'

'Okay,' said Liz, 'but aren't there other things to talk about?'

'Fine, go ahead, you want to talk, then you do the talking,' he said, picking up his glass again and sitting back.

Liz decided to push ahead. She'd been wanting his input on something for a while anyway.

'Well, you know my work hasn't been very fulfilling for some time,' she said.

He nodded.

'So I've been toying with the idea of going back into surgery.'

'Why would you want to do that?' He frowned.

'Same reason you're doing it. Because it's exciting, and a challenge . . .'

'That's not why I'm doing it. You know I don't really have a choice, I'm the breadwinner. Do you have any idea how often I look at your life and envy it? Regular office hours are something I can only dream about.'

'Then why didn't you do another specialty?'

He rubbed his eyes. 'Liz, you know all the reasons why. I was already a surgeon by the time Danny was diagnosed. To start all over again then would have been impossible, the study, the hours. Why do you want to go over old ground?'

'I don't,' she said. 'I'm just saying, things aren't as green as you imagine on my side of the fence. I've never stopped missing surgery, you know how much I loved it.'

'You shouldn't be thinking the grass is greener for me either,' said Andrew. 'Don't forget the hours, the stress . . . It'd impact on our time together.'

'So what are you saying? I should put my life on hold so I'm available at your beck and call, whenever you have a spare moment to drop in for a quickie?'

'Hey,' he said, putting his glass down and turning to her. 'What's going on?'

'Andrew, you're it, you're the only partner I've got. I would appreciate your support when I share things like this with you.'

'Okay, but Liz, you have to know you'd be a long shot for a surgery program.'

'I realise that, but I've been looking at the criteria –'

'You have? So you're serious about this?'

'That's what I've been trying to tell you,' she insisted. 'Anyway, a letter of recommendation from a surgeon of your reputation –'

'Liz, you can't ask me to do that.'

She stared at him. 'Why not?'

'Well, ethically . . .' He just shrugged, like it was so obvious.

'Andrew, you worked with me, you were my supervising registrar.'

'Ten years ago,' he reminded her. 'And yes, you showed promise back then, but I don't know what kind of weight that would hold now. And anyway, you know I can't write a letter . . .'

'Because we're sleeping together,' she said flatly.

'It opens us up to all kinds of scrutiny, if someone wanted to dig a bit and challenge it.'

'I don't believe I'm hearing this.' Liz shook her head, slamming her glass down on the coffee table. She got up off the sofa and walked over to the window.

Andrew followed her across the room.

'I have made so many sacrifices and compromises for you,' said Liz, without looking at him, 'and for your wife, and for your kids. People I don't even know. Danny's needs are paramount, and you can't forget about Samantha, and then Jennifer needs support, so your job is vital. And I come last.'

'No you don't,' he said, placing his hands gently on her shoulders. 'Not to me.' He turned her around then, to face him. 'I know it doesn't always seem that way to you, and I'm sorry for that. But you have to know that you are so precious to me, you are the best part of my life. And because of you, and only you, I can face the rest of it.' He held her face in his hands. 'You're the only thing keeping me together, Liz, and that makes you more important to me than anything else.'

*

Later, after they'd had sex, and Andrew had left, Liz lay awake staring at the ceiling for a long time. She knew she was important to him, she knew his life was hard and that she made it easier. She gave him something he couldn't get anywhere else. It was selfish to think about herself, her needs, when his needs were so much greater, when he needed her so very much. That's what love was all about, wasn't it?

But there was a voice inside her that had been murmuring away in the background for a while now. Lately it had started to grow louder and more insistent.

What's in it for me?

Surry Hills

By the time Ellen and Liz arrived at the bridal *salon*, as Emma insisted on referring to it, Cara had already been and gone and Tayla was standing on a podium while a seamstress knelt at her feet, pinning up the hem.

'Hi,' Evie greeted them with a forced smile.

'You look great,' said Ellen, kissing her on the cheek.

'How much weight have you lost?' Liz added as she kissed her on the other cheek.

'I'm not sure.' She shrugged. 'I haven't really been keeping track.'

'Okay Tayla, I think you're done,' Emma was saying. 'You can take her back to get changed now, Evie.'

'Wow,' Ellen turned to Tayla, 'don't you look gorgeous.'

Tayla was clearly chuffed.

'That's a beautiful shade,' Liz remarked. 'What do you call that, Em?'

'Champagne,' she said briskly.

'So is that just for Tayla?' Ellen asked. 'Or are you thinking about it for everyone?'

'I'm not thinking about it – I've decided. This is the colour. Kate's already in the dressing room getting changed, so hurry along, Liz, and we'll get this over and done with as quickly as possible.'

As they ducked behind the curtains, Ellen whispered to Liz, 'What's her hurry?'

'I don't know. She must have to *dash* off somewhere.'

'Yoo-hoo, Kate, I'm here,' Ellen called.

A moment later Kate stepped out of one of the cubicles. She looked lovely; the dress was simple but beautifully cut, and the colour was perfect. 'You look stunning. Come on, let's go show Aunty Em, I think she's going to be very pleased with the effect.'

She was, though still oddly businesslike about it all. Kate was up on the podium having her hem adjusted when Liz, Evie and Tayla rejoined them.

'I really do like this colour,' said Liz, doing a twirl in front of the mirror.

'I'm glad you approve,' said Emma, 'but I was having it anyway.'

Liz and Ellen glanced at each other. What was she so tetchy about?

'Why are we just standing here, Mother?' Tayla whined, tugging on Evie's arm. 'We have to go, it's four o'clock already.'

Evie sighed. 'It's a sleepover, Tayla, you'll be there all night. Another half an hour is not going to make a difference.'

'But everyone else was getting there at four!' she carped.

'Hey, Tayla,' Kate said, 'you know it's so not cool to be the first at a party. The coolest people arrive after everyone's there and make an entrance. And how many of your friends will be able to say they've been to get fitted for their bridesmaid dress?'

That got her thinking, and shut her up in the bargain. Evie mouthed a silent 'Thank you' to Kate. 'Still, we better be on our way. Sorry we don't have more time. Haven't seen you all in a while.'

'Hmm,' Liz agreed. 'Everything okay?'

'Yeah, busy, as always.'

'Mo*therrr*!'

'Okay, bye everyone.'

'So am I done now too, Aunty Em?' Kate asked after they left in a flurry of hugs and kisses.

'Yes, sure, you can go and get changed again.'

'Great, thanks, I need to get going as well.'

'Oh, okay,' said Ellen. 'The thing is, I drove Aunty Liz here, so if you can just wait till she's finished –'

'It's all right, Mum. I'm meeting some friends in the city,' she said, stepping down off the podium.

'Oh, you're not going back to your father's?'

'No. Dad's got something on tonight anyway.'

Ellen felt a ripple of irritation down her spine. So Tim couldn't even rearrange his hectic new social life around one weekend a fortnight?

'What about Sam? What's he going to do?' she asked Kate.

'I don't know.' She shrugged.

As she disappeared behind the curtains, Ellen took out her phone and flipped it open. 'I should ring and find out what's happening with Sam.'

'No, you shouldn't,' said Liz, quickly snatching the phone from her.

Ellen blinked. 'What are you doing?'

'Saving you from yourself,' she said. 'Sam is Tim's responsibility this weekend.'

'But if he's not taking that responsibility seriously –'

'– it's none of your concern,' Liz finished.

'She's right,' Emma chimed in. She'd been circling Liz, pulling and tucking and adjusting the dress as she went.

Ellen regarded them both, crossing her arms. 'You know, they are my kids, I think I know what's best for them.'

'I'm sure you do,' Emma said, yanking Liz's straps in at the back so the bodice lifted. 'But they're Tim's kids too, so he gets to do what he thinks is best when they're with him.' She came around in front of Liz. 'Ah, there's your cleavage! I knew it had to be in there somewhere.'

Liz pulled a face.

'Can I have my phone back?' Ellen asked her.

'Not if you're going to call Tim,' said Liz.

'I'm not going to call Tim.'

'Are you going to call Sam?'

'Are you telling me now I can't call my own son?'

'I just don't think you should do it tonight, you'll only make yourself upset.'

'I'm already upset,' she said. 'Now I'll be worried about him all night as well.'

'How about I buy you a drink when we're finished here?' said Liz. 'Take your mind off it.'

Ellen gave a grudging shrug.

'Won't be much longer,' Emma said sharply. 'We just need to do your hem,' she added, helping Liz up onto the dais.

'That's fine,' said Ellen. 'No hurry.'

'Well, I don't want to take up your time when you've obviously got other places to be.'

'We're only going for a drink,' said Liz. 'Have you got to be somewhere?'

'No,' she said simply, glancing at her watch. 'Not for hours anyway.'

'So what's the big rush?' Liz persisted.

'I don't want to hold you up.'

'Would you stop saying that?' said Ellen. 'We only just decided to go and have a drink. It's not like we had big plans or anything.'

'Why don't you come with us if you're not doing anything?' Liz suggested.

'That's all right,' said Emma. 'You've already made your plans.'

'What plans? We just decided. Do you know any places we could go around here?'

'I know a few.'

'Good, then we can walk.'

'Will my car be all right? It's parked on the street,' said Ellen.

'Of course. Surry Hills isn't what it used to be,' said Emma.

'So you'll come?' Liz asked her.

Emma hesitated for a moment, then the beginnings of a smile hovered around her lips. 'Okay, then, I guess you talked me into it.'

*

'I think we should have champagne,' Liz announced, studying the wine list. 'Seems appropriate – champagne to toast the champagne.'

Emma had led them up the street and around the corner into the next block, to quite a glam little bar that was decked out all retro style.

'So you do like the colour?' said Emma, after Liz had ordered the champagne.

'I really do,' said Liz.

Ellen was nodding. 'And it looks so good on everyone. How did you come up with it?'

'Oh, it's all right,' she dismissed. 'You don't have to pretend to be interested.'

'But I am interested.'

'I'm interested too,' said Liz. 'You haven't told us anything lately. You haven't sent any emails for a while either. Is everything okay?'

Emma glanced around, avoiding eye contact with either of them. 'Oh, well, I think I was a bit too concerned with pleasing everyone, and getting everyone's input. I needed to remember whose wedding it was and make a few decisions on my own.'

'Well, this one was a good one,' said Ellen. 'I remember you said that once you had the colour, everything else would fall into place?'

'That's right.'

'So?' Liz prompted when she didn't elaborate. 'Tell us.'

'It's okay, you don't have to act interested.'

'Would you stop saying that, Em?' said Liz. 'You've gone from the sublime to the ridiculous. Are we going to have to beg?'

That was all the encouragement she needed, and Emma launched into a lengthy description of her quest for the perfect bouquet. The waiter returned with the champagne and they toasted the bridesmaid dresses. Emma had moved on to menus by the time the waiter returned to top up their glasses.

'Anyway, that's enough about the wedding,' she said finally, sensing their interest flagging. 'What's going on with you two?'

'Well, since you asked,' said Liz, 'I'm toying with the idea of going back into surgery.'

'You're kidding?' said Ellen.

'Can you do that?' asked Emma. 'Is it possible?'

'Probably not,' she said with a shrug. 'I'm probably having myself on. I'm getting too old, I'd be competing for a place along with all the young guns straight out of medical school.'

'So what's brought this on?' Ellen asked her.

'I always wanted to be a surgeon. The only thing I wanted to do more was have a family, so I took the safe option, a specialty with no emergencies, regular hours.'

'I didn't realise that,' Emma said.

'So much for being the brains of the family, eh?' Liz gave a lame smile.

'You're still young enough to have a family,' Ellen said pointedly. 'If you put yourself out there.'

'And now that's enough about me,' said Liz. 'Your turn.'

Ellen glanced warily at them. 'I'm thinking of applying for a job in a private school.'

Emma's eyes widened. 'Ooh, what will Mum and Dad have to say about that?'

'I know,' Ellen groaned. 'That's the only thing stopping me.'

'Nonsense,' Liz declared. 'They coped when I went into private practice.'

'That's because you can do no wrong,' returned Ellen. 'You're a *specialist*.' Emma chimed in on the word 'specialist'.

Liz stared at them. 'Oh that's crap. If anyone can do no wrong, it's you, Ellen.'

'We'll see about that if I leave the public system.'

'So you really are going for this job?' said Emma. 'You're not just thinking about it?'

'I don't know,' she sighed. 'I don't know if I even want to go into the private system, but money's so tight at the moment, I have to do something. But it all feels too hard. You should see the application alone. And then if I actually get an interview, well, look at me. I just haven't had the time to fuss over myself lately. Look at my regrowth,' she said, dipping her head.

'I noticed,' said Emma.

'And I don't have anything decent to wear for an interview.'

'I can help you with all that,' said Emma.

'Thanks Em, but I wouldn't fit into any of your clothes.'

'Of course not,' she dismissed, like it was a given. 'I'm talking about taking you out shopping.'

'I can't afford it right now, Emma. That's why I need the job.'

'You don't understand,' she persisted. 'I have sources. I can take you direct to designers and probably find you samples. You'd be surprised how inexpensive they can be.'

'I'm sure I would be.' Surprised at what Emma would rate as inexpensive. 'Look Emma, it's really nice of you, but I just can't be thinking of new clothes for myself now, with all the expenses for the wedding.'

Emma frowned. 'What expenses do you have for the wedding?'

'Kate's dress, and shoes, and well . . . everything.'

'But you're not paying for any of that.'

'That's really generous, Em, but I can't expect you to do that, and it isn't fair to everyone else –'

'What are you talking about?' said Emma. 'I'm paying for everyone else.'

'You don't have to do that, I can afford it,' said Liz.

'That's got nothing to do with it,' said Emma. 'What planet are you girls from? The bride pays for her bridesmaids, that's basic etiquette.'

'I don't remember paying for yours,' Ellen mused.

'Of course you didn't – you were nineteen years old and we were all still living at home. Mum and Dad paid for everything.'

Ellen was frowning. 'Still, I don't know . . .'

Emma waved her hand. 'It's already taken care of. You're not even going to know how much the dresses cost.'

'Seriously?'

'End of discussion,' Emma said firmly.

'Well, in that case, let's order another bottle of champagne,' Ellen declared happily. 'On me.'

'Better make it on me,' said Liz, beckoning the waiter. 'You still have your car to pay for.'

'What happened to your car?' Emma asked.

'You haven't heard?' said Ellen.

'No one tells me anything.'

'So that means you don't know about the hot mechanic, either,' Liz grinned.

'There's a hot mechanic involved?' Emma exclaimed.

Ellen pulled a face. 'Okay, exactly when did I ever say he was hot, Liz?'

'Well, is he?'

'I don't know,' she said. 'I don't look at him that way, he's my mechanic.'

'You are such a snob, Ellen.' Emma shook her head.

'That's what I said!' Liz declared.

'You needn't get smug, you're just as bad,' said Emma. 'You both think anyone who doesn't have a university degree is beneath you.'

'What?' 'That is so not true!' 'Since when?' Ellen and Liz spoke over the top of each other in the rush to defend themselves.

'Then what's wrong with the mechanic?' asked Emma.

'Nothing's wrong with the mechanic,' Ellen cried. 'But he is just my mechanic – and that's not meant as a slur, merely a statement of fact.'

'So would you go out with him if he asked?' Emma persisted.

'He did ask her to have a drink with him,' Liz told her. 'But she declined.'

'Did you now?' Emma raised an eyebrow.

Ellen groaned. 'He politely offered me a beer when I bought him some as a thankyou.'

'A thankyou for what?'

'For fixing my car . . . he's my mechanic!'

'You don't even call the poor man by his name,' Emma tuttutted. She was enjoying this.

'Oh, she does,' said Liz. 'It's Flynn, isn't it?'

'Ooh, Flynn?' said Emma. 'As in Errol? And you know what they used to say about him. "In like . . ."'

'Indeed.'

'It's not *Flynn*,' said Ellen, 'it's *Finn*.'

'Still works . . . in like –'

'Stop!' Ellen held up her hands in defeat with a laugh. 'This is so ridiculous.'

'What are you so afraid of, Ellen?' said Liz, not laughing along.

'I'm not afraid of anything,' she protested.

'Sounds to me like you're a little afraid,' said Emma.

'And you sound like Eddie,' said Ellen. 'He wants to take me hang-gliding to help me get over my supposed fears.'

'So he rang?' said Liz.

'Yes, and that's his solution. But then he thinks hang-gliding is the solution to everything. I don't have to step off a cliff with only a bit of nylon to keep me alive to prove that I'm brave.'

'Okay, then you shouldn't be so afraid of putting yourself out there, Len,' said Liz.

'I'm not afraid,' she insisted.

'Then why aren't you doing it?' Liz persisted. 'I know it's hard. But don't you want to experience passion again in your lifetime? Or even for the first time?'

'She's right,' Emma agreed. 'You can't live the rest of your life without a little passion.'

'Well, I just might have to,' said Ellen.

'Why?'

'You're saying it like I have a choice.'

'Well, don't you?' said Liz.

'I don't subscribe to the theory that there's one true love for everybody.'

'Now you're saying you don't believe in true love?' asked Emma.

'Of course I believe in true love, look at Mum and Dad. And I see other couples, there's no denying that they have something really special together.'

'Blake and I for example.'

'That's right.' Ellen glanced sideways at Liz. 'Like you and Blake. But saying that everyone can have that is like saying that everyone can be famous, or everyone can win the lottery. It doesn't happen like that. Most people go through life in mundane jobs, and they never so much as win a scratchie.'

'But finding true love is not as impossible as winning the lottery,' said Emma.

'Sure, and some people do win the lottery, some people become famous and some people experience true love,' said Ellen. 'It's when we expect, or plan our whole lives around it, that we run into problems.'

Liz didn't like where this was heading – right for a raw nerve. 'Well, I'm depressed now,' she sighed. She looked around. 'Where's that waiter?'

Ellen bit her lip. 'Oh damn, I forgot, I drove. Maybe I shouldn't have anything more to drink.'

'Leave it and catch a taxi home,' Emma suggested. 'You can come back and pick it up tomorrow.'

'We'll share a taxi,' said Liz. 'You can stay at my place and I'll drop you back to your car in the morning.'

'Beats going home to an empty house,' said Ellen.

'What about you, Em? Can you stay?' Liz asked.

She took out her iPhone and checked the screen. 'I'm waiting to hear from Blake, he was going to organise something for later.' She looked at her sisters. 'But you know what? I'll just tell him he can pick me up on the way.'

'Okay, great,' said Liz, waving more insistently for the waiter.

Ellen looked at Emma. 'You're sure the car will be all right?'

'Of course, I told you, Surry Hills isn't what it used to be.'

The morning after

Ellen told Liz just to drop her off at the corner. The street where she'd parked the car yesterday was one way, and Liz would have to do a huge loop to get back in the direction of home.

'Okay. Well, feel better,' said Liz.

'You too.' Ellen gave her a feeble smile before closing the car door and stepping up onto the footpath. They were both paying for last night's overindulgence. By the time Blake had come to pick up Emma it was nine o'clock, and they hadn't had anything to eat. Liz and Ellen had decided to go back to Liz's, and they'd picked up food on the way, but also more wine. That had been their undoing. At least Ellen would have a few hours to recover before the kids were due home.

She strolled up the street towards her car. Surry Hills may have become gentrified over the past decade or so, but it was still a bit grungy for Ellen's liking, especially in the harsh light of morning, and with a hangover. She was relieved when her car came into view, right where she'd left it. She stepped off the kerb and walked around to the driver's side as she dug in her handbag for her keys. She slipped her sunglasses up onto her head so she could see inside the dark lining of her bag, and then something caught her eye. Ellen's gaze was drawn to the side of her car, and the huge yawning dent running along the length of it. Her heart jump-started, racing along as she began to shake, frantically looking around in a futile attempt to see who was responsible. There was nobody there, of course, it had probably happened through the night anyway. She checked the windscreen, but there was no note, no slip of paper with a phone number, details from a witness . . . nothing. Someone had rammed into her car. This wasn't a mere sideswipe, or an accidental clip by a passing car, unbeknownst to the driver. No, whoever did this had to have known what they had done, and they drove off regardless. Bastards!

Ellen felt her throat tightening and tears welling. She had to get off the street and into the car. She wasn't even sure she'd be able to get the door open. She found the keys in her bag and unlocked the door but she really had to reef at the handle, and as soon as it released, the alarm went off. Bugger, this had obviously screwed the system somehow. She closed the door again and fiddled with the remote lock for a few minutes, her hands shaking the whole time, until she was finally able to open the door without setting off the alarm. She dived into the car and closed the door. Only then did Ellen allow the tears to flow. And they flowed, in great rolling waves, as she hugged the steering wheel and sobbed her heart out.

What next? Plague, pestilence? Locusts, for crying out loud? Was this some kind of karmic payback for daring to end her marriage? But people did that every day, and she hadn't abandoned her kids or had an affair, or done anything bad. How come Tim got to start a whole new life without a hitch? What had she done to deserve all this?

Ellen sobbed till she was out of breath and out of tears. Finally she sat back against the seat, staring out through the windscreen. She didn't know how she was going to afford to fix this, or what she was going to do, or anything, she just needed to get out of this place and go home and be alone. She wasn't going to phone Liz, she wasn't going to tell anyone right now, she didn't want to be jollied out of it. She wanted to wallow in abject misery, and feel badly done by, and rail against the world, and she didn't want anyone telling her she shouldn't feel that way.

So she went home and she was duly miserable, and she felt incredibly alone. When Tim dropped the kids off she pretended she was in the middle of something and had no time to stop and chat. She'd put the car away in the garage so he wouldn't see it; she just couldn't be bothered telling him what had happened, mostly because she didn't think she could handle his disinterest. And Ellen thought she might hit him if he said anything remotely accusing, like 'Why would you leave your car overnight around there?'

No, she would deal with this one on her own. That was how things were going to be from now on, so she might as well get used to it.

The next day

Ellen turned into the driveway of Southside Auto Care and pulled in over near the fence. It was becoming her regular parking spot. She'd called the school to tell them she wouldn't be coming in today. At first she was just going to get someone to cover her morning classes, but then she thought, bugger it, why shouldn't she take the whole day off? She barely ever took time off. She hadn't even lost one day's work throughout the disintegration of her marriage. She got out of the car and peered into the garage. Someone was working on a car up on the hoist, but it wasn't Finn. She couldn't see behind the counter in the shop from out here. Maybe he was at his desk, or on the phone. She hoped so. She hadn't even considered the possibility that he might take the odd day off, or have to go out for a while. Maybe she should have just rung to get the phone number for the smash repair place, but she needed to talk to someone, and Finn seemed like the right person to talk to – the ideal person, in fact. He obviously had a relationship with the smash repairers, he'd have some idea about what it was likely to cost, and she was hoping he could suggest the minimum repairs she could get away with. The doors did open and close, though she was not sure how waterproof they were now. And there was the issue of the alarm.

As she walked towards the garage, she was relieved to see Finn appear through a side door. He didn't notice her at first, not until she came closer, close enough to see the surprise register on his face.

'Ellen,' he said. 'Is everything okay with the car?'

'No, it's not actually . . . I mean, yes, the car's running fine, it's great,' she added quickly, seeing his concern. 'But, um,' she swallowed, 'someone ran into me.'

'What, just now?' he said, faintly alarmed, coming towards her.

'No, no, it happened on the weekend.'

'Jeez, are you okay?'

Something in his voice brought a lump to her throat. Cripes, don't start crying now. She swallowed. 'Um, yes, I'm fine, I wasn't in the car. It was parked at the time.'

'Well, that's good,' he said. 'Not that it's good your car got hit, just that you weren't in it. Is there much damage?'

'All down the side, both doors are dented.'

'That's not so good. Did you get their details?'

'No,' she sighed. 'Hit and run. I didn't even see it happen.'

'Bastards,' he muttered. 'But you've got insurance, right?'

'Yes but –'

'Did you drive it here?' he asked, looking out at the line of cars parked against the fence. 'The car is drivable, I assume?'

'Oh, yes, I can drive it . . . it's over there.'

Finn took off towards the car and Ellen followed him. He gave a low whistle when he saw the dent. 'They really did some damage, didn't they? Any idea how it happened?'

Ellen shrugged. 'It was in a narrow street in Surry Hills. I don't know if someone backed into it trying to park, maybe?'

'I doubt it, they would have had some momentum behind them to have that much impact. Probably drunk as well, that's why they didn't hang around.' He shook his head, rubbing his jaw with his hand. 'Well, let's take it around to my guys now, get it sorted right away.'

Ellen just stared up at him. He was taking on the problem like it was his own. She was going to cry.

He turned around to look at her. 'Sorry, Ellen,' he said. 'Am I railroading you? I just assumed you wanted to use my smash repair guys.'

She stirred. 'Yes, absolutely, I do,' she assured him. 'That's why I'm here. But I don't want to put you out, Finn. You can just give me the phone number.'

He shook his head, dismissing that idea. 'You're not putting me out.'

'But . . .' She hesitated.

'What is it?'

'I don't know if I should even go ahead with the work. I'm worried about what it's going to cost.'

'But you said you have insurance? Is it comprehensive?'

'Yes, of course, so I don't want to lose my no-claim bonus.'

He smiled then. 'Tell me, have you ever made a claim?'

'No, that's why I still have a no-claim bonus.'

'And how long have you been insured?'

'Oh, gosh, I don't know. As long as I've had the car, I guess. Actually even before that – we transferred it over from the old car.'

'Then I guarantee you won't lose your bonus,' he assured her.

'Really? But how can that be if I claim –'

'Look, I'll explain on the way over.' He started to walk back to the garage.

'Finn!'

He turned around.

'Are you sure?' she said. 'Is this convenient right now?'

'Yeah, no worries,' he said, walking backwards. 'I'll just let Dave know to mind the shop.'

A few minutes later Finn climbed into the passenger seat beside Ellen and directed her out of the station and up the side street to their left.

'Are you okay?' he asked, looking at her.

'I'm just a bit confused about all this,' she said. 'I was hoping you could tell me how much you think it's likely to cost, if it would be better for me to pay for it myself. Maybe they could get away with a partial repair job?'

He shook his head. 'You're going to have to fix it properly, Ellen. It'll never get through rego like this. And anyway it's easily going to cost over two Ks.'

'Excuse me?' she said, stunned.

'Ellen, two doors have to be replaced.'

'Replaced? They can't just beat them out?'

'That's not how it's done these days,' he said with a smile. 'But it's going to be okay, I doubt you'll have to pay anything.'

'Seriously?' she said. 'What about an excess?'

'Maybe you'll have to pay a small excess,' he allowed. 'Depends on your insurer. Some of them have safe driver arrangements, you're rated on the number of years you've had insurance without a claim. If you've been insured for longer than ten years and you've never made a claim, you'll be fine. Did you bring your papers?'

'No,' she said weakly.

'But you do know who you're insured with?'

She nodded.

He gave her a reassuring smile. 'It's going to be okay, Ellen. Trust me.'

She did trust him, strangely, but she should never have trusted Tim. Ellen had always left this kind of thing to him. It was probably sexist, she realised, but as she had to handle just about everything else, she figured it was reasonable for him to be responsible for matters relating to the car. They'd had one or two incidents over the years, nothing major, small bingles in carparks, that kind of thing, and Tim had always insisted they must never claim on their insurance. Ellen remembered being annoyed one time – why were they paying insurance if they were never going to use it? Tim had insisted that it was for major accidents only, if they wrote off the car, or someone else's.

The smash repairers turned out to be only a few blocks away. As soon as Ellen pulled up Finn jumped out of the car and walked straight over to a guy in overalls. They were in conversation when Ellen joined them.

'This is Jake, Ellen,' Finn introduced them. 'He's going to write up the quote.'

'I'll just go get the paperwork,' he said, excusing himself.

Ellen turned to Finn. 'But if I'm going through insurance, won't I have to get three quotes?'

Finn scratched his head, smiling. 'You really haven't dealt with this kind of thing in a long time, have you?' he said. 'You don't have to get three quotes anymore. This is an approved repairer, and everything's standardised now. They'll send an assessor out this week, and they decide how much the work will cost, so there's no need to get multiple quotes.'

Jake returned and handed Ellen a clipboard with a form attached. 'Just fill in the details that you know,' he said. 'Have you got your keys? I'll move the car into the workshop.'

'Oh, sure,' said Ellen, handing them over.

'Come into the office,' said Finn. 'You'll be more comfortable there.'

Ellen followed him inside, and Finn indicated for her to take a seat at the desk where she could fill in the form. It was fairly basic, her personal information, the name of her insurer, make of car, but then it moved on to details about the accident.

'I'm not sure about all of this,' she said to Finn eventually.

He took the form from her and scanned it. 'This is enough to go on with,' he said, as he sat down at the other side of the desk and picked up the phone. Was he going to call the insurer? Seemed like it. Next thing he was going through the details, checking boxes as he spoke, talking schedules and appointments. He hung up the phone and looked at her. 'All set.'

Ellen frowned. 'You seem to know a lot about all this. Do you moonlight here or something?'

Jake came back into the office then. 'Got the paperwork, boss? I'll start marking up the repairs.'

Finn handed him the clipboard and Jake glanced over it, before giving Ellen a nod and a wink. 'Don't worry, Ms Cosgrove, we'll get it back to you as good as new,' he said as he walked back out of the office.

Ellen looked at Finn, raising an eyebrow. 'Boss?'

He shrugged sheepishly. 'Yeah, I kind of . . . own the place.'

She frowned. 'What about the garage?'

'Mine too.' He stood up. 'Come on, I'll buy you a cup of coffee.'

He led Ellen around a corner to a small kitchenette, where a coffee machine took up most of the bench.

'This is buying me a cup of coffee?' Ellen said wryly.

'Well, I do pay for it,' he said, rinsing out a couple of mugs. 'How do you take it?'

Finn made the coffee and passed her a cup, then he pushed open a door that led outside to a large vacant lot behind the workshop. Old tyres and car panels were discarded among the overgrown weeds, while a couple of rusted-out car wrecks languished in one corner. Finn overturned an old milk crate for Ellen to sit, then one for himself.

As he sat down he turned to her with a grin. 'There, don't say I don't take you anywhere nice,' he said.

Ellen smiled.

'Ah, look at that,' he declared. 'Finally a smile.'

'You think I had any reason to smile today?'

'Yeah, I do actually.'

'And how do you figure that?'

'Okay,' he began, 'you thought you were going to have to pay for the repairs yourself or lose your bonus, but instead, everything's covered. And you know what else? The impact won't have affected anything mechanical, including any of my hard work of the past few weeks. If you were going to get hit, it was the best place to get hit, unless you were in it, which you weren't, so, it's a win-win.'

Ellen shook her head in wonder. 'You're a real glass half-full kind of guy, aren't you?' she said.

'It's better than the alternative.'

'Yeah, well, okay for you to say. My glass seems to be emptying out so fast these days I can't even get it to half-full. When I came back and saw the car the other day . . .' She paused, shaking her head, feeling teary again. 'I just don't know how much more of this I can take. It feels like I'm paying for something bad I did, like the whole world is against me.'

'You can't think like that, Ellen.'

'Even when all evidence points to the contrary?'

He looked at her directly. 'So you really believe the cosmos is somehow pitted against you? Sorry to burst your bubble, Ellen, but you're just not that significant, you're one person out of over seven billion across the planet. Now if you were in the path of that tsunami way back, or in Haiti when the earthquake hit . . . or let's face it, if you were born in some poverty-stricken country in Africa, maybe you've got a right to feel like you've been dealt a dud hand. But you live in one of the richest countries in the world. You were born lucky. You're just having a run of bad luck at the moment. And when it passes, which it will, you won't wake up dirt poor in a hut in Africa, wondering if you're going to get anything to eat that day.'

'That's very philosophical, for –'

'A lowly mechanic?' he finished, raising an eyebrow.

'I was going to say "for a Monday morning".'

He smiled, putting his cup down on the ground beside him and resting his elbows on his knees. 'Look, I've been where you are before, and it sucks. But you only make it harder for yourself if you think the whole world is against you. It doesn't do you any good.'

'It's just hard sometimes,' she said, 'when everything seems to be going wrong.'

'Depends which way you look at it. It is really bad luck that some dickhead ran into your car, but it's really good luck that you have insurance. And it was really bad luck that your car broke down the other week, but how lucky are you that when it did, the tow-truck driver brought you to my place?'

Ellen grinned. She had to admit that was probably the best bit of luck she'd had in a long time. 'How am I going to repay you?' she said sincerely.

'Fortnightly,' he said, picking up his coffee cup again. 'It's all set out in that payment schedule I gave you.'

Winter

Liz buzzed the inter-office intercom. 'Michelle, can you come in here for a moment?'

Liz had been checking off her appointments for the afternoon on the computer. Michelle walked into the office and sat down on the other side of the desk.

'What's up?'

'I just noticed this double appointment booked in for this afternoon. What that's about?'

'Oh, yeah, I was going to talk to you about it,' she said. 'This woman rang, a few weeks ago now, wanting to book two full appointments, the last of the day. She insisted, said she'd pay for both. She has a disabled son, apparently, who needs treatment for eczema, and she wanted to see you first herself, before she brings him in. She wanted to make sure she had plenty of time.'

'What kind of disability?' asked Liz.

'She didn't say.'

'Well, she doesn't have to pay for two appointments,' said Liz. 'Only bill her for one.'

When the woman walked into the office later that afternoon, she looked fragile and weary, even though she was only around Liz's age. She offered her a seat.

'What can I do for you, Ms Harris?'

'Please, call me Julie,' she said. 'Okay, well, here it is. My son, Alex, is autistic,' she said, catching Liz by surprise. 'And he has severe eczema. He can't cope with new people, and he certainly can't tolerate being touched by anyone he doesn't know. Even then . . .' She paused. 'Anyway, we've tried to treat it ourselves, with medical advice, of course. But it's just not getting any better, and the poor kid gets so agitated, he scratches himself raw. Someone has to look at him. You came highly recommended.'

Liz nodded. 'I'd like to help in whatever way I can,' she assured her. 'But you need to be prepared – eczema is a complicated condition, very frustrating for the patient and the doctor, let me tell you. It's usually caused by a whole raft of irritants and agents that are difficult, if not impossible, to isolate. I assume you've been down the whole food allergy route?'

'Of course,' she said. 'We have him off dairy at the moment, but we've tried cutting out a lot of different foods that haven't really made any difference in the end.'

'That's right, because it's never one thing alone . . . if only.' Liz smiled sympathetically. 'There are environmental allergens as well, and as I imagine you know already, they're almost impossible to eradicate entirely – house mites, grass pollens, pollution.' She paused. 'Having said that, the accepted and most successful approach is not to aim to cure, but to treat the individual. That will be my primary focus with Alex, the other will be to stop him from scratching. That's hard for anyone, children as well as adults. I imagine it's very difficult in Alex's case.'

'That's why we're here,' said Julie. 'I know it's a big ask, but if you can get him to trust you . . . it will take time, and a lot of patience, but if Alex believes what you tell him, well, anything's possible. He's a very determined boy when he puts his mind to it.'

Julie went on to explain how Alex had to be handled – he couldn't be touched at all, under any circumstances, which was the first hurdle. He may not even let Liz look at the affected areas this time, they'd have to wait and see. She should avoid making eye contact, but she should address him directly. He didn't like being talked about in the third person.

'He might have become agitated sitting around in the waiting room,' Julie explained, 'so my husband has taken him for a walk. I said I'd call as soon as you're ready to see him.'

'Please, go ahead,' said Liz. 'Do you need to use the phone?'

'No, it's okay, I have my mobile,' she said. 'I'll wait for them out at the lifts. Will it be okay to walk him straight in?'

'Of course, I'll let my assistant know.'

'Probably best if she doesn't speak to him, or acknowledge us.'

'I'll tell her.' As she started for the door, Liz stopped her. 'Julie?' she said.

She turned around.

'Do you mind if I ask you a question?'

'No, of course not.'

Liz sat back in her chair. 'How do you do it, how do you cope?'

Julie shrugged. 'Like they say, one day at a time. It's not all hard, he really is a great kid.'

'I'm sure he is. I'm just wondering about the . . . relentlessness, I suppose.'

'I couldn't do it alone,' she said. 'My husband is amazing. He's always been completely involved, he's so good with him.'

'Well, Alex is his son, too.'

Julie shook her head, taking a few steps back towards the desk. 'That's the thing, he's not. I mean, Neil considers Alex his own, but Alex's father left about a year after he was diagnosed. He couldn't deal with it. Then when he realised he missed him and he wanted to be part of his life, Alex didn't know him anymore, or he didn't want to know him. They see each other occasionally, but they can't get established. Neil is with him every day. He's put in the hard yards. They're bonded for life now.'

*

Before Liz left her office that afternoon, she called Andrew to see if he was still at work. His secretary told her he was in surgery but that he should be through within the hour if she wanted to try calling his mobile then.

Liz had a better idea. She drove to the hospital and parked in the visiting doctors' carpark. She was waiting out in the corridor when Andrew came out of surgery. He was talking with some colleagues when he noticed her. He excused himself and walked up to where she stood, his expression curious, to say the least.

'Liz, what are you doing here? Are you visiting a patient?'

'No, I came to see you,' she said plainly.

He looked around uneasily. 'I wasn't going to be able to see you tonight,' he said in a low voice. 'Jennifer's expecting me home for dinner.'

'That's fine,' said Liz. 'I just want to talk to you about something. Have you got time for a coffee?'

He scratched his forehead, checking his watch. 'Okay, a quick one. I have to get changed first.'

'I'll wait.'

He sighed. 'All right. Meet me in the staff cafeteria. I'll be about ten minutes.'

*

'So, what did you have to talk about so urgently?' said Andrew when he rejoined her in the cafeteria, dressed in his civvies.

Liz took a breath. 'I had a patient today, an autistic boy.'

His curiosity now morphed into wariness. She could see it in his eyes.

'Poor kid's riddled with eczema, it's going to be a long road, but we established a tiny bit of rapport today.' Liz paused, but Andrew remained stonily silent. 'He was a funny kid, really. Was only interested in facts, he kept insisting I told him the facts. So that's what I gave him – facts, statistics. He wanted to know exactly what the cream I prescribed was made of, how it worked, and I had to use the terminology, not simplify anything. He was an extraordinarily bright kid, really interesting, actually.'

'Why are you telling me this?' Andrew said bluntly.

'I don't know,' said Liz. 'It's just . . . well, it's weird. Autism has had a profound influence on my life, but I don't really know anything about it. And I certainly haven't had anything to do with it.'

'So you think now you've met one, you know it all,' he said tightly. 'That all autistic kids are the same?'

'Of course I'm not saying that –'

'Jesus, Liz.' He was shaking his head, clearly annoyed. 'You think they're all like Rainman? I wish. I actually hoped that was how it was going to be with Danny, but it's nothing like that. He regressed, he's lost language, he can barely communicate. If we tried to bring him to your rooms, he'd be more likely to have a fit and start smashing things than sit down and listen to you.'

'I know, I understand Danny's different.'

'Then what is your point?'

Liz sighed. 'I just wanted to talk about it,' she said, beginning to wish she hadn't. 'This boy, he had an unusual background, his dad left when he was quite young, but his mother remarried, and this man, his stepdad, is wonderful –'

'What the hell are you suggesting now?' Andrew said angrily. 'That I leave Danny so Jen can find another guy, better than me?'

'Would you stop taking everything I say as some kind of accusation?' said Liz. 'I just wanted to talk about it. It occurred to me that this boy obviously got very used to someone else, someone who's been really good for him. You decided early on that any change could only be bad for Danny. You don't know that.'

He dropped his head, dragging his fingers through his hair, before he looked up again, meeting her eyes. 'This isn't the right time, Liz. Danny hasn't adjusted to high school at all, he's getting further behind. They've had to change his aide three times this year, no one wants to work with him. He's too aggressive, too unpredictable. Jennifer and I had to have a meeting with the principal and the counsellor a few weeks ago. They're suggesting a special school.'

'Andrew . . .' Liz shook her head. 'Why haven't you told me this?'

He took a while before he answered her. 'I didn't want to tell you because you know what it means for us, for you and me.' He paused again. 'How many more promises can I break before you say you've had enough?' His eyes were glassy, staring at her. 'And right now, I can't see an end to this, ever. Jen's a mess, I couldn't walk out on her now. And what about Samantha? She's getting lost in all this. Everything has been for Danny, but despite all the therapies and special programs, all the money, he's going backwards. We've tried everything. So now I think it's my fault, because I haven't been around.'

'You can't blame yourself,' said Liz, on automatic pilot, as she felt her insides recoil. This was her role, to help Andrew cope.

They sat there for a while, not touching their coffees, not saying anything.

'I have to go,' he said finally. 'I'm expected. I wish I could stay . . .'

'Never mind,' said Liz. 'I understand.'

Parramatta Park

'He wants to go again.'

Steve looked at Evie. They had met at the same place, but Steve led her on a different route this time.

'Craig. He wants to go to the club again.'

'How do you feel about that?'

'You know exactly how I feel about it.'

'So have you told Craig?'

She shook her head. 'I haven't wanted to bring it up, I was hoping he'd forget about it.'

'Ah, the always successful head-in-the-sand technique.'

Evie gave him a weak smile.

'You really should just tell him it's not your thing, that you tried but you couldn't go through with it.'

'But I didn't try, did I?' said Evie. 'That's what he'll say.'

'Well, you can only lead a horse to water . . .'

'The thing is, I can't help feeling that if I refuse to go with him, he'll go off looking for another avenue. I mean, he more or less told me straight that he wants to try sex with someone other than me, at least once in his life. What if he finds someone he'd rather be with?'

'That's what's kept me going with Cheryl,' said Steve. 'Hey, why don't you let me know when you're going and I'll arrange for us to go the same night. Then we can just hang out at the bar like last time.'

'That's really nice of you, Steve, but I can't expect you to do that every time, and sooner or later Craig is going to want me to . . .'

Evie took a deep breath. '. . . to join in. I mean that's the whole point, isn't it?'

Steve nodded. 'But you're not going to be able to do that, are you?' he said plainly. 'You have to talk to him, Evie.'

But Evie couldn't find the right moment – either the kids were around, or Craig was engrossed in some TV show, or asleep in front of some other TV show. She kept thinking that maybe she should try it . . . or at least be open-minded about it. Steve was a nice guy, a really nice guy. He wasn't a weirdo, or a pervert, and yet he was the one who'd suggested it in his relationship. Yes, it had backfired now, but Evie certainly didn't doubt that he loved his wife. Maybe, if Evie willingly joined in, that might be enough for Craig. He'd realise that he loved her and only wanted her, that he didn't want to see her with other men . . .

That's when all the rationalising came to a screeching halt inside her brain, like a needle scraping across an old vinyl record. It was all very well to theorise about this, but the reality was that Evie would have to engage in some sort of sexual activity with people she didn't know. And Steve was right, she really didn't think she was capable of that.

Friday

As Ellen walked back to her car she was amazed yet again by how, well, ordinary it looked. You could never tell the whole side had been crushed in only a couple of weeks ago. She supposed it shouldn't surprise her – the doors had actually been replaced, but the paintwork was seamless. Just as Jake had promised, they'd brought it back as good as new.

Which was a little how Ellen herself was feeling right now. She pressed the remote lock, which was working perfectly again, opened the door . . . but then she stopped herself. She dropped her handbag on the driver's seat, before slipping off her beautiful new jacket. She opened the back door and laid it carefully across the seat. Her beautiful new *Prada* jacket – the devil wasn't wearing Prada today, she was. Never in her life had she imagined owning anything by Prada, and here she was, dressed in an entire suit. She felt as though she was an actor playing herself in a movie.

Something had shifted for Ellen in the past few weeks, since that day she had sat on the upturned milk crate, having coffee with Finn. He was right. Whether she was a victim or not, she had decided she had to stop *feeling* like a victim. She was going to stop letting things get her down and take charge of her life. That meant she had to do what was best for her and the kids and not worry about what people thought. So she went ahead and applied for the position at the private school – she would deal with her parents if she actually got the job. After all, they'd up and sold the house without consideration of any of them, so they were going to have to respect her decisions as well.

Getting an interview buoyed her resolve, but it also sent her into a spin. She had to find time to get to the hairdressers, and what the hell was she going to wear? So she decided once again to bite the bullet and take Emma up on her offer.

'Oh my God!' Emma exclaimed when she called. 'This is fantastic!'

'Are you sure you've got the time, with the wedding and all?'

'Are you kidding me? I'll make the time,' she declared. 'I've been wanting to get my hands on you forever.'

'You have?' Ellen said nervously.

'This is what I do,' said Emma. 'Trust me.'

So she did. Emma dragged her around to designers' warehouses in back alleys in places Ellen didn't even know existed – these were not for the general public. And she had her try on clothes Ellen would never have chosen for herself.

'You don't wear clothes that flatter you,' Emma said. 'You just cover yourself up, and you've still got a nice figure, Ellen. It's not perfect, but whose is?'

'Yours comes pretty close,' Ellen muttered.

'Ha,' she scoffed, 'I just know what to wear. I've got the Beckett backside.'

'Well, I got the Turner boobs.' All the Turner women, their mother included, had ample bosoms, which was all well and good when you were sixteen and they sat up all on their own. Not so good once you were the wrong side of thirty and had to wear scaffolding for a bra.

Emma rolled her eyes. 'I can't stand women who complain about having big tits, I mean, *come on!*'

'But I'm all out of proportion,' Ellen complained. 'I've never been able to find a jacket that fits me properly.'

'Trust me, I will.'

And she did. Ellen felt like a different person in the classic black suit. Somehow it gave her an entirely new silhouette. It was all in the cut, Ellen had always heard, now she understood. She looked taller, more elegant. She looked . . .

'Amazing!' Emma declared. 'Now we have to find the right shoes.'

'No way – no, I can't wear heels like that,' Ellen insisted when Emma took her to yet another back-alley place and picked out two beautiful pairs of shoes for her to try.

'I bet the last pair of shoes you bought cost, what, sixty dollars?' said Emma. 'Maybe eighty? It's no wonder you won't wear heels, Ellen. Quality costs.'

When Ellen tried the shoes, she had some idea of how Cinderella must have felt when she put on those glass slippers. And she understood how all the celebrities were able to walk in them. They were a feat of engineering beyond her meagre comprehension, or her meagre income. But in the end, a deal was struck, and Ellen had the feeling she'd paid for little more than the box they came in.

Her younger sister had a lot more pull than Ellen had ever given her credit for. No one in the family had ever really given Emma her due – teaching, doctoring, mothering, even hang-gliding had more status in their collective eyes. Ellen was as guilty of it as anyone.

'Now we have to get the rest of you up to scratch,' Emma announced when the shopping was complete.

'What do you mean?'

'Your interview's Friday, right?' Emma said, scrolling through her diary on her phone.

'Yeah, we scheduled it for after school, so it wouldn't interfere –'

'Well, you can forget that, you're certainly not going to work first.'

'What?'

'Ellen,' she said, looking at her directly, 'I've seen how you look after a day at school – that will never do.'

Emma finally talked her into taking the day off and arranged to pick her up at nine.

'Why so early?' Ellen asked. 'The interview's not till four.'

'We've got a lot of work to do before then.'

When they'd pulled up at the salon spa that morning, Ellen had baulked. 'Emma, I can't afford this. I mean I know you got me the suit for less than cost, but –'

'Don't worry about it,' Emma dismissed. 'This is a freebie. I'm calling in some favours. And believe me, they owe me big-time.'

And so she spent the day being preened and plucked and waxed and generally slapped into shape. The first hour or two were all about pampering – a massage and a facial followed by a deep relaxation bath with rose petals and essential oils and God knows what else. Ellen felt a little like she was stewing in herbal tea, but she had to admit it was quite relaxing. Then the real work began, starting with a pedicure – the first in her life – followed by a manicure. Then it was time to attack her hair. Ellen had worn her hair in the same style for more years than she could remember. She had been going to the same hairdresser and when she occasionally suggested a change, showed her a photograph, the hairdresser would agree, but her hair never looked any different afterwards. Ellen blamed her hair.

'I blame your hairdresser,' Emma snorted. 'You've got good hair, Ellen, we all do actually – fortunately both the Becketts and the Turners helped us out there. But you need to get some shape into yours to suit your face.'

'Not too short!' she warned. 'I like to put it up in a clip or a ponytail.'

Ellen curled her lip. 'So I've noticed. You're not going to want to do that after Rene finishes with it.'

Rene was a tall, slender, terribly attractive man, with some kind of South American lineage, Ellen guessed. But he looked at her hair with such disdain Ellen was embarrassed by it. He tuttutted and shook his head, despairing at the amateur colour job, the dreadful condition, the way it had been hacked, according to him.

'But don't worry, I will fix,' he told Emma.

Ellen had never spent so long in a hairdresser's chair in all her life, she even nodded off a couple of times, till Rene would come along and yank her back to life, inspecting the foils, sending her off to the basins, and then back again for another application of colour and more foils. She couldn't watch when he started to cut. She couldn't tell what he was doing, but he seemed to be taking off an awful lot, and Ellen was too intimidated to tell him not too much. But when he began to blow-dry it, and it fell into perfect golden waves around her face, Ellen almost didn't recognise herself. She had to blink back tears.

'Beautiful,' Emma said proudly, as though she'd done it herself.

The final step was makeup, and after that Ellen really didn't recognise herself. How did they make her eyes look so big, her skin so smooth? And where had her double chin gone? All that, but she didn't really look 'made up', she looked quite natural, and . . . well, damn it, she looked *attractive*. Ellen had never considered herself very attractive; maybe when she was young she was all right, but as the saying went, her looks had faded. This was like they'd filled them all in again.

Emma snapped her out of her reverie. 'Come on, we have to get you home and dressed. We're not going to waste all this by making you late for your interview.'

When she was finally dressed in the complete outfit, shoes and all, Ellen looked at the full effect in the mirror in her bedroom, and she was bowled over. Tears sprung into her eyes.

Emma came to stand behind her. 'Look at you.'

'It's unbelievable,' said Ellen. 'You know, if you took a photo of me right now, and I saw it, without having seen myself, in the flesh . . .'

Emma was frowning.

'Just go with me,' said Ellen. 'What I'm trying to say is that if I saw a photo of myself looking like this, I wouldn't know it was me.'

Emma smiled then. 'You know what my philosophy is?'

'Yeah, yeah, I know, I should be taking better care of myself.'

'No, that's not what I was going to say. I realise most women can't go to this much trouble every day, or even every week.'

'Or even every month,' Ellen muttered.

Emma nodded. 'It's a huge commitment, and the problem is, once you get started, you can't stop.' She looked a little wistful. 'Sometimes I wonder what Blake would do if I let myself go. That's why I'm scared to have babies. I mean, I know I could bounce back, but it's hard to look like this when you're in labour.'

Ellen saw something in her eyes she hadn't seen before, vulnerability perhaps?

'I'm sure Blake would love you no matter how you looked.'

Emma gave a dismissive little laugh. 'Anyway, I was saying, my philosophy – or maybe it's not so much a philosophy as a tip – but I believe that every woman should have a makeover, or a professional photo shoot, at least once in their lives. Because even if they don't want to go to the trouble every day of making themselves beautiful, at least they'll know that they can look as good as the women on the covers of magazines if they want to. And then they can feel better about themselves the rest of the time.'

Catching sight of herself in the mirror again, Ellen felt bad for every time she'd ever dismissed Emma's work. She knew this was all only surface stuff and what was inside was more important, but today she didn't care, today she felt beautiful, and she hadn't felt beautiful in a very long time.

'Well I don't know how to thank you,' she said in a small voice, her lip trembling.

'Uh-oh!' Emma scolded. 'You'll ruin your makeup. Okay, there's just one more thing. Where's your handbag?'

Ellen picked up the bag she'd been carting around all day.

'I thought as much,' said Emma, dashing out to the hall and coming back with a designer carrier bag.

'What's this?' said Ellen when she handed it to her.

'Take a look.'

Ellen lifted out a gorgeous red leather tote, the kind she'd only seen in magazines or in movies on the arms of actresses. 'Oh my God,' she exclaimed. 'Are you lending me this for the interview?'

'No, silly, I'm giving it to you. It's my good-luck gift.'

Now Ellen couldn't speak at all. The tears were choking her throat.

'I said no crying!' Emma ordered. 'You'll ruin your makeup!'

So instead Ellen stepped forward and put her arms around her sister.

'Don't crush your shirt! Careful!'

When she stepped back, she was pretty sure Emma had tears in her eyes as well.

'Okay, so go knock 'em dead.'

*

Ellen slid carefully into the driver's seat now, smoothing out her skirt. She pulled the car door closed and took a deep breath, smiling happily. The interview had gone well. How could it not – she felt like she could do anything the way she looked.

So what now? She didn't want to put all this to waste and just go home and watch a movie on her own. The kids were at Tim's, so she couldn't even show off to them. She wanted to celebrate ... She knew Emma was busy; she wondered if Liz was free for a drink. Ellen tapped her manicured nails on the steering wheel, thinking, and then she had a better idea. Her next payment to Finn was due, she should have transferred it today but it had slipped her mind, not surprisingly. She could just drive over there and pay in person. Her heart skipped a beat as she started up the engine. Her sisters said she had to put herself out there, but this wasn't that. She was just ... broadening her social circle. Finn could be counted as a friend now, and Ellen had to develop new friendships ... with other single people. That's all it was.

When she arrived at the garage, she pulled into her regular spot and cut the engine. She quickly checked herself in the rearview mirror. Boy, she didn't even need to touch up her lipstick, this makeup was so good. She smiled at herself, picked up the red handbag and stepped out of the car.

As she walked across the tarmac to the office, Ellen became conscious that she was even walking a little differently in these shoes, in this skirt. Perhaps it was the entire outfit, or perhaps it was just that she *was* conscious, but there was a slight sway to her hips. Now she just had to make sure she didn't trip and fall over, that would certainly ruin the effect.

She heard a wolf-whistle and looked across to see Finn standing in the entrance to the workshop, holding his regular Friday afternoon beer, gazing at her with obvious admiration.

'Ellen,' he said in a quizzical tone, 'is that you?'

She smiled and turned to walk towards him. 'It's a version of me,' she said. 'New and improved.'

'I liked the old Ellen well enough,' he said as she came closer. 'But this is not bad.'

'Not bad?' she said, raising an eyebrow as she stopped in front of him.

'Not bad at all.'

Ellen felt a frisson, like electricity passing between them. She hoped she wasn't blushing, but no matter, the makeup would hide it. Finn was staring at her, and she realised that she was staring back. Someone had to say something.

'So I was just passing,' she began, 'and I realised I hadn't paid my account today. I thought I might as well do it in person.'

'I'm glad you did,' he said. 'Where have you been? Doesn't look like it was a regular school day.'

'I had an interview this afternoon, at a private school.'

'Ah,' he nodded. 'That explains it. How'd it go?'

'It went pretty well, I think.'

'I'm not surprised, you look like you'd fit right in,' he said. 'Well, I reckon this calls for a drink, to celebrate.'

She smiled. 'Maybe I could stomach a beer, just this once.'

'No way, we can't hang around here with you all dressed up like that,' said Finn. 'I know a nice place up the road we can go.'

Ellen wasn't expecting that. 'Oh, are you sure?'

'Yeah, Dave's still here, he's working on a mate's car. He can close up.' He looked at her. 'You don't have to be somewhere?'

'No . . .' she said meekly.

He nodded. 'Good. Give me a sec and I'll clean up, change out of this shirt. So I'm fit to be seen with you.'

As soon as he turned away, Ellen began to feel twitchy. She started to pace. Was this *something* like a date? Because if it was, she should really slow down and think it out more. You don't just drop in on someone, casually, on a Friday afternoon and *start* something. No, it wasn't anything. He was her mechanic, for godsakes, and they had become friends, wasn't that nice? To have someone she could go out for a drink with, someone who wasn't one of her sisters. It definitely wasn't *something*.

She peered into the workshop. Finn was standing at a sink at the back wall, his shirt off, splashing water over himself. He straightened, reached for a towel on a hook on the wall, and turned around, drying himself while he spoke to Dave, who was bent over under the hood of a car. Ellen just stood there, staring, following the path of the towel, across his chest, his shoulders, his arms, his abs . . . Her mouth went dry . . . probably because it was hanging open, she realised, closing it quickly and looking away. But her heart was still fluttering erratically. What was that about? Couldn't she even look at a man with his shirt off without going weak at the knees? Clearly she'd been deprived of sex for way too long. God, why did she have to go and think about sex?

'Ellen?'

She swung around with a start.

'Wow, where were you just then?' Finn was smiling at her as he buttoned up his shirt, from the bottom up, which meant his chest was exposed, smack in front of her. 'Ellen?'

'Huh?' She jerked her head back, making eye contact . . . keep making eye contact, look him in the eye, for godsakes.

'You were a million miles away.'

Not nearly that far. Ellen swallowed. 'Oh, just . . . going over the interview in my head.'

'Well, you can tell me all about it over a drink,' he said. 'You want me to drive, or you can drive, whatever . . .'

'No, you drive,' she said quickly. She was afraid her powers of concentration were not up to the task right now.

*

They drove all the way to the point at Abbotsford, and the Rowing Club.

'This all right with you?' Finn asked when he pulled up in the parking lot.

'Oh sure,' she said. 'It's a bit fancy.' Not really his style, she would have thought, but she kept that to herself.

'I think they'll let you in, you look pretty fancy,' he said with a grin.

They went inside and found a table out on the deck, overlooking the water. Finn went to the bar to get the drinks. When he returned, they toasted to her success and he asked her all about the interview. There was a panel of five, she told him, comprising the principal, the deputy responsible for curriculum, a parent representative, plus the head teachers from both the English and History departments. It had been thorough, but polite, she hadn't felt particularly put on the spot at any time. As far as interviews went, it had leaned more on the side of conversation than interrogation.

'That's good, isn't it?' Finn asked.

'I think so,' she said, reflecting. 'That's as long as they were taking me seriously and not just filling in time. If they were really interested, maybe they would have been more rigorous, put me on the spot . . .'

'Hey, is that your glass half-empty?'

Ellen glanced down at her wine. 'No, it's fine.' She looked up at him and he was grinning at her. 'Oh, okay, I get it. I'll rephrase – it was a good interview, very positive.'

'Is this something you've always wanted?' he asked.

'No way.' She shook her head. 'I come from a family of public school teachers, I never dreamed I'd be doing this.'

'So why are you?'

'I need the money,' she said simply. 'There's this standover mechanic I owe big-time.'

He grinned, shaking his head. 'I really hope that's not the reason.'

'No,' she assured him. 'I'm just sick of only barely making ends meet. I'm on my own now, I have to find a way to earn more money.'

'Gee,' he said, sitting back and holding his hands up as though he was weighing things on a scale. 'Money or principles? It's a tough one.'

'Don't be awful,' she protested. 'It's not like I'm going to work for the enemy, sell state secrets or anything.'

'No, just your soul.'

Ellen was intrigued. 'You've really got something against private schools, haven't you? What, did the poncy kids on the bus tease you when you were a kid?'

He considered her for a moment. 'Look, I'm just saying . . . what if there were no private schools?'

'What, and no religion too?' Ellen raised an eyebrow. 'You sound like a John Lennon song.'

'Nothing wrong with that,' he returned. 'I just think there should be a level playing field.'

'It's never a level playing field, Finn,' she said. 'I realise kids from private schools have an advantage, but so do kids in public schools from better areas. It's wealth that makes the difference.'

'I don't know,' he said. 'What about the old boys' networks? I went to a private school and –'

'You did?'

He looked at her. 'You don't have to look so surprised.'

'Well, do you mean *private* private, or a local catholic school?'

He smiled. 'I didn't take you for a snob, Ellen.'

She'd had quite enough of being accused of that. 'It's a valid question,' she insisted.

'I went to one of the poncy ones, straw boaters, the whole deal.'

So how did he end up as a mechanic, she wondered, albeit a successful one?

He was watching her. 'You want to know how I ended up here, don't you?'

Ellen shrugged. 'It must be an interesting story . . .'

He took a sip of his beer. 'Okay, I did all right at school, and I got into Mechanical Engineering at Sydney Uni.' He took a breath. 'Then when I was in second year, my father did the whole clichéd middle-age crisis thing and ran off with a younger woman. And then they stripped my mum of nearly everything. She got the house, mortgage and all, but she couldn't afford it. So we had to sell up. My sister was at the corresponding poncy girls' private school in the area, and she only had a year to go, so I deferred uni and got a job to help out so at least she could finish.'

Ellen was intrigued. 'That's the most you've ever told me about yourself.'

'That's the most you've ever asked.'

And now she had so many more questions. Her perception of him had just done a one-eighty-degree flip. Maybe she *was* a snob? 'Your sister must have appreciated what you did.'

He shrugged. 'She never knew. She thought I was a dropout. She went on to marry a bloke from my school, and well, now they've got their kids at the same poncy private schools and they're vaguely amused by their uncle the mechanic.'

'Wow,' Ellen said in a low voice. 'No wonder you've got a thing against private schools.' Just then her phone beeped with a message. 'Sorry, I should check that . . . the kids.'

'Sure, go ahead.'

She took her phone out of her bag and flipped it open. It was from Kate. *Hey Mum, just got home. Where r u?*

'That's odd,' said Ellen.

'What is it?'

'My daughter,' she said, frowning at the screen of her phone. 'She's at home, wondering where I am. She's supposed to be with her father this weekend.' She looked across at him. 'I'm sorry, Finn. I think I should go home, find out what's happened.'

'Of course, I understand,' he said. He picked up his beer and drained the rest of it. 'I'll take you back to your car.'

She apologised a couple more times on the short trip back to the garage, but he dismissed it. She probably shouldn't make too big a deal about it. They were just friends, after all.

'Thanks for the drink, Finn,' she said as he pulled up next to her car.

'My pleasure. I'm glad we got to do it.'

'Oh,' she just remembered, 'I didn't make the payment.'

'I know you're good for it, Ellen,' he said with a grin. 'And anyway, I know where you live.'

'I'll transfer it online tomorrow, or tonight if I get the chance.'

'Don't worry about it. I hope everything's okay with your daughter.'

'Thanks.'

He waited until she drove away in her car, giving her a toot as she pulled off up the road towards home. Ellen hoped everything was okay with Kate too. She tried not to think the worst, not that she could imagine what the worst might be. In fact, it was probably nothing. But she couldn't help wondering why Tim had let Kate go home. Why he wouldn't check with her first? She was more than happy for Kate to come home, but she didn't like the feeling that it was expected that she would be there. When Ellen arrived at the house, she parked in the garage and came in the back way. Kate was standing at the fridge, the door wide open, staring inside.

'Hey, you look great, Mum,' she said. 'Where've you been?'

'I had that interview today.'

'Wow, it went late,' said Kate.

'I met a friend for a drink afterwards.'

Her face dropped. 'You didn't have to come home . . .'

'No, I wanted to,' Ellen assured her. 'Is everything okay, though? You didn't want to stay at Dad's?'

The fridge started to beep and Kate closed the door. 'He was going out, and Sam was going to stay at a friend's for the night, so I thought I might as well come home. That's okay, isn't it?'

Ellen suppressed the rage building inside her, clenching her fists so her newly manicured nails dug into her palms. 'Of course it's okay. I'm glad you're here. It's Friday night, what do you say to pizza and Netflix?'

'I say yay, there's nothing in the fridge.'

'Just let me get out of these clothes,' she said, heading for the hall.

'You really do look great,' Kate called after her. 'I like your hair.'

'Thanks, honey.'

Ellen got to her room and closed the door, leaning against it, breathing hard. She was furious. What the hell was Tim playing at? She felt like calling him now, but he was 'out', so it would be another one of those smug, disinterested exchanges where he'd insist there was nothing he could do. But she was going to have to talk to him about this – she would call him tomorrow and insist. If he was seeing someone, they needed to start making some ground rules. And she might take this opportunity to sound out Kate, get a sense of how she was feeling about the situation.

*

'Well, that was lame,' Kate announced as the closing credits rolled.

Ellen was pleased her daughter showed some discernment. It was a typical romcom, but not a very good one. No prizes for guessing who was going to end up with whom – that was what you expected from a romcom, just like you expected James Bond to survive whatever was thrown at him. But you expected the journey to be interesting at least.

'Do you want that?' Kate asked, pointing to the last piece of pizza.

'No, you have it,' said Ellen. 'So what didn't you like about the film?'

'I don't know.' She shrugged. 'They always show these smart, savvy women falling over themselves for the attention of some wanker. Like you're not a whole person until you're half of a couple.'

'What did you expect from a romcom?'

'Oh, I know,' she said. 'I don't know why I always go for them. Must be imprinted in our DNA.' She took a bite of the pizza and chewed it thoughtfully. 'I mean, look at you, Mum,' she went on, swallowing. 'You're a strong, independent woman. You don't need a man to make you feel whole.'

Ellen was surprised, and quite chuffed that her daughter obviously didn't consider her pathetic because she was single. Strike one for her.

'Still,' she said carefully, 'you realise, Kate, one day I might start seeing other people. And Dad too. Would you be all right with that?'

Kate turned her head abruptly to look at her mother. 'Would you?'

Ellen wasn't sure what she meant. 'Would I be all right about seeing someone?'

'No.' She tossed the pizza crust into the box. 'About Dad seeing someone?'

'Of course,' she said. 'We're separated. He's allowed to move on.'

'Yeah?'

'Yeah,' Ellen insisted. She wondered if she should push it further. Perhaps if she just suggested . . . 'In fact, you know, I think your father may even be seeing someone now.'

Kate looked dismayed.

'Don't worry,' she assured her quickly, 'I'm sure it's only casual if he is, and I don't know, I'm only guessing.'

And then Kate burst into tears. Now Ellen was dismayed. God, she shouldn't have said anything. She brought her arms around Kate and hugged her, rubbing her back. 'It's okay, honey.'

'He told me not to tell you,' she cried into her shoulder.

Ellen's heart felt as though it had stopped. 'What?' She pulled back to look at Kate.

'Dad. He told me not to tell you he's got a girlfriend.'

Ellen was so stunned she couldn't speak. Fortunately she didn't have to, because for the next five or ten minutes Kate poured out everything she knew. Her father had met this woman

on the internet . . . he'd been internet dating since the split . . .
had gone out with about half-a-dozen women . . . Ellen couldn't
take it all in, and she didn't try. Instead she took the chance
to calm down, think about how to proceed, what to say to her
daughter about her phenomenally inept father.

'I hated keeping secrets from you, Mum,' Kate said finally,
blowing her nose with a tissue from the box Ellen passed her.

'Dad shouldn't have asked you to do that,' Ellen said, keeping
her tone calm and even, not accusing. 'And I'm going to have a
word with him –'

'Don't tell him I told you,' Kate pleaded.

'Hey, you didn't tell me, I'd already guessed,' Ellen reminded her.
'This isn't your fault, Katie, you've done nothing wrong here. Silly
old Dad,' she said, trying to sound amused and affectionate, while
feeling neither. 'I don't know what he was thinking. He doesn't need
to lie about seeing other people. We're separated, it's allowed.'

'Are you seeing anyone?'

'Of course not.'

Kate frowned.

'Of course not,' she repeated in a more casual tone, 'because I
would have told you, and I would have told Dad, and no one would
be keeping secrets. You see, Dad and I just haven't had a chance to
discuss how to handle this kind of thing with you kids. And well,
you know your dad, he's not real great with this stuff, so he was just
trying to do what he felt was right, and he got . . . confused.' God,
it's a wonder lightning didn't strike her, the fibs she was sprouting.
But it was for the greater good, right now. She was going to put Tim
straight as soon as was humanly possible. If she didn't kill him first.

Kate gave a loud sigh. 'I'm so glad it's all out in the open.'

'So am I, honey. So am I.'

The next day

Ellen was already waiting at the café when Tim walked in. She'd called him first thing this morning, she couldn't have cared less if she'd interrupted some cosy little tête-à-tête.

'We have to talk,' she'd snapped when he'd answered the phone.

'Oh, well, this is not a good time,' he'd said in a hushed tone.

'I don't mean now, on the phone, we need to talk face to face. Today.'

'I don't think I can do that –'

'Well think again. I've had Kate in tears last night, she told me everything, so it's time I got it from the horse's mouth, or should I say "arse".'

There was silence for a moment while he contemplated the inevitable.

'I have to pick up Sam at three, you want to meet somewhere before that?'

'One-thirty, at that café on the strip near the fruit shop. You know the one I'm talking about?'

'Yeah.'

He was approaching her table now, looking sheepish, nervous, possibly even a little fearful. Good.

The waitress arrived with Ellen's coffee as Tim went to sit down opposite her. 'Can I get you something?' she asked.

'Ah, yeah, I'll have a soy latte.'

Ellen rolled her eyes as the waitress walked away. 'You've got to be kidding. Soy latte?'

'What?' he defended. 'It's nice. You should try it.'

'I have, it tastes like coffee-flavoured baby formula.'

He ignored that.

'So,' she went on, 'jazz, soy lattes – you're really reinventing yourself, aren't you?'

'Is that what you wanted to talk about?'

'Oh, I think you know what I want to talk about, Tim.' She gazed directly into his eyes. 'You've got something to tell me, I believe?'

He sighed. 'Okay, so you know,' he said, raising his hands as though in defeat. 'I was going to tell you, eventually, I just thought it was my business.'

'It was your business, until you told the kids, and then, incredibly, told them not to tell me.'

Tim was shaking his head. 'I can't believe Kate told you that.'

'Why, isn't it true?'

'No, but that's the point, I asked her specifically not to,' he said. 'Kate's always been on your side.'

Ellen felt like she was dealing with an adolescent. The waitress returned with Tim's new lifestyle brew.

'Tim,' Ellen said, speaking slowly and carefully, 'do you not have any appreciation of the fact that it was totally inappropriate for you to tell Kate all about your love life and then tell her to keep secrets from her mother?'

Tim seemed to be mulling that over. 'Well, when you put it like that . . .'

Ellen closed her eyes for a second, composing herself. 'Why would you do that, Tim? I'm really struggling to understand.'

'Well, like I said,' he began, pouring enough sugar into his coffee to make the gunk drinkable, 'I thought it was my business. But I also didn't want to upset you.'

Ellen blinked. 'Pardon?'

'I didn't want to upset you,' he repeated. 'Like you are right now.'

'Exactly why do you think I'm upset, Tim?' she asked.

'Well, I realise it must be hard for you to think of me with another woman.'

Ellen snorted before she could contain herself, and then she broke into full-scale peals of laughter. Tim sat stony-faced watching her.

'Oh, it is hard to imagine you with another woman, Tim,' she was eventually able to say, wiping tears from her eyes, 'but not for the reason you're thinking.'

'So you're resorting to insults, Ellen? Very mature.'

Ellen shook her head. 'You're the one who's insulting, Tim. I couldn't care less what you do in your own time, our marriage has been over for so long I couldn't feel jealous if I tried.'

He seemed a little miffed at that.

'You need to understand this whole situation a lot better, Tim. You put Kate in a terrible position, she was so distressed last night. Don't you even care about that?'

'Of course I care. I didn't mean for that to happen. I didn't do it maliciously.'

'Oh, for Chrissakes, can we not revert to that defence?' said Ellen. 'I should hope you didn't maliciously set out to upset your daughter. But you did anyway, by being thoughtless and self-centred. So can we agree now that stuff like this doesn't go through the kids first? And that we never, and I mean *never*, ask them to keep secrets from the other parent?'

'What if it's about a birthday gift or something?'

Ellen wondered if he'd always been this thick. 'Tim, are you actually *trying* to be obtuse?'

'Sorry, okay, I get it.'

'And while we're establishing ground rules,' Ellen continued, 'another thing I have to insist on is that you didn't let Kate come home whenever she wants if it's your weekend.'

'Well, I don't know how I can stop her,' said Tim. 'She's a young adult, Len. At her age you were pregnant and we were about to get married.'

'I was a little older than she is now,' Ellen corrected him. 'But this has nothing to do with whether she's old enough to come and go as she pleases. The point is, what if I wasn't alone?'

'What do you mean?' He frowned.

'What if I was with someone?' she said, spelling it out for him.

'Were you?'

'I don't have to tell you that.'

'Oh, but I have to tell you.'

She rolled her eyes. 'Tim, you only have to tell me before you tell the kids. If it doesn't involve the kids, your private life is your own business. And I have a right to the same privacy on my weekends off, and a chance to pursue a life for myself without thinking the kids are going to walk in on me.'

Tim looked quite pale at that idea. 'What am I supposed to do? I can't physically stop her.'

'Tim, I don't blame Kate for not wanting to hang around in your empty flat last night. But it's your weekend, and you should have made the kids a priority, not packed Sam off to a friend's place and left Kate to her own devices.'

'But I had something on.'

'Well, bad luck,' said Ellen. 'These are the sacrifices we have to make when we're parents. You have seventy-five percent of the time to do whatever the hell you want, is it so hard for you to give them twenty-five percent?'

He looked chastened. 'I guess not.'

Ellen sighed. She hoped she'd finally got that through his thick head, though she had to wonder. 'Now, how are you going to proceed?'

'What do you mean?'

'The new girlfriend,' Ellen said plainly. 'Is it serious, do you want the kids to meet her?'

He shrugged. 'What do you mean by serious? I'm not thinking of marrying her or anything.'

'But it's a steady relationship?'

'Yeah,' he sighed. 'I have been thinking it's time they met her.'

Ellen thought about it. 'Okay, I'm going to be honest – it's weird for me not knowing who she is, when my kids are potentially going to have a lot to do with her. I mean, I never let them stay the night at a friend's place before I meet the parents.'

'Do you want to meet her first?' he suggested.

'No, that'd be weirder.' Ellen tried not to grimace. 'I don't know, I've never done this before.' She paused, thinking. 'I suppose I should know the basics, where she lives, what she does for work. Her name for a start.'

'Oh, right,' he said. 'Well, her name's Therése – you know, with the accent. Not Ther*eez*, she hates that. She lives in the city . . .

Oh, and you don't have to worry, she's got plenty of money,' he added, his eyes widening. Ellen wasn't sure why that was her worry. 'And, um, well, she's very accomplished, she's travelled the world, even lived overseas for a while. She has a law degree, but she isn't a lawyer, she's some kind of consultant, very well regarded. She's on boards and stuff like that.'

Ellen was beginning to wonder what this superwoman saw in Tim.

'But . . .' He was frowning.

'But what?'

He looked uneasy. 'Well, she's pretty amazing, really accomplished . . .'

'Yeah, you said.'

'But she's . . . well, she's . . . she's not exactly . . .'

Ellen was waiting.

'She's not that attractive.'

*

'You should have said, well, lightning's not going to strike twice.'

Ellen looked at Finn, not understanding.

'You know, that he can't expect to find someone as attractive as you again . . .'

She smiled then, maybe even blushed a little. But it was nice of him to say that, to make her feel better. Finn had a knack of saying the right thing at the right time, which was probably what had drawn her over here after she left Tim at the café. Kate was going back to her father's sometime today, so Ellen would be going home to an empty house, and she just had to debrief after her meeting with Tim or her brain was likely to implode. Back in the car, she'd picked up her phone, contemplating who she could call as she scrolled past Emma, then Evie . . . no, Liz was the best person . . . but then she'd come to Finn. She'd pressed Call before she'd thought about what she was doing. When he answered she made some excuse about paying her account, and he said to come on over.

'I just can't believe Tim would say something like that,' Ellen went on. 'I mean, what kind of message is he sending the kids, telling them his girlfriend's not all that attractive?'

'Do you think he actually said that to them?' Finn asked.

'I wouldn't put it past him. He seems to have no idea of what's appropriate for a father to say to his children, let alone for a man to say to his estranged wife. You know what he told me, in all innocence? He said he'd joined a couple of internet dating sites *before* we separated, and he'd made lists all ready to go, but he swore to me that he never actually contacted anyone until after we were separated.' Ellen shook her head. 'He's such a . . . a nong. How did I put up with him for so long?'

'Got me.' Finn shrugged.

'And the ego,' she rolled her eyes. 'He said he didn't want to upset me, that's why he didn't tell me about the girlfriend.'

'Well, you do seem kind of upset . . .'

'No, I'm upset that he thinks I'd get upset! And he didn't stop there. He kept telling me I should go on the internet myself, that he understands how hard it is to put yourself out there but that I just have to be brave. How dare he start giving me dating advice? Like he's suddenly some kind of guru, when all he's done is snare himself a rich, "not very attractive" woman and is sitting back, hitching a ride on her coat tails. What's he done that's so "brave"?'

Ellen stopped, noticing Finn's slightly startled expression. 'I'm sorry, I'm getting worked up. And I'm holding you up.'

He shook his head. 'I've got nothing better to do. Do you want a drink?'

'Yes please,' she sighed. 'That's only if you were going to have one?'

He nodded. 'But I've only got beer.'

'I don't care, as long as it's alcohol!'

He ducked out the back and came back with two bottles, passing one to Ellen. He clinked his against hers. 'To better days.'

'I'll drink to that.' She took a sip and grimaced, swallowing it down.

Finn smiled, watching her. 'I've got something that might help.' He disappeared out the back again.

'I'm not sure I'd like lemonade,' she called after him, 'it might be a bit sickly.'

He reappeared holding a couple of wedges of lemon. 'Not lemonade, the real thing. There's a lemon tree growing over the back fence,' he explained as he took her bottle and proceeded to push one wedge down into the neck. 'I pick up whatever drops on the ground. Or looks like it's going to,' he added with a grin.

Ellen was watching him. 'I've seen this, does it really make much difference?'

'The trick is,' he said, pressing the flat of his palm over the top of her bottle, 'to mix it right through.' He turned the bottle upside down and the lemon rose right up into the base and bobbed around. 'That ought to do it,' he said, turning it upright again and passing it back to her.

'Thanks.' Ellen took a tentative sip. 'Hmm, that's not bad.' She took a couple more swigs while Finn did the lemon trick to his own bottle. She started to feel a little buzz, and a sense that the tight coil of righteous indignation inside her was starting to unwind.

'Have you ever tried the internet?' she asked Finn.

'What, dating?' He shook his head. 'Nuh.'

'You are single?'

'Don't you think I would have mentioned it before now if I wasn't?'

She wasn't sure what he meant by that.

'How long have you been single?' she persisted, leaning her elbow on the counter and propping her chin in her hand.

'Depends how you calculate it. I haven't been in a long-term relationship for a while.'

'Why not?'

He gave her a slightly quizzical smile. 'I don't know. I don't think I've got commitment issues or anything, if that's what you're asking.'

'No, no, I'm just saying, you're a good-looking man, you've got a full head of hair, you're in the prime demographic, and it's a buyer's market. I'm surprised you haven't been snapped up.'

'What can I say?' He shrugged. 'You don't meet many girls in my line of work.'

'What about customers?'

'Most of them are married.'

'I wasn't,' she said. 'I mean, I'm not. Well, actually, officially I am, but not really, you know?'

'I know.'

She took a long swig of her beer and sighed deeply. 'Can I ask you something, as a man?'

'But you're not a man.'

Ellen frowned. 'Will you answer me as a man, I mean?'

'Well, I can't very well answer you any other way.'

She pulled a face. 'I want a man's perspective on something, an honest perspective.'

'I'll do my best.'

'What's it like having sex with someone for the first time?'

He sputtered a little on his beer. 'Wow, I didn't see that coming.'

'I'm sorry, am I being too personal?'

'Well, I don't think you could get much more personal, but it's okay.'

''Cause I was just wondering, that's all, how a man feels "putting himself out there",' said Ellen. 'Everyone keeps saying that's what I have to do – put myself out there. What does that even mean? And how do you do it? It's terrifying.'

'It can be terrifying for men, as well,' said Finn. 'You know, all the approaching has to be done by us, we're the ones who have to risk rejection.'

'I guess, but women are only rejecting a lot of the time because they're so terrified.' She drank down another mouthful of beer. 'I know I am.'

'Are you?'

'Not of meeting guys, or talking to them . . .'

'Obviously not.'

'Or even going out for dinner . . . but having sex?' She shuddered. 'Can I tell you something?'

'I have a feeling you're going to anyway.'

'I haven't had sex with anyone but my husband. How pathetic is that?'

'Well, you were only young when you got married,' he pointed out.

'How do you know that?'

'You told me your daughter's nearly nineteen, right? You must have been very young. Maybe twelve?'

Ellen smiled then. 'Resorting to flattery, eh?'

'I just think you're worrying about nothing – guys aren't as fussy as you think.'

'I liked it more when you were being flattering.'

'I knew that wasn't going to come out right,' Finn said with a rueful smile. 'What I'm trying to say is that men love women, and men love sex, and if they get some, mostly they're just grateful. They don't call it getting lucky for nothing.'

'I'm still terrified,' she muttered.

'You've got to face your fears sometime.'

'But facing your fears doesn't usually involve getting naked,' she pointed out, taking another swig of beer.

He smiled. 'What do I keep telling you? A guy would consider himself lucky.'

'I'll take that as a compliment.'

'You should.'

'But look, I'm going to be frank now.'

'You haven't been frank so far?'

'Tim and I didn't have a great sex life, even before our marriage went down the gurgler,' she said. 'I'm just so out of practice.'

'You know what they say, it's like riding a bike.'

'What? Sweaty and uncomfortable? Leaves you a little sore in the saddle?'

He laughed then, a big laugh, throwing back his head. 'You crack me up.'

Ellen couldn't remember anyone saying that about her. But then, life hadn't given her much to be funny about for quite a while. She drained her beer and set it back on the counter.

'That seemed to go down easily enough.' Finn said. 'Do you want another?'

It was tempting. She was having a nice time, and she was feeling quite a buzz – from one beer. Probably because she hadn't eaten anything all day, she just realised, she'd been so worked up about Tim. But that had all gone away, talking to Finn. He was so easy to talk to . . . maybe a little too easy, the things she'd just said . . . She really should have something to eat before she drank any more. Maybe it was better to bid a dignified retreat while she still could.

'No, I've held you up long enough,' she said, picking up her bag. 'Thanks for listening, really Finn. I appreciate it.'

'Any time,' he said.

She walked towards the door.

'Hey Ellen?'

She turned around.

'If I can ever be of any assistance . . .'

She raised an eyebrow.

'You know, if you want to get some practice in.' He was grinning that big cheeky grin of his. 'I'm just saying, you let me service your car . . .'

'Bye Finn,' she said with a smile, walking out the door.

*

All the way home Ellen couldn't stop thinking about what Finn had said. And she couldn't stop imagining him without a shirt on. And once she was home, she couldn't stop imagining him without a shirt on, saying what he'd said, and then making mad passionate love to her on the floor of his office. Feeling flushed and lightheaded – because she hadn't eaten, that's what it had to be – she made herself a toasted sandwich, and then she made herself eat it before she opened a bottle of wine. She drank down a glass too quickly and refilled it straightaway. Then she happened to glance at the time on the stove. God, it was barely five o'clock. This was not good. She was about to tip the glass into the sink when she thought better of it. She'd save it for later, and right now she'd have a shower, clear her head, get dressed into her most unsexy flannel pyjamas, and settle down to watch a very unsexy movie. After the disappointment last night on Netflix, Ellen went to check their own collection of DVDs. She had to find something that would take her mind off . . . well, Finn. She couldn't believe the things that had come out of her mouth today. If a man had spoken to her the way she spoke to him, she'd have thought he was sleazy, taken it as a come-on and given him short shrift. But Finn hadn't given her short shrift at all. He'd offered her another beer, and offered her his services . . .

Ellen shook her head to clear it. What was the matter with her? Sex deprivation, that's what it was. How long can someone go without sex before they start to see everybody as a prospect?

Finally she spotted the perfect distraction – *To Kill A Mockingbird*. She would not be having any lurid fantasies involving sex on the floor of a service station while Atticus Finch was championing civil rights. That would be unseemly.

Showered and pyjamaed, Ellen curled up on the sofa with her glass of wine and started the DVD. She'd loved this movie ever since the first time she'd seen it as a little girl. When she got a little older, she developed a crush on Gregory Peck, but it was one of those very chaste crushes, like the ones you have for priests. Watching him now, he reminded her of Finn, somehow. They were nothing alike . . . well, they were both tall with dark hair, but that was where the resemblance ended. There was something though . . . the mannerisms? Maybe it was the essential kindness of the man. Finn had always been very kind to her, she reflected rather wistfully as she drained her glass. She tottered off to the fridge and brought the bottle of wine back with her, filling her glass again. She may as well leave the bottle here, it didn't need to be completely chilled on a cool night like tonight.

She settled back on the sofa and sipped her wine. Maybe it was the voice? Ellen liked a deep voice on a man. Well, who didn't? But it was the *depth* of the deepness . . . she didn't mean Barry White deep, but like Gregory Atticus here. Depth with gravity, with kindness, with understanding. Just like Finn's. Ellen drained another glass and refilled it absently, staring at the screen. Their builds were different, Finn was more . . . built, was that the expression? She started to wonder what Atticus Finn would look like without a shirt.

Okay, that was quite enough. She snatched up the remote and stopped the film. What was going on with her? When she and Tim separated, the last thing on her mind had been finding another man. She'd had quite enough of married life by that stage, and the thought of settling down into another rut held no appeal in the slightest. She had been so lonely in the marriage, she couldn't imagine that life without a partner could be any lonelier. But it was a different kind of loneliness now. It had probably been short-sighted of her, but while Ellen had been relieved to move on and not be somebody's – namely Tim's – wife anymore, she hadn't really thought about the fact that she wouldn't be a mother full-time anymore, that her family life would become fragmented, divided up into allotted portions. As her marriage had died off, her kids had filled the void. They were her life. What was she supposed to do with herself when they weren't around?

Ellen drained her glass and stared at the bottle. That's what she did with herself – she sat around on a Saturday night alone, in her pyjamas, drinking too much and feeling sorry for herself.

Her mind drifted back to Finn, and what he'd said. Was he serious? Was he actually interested in her? He said she was attractive, several times. They'd gone out for a drink together only yesterday. Did that count as a date? What was that remark he'd made today . . . her head was getting a bit fuzzy . . . when she'd asked him if he was married? He said that he would have told her by now. Why would he have had to tell her if he was married? Surely he was indicating that there was something developing . . . possibly . . .

Oh, how was she supposed to know? Ellen had never really dated before. There had been a couple of boys in high school, a pash at a dance, and then she'd met Tim. She tried to remember what had attracted her to him; it was so hard sometimes to see past the man he had become. But he was a boy then. A nice, considerate, gentle sort of boy, who didn't scare her like a lot of boys did. She didn't know why boys should scare her, she could hardly be described as timid. But she knew nothing about boys, she hadn't even seen one naked until Eddie was born. She could remember how they had all been so fascinated by his anatomy, standing around ogling at nappy change time, giggling when the poor kid would get a prepubescent erection in the morning – it was a wonder he hadn't grown up with some major issues.

And so Tim became her boyfriend. It felt safe to be somebody's girlfriend. It gave you an identity, and you weren't there for the taking anymore. After they were going out for about a year they tried sex, with rather clumsy results, but again, it was a bit of a relief to get that out of the way with someone who was safe. Tim hardly knew what he was doing either, but they fumbled through, and being teenagers with the requisite raging hormones, they got the hang of it well enough. Well enough for her to get pregnant.

Life had taken over from there. There were no choices to make, it seemed, even though they made dozens and dozens of choices from then on in, but in reality, they were just reactions to the situation they'd found themselves in. We're having a baby, we should get married, we should have another baby so they're not too far apart, we should buy a house now Tim's graduated and working full-time, she should go back and finish her degree, she should do teaching, it's a good career for a mum . . .

And so it went on. But now her kids were spending the weekend with her estranged husband and she was sitting in her pyjamas alone on a Saturday night. Now, she had some choices to make, and she didn't know how to go about it.

Was Finn there for the choosing? Could it work with him? But there was the thing – did it have to work with him? She was an adult now, a *consenting* adult was the popular term. What exactly did that mean? That you give your consent to have sex, freely, without expectation, without ties, without obligation. Was that possible? Was that what she wanted? How would she know? She'd never had sex with anyone but Tim. She had no idea how it would feel. And she never would until she gave it a try.

This made hang-gliding look easy.

Ellen stared at her phone on the coffee table. Her heart was pounding against her rib cage, vibrating right up into her ears. She was well aware she'd had too much to drink, she wouldn't even be considering this if she hadn't. But she also knew that if she didn't act now, she never would, that she'd wake up tomorrow morning and remember what she'd contemplated and be incredibly relieved she hadn't done anything about it. And then she would stop going around to Finn's garage, she'd pay off the rest of her account online, and she'd probably even try to find a new mechanic. And she'd regret it. Granted, she might also regret having sex with him, but what was she likely to regret more?

She lurched forward and grabbed the phone. Her hands were trembling as she scrolled through the numbers and pressed Finn's.

He answered almost straightaway, which was just as well or she probably would have hung up.

'Hello.'

She took a breath. 'Hi . . . it's Ellen.'

'I know.'

Great, what was she supposed to say now?

'You got home all right?' he asked.

'Yes, thanks. Oh, are you at home? Am I interrupting anything?'

'No, I'm just watching telly. It's a big Saturday night in.'

Ellen was trembling all over now. And she'd gotten hot all of a sudden. She held out the front of her pyjama top and blew on herself.

'So, what are you doing?' he asked after a while.

'Oh nothing,' she said quickly, dropping her top again as if he could see her. She took a breath. Of course he couldn't see her. 'I'm just watching telly too.'

'Hm.'

There was a pause. What the hell was she thinking? What was she going to say to him? This was such a stupid idea.

'So . . .?' he prompted after a while.

'What?'

'Ellen, you called me.'

She sighed. 'Yeah, I did. I think I shouldn't have, I'm sorry –'

'No, no, wait on,' he said. 'What's up? Did you want to talk?'

'Oh, sure, yeah . . . I guess.'

'What did you want to talk about?'

Okay, this was it, speak up or forever hold your tongue. Or was it peace? She took a gulp of her wine. 'I was thinking about what you said today.'

'Oh?'

He wasn't going to throw her a line at all.

'As I was leaving,' she added.

'Oohhh,' he said like now he understood.

'Well, I was wondering if you meant it,' she blurted.

There was a pause. Shit.

'Ellen . . .'

His tone . . . this was excruciating. 'Never mind, I shouldn't have bothered you –'

'Wait, just wait a minute,' he said over the top of her. She was quiet. 'Are you still there?'

'Yes.'

'Ellen,' he started again. 'Well, yeah, of course I meant it, but I didn't mean it . . . I mean, I wouldn't throw you a cheap line like that and expect you to take me seriously.' Now he sounded like he was nervous. She heard him take a breath. 'I was flirting with you, you know?'

Ellen wasn't sure how to take that. 'Did you mean to?'

'Sorry?'

'Did you mean to flirt?' That didn't make sense. 'Were you flirting with intention?'

There was another pause, another deep breath. 'Well, yeah . . .'

'Okay then,' she said. 'So what happens now?'

'Sorry?'

Ellen sighed. 'Listen Finn, we're adults, aren't we? And I think we get along, there's obviously some mutual attraction, and we could spend the next . . . who knows, maybe months, playing this game – a bit of flirting, having a drink, maybe graduating to a whole meal – until we finally make it into bed, which is where we've been aiming for the whole time.'

God, she couldn't believe she just said that. Maybe Finn couldn't either, there was only silence on the phone line, she couldn't even hear him breathing now.

'Finn?'

'Exactly how much have you had to drink, Ellen?' he said finally.

'Not that much,' she said, glancing at the half-empty bottle. 'The fact is, I do know what I'm saying, Finn, and I also realise I wouldn't be saying any of this if I hadn't had a drink, but is that such a bad thing?'

He didn't respond. He liked these long silences.

'I'm going to get a complex soon if you don't say something.'

'What do you want me to say?'

'That you're coming over.'

'What, now?'

'This is what I've been getting at,' said Ellen. 'I need to have sex. I need to get it out of the way so it's not so scary. And I trust you, Finn, you've been really decent to me. I just think this is far better than picking up some random guy in a bar, or online. But that doesn't mean I expect anything to come of this, Finn, I promise. We can even pretend like it didn't happen afterwards, if that's the way we feel. I don't want to lose you as a friend, or a mechanic for that matter.'

She gave an awkward laugh then, which was met with total silence.

'This is a strictly limited offer, Finn. Honestly, if you don't say something soon –'

'I'm on my way.'

Ellen hung up the phone and realised what she'd done. But there was no going back now. She jumped up off the sofa, grabbing the wine bottle and putting it back in the fridge. Then she ran up the hall to her bedroom, stopping dead in the doorway as she was confronted with the bed. The bed that she and Tim had shared. What was her problem? There hadn't been much going on in it for some time, so she wasn't going to get all weird about it. She didn't have time to change the sheets, but they were only a couple of days old. She did, however, need to change herself. She started frantically rummaging through her wardrobe for something that wouldn't look like she had dressed specially; on the other hand, she did want to look at least a little sexy. Who was she kidding, she didn't own any clothes that were sexy. She finally pulled a simple long-sleeved black top off its hanger and grabbed her good jeans. It was when she went to investigate her underwear drawer that she realised the true extent of her lack of sexy apparel. Her underpants were serviceable, that was the best that could be said about them, and she had one black bra that didn't look like a safety harness, much. God, she really hadn't thought this through. Perhaps a little forward planning would have been a good thing.

Too late now. She stripped off her flannel pyjamas and doused herself in perfume, then quickly got dressed. She didn't stop to check how she looked in her underwear, in fact she avoided the mirror altogether. She didn't need to know how she looked because there was nothing she could do about it now anyway. She was just putting a brush through her hair when she heard the door knocker.

Ellen took a deep breath, and then another one, and then she walked calmly up the hallway and opened the door. Finn stood under the porchlight, looking faintly nervous and, it had to be said, very attractive. She supposed he'd always looked like this, she just hadn't let herself dwell on it. She'd noticed his smile more than anything, and his bare chest.

Ellen had a sudden mental image of herself sitting opposite Tim saying, '. . . and he's *very* attractive.'

'Hi,' said Finn, his voice a little gravelly.

'Come in.' Ellen stepped back as he walked past, and he leaned down to kiss her on the cheek, which she wasn't expecting, so their faces bumped awkwardly. 'Come on through,' she said.

He followed her down the hall to the kitchen. 'Nice place,' he remarked.

'Thanks.'

He turned to look at her. 'And you look nice.'

'It's okay, you don't have to do that.'

'What do you mean?'

'You know, you don't need to butter me up, you're going to get laid anyway.'

He looked embarrassed. That might have been going too far. But Ellen was embarrassed too, she was just expressing it in a different way – by making inappropriate comments. Move on.

'Would you like a drink?' she asked.

'I brought wine,' he said, holding up a bottle.

'Oh, I'd better not drink red, makes me sleepy.'

'Sorry.' He put it down on the kitchen table. 'It's just what I had at home.'

'Don't apologise,' said Ellen. 'I'll get you a glass.'

'No, not if you're not having any.'

'I've got some white in the fridge,' she assured him. 'I'll have that.'

Besides, it gave her something to do. She got them each a clean glass from the cupboard, and retrieved the white from the fridge and filled her glass. Finn poured himself a glass of the red and picked it up.

'What shall we drink to?' he said.

Every phrase that went through Ellen's head sounded like a tawdry come-on. 'To good friends,' she said finally.

'I'll drink to that,' he said, holding up his glass.

Ellen took a gulp of her wine. 'Jeez, this was a lot easier on the phone.'

'Yeah,' he said awkwardly. 'Maybe we should sit down, relax.'

She knew she wasn't going to be able to do that. 'No, you know what?' said Ellen, putting her glass down on the table. 'We should just get on with it.'

'What?'

'Come with me,' she said, grabbing his hand and leading him back up the hallway towards her bedroom.

But Finn stopped abruptly, pulling his hand free. 'What are you doing, Ellen?'

She turned around. 'We both know why you're here, so why hang around drinking wine and making small talk?'

He folded his arms. 'What has gotten into you?'

She blinked, staring up at him.

'I'm not a performing monkey, you know, Ellen,' he said. 'Can you imagine if this was reversed?'

She caught her breath. 'Oh my God, I probably would have slapped your face.' She swallowed. 'I'm so sorry, Finn. I don't know what I'm doing, I don't know what I was thinking. I'm so bad at this.' She was choking up. She turned around because she couldn't look at him. 'I understand if you just want to go.'

She felt his hands on her shoulders, turning her around again. 'I'm not going, and I'm not going to slap you either.'

Ellen looked up at him and he smiled at her.

'Why don't we go and drink some wine and make small talk?'

She smiled back. 'I'd like that.'

*

'It's just so much harder for a woman after a marriage break-up,' Ellen was saying, once they were ensconced on the sofa, drinking their wine and making not so small talk. 'I mean, even in our case, where it was completely mutual, Tim gets to start this whole new life. He only has the kids a quarter of the time, he pays the standard child support, but because there's a whole lot of men out there who don't even do that, he's considered some kind of hero. It's like the base line is "bastard", anything above that and you're father of the year. Who ever says to the woman, the mother, wow, you're doing an amazing job there, you're really going the extra mile?'

'That's true,' said Finn, 'but your kids will always be much closer to you than Tim.'

'I know, and honestly, I wouldn't have it any other way. If anything I wish they could be with me the whole time,' she admitted. 'And I certainly couldn't bear to have them any less than I do now. But men seem to be able to detach themselves a lot easier.'

'That's a bit of a generalisation,' said Finn. 'Sometimes we don't get a choice.'

Ellen looked at him, frowning.

'I have a son,' he said.

'You do?'

He nodded. 'Josh. He's all grown up, he's a year or so older than your Kate. He's at uni in Queensland.'

'So you were married?' Ellen asked.

'No,' he said. 'His mum and I were very young, and very foolish, and she ended up pregnant. I was working by then, and my sister had finished school, so I tried to do the right thing. We both tried, but a few months after Josh was born we gave up pretending that we had any hope of making it as a couple. It was all good though, I had him most weekends for the first couple of years. Then Trace . . . Josh's mum, Tracey, she met someone, and they wanted to move to Queensland, with Josh, of course. I tried to fight it at first, got a lawyer and everything, but then I realised it was going to get really nasty. Trace and I had always got on well, which was much better for Josh, and I could see how happy she was with this guy, which could only make her a better parent. So I let him go.'

He paused, taking a breath. 'But it was a wrench, being so far away from him. I flew up every second weekend, but we had to stay in motels, it wasn't ideal. Anyway, long story short, I ended up taking a job on an oil rig so I could work for blocks of time and then get weeks off at a time. Trace was really happy for me to have him because she was working, but I think she also wanted to spend time with her new bloke, which was fair enough too. I had Josh every school holidays, and I took him all over Australia. We had a pretty great time.'

'Sounds like you made it up to him.'

'I guess,' said Finn. 'When he got into his senior years, we had to pull back a bit, only one big trip a year. And he started to get his own life as well, wanted to hang out with his mates in the holidays.'

'Are you close to him now?'

'Yeah, I think so. I hope so,' said Finn. 'We had a lot of fun, and did a lot together, but you know, I still missed having breakfast with him in the morning before school, weekends making him do his chores, just being a regular dad.' He looked at her. 'That's what I started out saying – try not to compare yourself to your ex, think of yourself as lucky that you get to be with them so much more.'

'See the glass as half-full.' Ellen nodded. She looked at her own glass then. 'Which you can't do when it's empty. Maybe I will have some of that red after all.'

Morning

Ellen stirred, rolling over onto her back. What day was it? Then she felt movement in the bed next to her. She opened her eyes. The room was dim, the blinds and curtains drawn, the door shut.

'Hi.'

Ellen slowly turned her head to see Finn, waking up beside her.

Scenes from last night flittered across her brain like a film montage, but the last thing she remembered they were sitting on the sofa together. How did they get here?

'Did we . . .?'

'It was that memorable you have to ask?' Finn said, his voice all husky from sleep.

Shit. Ellen really couldn't remember. But she was still dressed under these covers. Well, mostly dressed. No jeans, but everything else was in place, even her bra. Surely they hadn't . . .?

'We didn't,' Finn was saying.

Ellen turned over onto her side to face him. 'What happened?'

'You shouldn't have started on the red wine,' he murmured. 'You said it would make you sleepy.'

'So I fell asleep. Not in the middle of things, I hope?'

He shook his head. 'No, we didn't even get started.'

'Exciting night for you then.'

He smiled, rolling onto his side now, facing her.

'Why did you stay?' Ellen asked him.

'You asked me to. When you started to nod off, I tried to get you to go to bed, but you were determined to go through with it. That's what you kept saying. And you started trying to get your jeans off, but you couldn't quite manage, and then you kind of passed out on the bed, with your jeans around your knees.'

She pulled a face. 'That would have been a good look.'

'It wasn't bad.' He smiled sleepily. 'Anyway, I tucked you in, but you hung onto me and asked me not to go. I thought I'd just stay till you were sound asleep . . . and that's the last thought I remember having. Except for when I got cold sometime through the night and climbed in under the covers.'

Ellen shifted, and her leg brushed against his. 'And took off your jeans?'

'Bit uncomfortable to sleep in.'

Ellen stifled a yawn. 'Well, thank you.'

'What for?'

'For coming and for staying.'

'Thanks for inviting me.'

Her face was close to his. He looked all ruffled and sleepy, and quite adorable. Ellen brought her hand up from under the covers to smooth his hair, and then she couldn't recall what happened next. Was it his leg that slid across hers, or the other way round? His arm came around her pulling her in close while they kissed, but who kissed who first? Hard to say. It was as though their bodies moved by instinct, coiling around each other, their remaining clothes slithering off of their own accord, till Ellen heard herself moaning as she felt his skin against hers, then his mouth, his tongue . . . She was breathing faster, her heart was racing, and as he pushed up inside her she was completely overwhelmed. She couldn't think straight anymore, she couldn't think at all, she was all nerve endings, wired, intoxicated. Was it him thrusting, or was she doing that, and did he bring her up on top of him, or was it her, pushing him over, straddling him as she rocked harder and harder against him till she almost blacked out.

Ellen fell back onto the bed, gasping for breath, stunned. What the hell just happened? She could hear Finn breathing just as hard.

She turned her head to look at him, and he turned to look at her. He seemed a bit stunned as well.

The phone rang.

'Oh shit,' she breathed.

'Leave it.'

'I can't . . . the kids.'

'Oh, yeah.'

Ellen reached for the phone on the bedside table as she dragged herself up to sit.

'So, how did it go?'

What? It was Emma, was she psychic or something?

'Um –'

'Were you fabulous? I bet you were!'

Ellen's heart was pounding as she tried to catch her breath and collect her thoughts.

'Are you okay? Did you have to run for the phone?' Emma asked.

'Um, just from the bathroom, I'm fine.'

'Sorry I didn't call yesterday, I got completely caught up – we had our first meeting on site, at the venue, and well, thank goodness we're still a couple of months out is all I can say. I had to wonder if they'd even read any of my emails. But that's enough about me. Tell me all about the interview!'

Ellen's brain finally caught up and she sighed with relief. 'Oh, it went really well, thanks, Em.'

'So what do you think of your chances?'

'I don't know . . .' Ellen flinched a little as she felt Finn's hand on her back. It was just an affectionate touch, familiar even. But Ellen felt uncomfortable, naked . . . probably because she was naked. And she didn't want to sit here naked talking to her sister while he watched. That felt weird. She drew the sheet partway around herself.

'They said it'll be at least a couple of weeks before they let us know,' she said into the phone.

'That long?' Emma remarked. 'How many people did they interview for the position, do you know?'

'No idea.' Ellen was scanning the room for something she could grab to cover herself with. 'Ah, let me think, there was a woman ahead of me, and two more waiting when I came out. And I think the interviews had been going all day.'

'Well, that would amount to quite a few,' said Emma. 'Let's see, that's . . .'

Ellen didn't want to cut Emma off after she'd been so good to her, but she was finding it hard to concentrate. She lurched from the bed to the door, grabbed her robe off the hook and wrapped it haphazardly around herself as she opened the door and ducked out. She didn't look back at Finn, she didn't want to see the expression on his face.

'– so there could be as many as twenty, maybe even more. Is that usual for a teaching position?'

'Honestly, Em, I wouldn't know,' said Ellen. Now that she was out of Finn's sight, she put the robe on properly, crossing it right over in front and holding the phone under her chin as she tied the sash firmly. 'It's different in the public system, your number comes up and the interview is more or less a formality. I don't know how many people usually apply for a job in a private school.'

'Well, we'll just have to keep our fingers crossed,' she said. 'What else have you been up to?'

'Nothing,' she blurted a little too quickly. 'Um, you know, the kids are with Tim this weekend, I've just been hanging around.'

'Oh Ellen,' said Emma. 'You can't keep this up. You've got to start putting yourself out there. You have to make a life for yourself.'

Ellen had a momentary impulse to tell Emma who was in her bed right now, but that would only complicate matters. She didn't even know what to do about the fact that he was still in her bed. One thing for sure, she wasn't going back in there, she didn't want to give him any ideas about cosy Sundays sleeping in and breakfast in bed. No, this was supposed to be easy, unfettered, two consenting adults, all that . . . and now she didn't know how to get rid of him so that she could deal with what just happened.

'I'm trying,' said Ellen. 'I really am. It's just going to take time.'

'I suppose,' Emma sighed. 'But you don't want to lose your last real window of opportunity.'

'Pardon?'

'This side of forty you've got more chance of finding someone than after you go over to the dark side.'

'This is doing wonders for my morale,' Ellen said drily.

'I'm only telling it like it is,' said Emma. 'But I have to dash, we're meeting some people for brunch.'

'Okay, thanks for the call, and you know, I haven't even thanked you properly for Friday –'

'Yes you did,' she dismissed. 'Besides, I think I had more fun than you did.'

Emma rang off and Ellen put down the phone. Her heartbeat had settled back to a normal rhythm, and she wasn't breathless anymore. But she still felt like she'd been run over by a truck . . . in a good way, she supposed. She lowered herself onto a kitchen chair and leaned her elbows on the table as she cupped her chin in her hands, staring out in front of her. Okay, she'd done it. She'd had sex with someone other than Tim. But it was not like any sex she'd ever had with Tim. She'd really lost it in there, and that was freaking her out. Ellen was not accustomed to being out of control, especially with a virtual stranger. She supposed Finn wasn't exactly a stranger, but it's not as though they were close . . . well, they were now . . . No, they weren't!

She couldn't make a big deal about this. She was the one who said let's just do it, get it out of the way, obligation-free, consenting adults and all that. Only now she felt like an adolescent. How had she got to this age and never had sex like that before? Somewhere, quite deep inside her, she felt a little pissed off.

'Ellen?'

She jumped, looking up.

'Sorry, I didn't mean to startle you.'

It was Finn, fully dressed, gazing down at her, bringing his hand to rest on her shoulder in that same affectionate, familiar way. Ellen stood abruptly and moved out of his reach. She needed distance if she was going to keep her head around him.

'Is everything all right?' he asked. 'Are you okay?'

She nodded. 'I'm fine. Great. All is well.'

'Okay,' he said, a little bemused.

'So, um,' she said, putting more distance between them by backing into the furthest corner of the kitchen. 'Can I get you anything . . . before you head off?'

She saw it, unmistakably, the penny dropping, along with his face.

'No,' he said. 'Thanks. I'll get out of your way.'

Now she felt mean. She had no idea how to do this. She just knew she couldn't be around him right now, she wouldn't be able to think straight. And she had to get her thoughts into some kind of order. She followed him up to the front door and he turned around to look at her.

'Ellen,' he said, 'I can't just not say anything, it seems like bad manners, if nothing else.'

She couldn't look him in the eye.

'I wanted you to know that I'm not irresponsible, I did bring protection, but it all happened so fast . . .'

Oh God, they were going to have that conversation.

'It's okay,' she blurted. 'I've got an IUD.'

'Oh . . . right then.' He took a breath. 'But contraception isn't the only issue.'

Ellen looked up at him then, her eyes wide.

'I know you haven't been with anyone,' Finn said quickly. 'I just wanted to reassure you that you won't catch anything from me.'

She dropped her gaze again. 'Okay, so can we stop talking about it now?'

Ellen should have been better at all this, she was a high school teacher, for crying out loud.

She felt Finn's hand on her arm again. 'I had a nice time, Ellen, a really nice time. I'm sorry if I disappointed you somehow –'

'No,' she said quickly. 'No, I'm not disappointed, you weren't disappointing. I just need some time to . . . to process . . . I don't know.'

'Okay,' he said. 'Call me when you have. If that's what you want.'

She nodded, still not making eye contact. He drew closer, his cheek brushed against hers and she jerked back.

'For Chrissakes, Ellen,' he muttered, and taking hold of her face with both hands, he tipped her head back and brought his lips down onto hers in a firm kiss. Then he released her again. He opened the door, looking back at her.

'Bye Ellen,' he said.

She swallowed. 'Bye.'

*

Ellen spent most of the day in a daze – luckily housework didn't require much brain power. She busied herself with mundane chores while her mind went around in circles, getting nowhere.

It was surreal speaking to Tim when he dropped the kids off. She wondered if he could tell . . . She wondered if he'd had the same experience with Thérése. It would be fascinating to know, though maybe not. He was the only person she knew in her exact situation. But was it exact? He was a man after all; sex was different for men. There was one result, and one result only for them. Whereas, Ellen was coming to realise, there more ways for a woman to skin a cat.

She really had to work on her metaphors.

Tim was still talking, she had to focus. The kids had met Thérése today, he reported. It had seemed to go well. Ellen's mind drifted imagining Finn meeting Kate and Sam . . .

'So you will talk to them?' Tim was saying.

'Hm?'

'Make sure they were okay about today?'

'Oh, of course,' Ellen roused herself. 'I'll talk to them.'

Sam had worked his way through half the contents of the fridge by the time Ellen came back down the hall. She wanted to say, 'Doesn't your father feed you?' but decided to bite her tongue.

'Did you have a good weekend?' she asked instead.

Sam shrugged. 'I've got homework,' he said, heading for the hall.

She also wanted to say, 'Doesn't your father make you do your homework?' but instead she just said, 'Please take your things with you.'

Ellen turned to Kate, who was sitting at the table, a range of snacks spread out in front of her. 'Seriously, does Dad not have any food at his place?'

Kate grinned. 'Not any good stuff.'

Ellen took a seat opposite her. 'So, how'd it go?'

Kate looked at her. 'We met her, did Dad tell you?'

Ellen nodded.

'We had the big "talk" on Saturday night, and then we had lunch with her today.'

'How was that?'

Kate shrugged. 'It was okay, she seems okay.'

'Is something wrong?'

She sighed, shaking her head. 'Dad's just so hopeless. He warned us ahead that she wasn't very attractive. Can you believe he'd say that?'

Unfortunately, she could, all too well. Ellen automatically began to think of a way to explain his behaviour, and then it occurred to her she didn't have to defend him, that wasn't her job anymore. She shouldn't criticise or belittle him, of course, but she didn't have to defend him, make excuses for him. He had to do that for himself now.

'I was expecting some horrible deformed witch with a wart on her nose,' Kate was saying, 'but she was all right. She's kind of a biggish woman, but there's nothing wrong with that.'

'Of course there isn't,' said Ellen. 'How was Sam?'

'Quiet,' she said. 'He's sixteen, Mum, he doesn't have a lot to say to a middle-aged woman.'

'She's middle-aged?'

'I guess, she's about the same age as you anyway.'

'Thanks.'

Kate grinned. 'Sorry, Ma.'

Ellen looked at her. 'You seem a lot brighter.'

'I'm just relieved there are no more secrets,' she said. 'You know, I understood why you didn't tell us you were separating, I really did, but one thing I counted on after that was that you promised from then on you'd tell us everything. I know you'd never keep anything from us, Mum. And now Dad's got no reason to either.'

Later, when dinner was almost ready, Ellen went into Sam's room.

'Oh, so you're doing an assignment all about Facebook?' she remarked as she came closer.

'Mu-um,' he groaned, clicking on the mouse to bring up his homework. 'See, I'm doin' it.'

Ellen sat herself on the edge of the bed. 'So, you met Dad's friend today,' she said, cutting to the chase.

Sam glanced in her direction, then back at the screen. 'Mm.'

'Was that okay?'

He shrugged.

'You don't have to tell me, Sam, you don't have to talk about it at all if you don't want to,' Ellen said plainly. 'But I just want you to know that it is okay to talk, if and whenever you want to.'

After a moment, he said, 'It's just weird.'

'Weird talking to me, or do you mean it was weird today?'

'It's all weird.' He swivelled his chair to face her, though he still didn't meet her eyes.

'I can imagine,' said Ellen. 'Of course it's going to be weird, your parents dating other people.'

He finally looked at her then. 'Are you going to start dating?'

Ellen could see the anxiety in his eyes. 'It's not something I'm thinking about right now.' God, did that constitute a lie? 'It's just not a priority for me, okay? So don't worry about it.' She stood up and walked towards the door. 'Dinner'll be about ten minutes.'

''Kay . . . Thanks Mum,' he added, and Ellen could hear the relief in his voice.

Pyrmont

Emma walked into the apartment, absolutely exhausted. She had squeezed in extra clients almost every day lately, trying to get ahead before the wedding. She'd heard people say that as the big day drew near, you started to look forward to the honeymoon more than the wedding, simply because you were so desperate for a holiday. Emma was beginning to understand the sentiment.

'Hi darling,' she said as she walked through to the living room.

Blake was hunched over the dining room table, his laptop open in front of him, and papers spread out all around him.

'Did you have to bring work home?' she asked.

He turned to look at her. 'No,' he said. 'I'm taking a look at the wedding, actually.'

'Oh, are you?' She smiled, leaning down to kiss him, but he just offered his cheek. 'I'm so glad you're finally taking an interest.'

'So am I,' he said gruffly. 'Take a seat.'

Emma was wondering what this was all about. She noticed a glass of wine at his elbow. 'Do you mind if I get myself a drink first?'

'Go ahead, I'll have a top-up while you're there.' He picked up his glass and threw back what was left, before passing it to her.

'Okay,' she said brightly.

Well, he was in a mood. She went into the kitchen and opened the fridge. A few minutes later she returned to the table with his refilled glass, and a platter of cheese and olives and crackers. Maybe his blood sugar was low. He mustn't have eaten yet.

She fetched her glass and joined him, pulling out the chair next to him and sitting down.

He looked at her. 'I picked up the mail on my way up this afternoon,' he began. 'And the quote from the reception place was there.'

'Oh good,' said Emma, leaning forward. 'Let me see.'

He held up a piece of paper, but he didn't pass it to her. 'It's not the final figure,' he said, 'because the numbers haven't been confirmed yet, according to them.'

'Hm, that's true,' she nodded, 'but it'll give us an idea.'

'An idea?' he exclaimed. 'They've quoted for three hundred guests, Emma!'

She shrugged. 'Well, that was the ballpark . . .'

'Have you any idea how much this is going to cost?'

Emma detected a certain level of anger in his voice.

'Of course,' she said lightly. 'At one hundred and –'

'I can do the maths, Emma.' Oh, he was definitely angry. 'And then I started investigating. The flowers alone are coming in over three thousand.'

'That's how much they cost. They have to import the –'

'And that's not all,' he went on, interrupting her. 'I found your folder.' He snatched it up off the table and waved it in the air.

'It's not like I was hiding it from you.'

'According to this, we're paying for the bridesmaid dresses, shoes, even the jewellery, for godsakes.'

'The jewellery is the traditional gift.'

'It's all a gift, we're paying for the lot.'

'That's what's expected, Blake, it's etiquette.'

He sat back in his chair, picking up his glass. 'This has gotten out of hand, Emma. We can't afford this.'

'Of course we can,' she insisted. 'I've been keeping track.'

'So what kind of a crazy budget did you set in the first place?'

Emma wasn't going to let this escalate, she had to keep calm. 'We have discussed all of this, Blake. I've always kept you informed. It's not my fault that you weren't interested, that you left everything to me.'

'Because I didn't realise you were insane,' he spat.

'Blake,' she said, hurt, 'that's not necessary. What exactly is the problem here? I'm fully aware of what we can afford, and I am working to a budget. But this is the most important day of our lives.'

'No, it's not,' he retorted. 'It's a ridiculous big circus that you wanted to throw to impress everyone. I wish I'd never asked you.'

Emma could feel tears stinging her eyes. 'Do you mean that?'

He sighed, looking at her. 'Don't get upset . . .'

'What do you expect?' she said tearfully. 'Barely a couple of months out from the wedding and you say something like that?'

'I didn't mean I don't want to marry you,' he said. 'But I would have been happy with a service in a registry office.'

'Well, I wouldn't have,' she sniffed, 'and you knew that when you asked me.'

He reached over and took her hand. 'Look, this is just a lot to take in, Em. You know I didn't get a bonus the last couple of years, and they're probably not going to give them out this year, now that we're barely clawing our way back.'

'I didn't factor in bonuses,' she insisted. 'I'm not an idiot, Blake.'

'I know you're not . . . I'm sorry.' He leaned his elbows on the table and dropped his head in his hands.

Emma was watching him. 'What's this about, Blake? What's really bothering you?'

'Nothing, it doesn't matter.'

'Yes it does. Talk to me.'

He sighed heavily, lifting his head to look at her again. 'It's just, the bigger this thing gets the less it seems to have anything to do with you and me.' He paused. 'I keep thinking about that legend, the one about Icarus.'

'Who flew too close to the sun?'

Blake nodded. 'And his wings melted, and he plummeted back to earth. What happens after all this is over, and you don't have your wedding to dream about anymore, and it's just you and me and reality?'

'What are you getting at?'

'My parents divorced, one of my sisters is divorced, the other one never wants to get married.' He sighed. 'It seems to me if you don't get married, you can't get divorced.'

'Blake,' said Emma, sliding off her chair and over onto his lap, facing him. 'We're not going to get divorced.'

'How do you know that?'

'Because if you did anything that would make me want to divorce you, I'd kill you first.'

His face broke into a smile finally.

'Blake, I love you. You think the piece of paper doesn't make any difference, well, neither do I, in that sense. It may not keep us together, but it's not going to drive us apart either.'

Emma leaned in to kiss him, and slowly he responded, circling his arms around her. After a while, she drew back to look at him.

'What can I do to make you feel better about the wedding?' she said. 'I'm afraid most of this has already been ordered, deposits have been paid . . .'

'It's okay,' said Blake. 'I want you to be happy.'

'And I want you to be happy,' she insisted. 'I could bring down the guest list a bit. Would that help?'

'It wouldn't hurt.'

'Done.' She looped her arms around his neck. 'Do you still love me?'

'I never stopped loving you.'

'And you better never stop,' she said, leaning in to kiss him.

Saturday

'I can't believe this is it,' Evie said wistfully, sipping her tea.

'You're telling me,' Liz grumbled.

The removalists were coming during the week, and Edward and Evelyn would be walking away from their house for the last time, and hopping straight onto a plane to Peru, their sadness at leaving being quite effectively quashed by their excitement about the trip. It had all come about because their apartment was not going to be settled for another month, and when they looked at their temporary accommodation options – including offers from all their children to stay with them – it suddenly occurred to them that they might as well get started on their travels.

So the family had been summoned to clear out anything that still belonged to them, as well as to help their parents cull the cumulus of forty years.

'This is your last chance if you want anything,' Edward announced as everyone gathered in the kitchen, 'or else it's all going to Vinnies.'

'Nothing's going to Vinnies,' said Liz. 'I'm taking anything and everything you don't want. Everyone hear that? I have first dibs.'

'But Elizabeth, darling,' her mother protested, 'there'll just be a lot of old mismatched crockery, that kind of thing. You don't want any of that.'

That was exactly what she wanted. Everything in Liz's flat was matching, out of the box, new. You couldn't make a home out of stuff like that.

'I'll be the judge of that, thanks, Mum.'

'How long is this going to take?' Tayla whined.

'Tayla,' Evie chided. 'It'll take as long as it takes. Grandma and Grandad need our help.'

'But you said it'd be fun, it sounds like just a lot of cleaning up.'

'What's your rush, missie?' said her grandmother, coming to put an arm around her shoulders. 'You're staying the night with us tonight, aren't you?'

'Ooh, someone's going to get spoilt!' said Liz.

'We should get started on the shed, eh Dad?' said Eddie. 'You ready for some serious male bonding, Sam?' he added, slapping his nephew on the back.

'Boys and their sheds.' Evelyn rolled her eyes.

'This is really sexist, you know,' said Kate. 'The men in the yard, the women in the kitchen.' She gave her head a dramatic shake. 'I thought better of you, Grandma and Grandad.'

'Katie, you're more than welcome to come and fossick around among the spiders with us,' her grandfather said with a wink.

'It's not the spiders I'd be worried about,' said Ellen. 'It's the rats' nests.'

'Seriously?' Kate grimaced.

All the women nodded.

'Fine, I'll conform to sexist stereotyping and help Grandma in the kitchen,' she said airily.

'Yoo-hoo?'

'Is that Emma?' Edward walked into the hall, backing into the kitchen again as Emma breezed through, carrying a large cake box.

'What are you doing here, Emma?' her mother asked her. 'I said you didn't to have to come today. You must be so busy with all your wedding preparations.'

'I am,' she returned, dumping the box on the kitchen bench. 'But I figured if I didn't come today, I wouldn't see either of you until Dad's walking me down the aisle.' She opened the box. 'That's if you make it back in time.'

'Donuts!' Tayla exclaimed.

'Now, now, Em,' said her dad, putting his arm around her and kissing her cheek as he reached for a donut, 'we'll be back in plenty of time for your wedding.'

'As long as you don't get sick or have an accident trekking up to Machu Picchu,' she returned. 'Have you two really considered what you'll be doing? Climbing hundreds of stairs, four to five hours a day, at an altitude above four thousand metres. There's not much oxygen up that high, the statistics of people having heart attacks –'

'Emma!' everyone chorused.

'I'm just saying, I hope you understand the risks. But it's only my wedding, so . . .' She shrugged. 'I'll get started up in our old room.'

She brushed her hands together and walked briskly out of the kitchen again.

'Is it really as dangerous as Aunty Em says?' Kate asked tentatively.

'No, of course not,' Eddie assured her.

'No offence, Uncle Eddie, but you jump off cliffs for a living.'

'And you sound just like your mother,' he muttered.

'Nothing wrong with that,' said Ellen.

Evelyn came over to her granddaughter and patted her arm reassuringly. 'It will be challenging, Kate, but not dangerous,' she said. 'You mustn't pay attention to Aunty Emma.'

'Because no one else does,' Ellen said, but she wasn't joking.

'What are you saying, Ellen?' her mother asked.

'I think we were all so determined not to let Emma go overboard that we've ended up virtually ignoring her wedding.'

Everyone looked a little sheepish.

'I'll go up and talk to her,' said Ellen.

Liz dropped her half-eaten donut back in the box. 'No, I'll go,' she said with a resigned sigh. 'I'm maid of honour.'

She walked up the stairs to the room she had shared with Emma, what felt like a hundred years ago. As she pushed back the door, Emma was standing in front of the open wardrobe, her hands on her hips.

'Are you okay?' Liz asked.

She turned around. 'I suppose everyone thinks I'm a bitch.'

'No,' Liz said carefully, walking into the room. 'You're just stressed about the wedding, that's natural.'

'It's not just about the wedding. I'm worried about them. They're too old to be making that trip.'

'Em, Mum and Dad are in really good shape, they've been cleared by their doctors.' She dropped down on the bed. 'They will make it back, your wedding's important to them.'

Emma shook her head with a disdainful grunt. 'I don't think this wedding is very important to anyone. Blake has put more effort into his buck's weekend. You know what he's planning?' She didn't wait for Liz to hazard a guess. 'White-water rafting! A week before the wedding. I mean, Blake is fit, but he plays racquetball and works out at the gym, he's not an extreme sports kind of guy. He's going to end up drowning himself, ruining everything.'

A drowned groom would definitely put a dampener on the proceedings, but Liz decided not to wade into that one. 'So what are you doing for your hens' night?'

Emma looked at her. 'You tell me, Liz.'

'What do you mean?'

'The maid of honour usually organises it.'

Liz's face dropped. 'Oh my God, I'm so sorry, Em. I've never done this before. I didn't think about it.'

'Don't worry, you're not the only one,' she muttered, dragging a box out of the way.

'Ellen or Evie would have been much better at this. They've been through a wedding, they know what you're supposed to do.' Liz paused. 'Sometimes I wonder why you picked me.'

Emma sat on the bed next to her. 'How many years did you and I share this room?'

Liz shrugged.

'Don't you remember, when Evie was born, they put all three of us in here together, until Ellen complained so much, they closed in part of the verandah so she could have a room to herself.'

'And you were supposed to get that room when she left home,' Liz recalled. 'But Eddie was, what, about seven by then? And Mum and Dad said he couldn't keep sharing with Evie, it wasn't fair, so he got Ellen's old room.'

Emma nodded.

'Then you tried to kick me out,' said Liz with a smile, 'or to swap with Evie.'

'You were impossible to live with. You were such a slob.'

'I know,' Liz said. 'And you were so neat. So you moved out. You were the most independent of all of us. Mum and Dad had to virtually kick me out.'

'As if they would have ever kicked you out,' she scoffed. 'They would have had a conniption if you'd even talked about moving out before you graduated.' She paused. 'Anyway, I was around the same age Ellen and Evie were when they moved out. It wasn't that big a deal.'

'They both moved out to get married,' Liz reminded her. 'But you made your own way. I remember thinking you were really brave.'

'You did?'

She nodded. 'I also thought you were slightly mad.'

That finally drew a smile out of Emma.

'I've been really slack about your wedding, and I'm sorry,' said Liz. 'But I'm going to make it up to you. I'll organise this hens' night. Do you have anything in mind?'

Emma gave her head a coy tilt. 'I had been thinking a high tea might be nice.'

'Pardon?'

'A high tea,' she repeated. 'They're quite the thing these days. There are a few places that do them in the city, tea rooms, some of the big hotels. I can give you a list.'

Liz frowned. 'And so, at these high teas . . . you have tea?'

Emma looked at her. 'Of course. What did you expect?'

'It just doesn't sound like much of a hens' night.'

'Liz, my friends are not going to come on a pub crawl with me wearing a nylon veil on my head.'

Pity. 'Okay, if that's what you want,' she said, slapping her thighs. 'I'm onto it. Is there anything else I'm supposed to be doing?'

'Well,' she hesitated. 'I have my final dress fitting in a few weeks.'

'That sounds like something I should be there for, right?'

Emma shrugged. 'It'd be nice if someone saw it before the big day. Or else it's taking the surprise element to a whole other level.'

'Okay, email me the details, and cc them to Michelle, would you?'

Emma smiled. 'So she remembers if you don't?'

'So she keeps my schedule clear,' said Liz. 'And it can't hurt to have someone else on the case.'

Just then Ellen came rushing into the room and shut the door, leaning back against it. 'I might not have long, Kate and Evie have started on the kitchen with Mum –'

'Hey,' Liz said, getting up, 'I said I have first dibs.'

'Just wait,' said Ellen, holding up her hands. 'I have to talk to you in private.'

'Oh,' said Emma, getting up as well. 'I'll go then, leave you two to it.'

Ellen shook her head. 'No, don't go, Emma. I could use your perspective as well. You've got more experience than I have in this.'

'What is it?'

'Okay, well . . .' She hesitated. 'Look, before I start, this really is in the vault, okay? You can't tell anyone.'

'This is getting good,' said Liz, plonking back down on the bed and hugging her knees to herself. 'Out with it.'

'Okay.' She closed her eyes. 'I did it with the mechanic.'

Ellen opened her eyes again as they both gasped.

'You're not still referring to him as the mechanic?' said Liz.

'She's a snob, what did I tell you?' Emma said, sitting down again.

'Of course I don't call him the mechanic. That was just so you'd know who I was talking about.'

'Yes, because we get mixed up with all the guys you've had lined up waiting to go,' Emma said wryly.

'Well I remember his name,' said Liz. 'It's Flynn, right?'

'Finn,' Ellen corrected her. 'Short for Finlayson.'

'You slept with him and you still don't call him by his first name?' Emma remarked.

'No one calls him by his first name, I don't even know what it is.'

'Don't you think it's time you found out?'

'Fine, I'll make that a priority and get back to you,' said Ellen. 'But for now, can you please just hear me out? Especially before anyone comes.' She glanced over her shoulder at the closed door. 'I obviously don't want Kate to hear any of this. Or Evie, for that matter.'

'Why not Evie?' Liz asked.

'Oh, you know, Evie's so sweet, but she's a bit naive,' she said, taking a tentative step away from the door. 'I don't want to shock her.

She probably expects me to be well and truly divorced before I start sleeping around, or even dating.'

'Oh, I don't know if Evie's as naive as you imagine,' said Liz in her defence. 'You never know what they get up to in the suburbs.'

'Yeah right,' Emma said dubiously. 'Go on, Ellen.'

She bit her lip, looking at her sisters. 'God, I don't know how to put this.'

Liz raised an eyebrow. 'Wow, this really is getting good.'

'Just say it,' said Emma.

'Yeah, you can tell me anything, I'm a doctor.'

Ellen took a breath. 'Okay, well, you know I haven't been with anyone but Tim.'

They nodded.

'So I don't know what's normal.'

'Because Tim isn't?' Liz snorted a laugh. Emma grinned, nudging her.

'I'm sure Tim's quite normal,' said Ellen. 'Maybe just a little . . . unimaginative. Or maybe I should say ineffectual?'

'What are you getting at?' Emma frowned.

'Did Finn do something *ab*normal?' Liz asked, her eyes wide.

'No, that is, nothing bad, or weird, or kinky. But it wasn't normal for me,' said Ellen. 'I don't know what's normal. I've got nothing to compare it to.'

'For crying out loud, what did he do?' sighed Liz. 'Just spit it out.'

Ellen closed her eyes again. 'I can't say it.'

'Oh come on, we're your sisters,' Emma said.

'And I'm a doctor, you can tell me anything,' Liz tried again.

'Oh, it's not you guys, it's me.'

'Since when did you become so squeamish about sex?' said Liz.

'Since forever, I suppose,' said Ellen. 'I'm not used to talking about it. I haven't even had anything to talk about for years.'

'Okay, well use a euphemism if you have to,' Liz suggested.

'A euphemism,' she pondered. 'All right, that's good, in case we're interrupted.' Ellen glanced over her shoulder again. 'Okay, I've got it. Tim Tams.'

'Tim Tams?' said Liz. 'Do they represent sex?'

'Works for me.' Emma grinned. 'They're better than sex, depending on your mood.'

'Well, they're more than that,' Ellen said. 'Let's say that coffee represents sex, whereas Tim Tams . . .'

'Ohh,' Liz nodded. 'I think I'm with you now.'

'You are?' Emma frowned.

'Listen, here it is,' said Ellen. 'Tim Tams are great with coffee, right? But say you start eating your Tim Tam while your coffee is getting ready, and you eat it all. Well, it's still great, it's still a Tim Tam. But if you have your Tim Tam with your coffee, it's even better, don't you think?'

They both nodded thoughtfully.

'Best way to eat a Tim Tam,' said Liz, 'is when you bite off either end and suck the coffee through.'

Ellen gave a wistful sigh.

'So that's what you did with Finn?' Liz exclaimed. 'You sucked that coffee through that Tim Tam till it disintegrated into a big chocolatey –'

'Hold on,' said Emma, raising her hands. 'Are we talking orgasms or oral sex now?'

'Shh,' Ellen said. 'Keep your voice down! I'm talking about the first one,' she added in a small voice.

Emma's jaw dropped. 'Are you saying you never had an org- . . . a Tim Tam with Tim?'

'Sounds like she had Tim without the Tam,' Liz chuckled.

Ellen rolled her eyes. 'No, of course I've had Tim Tams, I've just always had them first. Sometimes I still had some Tim Tam left to have with my coffee . . .'

'But you're saying you never sucked coffee through a Tim Tam, the whole of your marriage?' said Liz.

'I really wish you wouldn't use that analogy,' Emma muttered in distaste.

'To answer your question, Liz,' said Ellen, 'I could count the times on one hand. And have fingers left over.'

'Are you serious?' said Emma.

'Yes,' she said weakly. 'I thought it was a fluke if it happened. But you're saying not?'

Liz shook her head. 'I mean, it's different for different women, and it's not guaranteed every time, but I'd say more often than not.' She looked at Emma, who nodded in agreement.

'Damn!' said Ellen, dropping down to sit on a box. 'I feel so ripped off. I mean, now I get what all the fuss is about. I thought my head was going to explode the other day,' she added glumly.

'I think Lenny's found her groove.' Emma grinned, as she and Liz held their hands up to high-five Ellen, but she just sat there, her chin in her hands.

'Why are you so miserable?' Liz said. 'You've opened up Pandora's box now, honey, there'll be no stopping you.'

'You don't understand,' Ellen sighed. 'I don't think I can keep seeing Finn.'

'Why not?' Emma asked.

'It's complicated.'

'How?'

'Well, you know Tim has a girlfriend?'

'Tim?' Liz exclaimed.

'Has a girlfriend?' Emma added. 'I didn't know. Did you know?' She glanced at Liz.

Liz shook her head. 'I didn't know.'

'Yeah, well, it only came out last week,' said Ellen. 'Anyway, he handled it really badly.'

'Why does that not surprise me?' Liz sighed. 'What did he do?'

'He told the kids and then he told them not to tell me.'

'What a blockhead.'

'Hm, so anyway I had to confront him, and we've sorted it out, but the kids are still a bit . . . shell-shocked, I suppose. They've both more or less indicated that they're glad I'm not dating anyone so they don't have to deal with that as well.'

'But that's not fair,' said Emma.

'Welcome to my world.'

Liz was thinking. 'Look, you have every second weekend to yourself, Len, you have opportunity. The kids don't have to know everything you get up to.'

'But I promised them there'd be no more secrets. I don't know if I should do it on the sly.'

'Sex on the sly could be pretty exciting,' said Liz.

'And she'd know.' Emma nodded.

'Shut up,' said Liz. 'Look, I'm sure Finn would understand why you have to keep it under wraps for a while, give the kids some time.'

'I don't know,' said Ellen. 'I don't even know if he wants to take things further. I don't even know if I do.'

'Are you kidding?' said Liz. 'Why wouldn't you? When you can have all the Tim Tams you want.'

'The thing is,' said Ellen, 'when I invited him over the other night, I made it very clear that I had no expectations of anything else. I just wanted sex.'

'Listen to you!' Liz declared.

'Did you actually say that to him?' Emma was shocked.

'I know it sounds pretty strong,' Ellen defended herself, 'but you have to understand the context. He had been flirting with me, and I'd had a few drinks . . . I don't know, I seized the moment.'

'My sister the barracuda,' Liz remarked.

'Don't call me that,' she chided. 'Look, you're the ones who kept telling me I had to get out there, and you have no idea how terrifying that is at my age, after so many years. Finn is a good guy, I trust him. It felt like a safer option than picking up someone random.'

'I'm not criticising you, Len,' said Liz. 'I just never expected it of you.'

'I never expected it of myself,' she agreed. 'But it doesn't matter anyway, it is what it is. I can't have any expectations of him. That was the deal.'

'Don't be so hasty,' said Emma. 'Did he say anything afterwards?'

Ellen nodded. 'He said I should call him, if I wanted to.'

'Well there you go!' said Liz.

'He was probably only being polite.'

'Uh-uh,' Emma shook her head. 'When they say *they'll* call you, that's when they're being polite.'

'She's right,' said Liz. 'He's leaving it up to you.'

'Well what'll I do?'

'Call him!' they cried in unison.

Ellen looked at them. 'I don't know, I don't know if I'm ready to start something. Isn't it too soon?'

'Not for Tim, obviously,' Emma pointed out. 'And if it's good for the goose . . .'

'But what if it ends badly?'

'You're such a pessimist,' said Liz.

'That's what he says,' Ellen sighed.

'Who?'

'Finn. See, he really has become a friend, and I wouldn't want to risk losing him as a friend.' She paused. 'Not to mention as a mechanic,' she added. 'Good mechanics are hard to come by.'

'Listen, mechanics are easier to come by than Tim Tams,' said Emma. 'In this context anyway.'

'Words of wisdom,' Liz nodded. 'Have a bit of fun, Lenny. Don't you think it's about time? You've been married since you were a child, and only keeping up appearances for half of that. Stop stressing about what might happen and just – how did you put it before? – seize the moment. Think about it, this is your chance to have your Tim Tams –'

'– and eat them too!' Emma finished, and then she snorted a laugh. Liz looked at Ellen, and they both started to laugh, and pretty soon all three of them were rolling around in stitches.

'What's so funny?'

They all looked around. Evie was standing in the doorway, staring at them.

'We were just talking about how much we love Tim Tams,' said Liz.

Evie sighed. 'I haven't had a Tim Tam in ages. Truth is, I don't even like them much anymore, they seem a bit sickly.'

The other three glanced at each other and burst into fresh peals of laughter all over again.

'What is so funny?' Evie repeated, getting a little frustrated.

'It's nothing,' Ellen assured her, catching her breath. 'We're just being very silly. I think this room is making us regress into adolescents again.'

'Oh, right,' said Evie in a flat voice.

'Is everything okay, Evie?' Ellen asked. 'You don't seem like yourself.'

There was a pause before she answered: 'Everything's fine,' she said, mustering a smile. 'Mum just sent me up to get you, Liz. She's about to start packing a box to take to Vinnies.'

'Not if I have anything to say about it,' said Liz, getting up off the bed.

*

Evie was running late getting back from her parents', and Craig was already dressed and raring to go, pacing the floor when she came in through the door. She knew she'd dawdled, finding one excuse after the other to delay leaving, until her mother had said plainly, 'Evie, aren't you and Craig going out tonight?'

'Ooh,' said Liz. 'Big night out, is it? Or a romantic dinner for two?'

'It's nothing,' she said. 'We're just meeting some friends.'

'You don't have to look so excited about it,' Liz said drolly.

'I don't even know them all that well,' Evie said. 'Craig organised it, it was his idea.'

She wished she could talk to her sisters about what was going on, just blurt it all out. But she couldn't, she had to sort this out with Craig, one way or another. If she told anyone, they'd never be able to look at him the same way again. It was hard enough for Evie.

So although she was late, she didn't hurry home; even on the freeway, she drove under the speed limit. She was glad when she came to a red light, annoyed when too many of them stayed stubbornly green as she approached.

'Evie,' Craig said when she finally arrived home, 'do you know what time it is? We're going to be late.'

'It's not like there's an official starting time,' she said sullenly.

'Well, can you hurry up now?'

She knew she couldn't get away with dawdling anymore, she was only putting off the inevitable. She came down the stairs twenty minutes later. Craig looked at her.

'You're wearing that again?'

She had on the same dress she'd worn the previous time. 'I don't own many dressy clothes, and nothing much fits me now anyway.'

'That doesn't fit you very well either,' he said with a slight curl of the lip.

It was true: the dress that had once not fitted her at all now fit her like a shirt on a fence, as her mum would put it, whatever that meant. Anyway, it was too big, it hung off her.

'You could have bought something new,' said Craig.

'Well, it's too late now,' she returned, picking up her purse and heading for the door. 'Are you coming?'

Craig rabbited on the whole way there, about his day, how he'd had to get up on a ladder and clean the gutters at his mum's because his dad was too lazy to do it, how she'd annoyed him with her incessant yabbering, how the boys had been playing up. It seemed as though they turned into the street all too soon. Craig parked on the opposite side to the house, a few doors up.

'There's a lot of cars here tonight,' he remarked, turning off the engine and taking the keys out of the ignition.

Evie didn't move, didn't lean down to pick up her purse, she just sat there, absolutely still. This was it. If she got out of the car with him now, she had to go through with it. She couldn't count on someone nice like Steve bailing her out, she wouldn't get away with that again anyway. But she finally knew for sure that no matter what it did to their marriage, no matter what Craig decided to do as a consequence, she couldn't go through with it. She was not going to get out of this car.

'Ev?' Craig prompted. 'Let's go.'

'I can't do it,' she said.

'What are you talking about?'

She took a breath. 'I can't do it, Craig. And I'm not going to, you can't make me.'

He sighed. 'Look, okay, I know you're nervous, Pud. But let's just go inside, have a drink. I bought a nice bottle of bubbly for you. Let's go in, relax, play it by ear.'

'No,' she said firmly, raising her voice. 'I mean it, Craig. I'm not going to do this.'

'You made an agreement, Evie –'

'No, I didn't!' she retorted angrily, finally turning her head to look at him. 'I've been railroaded into this from the start. I never wanted to do it. It was all your idea, and I've tried –'

'You haven't tried at all,' he sneered.

'I've done as much as I can do. I've faced it and I can't go through with it,' she cried. 'Don't you care how I feel?'

'Oh, that's rich,' he said. 'What about how I feel? This is like some kind of prick-tease, leading me along for weeks now, only to say no right at the last minute. Well, I don't care, you're coming,' he said, opening his door and getting out, slamming it again.

What was he going to do? Evie watched him walk around the front of the car and come around to her side. She flinched as he yanked open her door.

'I'm giving you one more chance,' he said. 'Get out of the car.'

She didn't move, didn't speak. She was trembling.

'Right,' he said, leaning in over her and releasing her seatbelt. Then he grabbed her by the arm.

'Craig!' she cried as he dragged her out onto the footpath. 'Let go of me,' she yelled, reefing her arm free. She turned and started to run up the street. He didn't follow her. Soon she heard the car start up and come after her, pulling in at the kerb where she had slowed to a walk. The window slid down.

'Get in the car, Evie,' he said grimly.

'I'm not going with you.'

'Look, okay, you won,' he said. 'Now get in the car.'

'No.'

'You're being stupid. You're in the middle of nowhere,' he said angrily. 'How are you going to get home?'

She didn't respond, she just kept walking.

'Get in the fucking car!' he shouted.

A porchlight came on outside the house she was passing. Evie came to a halt and for a split second she thought about making a run for the house, asking for help. But that was overdoing it. She didn't need to drag anyone else into this. And she wasn't actually frightened of Craig – what he'd done just then was completely out of character. She was pretty sure he'd surprised himself as much as her, which was why he hadn't come after her on foot. Besides, she felt strangely empowered. She had made her stand for tonight, and that was enough.

She leaned down to look at Craig through the window. 'Don't you lay another hand on me.'

'Don't worry, I have no intention of touching you,' he said.

She opened the door and got in, and he sped off up the street before she could even do up her seatbelt.

They didn't say a word for the whole drive home.

A week later

The letter was in the mailbox on Friday afternoon when Ellen arrived home from work. She knew what it was immediately, the school crest gave it away, but she probably would have guessed anyway from the thick, creamy, expensive stationery. She took it inside and slit the envelope open, drawing out the folded sheet. She sat down at the kitchen table. She knew this was going to be a rejection, the school would have phoned otherwise. Maybe she was a glass-half-empty kind of girl, but at least it didn't set her up for disappointment. She unfolded the single sheet and read.

Dear Ms Cosgrove

Thank you for applying for the position of senior teacher, English and History. While your application was impressive . . .

Ellen didn't need to read any further. She flicked the letter aside and pushed back her chair. Kicking off her shoes, she stood up and walked to the back window, staring out into the garden. So that was that. Just as well she hadn't mentioned it to her parents, they would never know she'd contemplated becoming a traitor to the cause of public education. She checked her wristwatch, they would be arriving in Lima soon. Ellen and the kids, as well as Liz and Eddie, had gone to see them off at the airport last night. Emma had hoped to get away, but she'd been held up on a shoot, and it was too far for Evie to make it on a school night, their parents had insisted. Besides, they were only going to be away for three or four weeks, they'd had longer holidays in the past and no one had made such a fuss. But this was the furthest they'd ever ventured, and it felt more momentous. With the house gone, it was like they were out there, free-falling, without an anchor to bring them home, without a home, in fact. But it didn't seem to bother them.

As Ellen watched her parents walk through the gate, holding hands, so excited to be heading off together, she'd felt a pang of envy at what they had together. Forty years already racked up, and they still had so much more ahead of them. Ellen would never have that, it was gone forever; in truth it had been gone for a long time. She'd lost the chance to grow old with the father of her children.

The shrill ring of the phone shattered the silence, along with her rather melancholy train of thought, which wasn't a bad thing.

'Hello Ellen?' It was Tim, sounding impatient, even a little annoyed. Great.

'Hi Tim,' she replied calmly. 'Is everything all right? Sam got home from training okay?'

'Yes, yes,' he dismissed. 'But everything's not all right.'

'What is it? Is Kate okay?'

'Both the children are fine,' he said firmly. 'They're in the kitchen now, having afternoon tea. They can't hear me in here.'

'Oh?' What was this about?

'The thing is, Ellen, I have to say I'm very disappointed right now, and I thought it was better to have it out with you. I mean, we are supposed to be amicable, right?'

'Right,' she said warily.

'Good then,' he said. 'Well, I just don't think you're making any sort of an effort to help the kids feel comfortable about Therése.'

'Pardon?'

'Sam is making it pretty clear that he doesn't want to have anything much to do with her.'

'And how is that my fault?'

'I just think if you were more positive it would make a difference.'

'Positive?' she said. 'What are you talking about? Look, Tim, I haven't said anything negative about her, I don't even know her.'

'Maybe that's the problem, maybe you should meet her.'

'I'm not interested in meeting her.'

'See? That's why Sam isn't interested in her either. He was always on your side.'

'Tim, it's not my job to smooth the way for you and your girlfriend,' she said angrily. She felt like yelling, I can't even have a boyfriend because you got in first! 'Maybe you should try being a little more positive yourself – you were the one who told the kids she wasn't very attractive.'

'I didn't say that.'

'Yes, you did,' she insisted. 'You said it to me as well.'

'No I didn't.'

'You think I'm making this up?'

'I never said she wasn't attractive – she's very attractive, she's just overweight, that's all.'

Ellen couldn't take any more of this. 'Listen, Tim, maybe you have to see this for what it is. I don't think Sam's got anything against Therése, but maybe when he has a weekend with you, he just wants to spend time with you.'

Tim had nothing to say to that.

'Now if you'll excuse me, this is my free weekend and I have better things to do.'

She hung up. She felt like throwing the phone across the room. What an imbecile! Thank God she wasn't going to grow old with him. Ellen stood there, breathing hard, staring at the phone in her hand.

'Have you called him yet?' Liz had asked her aside, last night at the airport.

'No,' she'd hissed back.

'Why not?'

'Because I haven't decided.'

'Think about it . . . all the Tim Tams you can eat.'

Ellen realised her hand was trembling. Why was she hesitating? Why shouldn't she have something for herself? Tim got to make a new life for himself, and now he was expecting her to talk up his girlfriend to the kids, pave the way, make it all nice and easy for him. Screw that. Screw sitting around being here for everyone else. She'd had enough.

She scrolled for Finn's number and pressed Call.

He picked up. 'Southside Auto Care.'

'Hi, it's Ellen,' she croaked, before clearing her throat.

'Oh,' he said. She could tell he wasn't expecting her, he mustn't have looked at his screen. Maybe he was busy. Maybe she should hang up. He wasn't saying anything.

'I'm sorry I haven't called,' she blurted.

'You're calling now.'

'I am.' She swallowed. 'Oh, I haven't transferred my payment today,' she said, remembering.

'Is that what you're calling about?'

'No, I just thought of it.'

'Would you mind holding a moment, please?' Finn said, suddenly businesslike.

'Of course.'

Ellen's heart was almost beating out of her chest, it was throbbing in her ears, competing with the hold music.

'Sorry about that,' Finn said, returning after a minute. 'You were saying?'

She hadn't been saying anything. She hadn't figured out what to say, she'd just called him. 'Um, you said I should call, if I wanted to. So I'm calling.'

'Okay.'

Ellen sighed. 'Is this a bad time, Finn?'

'It's just that I'm at work, I can't really talk, you know?'

Ellen wondered what that meant. If it was a statement of fact, or a hint.

'Okay, well, you could always come over later, if you want – you don't have to, or anything,' she added quickly. 'You know, no obligation. But, well, the kids are with Tim tonight, and I was just going to order pizza, watch a movie, so if you're not doing anything . . . if you're free . . . you could come over. If you want.'

There was a moment's silence before he answered. 'Is that what you want, Ellen?'

God, now what did that mean? Was he asking her, over the phone, if she wanted to have a relationship? How was she supposed to answer that?

'I don't know what you're asking exactly, Finn,' she said finally. 'All this tiptoeing around is getting exhausting, frankly.'

'You started it,' he said.

She smiled then, and she could imagine him smiling too. She really wanted to see that smile.

'I'd really like you to come over tonight.'

'Then that's what I'll do,' he said. 'I probably can't get away for another hour or so. See you around six?'

'Perfect.'

'Can I bring anything?'

'Just Tim Tams.' Shit, she said that out loud.

'What was that?' he asked.

'No, nothing, never mind, just bring yourself.'

*

Ellen had plenty of time to get ready without getting into a flap, but she got into a flap anyway. In a rather brazen display of optimism she went ahead and changed the sheets on her bed. Then she tidied the room, putting things out of sight that usually sat around not bothering anyone, like hand cream and the book she was reading. All the clear space suddenly made the dust noticeable. Ellen wasn't sure when she'd last dusted in here – she kept a clean house, but dusting her bedroom had never been a priority. It was now. When all surfaces were dust-free and shining, and she'd stopped sneezing, Ellen drew the curtains fully and started to play around with the lighting options. The bedside lamps were too bright, and she didn't have any lower wattage bulbs to replace them – she must remember to get some. She tried draping various scarves over the lamps, but then the place just looked like a bordello. Finally she decided they were going to have to stay off, though it was quite dark in here without any light at all. She glanced at the bedside clock and suddenly realised Finn would be on his way very soon. She rushed to the shower and was barely out and dressed when she heard the knock at the door.

When she opened it, Finn was standing there, smiling at her. 'Hi,' he said.

Ellen was so happy to see that smile. 'Come in,' she said, stepping back.

'I bought white this time,' he said, holding up a bottle as he walked through and Ellen closed the door.

'And I don't know if I heard this right . . .' he added, producing a packet of Tim Tams.

Ellen stared at them, and then she couldn't help it, she started to giggle.

Finn was watching her. 'What's so funny?'

'No, nothing,' she said, containing herself. 'I love Tim Tams, you have no idea. Thank you.'

And then, impulsively, she threw her arms around his neck and kissed him, really kissed him, which he obviously wasn't expecting, because he kind of stumbled back against the wall. He took a moment to catch up with her, but then he was kissing her back, and Ellen decided there was no time like the present . . . She manoeuvred him towards her bedroom door, and then all the way into the room, her mouth only leaving his when she pushed him down onto the bed.

'Ellen, I can't see you,' he said in the dark.

'That's okay,' she breathed. 'I'm sure we'll find our way.' She yanked her own top off and threw it aside, and then she started on the buttons of his shirt, when he grabbed her suddenly and flipped her over onto her back.

'Ow!'

'Sorry, did I hurt you?'

Ellen reached under herself. 'Oh, it's just the bottle.' She rolled it away and it fell onto the carpet with a thud. She went to draw his head down to kiss him again but he resisted.

'Ellen, what's the big hurry? I thought you said your kids were staying with their dad tonight?'

'They are,' she said, running her fingers across his chest. 'I just haven't been able to stop thinking about this, about being together. I don't want to wait.' She hooked one arm around his neck, bringing him close again to kiss him, as her other hand reached down for his belt buckle. He released a quiet groan. Ellen's heart was pounding, but something was different . . . she wasn't excited so much as oddly determined. She just had to push on, get him going, then everything else would fall into place, like last time.

And she did get him going. She could tell he was well on his way as he tugged impatiently at her clothes, while she deftly removed his, and they were finally naked against each other again. Something started to stir inside her belly, and she caught her breath as she felt his hand slide down to her inner thigh, but she stopped him. It must be all in the timing, they had to synchronise.

'No, it's okay, just come on,' she said, shifting her hips into place under his, and bringing her legs around him.

He was breathing hard. 'Are you sure?'

'Yes!' she insisted, pushing her pelvis up against him.

Ellen focused, trying to retrace or re-enact what had happened last time. As Finn built momentum, she rocked her hips against his in the same rhythm, but it didn't seem to be working. Maybe she should get on top, but she wasn't sure how to manage that now, in the middle of it all. Last time it had just happened.

He was thrusting faster now, and harder, and a vague, fleeting image of Tim crossed Ellen's mind, which she immediately blocked. Focus . . . time was running out . . .

Too late. There was the inevitable shudder and groan, before he collapsed against her, catching his breath. Ellen wanted to cry.

After a few moments he shifted his weight off her, and she heard a crackling sound.

'What's that?' Finn muttered to himself, and then he drew out the packet of biscuits.

Fucking Tim Tams.

He tossed them out of the way and turned to cuddle into her side, wrapping his arms around her and kissing her cheek. 'Are you okay?'

She made a kind of strangled noise in her throat.

'What is it?'

'Nothing . . . everything,' she gasped, her voice breaking. 'I'd just really like to know when something is going to go right for me for a change.'

'Hey Ellen,' he soothed, drawing her close. 'What's the matter?'

'I've tried, Finn,' she sobbed into his chest. 'I've really tried to do the glass half-full thing, and I know you said I shouldn't think the whole world is against me, but what am I supposed to think?'

'What's brought this on?' he said. 'What happened?'

'Everything! I didn't get the job, and I've had Tim on the phone telling me it's my fault the kids don't want to spend time with his girlfriend, and now, when all I wanted was to forget about all that and be with you, and have great sex, I couldn't even get that right!'

'What? I'm turning on this light,' said Finn, reaching for the switch on the lamp before she could stop him. She squinted as the light came on.

'Sorry, but I couldn't see your face.' He propped the pillows behind her, and drew the doona across them. 'Okay, from the start – you didn't get the job?'

She shook her head.

'Well, I don't think that's such a bad thing.'

'That's because you don't approve of private schools.'

'No, it's because you didn't want the job, Ellen, you wanted the money.'

She blinked. 'So I'm being punished for trying to make things a little easier for myself?'

He smiled. 'No, you just didn't get the job, probably because someone else was a better candidate. That's all. Not to punish you.'

She wiped her eyes with a corner of the sheet. 'What am I going to do now? I don't even know if I've got the energy for teaching anymore.'

'Then it's just as well you didn't get another teaching job,' he said wryly.

'I thought it might be easier in a private school. And you know, a change is as good as a holiday. Besides I don't know what else I can do. I left school, went to uni, had babies, went back to school. I've never known anything else.'

'Do you think that's a good enough reason to keep doing it?' Finn asked.

She looked at him.

'I remember being taught by teachers who should have left a long time ago. You're not being fair to yourself or your students.'

'But I don't know what else I can do,' she said again.

'I'm sure there's plenty you could do . . . just give yourself some time to think about it. Have you ever even done that?'

He had a point. Her life had been a series of chain reactions, she had never really considered what else she could do, what she might like to do . . . what else she was capable of doing. That was a scary thought, what if there wasn't anything? Better not say that to Finn, it was one of those glass half-empty ideas.

'And what was that you said about your ex?'

Ellen sighed loudly. 'He rang and told me off for not talking up his girlfriend to the kids so that they'll want to spend time with her.'

He started to laugh, rubbing his eyes. 'I'm sorry, I don't know your husband, I shouldn't have an opinion, but really, Ellen, was he always this dumb?'

She smiled. 'Thank you.'

'What for?'

'For being on my side,' she said. 'I'm sick of having to be so bloody amicable, and fair, and careful about everything I say. I just wish I didn't have to deal with him all the time. I mean, isn't that the point of being separated? It'd be fine by me if I never had to see him again, but that isn't possible because of the kids.'

'So that means you've got to try not to let him get to you so much,' said Finn. 'I wouldn't want to see you end up like my mum.'

Ellen looked at him.

'She had every right to be resentful and angry – my father was a pig to her, and he betrayed her – but she spent the rest of her life being miserable and feeling wronged.'

'What happened to her?'

'She got cancer, didn't even fight it, didn't want to,' he sighed. 'It was like the final, indisputable proof that she had got the raw end of the deal. She died four months after she was diagnosed.'

'I'm sorry.' Ellen stroked his cheek with the back of her hand. He had a bit of a three-day growth, he often did. She doubted Finn was making a fashion statement, but it suited him. He really was quite hot, she decided. Liz and Emma would approve.

'Hey, what's your name?' she asked.

'Hm?'

'What's your first name?'

'Why do you want to know that?'

'Well, I'm lying naked in bed beside you, it seems appropriate.'

'But I never use it, no one calls me by it.'

'Come on, what did your mother call you?'

He met her eyes then. 'I was named after my father. Michael John Finlayson. So not even my mother called me by my first name after he left.'

Their faces were level now, and very close, sharing the same pillow. Ellen inched towards him and pressed her lips against his. They lingered for a while, gradually building to a gentle, languorous, tender kiss. It was nice. It occurred to Ellen they had always kissed in such a frantic hurry . . .

Finn drew back to look at her. 'Before we get sidetracked,' he said in a low voice, 'there was something else you said. Something about not having great sex? A guy could get a complex, you know.'

'No, it's not you,' said Ellen. 'Last time, I mean the first time, that was amazing, Finn.'

'And you kicked me out straight afterwards.'

'I'm sorry, I was actually overwhelmed,' she tried to explain. 'I hadn't . . . well, it hadn't been like that for me before. I was right with you, you know, in sync, and that never used to happen with Tim. Maybe a few times, but I thought it was just a fluke. And then my sisters said it happens for them all the time, and I thought, wow, what have I been missing . . .?' She sighed. 'But now I think there must be something wrong with me. Last time was just a fluke as well.'

Finn lifted himself up on one elbow, frowning down at her. 'Ellen, I'm not sure if I'm getting this right. Are you saying . . . with your husband, you didn't . . .'

'Oh, no, I did, of course. Just, you know, not as a consequence of . . . um . . . you know.' She groaned. 'God, this is hard.'

He smiled at her. 'Funny how it's easier to do it than to talk about it.'

'Not so much for me.'

'Ellen,' he chided, stroking her hair from her forehead, 'there's nothing wrong with you. And I am going to prove it.' He kissed her lightly. 'You want to go for best out of three?'

She looked at him uncertainly. 'I don't know, what if it doesn't work again? I could end up with a phobia.'

'Oh, it'll work, trust me.'

'How can you be so sure? I don't know what the hell I'm doing, obviously. It's embarrassing, I'm a grown woman with two children, and no idea.'

'Well, I've got a few ideas,' he said, nuzzling into her neck.

'Have you now?'

He lifted his head to look at her. 'That was way too rushed just then, for one thing. You seemed to be in such a hurry.'

'But the first time was really fast.'

'It wasn't that fast.'

'I was just trying to . . . replicate it, I guess.'

'And there's your second mistake – you were thinking too much,' he said. 'It's not an intellectual exercise, Ellen. The first time, it just happened. It was amazing for me too, you know.'

'It was?'

'Hm.' He smiled at her. 'And I have vast sexual experience to compare it to.'

'Oh do you?' she said, raising an eyebrow.

'Well let's just say I've had more sexual partners than you.'

'Wow, that puts you right up there at two.' She grinned. 'Oh no, three, counting me.'

'See, so I know what I'm talking about.' He drew her close as he brought both arms right around her. 'And Ellen, you're a very sexy woman.'

'No I'm not,' she scoffed.

'Yes you are,' he returned, mimicking her tone. 'You don't have to try so hard,' he added, kissing her, 'or think so hard.' He kissed her again. 'Just relax. Go with it. Trust me . . .'

Monday

'Oh my God,' Ellen sighed into the phone. 'Oh my *God*!'

Liz was laughing. 'Oh yeah?'

'In almost every room of the house, in every position imaginable, and some I never had –'

'Okay, now you're skiting.'

'Oh Liz,' she sighed again. 'We didn't leave the house the entire weekend. You know when you do exercise you're not used to, and you discover muscles you never knew you had? Well I discovered erogenous zones I never knew I had.'

'Half your luck,' said Liz. 'We told you you could have your Tim Tams and eat them too.'

'I had so many Tim Tams I should be sick of them . . . but all I can think about is when I can have some more,' Ellen said wistfully. 'And now I have to wait two whole weeks.'

'Why?'

'The kids are with me next weekend.'

'You know you're not going to be able to keep up the subterfuge forever.'

'I don't know – how many years have you kept it up with Andrew?'

'Too many, believe me,' Liz said.

She had been avoiding Andrew since the day they'd talked at the hospital. The whole thing had left her feeling overwhelmed and confused, and she needed some space to work it out. Just because they weren't married didn't mean she didn't have an obligation to Andrew. What kind of person would she be if she left him when he needed her most? She loved Andrew, he had been a part of her life for a very long time. Liz didn't want to think she was the kind of person who would bail on someone she loved. But at the same time, she realised she was beginning to feel trapped.

'Anyway, I don't know if we have that sort of relationship,' Ellen was saying.

'What do you mean?'

'Well, we're just having fun, a lot of fun,' she added, her voice dropping. 'Once we start bringing the kids into it, well, it complicates things.'

'I guess, but it complicates things to keep it hidden as well.'

'Hm,' Ellen was thoughtful. 'Anyway, even if I was ready to introduce Finn to the kids, it doesn't solve my access problems. We wouldn't be going off to the bedroom for hot sex while they were in the house.'

'I take your point,' said Liz. 'Then you're just going to have to tell Tim that he has to start having Kate and Sam more often. Maybe they could go over one night a week for dinner as well.'

'You think?'

'Absolutely, why shouldn't he? A lot of divorced people share the parenting fifty-fifty these days.'

'Oh, I couldn't do that, I'd miss the kids too much.'

'But surely you could cope with one less night, considering the pay-off?'

'I think I could manage that.' Ellen grinned.

'And in the meantime, why don't I have the kids one night for a sleepover?' Liz suggested. 'I haven't done that in ages.'

'That's because they're sixteen and eighteen now,' Ellen reminded her.

'What? Are you saying they wouldn't want to come?' said Liz, crestfallen. 'I thought I was the cool aunty!'

'I'm sure you still are,' Ellen assured her. 'But they've grown up. They're past sleepovers at their aunty's, whether she's cool or not.'

'Well, that's it,' she said, resolved. 'I'm going to find something to lure them here.'

'You don't have to do that for me.'

'I'm not, I'm doing it for me,' she insisted. 'I'm crushed. I have to restore my image.'

The next day

Evie had slept in Tayla's bed that horrendous Saturday night, the only time she'd ever slept apart from Craig the whole of their married life, except for when she'd been in the hospital having babies. But she didn't sleep well, and she woke with the dawn the next morning. She decided to go straight over to her parents' place, before Craig woke up. She really didn't want to have to deal with him, with any of it. He'd stayed up drinking after they got home, watching television. Evie had heard him stumble up the stairs quite late, and had held her breath for a moment, but he'd headed straight for their bedroom. The only thing she heard after that was snoring.

She left a note so that he wouldn't phone her to find out what was going on for the day. It was just the bare details – that she would be at her mother's with Tayla, and that he shouldn't forget to pick up the boys.

Evie threw herself into the cleaning when she got to her parents' house. She was so glad to have something to do, she desperately needed the distraction. She didn't even care that Tayla complained most of the day, she switched off and let her grandparents deal with her. But as the afternoon wore on, she started to worry about the boys, and eventually they got their things together and left. It was only when Evie drove away that she remembered it would be the last time she'd see the house. Well, she was just going to have to go back over another day during the week, it was all too much to deal with at the moment.

She and Craig barely spoke that night. Evie didn't want to, and Craig didn't seem inclined to make any kind of approach either. He slumped off to the study after he'd said goodnight to the kids, she didn't care what he did as long as he stayed away from her.

But Evie really needed to talk to someone, and there was only one someone she could talk to. She sent a text to Steve to see if he wanted to meet for a walk the next morning. She felt a bit sad and lost when he didn't reply. It wasn't until the next morning that she finally received a text from him. He was away on business, all week. He promise he'd be in touch when he got back.

The week had dragged, and Evie felt just about ready to burst at the seams by the time he met her at their usual place the following week.

'Hey,' he said, smiling as he approached her. 'How are you?'

'Fine . . . no, I'm not fine, what am I saying? Why do I always say that? I really have to work on that.'

Steve looked at her, a bit bemused.

'Let's walk,' she said, scooping her arm through his and leading him along the track.

She launched into an account of that Saturday night but when she got to the part about Craig dragging her out of the car, Steve came to a sudden stop.

'Hold up a sec, Evie,' he protested. 'You're walking too fast and you're talking too fast.'

'Oh, sorry.'

He glanced around. 'Let's go sit over there, I want to listen to this properly.'

He led her across to a park bench looking out at the river, and they sat down. He turned to face her. 'So he dragged you out of the car?' he prompted her, frowning.

'Well, he dragged my arm. I was on my feet.'

'Are you okay?'

'Yeah, it was over in a few seconds. When I pulled my arm away, that was it, he didn't lay a finger on me after that. I think he was a bit shocked by what he'd done. He's never done anything like that before. I mean, he'll get the shits and slam a door, but that's about it.'

'You want to be careful though, Evie,' Steve said. 'You don't want him to start thinking it's okay to treat you like that.'

'I don't think that's going to happen,' she assured him. 'Anyway, I ran off up the street –'

'You did?' he said. 'Where did you think you were going to run to? It's outer suburbia, you weren't likely to find a cab.'

'I know,' she sighed. 'I didn't really think it through, I was just getting away from him right then. He came after me in the car, yelling at me to get in.'

'You weren't afraid?'

Evie shook her head. 'Even though he was obviously really pissed off, I knew he wouldn't hurt me. And in a funny way, I felt like I was the one with the power.'

'How so?'

'Well, Craig seemed like a bully in the playground, who can't do much more than give someone a shove or else he'll get into trouble himself.' She paused. 'I'd won, he knew it as well as I did. I'd stood up to him and there was nothing he could do about it.'

'You are amazing, Evie,' Steve said. His arm was resting on the back of the bench, and he gave her shoulder an affectionate squeeze.

'I don't know about that. I've still got to figure out what to do now,' she said. 'But it is such a relief that part's over. I've been living with this hanging over my head for months now. I feel free.'

'I'm glad,' he said, his hand lingering on her shoulder. 'So are you going to ask him to leave?'

Evie turned her head abruptly to look at him. 'That might be taking it a bit far.'

'Why?' Steve persisted. 'Do you honestly think you're going to be able to carry on as usual after this?'

'Well, you have,' she reminded him. 'Look how long you've stuck it out with Cheryl.'

'Yeah, and look where it's got me,' he said. 'Nothing's changed, Evie. I've been kidding myself, hanging in there, waiting for her to get it out of her system, like I told you. But I don't think she's ever going to. I think it's part of her lifestyle now.'

'I'm sorry, Steve,' said Evie, shifting to face him and putting a hand over his. 'I've been so caught up with my own problems, I haven't given you any chance to talk.'

He shook his head, taking hold of her hand. 'I don't mind, just being with you is the highlight of my week.' His other hand was still resting on her shoulder, and he moved to stroke her cheek.

Evie jerked back. 'What are you doing, Steve?'

He was gazing into her eyes. 'Evie, I've never met anyone like you, you're such a sweet person –'

'Stop it.' She took her hand out of his. 'Steve, you love Cheryl.'

'I don't know, I don't know whether I do anymore.'

'Well, I do,' said Evie. 'Look at what you've put up with all these years. You haven't hung in there for that long just to give up on her now.'

'That's the problem,' he said. 'It's like waiting and waiting for the share price to go up on stocks you've been holding on to for ages. But sometimes you just have to cut your losses and move on. Maybe it's time for me to make a new life, a new start.'

He went to reach for her again, but she held her hand up. 'Well, it's not going to happen with me, Steve,' Evie said emphatically. 'I like you, I like you a lot, in fact, but I think of you as a friend, a very good friend, but just a friend.'

He feigned an arrow hitting his heart, but he was smiling at the same time.

'Oh, come on,' she chided. 'You're just trying to find an easy way out. If you really don't think you want to be with Cheryl anymore, then do something about that. You don't fix things by just moving on to someone else. And I've got young children to consider, Steve. I've got to clean up the mess in my own backyard first.'

Spring

Liz had just managed to park her car when her phone rang, so she was able answer it, although when she saw it was Andrew, she nearly didn't.

'Hey hun,' he said, trying to sound casual, as though everything was fine and that great big elephant lurking in the corner of the room wasn't there at all. 'Listen, it looks like I'm free tonight. I'm on call, but things are really quiet here. I could get away.'

'Sorry, I'm due at Emma's final dress fitting,' she replied, opening the car door.

'Can't you get out of it?'

'No, Andrew, I can't,' she insisted, annoyed. 'I'm maid of honour.'

'I'm sorry, of course,' he said. 'It's just that I haven't seen you for weeks. Last Friday you took your niece and nephew to that comedy festival, and before that you were tied up helping your parents.'

'That's the way it goes sometimes, Andrew. I have a life too.' She picked up her bag and stepped out of the car.

'I know that,' he said, his voice a little strained. 'Is it going to take long, this fitting?'

Liz doubted it, but she didn't want to commit to anything. 'I really can't say,' she said evasively.

'Okay,' he sighed. 'Well, if you do finish up early, do you think you could give me a call later?'

'I'll do my best,' she said. 'But now I really am running late. I have to go.'

She dropped her phone into her handbag as she hurried up the street to the salon. Her last appointment had gone longer than scheduled, and then she'd hit a traffic snarl on Parramatta Road, and again on Cleveland Street. She hoped Emma wasn't going to be miffed – she could handle playing the supportive sister, but not under duress. She pushed back the door and burst in. All was quiet inside, strains of chamber music playing in the background. A woman stepped out from behind the wall of velvet drapes.

'Oh hi,' Liz said, still breathless. 'I'm here for Emma Beckett.'

'Of course, come through,' she said.

Liz followed her into the back, where Emma was standing on a dais in the most amazing dress Liz had ever seen, well, at least in real life. It was a creamy shade of white, and there were glass beads, probably crystal come to think of it, and what looked like tiny pearls sewn into it in intricate patterns. The bodice fitted her like a second skin, and the skirt fell in frothy folds, as though she was standing in the ocean and waves were breaking around her, swirling and foaming at her feet.

'You made it,' Emma said. 'I was beginning to wonder.'

'Em,' Liz was shaking her head as she came closer. 'This is . . . you look . . . wow . . .'

Emma smiled then. 'You like it?'

'It's stunning,' she said, finally finding a word to describe it. Because she had been stunned, literally, but in a totally good way. Emma really had a flair for this stuff. Liz wouldn't wear a dress like that in a million years, mostly because she could never pull it off. But there was no denying it was . . . stunning.

'You must be so happy with it,' said Liz, nodding politely at the seamstress.

'Oh, this is Sylvie,' said Emma. 'Sylvie – my sister, Liz, the maid of honour. Sylvie is my designer's right hand. We're almost done here. It just needed a few tucks.'

'She's lost weight,' Sylvie said, 'but we always allow for that, brides always lose weight.'

'All the stress, I suppose,' said Liz, dropping her handbag on a chair. She walked around the dais, looking at the dress from every angle, while the assistant finished up.

'That's it,' said Sylvie. 'Now we just have seventy-six buttons to undo to get her out of it.'

'I can do that,' Liz volunteered.

They both helped Emma off the dais, the assistant holding the train of the dress aloft. Liz followed her into the change room and began to undo the tiny pearl buttons, while Emma and Sylvie discussed the latest alterations. Liz was moving slowly and painstakingly down the row of buttons when her eyes were drawn to a mole on Emma's back. She bent closer to examine it, and her heart missed a beat. It fitted all the criteria – asymmetrical, ragged edge, variegated brown and inky black, and it was certainly greater than six millimetres in diameter. There was just one more thing.

'How long have you had this mole?' Liz asked Emma.

'What mole?'

'The one here on your back, just under your left shoulder blade.'

'I didn't know I had a mole there,' she said. 'Though I have had an itchy spot around there.'

Another bad sign. 'Emma, you should be aware of things like this,' Liz chided.

'But if I can't see it, how can I be aware of it?'

'Excuse me, Sylvie?' Liz said. 'Would you take a look at this?'

'Honestly Liz, don't make such a big deal.'

Sylvie came around behind Emma.

'Have you noticed this before?' Liz asked her, indicating the mole.

'Hm,' Sylvie looked closely. 'No, I don't think I have.'

'See, Liz, no one else would even notice it,' Emma insisted. 'You're just being paranoid because you're a dermatologist.'

'You're a dermatologist?' Sylvie remarked.

Liz nodded. 'How often has she had these dress fittings?'

'The schedule is roughly one a month, after the design is finalised.'

'And you're sure you haven't noticed this before now?'

'She didn't notice it now either,' Emma reminded her in a bored tone.

Sylvie was frowning as she stared at the mole. 'You know, it must have been smaller before. The early fittings are much more involved. When we were adjusting the curve of the bodice across the back here, for example, I'm sure we would have noticed it then.'

Liz's heart dropped. 'It needs looking at, Em.'

'Oh, you're overreacting,' she dismissed. 'Do you know how many years it is since I even exposed myself to the sun, let alone sunbaked? I'm super-careful. I only ever go to a solarium.'

Liz sighed loudly. 'Emma, solariums are worse! Didn't you believe me when I told you the dangers? I am a doctor, you know. I wasn't saying it for the sake of it.'

'Of course I believed you,' she returned. 'But then they brought in all these regulations, and my solarium was one of the first to put them into practice, before they were even mandatory. They had posters up everywhere with warnings, they upgraded their eye protection, and they did a complete skin assessment of all their clients, even if you'd been going for years. Then they designed an individual schedule so you could tan safely.'

Liz shook her head. 'I don't know when people are ever going to understand there's no such thing. Anyway, what's done is done. The important thing is to get this checked out as soon as possible.'

Emma gave a dismissive laugh. 'Not going to happen, Liz. I haven't got time to scratch myself at the moment. I swear every waking hour of every day from now until the wedding is already double-booked.'

'Emma, you cannot leave this,' Liz said firmly.

'I won't. I promise I'll have it checked out as soon as I'm back from the honeymoon. You can book me an appointment now, if you like.'

Liz knew it couldn't wait that long. But she also knew that scaring or bullying Emma into action wasn't going to work either. There was only one approach that would work with her sister.

'You know, Em, it's pretty ugly,' she said.

'What?'

'And it's sitting right above the edge of your dress, isn't it?' She looked at Sylvie for confirmation. 'It's quite prominent.'

'That's true,' Sylvie agreed.

'Worse, if it gets knocked it'll bleed all over the dress,' Liz went on. 'You don't want to risk that.'

Emma was craning around trying to get a good look at it. 'Isn't there some way of covering it up?'

'What, with a big piece of sticking plaster?' Liz pulled a face. 'It'll take me ten minutes in my rooms to whip it off and stitch it up.'

'But won't that leave a mark?'

'There might be a faint mark, but it'll be a lot less noticeable than this,' Liz assured her. 'Besides, it'll be all healed before the wedding, and there won't be a scar, I promise.'

Emma seemed to be contemplating her options. She turned around to face Liz, folding her arms.

'Okay,' she said finally. 'You can do it on one condition – that I don't hear another word about it before the wedding. Are we understood? I assume you're going to send it off for testing, so you can let me know the results when I get back from my honeymoon. I'll deal with it then. I mean it, I don't need anything else on my plate right now.'

'Sure,' Liz agreed. She should have crossed her fingers behind her back, but she was just going to take it one step at a time. 'So, I'll call Michelle to expect us soon, get things set up.'

Emma frowned. 'You want to do it right now? It's Friday afternoon.'

'Exactly,' Liz said, keeping her tone upbeat. 'My schedule was cleared this afternoon so that I could come here. So it's perfect, no waiting, you'll be in and out in no time. You don't want to put it off till next week, Em, you don't have the time. Let's get it out of the way now. Do you have to be somewhere?'

She looked at her watch. 'Not until later.' She still seemed unconvinced.

'The sooner you do it, the sooner it starts to heal,' Liz added as the final clincher.

Emma relented, and Liz called ahead to Michelle. As she promised, the procedure was quick and simple, and Liz saw her out of the office again not half an hour after they'd arrived.

'So that's the end of that,' said Emma as she got into the lift. 'Right?'

Liz just smiled as the lift doors closed. She was even more concerned once she'd examined the mole under the dermatoscope, not that she'd let on to Emma. She walked back into her office and through to the small examination-room-cum-surgery, where Michelle was placing the sample into the fridge for storage for pick-up after the weekend.

'No, I'm going to take that with me now,' Liz said, stopping her.

Michelle turned. 'What are you going to do with it?'

'I'll take it to the pathologists myself.'

'But they won't be open.'

'No, not for usual business, but they have staff there around the clock.'

Michelle looked at her. 'You're that worried?'

'Well, you saw it,' she said.

'Mm, it was nasty-looking, all right.'

'What bothers me is that Emma has no idea how long it's been there, or when it started to change or grow, but it has felt itchy. The woman fitting her dress couldn't remember it being that big a couple of months ago. I'm hoping we've caught it early, but we're guessing until we get these results.'

*

As Liz started up her car, she heard the beep of a text message. She picked up her phone to check it. It was Andrew. *How's it going there?*

She quickly keyed in her reply. *Something came up. Won't be able to meet.*

Exiting the carpark, her phone started to ring. Damn, she knew it would be Andrew. She picked it up.

'What's going on?' he asked.

'I'm driving, Andrew, I can't talk now.'

'Well, pull over.'

'I don't have time. I'll talk to you later,' she said. She turned the phone off and tossed it into her bag.

Ten minutes later, Liz pulled up in the near-empty carpark of the building that housed the pathology labs. She picked up the small cooler box from the passenger seat and carried it over to the front entrance where, as she expected, there was an after-hours buzzer. She pressed it and waited. Presently she could make out a figure approaching through the opaque glass, and a voice came over the intercom.

'Can I help you?'

'Yes, hi, I want to drop off a skin sample for urgent analysis.'

'I'm sorry, it's after hours.'

'I realise that,' said Liz. 'But like I said, this is urgent.'

'Who is this, please?'

'My name is Dr Beckett,' she said. 'I'm a local dermatologist, this is my regular pathology service. I have ID.'

There was a buzz and a click, and a woman opened the door, peering out at Liz who was already holding up her hospital ID.

'Good evening, Dr Beckett. I'm sorry about this, it's just not standard practice to receive random samples at the door.'

'Of course, but like I said,' for the third time, 'this is urgent.'

The woman looked pensive. 'I can't do this without authorisation. I'm going to have to check with someone.'

'Call Dr Tao.'

She blinked. 'Oh I can't possibly phone Dr Tao, he's the head of the whole practice! I can't just call him up on a Friday night.'

'He's an old friend of mine,' said Liz. 'Please, call him.'

She shrugged. 'I don't even have his number, outside of work.'

Liz took out her phone. 'I do.'

The woman brought her inside to the reception desk, where Liz insisted she phone the number so she could be assured everything was above board.

'Hello, Dr Tao? This is Jane Wilkie from the Spencer Street labs. I'm sorry to bother you at home . . . No sir, everything's fine. But there's a woman here who says she knows you, she gave me your number. A Dr Beckett? . . . Yes sir.' She held out the phone to Liz. 'He wants to talk to you.'

'Hi Richard, sorry about this.'

'Liz, long time no hear.'

'Hm, sorry about that as well. What can I say? Life's hectic.'

'Ah, it's the same for all of us. It's a mad world. What can I do for you?'

'I'm sorry to spring this on you. I have suspected melanoma tissue that needs analysis as soon as humanly possible. It's my sister's, and she's supposed to be getting married within the month.'

'Of course, Liz, whatever you need. But you do realise even on high priority you won't get the results until the middle of next week at least?'

'I know, that's why I have to get the ball rolling as soon as possible.'

'No problem. Put me back onto the receptionist, will you? Damn, what was her name?'

'I'll pass you back to *Jane*,' said Liz.

'Ah, thanks, Liz.'

'Thank you, Richard. I owe you.'

Friday night

'Are you okay now?' Liz asked Evie as she emerged from the bathroom.

She nodded. They had sent her off to the bathroom to wash her face and fix her makeup – they didn't think it was a good idea for Emma to walk in and see her tear-streaked face first off.

'So what now?' asked Ellen.

'Now we wait . . .'

The call had come through on Wednesday afternoon, from Richard Tao himself. Liz had picked up the phone with some trepidation when Michelle had announced him over the intercom. 'Hi Richard?'

'Hello, Liz,' he said. 'I told them at the clinic to let me know as soon as the results were in. I thought I should call you myself.'

She was not surprised by then to hear that it was bad news. It was at least a T3 malignant melanoma, making further tests and surgery imperative, not optional. No one knew exactly how long it took for a melanoma of that depth to penetrate below the dermis and become life-threatening – it could be weeks, it could be days. But one thing was for sure, it could not wait until after the wedding. Liz knew how stubborn Emma would be, she'd insist that they had made a deal and simply refuse to listen to her. So Liz was going to need reinforcements. She had to get all her sisters in a room together, and very soon. Emma was going to be the most difficult to pin down, so Liz had started with her.

'Now I know the high tea is only next week, but the girls and I want to have a drink with you before then.'

'What girls?'

'Your sisters, of course,' said Liz. 'Me, Ellen, Evie.'

'Seriously?'

'Yes.'

'When were you talking to them?' she asked, her tone highly suspicious.

'When I called about the high tea. We realised that we're not going to get a look-in at that, with so many people there, so we should find another time to have a drink together.'

'Oh,' said Emma, her voice softening. 'When were you thinking?'

'Tomorrow night.'

'Tomorrow? You're not giving me much of a heads-up. When did you all talk?'

'Oh, you know what it's like trying to find a night that suits everyone,' she said, evading the actual question. 'I just thought there was more chance you might be free on a weeknight.'

'Hmm, I have a late meeting . . .' Emma mused, checking her diary, Liz imagined. 'Actually Friday's just opened up. We had a cancellation, we were supposed to catch up with Damien and Cressida but he was called overseas unexpectedly, so we're going to have to reschedule. Heaven only knows when, I don't have another opening before the wedding.'

Liz didn't know or care about Damien and Cressida, they sounded like made-up people anyway. She wasn't comfortable at all about leaving it even one more day, but it was the only window she was going to get.

'Friday it is then, we'll meet at my place, I think six is good, you know, just come straight from work,' she blurted all at once before Emma could have second thoughts. Then she hung up.

Now she had to get the other two on board. Evie was a pushover; Liz concocted a story about Emma feeling ignored and that they needed to rally around her, and Evie gobbled up the bait without question. Then Liz rang Ellen.

'I'd love to,' Ellen responded when Liz outlined what she had in mind. 'But I have the kids.'

'They're old enough to stay on their own, Len.'

'I know that, but I only get alternate weekends with them, Liz, and they're busy with their friends most of the time. Friday nights are usually all we get to spend together.'

'Look, I wouldn't ask normally, but this is an emergency.'

'What do you mean?' said Ellen. 'You just said we were having drinks to cheer her up? And I think that's great, really, I do. But isn't there some other time we could do it?'

'No, there isn't.' Liz had hoped to avoid talking about it over the phone, but she had no choice. 'Ellen, I found a mole on Emma's back when I went for her dress fitting. I had it tested and it's a melanoma. It's malignant.'

'What?'

Liz had gone on to explain everything, including the promise she'd made to Emma.

'I need you with me when I break it to her, Len. We have to convince her that she has no choice, she has to have treatment as soon as possible, and we have to hope like hell that it hasn't spread already.'

Evie had taken the news badly, as expected, even though Liz had tried to reassure her that as long as they had caught it early, it was highly treatable. She didn't share her greatest fear that indeed they hadn't caught it early at all, and that it had metastasised. Liz hadn't even told Ellen that if it had, the survival rate was grim. It was basically considered incurable. She knew the chances of that were small, but without further tests any prognosis was still possible. And even if it had only spread as far as the lymph nodes and was in fact far more treatable, melanoma had a high incidence of recurrence, and survival rates reduced dramatically with each recurrence. This was the downside of being medically trained – she knew too much. She had to calm herself down and focus on taking it one step at a time.

When the doorbell sounded, everyone froze. Liz looked at her sisters. 'Let's try and act normal, natural, okay?'

They nodded and she went to open the door. Emma breezed in, pausing to air-kiss Liz, then swooping on the other two.

Liz had bought good champagne so that Emma would have nothing to turn her nose up at; besides, it felt like it was the least she could do. She popped the bottle and filled their glasses, before raising hers.

'To Emma and Blake, may you enjoy a very long life together.'

Oh God, she shouldn't have said that. Evie was tearing up already.

'Oh Evie,' Emma chided, putting her arm around her sister's shoulders. 'You're always so emotional.'

Ellen gave Evie a stern older sister glare, and she sniffed, composing herself before gulping down some of her wine.

'So let's sit down, relax,' suggested Liz. 'Tell us all about the madness, Em.'

'Madness is an understatement,' she replied, before launching into an animated, blow-by-blow account of the preparations she was immersed in at the minute. Liz found it hard to concentrate on what she was saying, and she could tell Ellen and Evie weren't even trying. Ellen's eyes kept darting from Emma to Liz expectantly, and Evie was barely holding back the tide of tears threatening to burst any minute. Her face was all pinched and she couldn't stop fidgeting. Liz knew she wouldn't be able to put it off much longer.

The banks finally broke, and Evie started to weep. Emma put a hand on her shoulder. 'I'm only talking about wedding cake and photographers, Ev. You're going to be a mess by the wedding at this rate.'

Evie looked plaintively across at Liz, and Ellen's eyes were still darting anxiously back and forth, her forehead knotted with tension.

Emma glanced around at her sisters, tracking the looks from one to another. 'What's going on here?' she said finally.

'I can't stand this anymore,' Evie gasped. 'Please tell her, Liz.'

'Tell me what?'

'Evie, you need to calm down,' Liz said, keeping her voice level. She turned to look at Emma. 'You know the mole I removed from your back? Well . . .'

She'd had to give this news before, many times. It was always difficult, but this . . . this was something else altogether. This was her sister. She took a breath.

'I'm afraid it's malignant, Em, and more advanced than we would have liked.'

Liz gave that a moment to sink in, but Emma was just sitting there, passive. So she pushed on.

'The results we have so far are not conclusive, we need to do more tests. But it appears to be at least a T3, which means the melanoma has penetrated the dermis, or worse. We need to test your lymph nodes as soon as possible to see how far it's spread, and to stop it spreading any further.'

Emma's expression didn't change. Nothing. She didn't flinch, she hardly even blinked. Eventually she spoke.

'I told you I didn't want to know, Liz. We had a deal.'

'I realise that,' said Liz, 'but when I agreed to that, I thought even if it was a melanoma it would be in situ, which is when it's all contained in the actual mole and hasn't started to penetrate the dermis yet. In that case, removing the mole is all that's needed. I didn't expect it was going to be a T3. If I did, I would have had you at the hospital that afternoon.'

Emma still remained strangely unmoved. 'Well, no you wouldn't have,' she returned. 'I had an engagement that evening, I wouldn't have let you go carting me off to the hospital, and now I wish I'd never let you talk me into removing the mole.'

'Emma, how can you say that?' said Ellen. 'Don't you understand what a melanoma is? It's cancer!'

'Enough with the drama.' Emma rolled her eyes. 'The fact is, if I hadn't asked Liz to my dress fitting, we'd be none the wiser.' An edge was creeping into her voice. 'So, that being the case, I would have gone ahead with my plans, feeling perfectly well, as I do now, until perhaps, just perhaps, Liz might have noticed the mole on the day of the wedding, when she was helping me adjust my veil or some such thing. And she might have had the same level of concern, but not even Liz would have thought she could whisk me away for a quick biopsy before the ceremony. And then I would be off on my honeymoon the next day, with a promise that I would have it checked out on my return, which is what I suggested last week. I should have stuck to my guns.'

Liz shook her head. 'But don't you see, Em, this is good news that we've caught it early, it's a stroke of luck. Between now and when you come back from your honeymoon is enough time for the cancer to spread, but we can arrest it now, before it has the chance.' She hoped.

'You're talking about a few weeks,' said Emma.

'It'll be more than a month,' Ellen pointed out.

'This is just scare tactics.'

'You want to be really scared, Emma?' said Liz. 'If it's already gone into the subcutaneous layer, every single day counts after that. We act now – hopefully before it's made it to the lymph nodes – and your survival rate is very high. We leave it, it can spread anywhere, to your liver, your lungs. And the fact is, melanoma that has metastasised . . .' She took a breath. 'It's terminal, Em.'

'What?' Ellen said, alarmed. 'But you are talking worst case?'

'I'm talking inevitable, if it isn't treated promptly,' said Liz. 'Melanoma is one of the most dangerous malignancies, we need to get things moving as quickly as possible, get you to the hospital at the very latest tomorrow morning. They'll do a scan, and then a surgeon will perform a sentinel node biopsy, as well as a wide excision to remove a margin of tissue from around the site of the original tumour, the mole. The biopsy results will take at least a few days and you might need further surgery after that to remove any affected lymph nodes. But the sooner we know what we're up against, the better.'

Emma was shaking her head. 'It's not possible, I just don't have that kind of time, Liz. You've obviously got no idea how much there is to do – weddings don't organise themselves, you know.'

'I can help,' Evie piped in. 'I'm completely available to do whatever needs doing.'

'I have to work,' said Ellen, 'but that still gives me plenty of time to help as well.'

'It's not that simple,' said Emma. 'Things are too far along now, it'd be more work getting you two up to speed than it would be to do it myself. Any way you look at this, it's simply impossible.'

'Nothing's impossible, Emma,' said Liz. 'This is too important.'

'Look,' she returned, clearly getting frustrated, 'if I go ahead with this now, I presume I'll end up with a big ugly gash across my back from that wide incision. And then you said there could be more surgery if it's in the lymph nodes? Have you forgotten, Liz,

I'm wearing a strapless dress? It's way too late in the day to be altering it now.'

'You don't do this, Emma,' said Liz, 'your chances of walking down the aisle in that dress at all are slim at best.'

'You don't know that, you don't know anything without more tests,' she scoffed. 'And those tests are going to ensure that everything is ruined, aren't they, Liz? And won't that make you happy?'

'What?'

'Oh, come on, I know how pissed off you are that you're the last one not married. While Blake and I weren't married, you didn't look so pathetic, hanging around waiting for a married man who's never going to leave his wife for you. Instead you could point the finger at poor ridiculous Emma, in her ridiculous job, hanging on to Blake, who was obviously just waiting for someone better to come along. Except he wasn't. He just didn't care about having a big wedding, but he knew how important it was to me and that's why he finally proposed.' She got to her feet. 'And that's why I'm going through with this wedding, and nothing's going to stop me, certainly not a stupid little mole on my back that's not even there anymore!'

'Emma, this is crazy,' Liz said. 'You're not being rational.'

'You have to listen to her,' Ellen insisted.

Evie could only sob, nodding in agreement.

'Oh for godsakes, Evie, would you stop crying?' Emma snapped. 'They've sucked you up into this little melodrama. For once in your life don't let them manipulate you.' She glared at Liz and Ellen. 'This is my moment, my time, and you're not going to take it away from me. You'll all finally see what I can do, and maybe you won't think that my life is so pointless.'

'I don't think your life is pointless at all,' Liz said seriously. 'That's why I'm trying to save it.'

Emma looked unfazed. 'Well I'm not going to let you ruin my wedding day,' she said, her voice quiet but determined. She walked back over to the coffee table and picked up her champagne glass, sculling back what was left. 'Thanks for the drink, girls. It's been a blast. See you at the church.'

With that she picked up her handbag and walked over to the door, letting herself out without looking back at them.

Ellen turned to Liz. 'You let her just walk out?'

'What else was I supposed to do? Crash tackle her to the floor and tie her up?'

'So you think it'll be okay to wait till after the wedding?'

'Of course I don't.' She picked up the phone. 'I'm calling Blake.'

*

After she'd pulled into her space in the basement carpark, Emma sat for a moment collecting her thoughts. Blake was already home, his car parked next to hers. She was wondering how best to play this with him. He was going to find out eventually, she was sure Liz would drag him into it. So it was better if it came from her first. She hadn't even mentioned the mole coming off yet, which had required a little subterfuge in the past week, mostly in the bathroom. Lucky they weren't having much sex at the moment, they were both too exhausted, so she had managed to keep herself covered up in bed.

So, she decided, offhand was the best approach.

'Oh, by the way, I had a mole taken off last week, turns out it's malignant.'

No, she couldn't use that word offhandedly. Malignant. What an ugly word it was, it actually sounded malignant.

How about, '. . . turns out it was a melanoma. But it's all gone now. I'll have some follow-up tests when we get back from our honeymoon, just to make sure.'

That was better.

She got out of the car and caught the lift up to their floor, rehearsing the words over in her head, practising the tone. The good thing was that she knew Blake wouldn't make a big deal about it. He would take her lead – if Emma was unconcerned, he would see no reason to be otherwise, and he certainly wouldn't waste energy stressing about it.

She stepped out of the lift and walked up the hall to the apartment. She let herself in, but before she had tossed her keys into the bowl or put her bag down, Blake was coming towards her up the hall.

'Emma, I've just spoken to Liz,' he said urgently, still holding the phone in his hand.

She sighed. 'Oh for goodness sake,' she said, making her annoyance plain. 'She wasn't going on about the mole, was she?'

'The mole?' he said. 'You mean the malignant melanoma?'

'Which is a mole by any other name,' she said lightly, walking past him out into the living room. 'Isn't mole an ugly name, I wonder who came up with it. I mean, freckle is cute, you can spin "freckle", you can't do much with "mole".'

'Emma, this sounds serious,' Blake persisted, following her.

She continued her way across to their bedroom. Don't get drawn into this, keep it offhand, appear unaffected. He will follow your lead.

'Liz is overreacting, Blake,' she said. 'You know she has a bee in her bonnet about solariums, she was just trying to frighten me.'

'I don't think so, Em. She explained everything to me, that it's a T3, which means it could have spread. You have to go and have more tests.'

'Of course I will,' she assured him, crossing to the walk-in and slipping off her shoes. 'I'm not stupid, Blake. I've told her to book me in for everything once we're back from the honeymoon.'

'Liz said you can't wait that long.'

'Dear oh dear, Blake,' she shook her head. 'I've never heard you pay so much attention to one of my sisters.'

'Emma, she's a doctor!'

'Which means she knows too much, and she's overreacting.'

'What's wrong with playing it safe?' he urged. 'Liz said it's only a couple of days in hospital.'

'Ha! Have you seen my schedule for the next few weeks, Blake? There are just not enough hours in the day already, and I certainly don't have a couple of days to spare –'

'Emma,' he interrupted firmly. 'I don't think you understand how serious this is.'

'No, it's you who doesn't understand what's really going on here,' she said, turning around to face him. 'You know what my sisters are like. They have seized on one tiny little mole to sabotage my wedding, because they can't stand that after all their gossiping and sniping that I'd never get you to marry me, that's exactly what's going to happen. They know my wedding will be amazing and they want to ruin it for me, because they're so miserable in their own lives. Liz has wasted more than a decade on an opportunistic adulterer, and Ellen's perfect marriage was a total lie, and Evie . . . well, Evie will go along with whatever they tell her to. But I'm not a such a pushover. I'm not going to let them win.'

Blake stood there, staring at her. 'Are you listening to yourself?' he said finally.

'What?'

'You're actually refusing treatment for cancer so that this fucking circus can go ahead?'

She didn't like his tone. 'I'm not refusing treatment, Blake, just delaying it. Why is everyone making such a big deal about this? I've got well and truly enough on my plate . . .'

While she changed her clothes inside the walk-in, Emma gave him a rundown of the next few days, partly to show him how impossible it was to fit in time-consuming tests and procedures, but mostly just to move the conversation along. Hopefully they could start to talk about something else. She'd had enough discussion about her mole for one night. When she walked out of the wardrobe a few minutes later, Blake had opened a suitcase on the bed and was zipping up his toiletries bag. He tossed it into the suitcase and went to walk past her.

'What are you doing?'

'I'm not going to be a part of this, Emma.'

She turned around, watching him as he plucked socks and underpants and T-shirts from his drawers.

'Blake, what are you talking about?'

'I've had enough,' he said, walking past her again and tossing the things into the bag. 'I can't do this anymore, I'm out.'

He walked back to the robe and started to take shirts off hangers.

'You have got to be kidding me,' Emma said. She was really beginning to get pissed off now. How dare Liz interfere like this? She had a good mind to ring her up and tell her off. And she was going to, but later – she had to deal with Blake's tantrum first.

'Stop this, Blake,' Emma said. 'We have enough to do without you pulling your entire wardrobe apart just to make a point.'

He didn't respond as he passed by her again with a pile of shirts over his arm. He started to pack them into the suitcase.

'This is all about the cost, isn't it?' said Emma.

Blake looked up at her then. 'You're kidding, you think that's what this is about?' He shook his head. 'Read my lips, Emma. I'm out. I'm leaving. It's over.'

She scowled at him. 'I know you never wanted this wedding, but this is low, to pull out now and to pretend to use my mole as your excuse.'

He ignored her, walking back into the robe and returning with a stack of jeans and trousers.

'I can't believe this,' she said, planting her hands on her hips. 'You must have been so thrilled when Liz called, handing you a pass-out on a silver platter. If you think anyone is going to see this as anything but you being a selfish, childish prat, then you're mistaken. I'll never forgive you, Blake. You don't get to ruin the wedding and then let things go back to the way they were. There's no coming back from this.'

Her voice was rising more shrilly as he moved around the room, calmly collecting his belongings, totally unmoved by what she was saying.

'You walk out of here, Blake,' she cried as he closed up his suitcase and picked it up off the bed, 'and that's it. I never want to see you again.'

He didn't even glance in her direction as he strode out of the bedroom. It was as though she wasn't there.

'Blake, I'm warning you, this is your last chance. I won't take you back if you do this to me.'

He picked up his laptop case and slung the strap over his shoulder, then he walked up the hall, took his keys from the bowl and left the apartment, without even looking back.

Emma stood there trembling so hard that her legs finally gave out and she collapsed onto the floor, sobbing.

*

There was nothing left for them to do at Liz's except sit around and wait until they heard from either Emma or Blake. Liz told Ellen and Evie they might as well go home, that she'd keep them posted of any developments.

'Are you sure?' said Ellen. 'I don't mind waiting with you. Tim has the kids for the night.'

Ellen had got straight to the point when she'd called Tim yesterday. 'Emma has a malignant melanoma. I need to be with her Friday night and I'd appreciate if the kids could stay with you so I don't have to worry about getting back to them.'

'Sure, of course,' he'd said, obviously shocked. 'How's Emma taking it?'

'We don't know yet.'

Liz assured Ellen now that she didn't need to wait around. 'It'll probably take Blake most of the night to talk her around anyway.' She looked across at Evie – her eyes were all swollen and red. 'You're exhausted, Evie, and you've got a drive ahead of you. I think you should both go home and we should all try to get a good night's sleep. Hopefully we'll need it because we'll be supporting Emma the rest of the weekend, and who knows how long after that . . .' she added, her voice trailing away.

Ellen nodded. 'You'll let us know if you hear anything, though?'

'Absolutely.'

When Ellen got into her car, she took out her phone and rang Finn. She just wanted to hear his voice. She'd done the same the night after Liz had called. She'd poured out the whole story to him, and he'd just listened. That was all she needed right now.

'How'd it go?' he asked when he picked up.

'Not very well.'

'Where are you now? Do you want me to come over?'

'I'm just leaving Liz's.'

'So come over here.'

'I don't think I'm going to be very good company, Finn.'

'Come on, you don't want to be on your own, Ellen. The kids are with Tim, aren't they?'

She hesitated. 'Well . . . I don't know where you live.'

*

Liz dashed to grab the phone when it started to ring, hoping it would be Blake or Emma. But it was only Andrew.

'How'd it go?' he asked.

Liz paused before answering him. She'd had to tell him what was going on. He'd been so upset by her brush-off last week he'd actually turned up at her apartment on the Saturday morning, something he'd never done in all their years together. Saturday mornings he was always too busy with the family. But apparently he had made some excuse to Jennifer about needing to check on a patient, and had subsequently fronted up at her place at eight thirty in the morning. He didn't call first, and that was unusual in itself. Liz was still in bed, though awake, and when she heard the quick knock followed by the key in the lock, it gave her a fright for a moment. Andrew sung out as soon as he opened the door and Liz scrambled off the bed, but suddenly he was in the doorway, blocking her way. He looked like he was scanning the room, as if he thought he was going to find someone there. When Liz suggested as much, he brushed it off, saying she was being paranoid.

'No, Andrew, you're the one showing up early on a Saturday morning, with no phone call or any warning at all, and barging in here before I can even get out of bed. What's going on?'

He dropped down to sit on the bed then, holding his head in his hands. 'It's been weeks, Liz. You were coming up with all these new excuses, comedy festivals and dress fittings, and then last night you didn't even bother with an excuse, you just hung up on me and then you turned your phone off. What was I supposed to think?'

Liz sighed quietly. She was only allowed to call Andrew at work. She did have his mobile number, but that was to be used only if it was absolutely essential and she couldn't get on to him any other way. He'd stored her number as 'Hospital records', because no one in that section would ever call a surgeon on his mobile, but Jennifer didn't know that. And Liz was only ever to text, *Please contact ASAP*. Then, when he was able, he would call her back.

So Liz felt like saying to him that she didn't care what he had been driven to think, whether he'd been worried or frustrated, if he didn't like being nudged out of her life without an explanation. But instead, she calmly told him what had happened with Emma the previous night. Although he was concerned for both Liz and her sister, the relief he obviously felt at there being a reasonable excuse for her behaviour drowned out everything else. And soon he was kissing her, and soon after they were making love. And then he was gone again, and Liz felt nothing but resentment.

He had kept in touch with her this week to find out Emma's results and had shown appropriate sympathy, if not exactly empathy. Then he'd called earlier to say he could probably make it over for a while tonight, so she'd told him what was going on.

And now Liz was sitting here, holding the phone to her ear, contemplating what to tell him. If she admitted that everyone had gone, he'd come over and they'd have sex, and then he'd go again. And he would feel a lot better, but she would not.

Finally Liz said, 'Um, I can't really talk right now, Andrew.'

'They're all still there?'

'Emma's being very stubborn,' she said, which was the truth.

'Okay.' He paused. 'So I guess I won't see you tonight.'

'No, it doesn't look like it.'

'She'll come around, Lizzie,' he said. 'You know this is just a standard reaction to the shock.'

'Mm.'

'If there's anything I can do . . .'

'I'll let you know.'

*

Evie arrived home to an empty house in darkness. She had arranged for Craig and the kids to go over to his mother's for dinner, though she'd let him think that it was his mother's idea. Unfortunately, as it turned out, she was unable to join them because she had to go and help Emma with something for the wedding. She could never have told Craig her sister simply needed cheering up. The chill between them had still not thawed. Weeks had passed and nothing had been said about that night, very little conversation had passed between them at all. They were polite but stilted; Evie focused on the kids,

Craig spent most of his time out in the garage or in front of the television. It seemed a married couple could carry on for quite an extended period without really communicating.

Evie was about to turn on the main lights now, but she hesitated. There was something comforting about the darkness, only the moonlight coming in through the windows, casting shadows across the carpet. Evie walked around the house, turning on a lamp here and there, enjoying the peace and the stillness. Time to herself to think.

The problem was that neither of them had the skills to deal with conflict. Evie had always just smoothed things over between them in the past, accommodated. But she wasn't prepared to do that this time. She didn't really want to be around Craig right now, but she wasn't sure if that was how she'd feel forever. And it was a huge step, an enormous, scary step to contemplate some kind of separation, even if it was only temporary. For the first time Evie realised just how brave Ellen had been. She and Craig were like two people on a raft in the middle of the ocean, with no oars or compass or anything, counting on the tide to bring them safely back to land.

But it was rapidly becoming clear to Evie that life was too short to drift along like that. Look at what was happening to Emma. She was only thirty-six . . . she was too young . . . it was only a mole . . .

Evie couldn't bear to contemplate it. Liz had to put the worst-case scenario to Emma to frighten her into action. Emma could not possibly die from a mole on her back, that would be so . . . pointless, wouldn't it? Not that there was anything stopping people from dying pointless deaths. It happened all the time.

No, she wasn't even going to think about that. Emma would come around, she was just in shock, and surely Blake would talk some sense into her? Surely she would listen to him?

Evie supposed she should call Craig, let him know she was home earlier than expected. She was going to have to tell him about Emma, but she was reluctant. This was the kind of thing that would brush everything else under the carpet. But she was going to have to tell him eventually – she had to be available for Emma, so he was going to have to step up and take over with the kids. She was not going to accommodate him this time. She walked over to bag on the kitchen bench, but then she stopped, her hand on her phone, unable to pick it up.

She turned away and strode out of the kitchen and up the stairs to her bedroom. She changed into her walking gear, laced up her shoes and picked up her hoodie. Downstairs she found the torch she kept in the hall cupboard. She'd never walked at night before, a torch was probably a good idea. She pulled on the hoodie and zipped it up, grabbed her keys and walked out through the front door, closing it behind her.

*

Ellen had made it to Finn's place without incident. He'd given her clear directions and it wasn't hard to find. She just had to stay on the main road around the corner from his garage, all the way till she turned off into his street in Abbotsford. She parked out the front and climbed out of the car, peering up at the house. It was a charming little single-fronted weatherboard cottage, very neat and tidy – at least it appeared to be in the half-light of the street lamps. She walked up to the gate where a pebble path led to the front porch, flanked on either side by a clipped hedge. She had to admit she was a little surprised. Somewhere in the back of her mind she'd imagined Finn living in an old fibro house with a great big yard full of old cars and spare parts and tyres. She could hear her sisters crying, 'Snob!' Maybe they were right.

Just then the front door opened. 'Hey,' Finn said, backlit by the light inside so that he was in silhouette. 'I thought I heard a car.'

Ellen just gazed up at him, and all the sadness and fear and turmoil she'd been suppressing all day rose up, threatening to engulf her.

'Are you okay?' he asked, stepping down off the threshold.

Ellen pushed through the gate and up the path to the steps, straight into his arms, where she collapsed into tears. She buried her face in his chest and he held her tight. 'It's okay, it's going to be okay,' he kept saying in a low voice, close to her ear. Eventually he drew her inside the house, closing the door behind them.

'You're freezing, Ellen,' he said, taking her hands in his and rubbing them. 'Didn't you have a jacket or something warm?'

She shook her head. It had been one of those four-seasons-in-one spring days, quite balmy when she'd left the house this morning, but the wind had come up and it was getting chilly now. She hadn't even thought to turn the heater on in the car, her mind had been on other things.

Finn was rubbing her arms now. 'Are you hungry, do you want something to eat?'

'No,' she said wearily.

'You look wrecked. Come in here and lie down for a while, let's warm you up.'

Ellen let him lead her into the bedroom off the hall. He threw back the doona and she dropped gratefully onto the bed, utterly drained. Finn took her shoes off her feet, then he climbed onto the bed behind her and covered them both with the doona, spooning into her back. His body was warm, the doona cosy; Ellen felt as though she was enclosed in a cocoon.

'Do you want to talk about it?' Finn said after a while.

'Hm . . .' she murmured. 'Emma's refusing to have follow-up tests or any treatment until after the honeymoon. Liz said that's too long to wait.'

'Why won't she listen to her? Liz is the doctor, isn't she?'

'She thinks we're just trying to sabotage her wedding because we're jealous.'

'Seriously?'

'It's my fault. Oh, we're all to blame in our different ways. But I never made it a secret that I thought she was frivolous, that what I did was so much more important, shaping young minds and all. And I had children of my own as well. What had she brought to the world?'

'That's not why this happened, Ellen.'

'Maybe not, but if it's even part of the reason she's reacting this way, I'll never forgive myself. The longer she waits, the greater the chance the cancer will spread, and Liz said when melanoma metastasises it's terminal.'

'You can't blame yourself.'

'I've just been wondering though,' Ellen murmured, 'the whole way here, how can I ever have treated her life as less important?'

Her voice caught in her throat, and Finn held her close as she wept quietly, until finally, overcome with exhaustion and grief, she drifted off to sleep.

*

As Evie approached the house, after walking for nearly an hour, she saw Craig's car parked next to hers in the driveway. Bugger. She hadn't thought about that, that he might get home before her. This would set him off.

She took a deep breath and walked determinedly up to the house, using her key to let herself in through the door.

'Evie, is that you?' he said, coming into the hall. 'Where the hell have you been?'

She put the torch down on the hall table. 'I went for a walk,' she said calmly.

'What the . . .?' he said. 'At this time of night? I've been worried out of my mind. Your car's here, and your phone's here, but you're nowhere to be found.'

'I needed to clear my head,' she said, unzipping her hoodie without meeting his eyes. 'Are the kids still awake?' she said, heading for the stairs.

He grabbed her arm. She stopped, looking down at his hand and then back up at him, her expression defiant. He released her.

'Emma has a melanoma,' Evie said, lowering her voice.

'What?'

'She has skin cancer. It's serious. So I needed to clear my head,' she repeated the words slowly and firmly.

He was just staring at her. 'Is she . . . are you all right?'

'I'm going up to see the kids,' she said, turning away and walking up the stairs.

Morning

'Ellen . . . Ellen . . .'

It was Finn, nudging her gently. Her brain slowly clicked into gear, and then she jumped, startled. 'What is it? What's happened?' she said urgently, scrambling to sit up.

'It's okay,' he said. 'Your phone was ringing. By the time I found it in your bag, it had stopped,' he said, handing it to her.

Ellen stared at the notification for the missed call, but she couldn't see clearly. Her eyes were still bleary from sleep, and the room was dark. 'What time is it?' she said, squinting at the screen.

'It's quarter to seven,' he said, reaching for the cord of the blind behind the bed and twisting it so that light slanted into the room.

Ellen blinked as her eyes adjusted. Finn was already dressed for work, she noticed. She looked down at the screen of her phone again. The missed call was from Liz. She pressed to call back, bringing the phone to her ear.

'Who was it?' he asked.

'Liz,' she said, pushing back the covers. Finn moved out of her way as she swung her legs over the edge of the bed.

'Hi, it's me,' she said when Liz answered.

'I've spent the night with Emma. Blake left her.'

'What?'

'Blake's gone,' Liz said. 'He walked out on her last night.'

'Oh my God, how's Emma?' She felt Finn's hand come to rest on her back.

'She's a mess, but she's prepared to go through with the tests. She's getting ready now, and then I'll take her to the hospital. Can you meet us there?'

'Yeah, of course,' she said, standing up, her head foggy. 'I have to change, and . . .'

'Take your time, no hurry,' said Liz. 'It's going to be a long day.'

'Okay, I'll see you as soon as I can get there.' She hung up the phone, spotting her shoes on the floor. She bent down to put them on.

'What's going on?' Finn asked, still sitting on the bed, watching her.

'Emma's agreed to have the tests,' she explained. 'I have to get to the hospital.'

'I made you tea,' he said, reaching for the cup on the bedside table.

'Sorry, I don't have time,' said Ellen. 'I'm going to have to go home first and shower and change, I've been in these clothes since yesterday morning.'

'I was going to make you some breakfast,' said Finn, getting to his feet.

'Thanks, but I really don't have time,' she repeated, looking around. 'Where's my bag?'

'It's out in the hall.'

Ellen dashed past him out of the room and picked up her bag from the floor, rummaging for her keys. She felt his hand on her shoulder.

'Ellen, promise me you'll eat,' he said. 'You're going to need something in your stomach.'

'Hm,' she said distractedly as she felt for her keys.

'Listen, I have to go into work, at least open up,' he said. 'I couldn't get onto Dave. But I could meet you at the hospital later.'

She looked up at him. 'Why would you do that?'

He shrugged. 'I don't know, for support.'

'That's not necessary, Finn.'

'I know it's not necessary, Ellen, I just want to . . . be there for you, I guess.'

'Look, I'll be with my sisters, we have each other, I'll be fine,' she said, hooking her bag over her shoulder.

'Okay,' he said, considering her. 'Whatever you want.'

He opened the door for her and stood back as she ducked out past him.

'Call me later?' he said as she stepped off the threshold.

She glanced back. 'I'll try.'

*

Evie hung up the phone and took a moment to catch her breath, blinking back tears. Poor Emma. And *damn* Blake to hell. She composed herself and then walked back out to the kitchen, where everyone was still eating breakfast.

'Craig, can I see you out here for a minute?' she said.

'I come too, Mummy?' said Cody, scrambling to get off his chair.

'No, honey. Finish your breakfast.'

'But I finshed orready.'

'Cody,' Craig said firmly, 'do as your mother says. We'll only be a minute.'

He followed her through the laundry and out the back door. Evie turned around to face him.

'Was that Emma on the phone?' he asked.

'No, it was Liz. She's taking Emma to the hospital. I have to meet them there, so you're going to have to mind the kids.'

'Yeah, sure.'

'I don't know how long I'll be, probably all day.'

'That's fine, take all the time you need, I'll handle things here.' He took a step towards her but she backed away. 'Evie, let's not keep this up now.'

'Craig,' she said, 'it's not going to go away because of this. We're going to have to deal with what happened, but now is not the time.'

He nodded. 'I know that. But –'

'Just do as I ask,' she said. 'And don't say anything to the kids. I'm just helping Aunty Emma with the wedding, okay?'

Craig looked at her, frowning. 'Is there still going to be a wedding?'

Evie felt a lump in her throat. 'I don't know what's going to happen,' she said, her voice wavering. 'For now we just have to get her through this.'

'Evie . . .'
'I have to get going,' she said, walking past him back to the door.
'Evie,' he said again.
She turned around to look at him.
'Tell Emma . . .'
'I will,' she said, and she opened the door and went inside.

Melanoma unit

'What can we do? I feel so helpless.'

'We just have to wait, Evie,' said Liz. 'These scans can take a while.'

Ellen and Evie hadn't seen Emma yet; she'd been taken off behind closed doors before they'd arrived at the hospital. Liz had been in and out, keeping them informed. She had given Emma a thorough examination and was relieved to report that there were no other suspect lesions. Now they were preparing Emma for a scan of her lymph nodes. Once that was underway, Liz had come through to wait with her sisters.

'So what is this scan?' Evie asked. 'Is it like an MRI?'

Liz shook her head. 'An MRI can't detect lymph nodes.'

'So this is to check if the cancer has spread to her lymph nodes?' said Ellen.

'No, you can only tell that by actually dissecting the nodes and examining them under a microscope.'

Evie frowned. 'But they couldn't do that to all her lymph nodes, could they?'

'No, of course not,' said Liz. 'They used to take out whole clusters in the most obvious area. But that can have some pretty nasty side effects. Somebody eventually worked out that there are sentinel nodes, which are the first nodes that will be reached by cancer cells when they spread. So nowadays they inject a radio-active tracing substance into the area of the original tumour, and it actually maps out the pattern the cancer would take, all the way to the sentinel nodes. Then they only have to remove those particular nodes for dissection. So Emma will only have a tiny scar, maybe a couple of centimetres under her arm, and none of the nasty side effects.'

'And that's it?' said Evie.

'Well, yes, for the biopsy. But they also have to do what's called a wide excision around where the melanoma was, and take a good chunk of the tissue away to be safe.'

'So they'll do the biopsy today?' asked Ellen.

Liz shook her head. 'They do that at the same time as the wide excision. Right now they're scanning to locate the sentinel lymph node in the first place. They'll take pictures, and then they'll actually mark the spot with an X on Emma's skin, so that Rob, the surgeon, knows where to go in.'

Evie frowned. 'That doesn't sound very high-tech.'

'He doesn't just go by that,' Liz assured her. 'He'll use a gamma probe to pick up the path of the tracer they use today, and he'll also inject a dye into the original site of the tumour, which will follow the lymph paths as well, so he can very precisely pinpoint the sentinel nodes.'

'It still seems like a risk to me to take only a couple,' said Evie. 'Wouldn't it be better if they just took out a bigger section, to be safe? Like they do with that other thing you said, the excision?'

'That's different,' said Liz. 'Like I said before, a block lymph dissection has some very nasty side effects. It can disrupt lymph drainage in the area, causing serious swelling and infection, mobility problems – it can be really awful. So this method avoids all that. Of course if they do find cancer cells in the sentinel node, they'll have to do a block dissection after that, but it's essential then, it's actually removing cancer cells you know are present. It's a bit extreme to do that just to check. But aside from all that, they actually get a much more accurate result this way.'

'Why is that?'

'Well, the pathologist can be way more thorough examining just two nodes, compared to twenty or more in a clump. This method has the highest reliability rate for detecting the spread of cancer.'

'Does that translate into survival rates?' asked Ellen.

'Not directly, but the fact is, early and accurate detection is the key, especially with melanoma. If they know exactly where the cancer cells are, they can get in and get them out as quickly as possible before they spread further.'

'So how soon can they do the surgery?'

'They usually schedule it the day after the scan, or sometimes later the same day if they start early,' said Liz. 'I had to call in a friend of mine especially to consult on a Saturday, and we both had to twist some arms to get Emma scanned today, but this way she'll be all ready for surgery on Monday.'

'They might put it off as late as Monday?' said Ellen.

'It's just going to be more difficult to get together a surgical team on a Sunday,' said Liz. 'But Rob is a really good guy, and an amazing surgeon. I trust him to do what's best. He'll only put it off till Monday if he thinks it's safe to do so.'

'And how long after that will we know if it's spread?'

'It takes around five to seven days for the full pathology report, maybe a little sooner for preliminary results.'

Evie groaned. 'I hate all this waiting,' she said, getting up and walking over to the window.

'You haven't told us what happened with Blake,' Ellen said to Liz.

She shook her head. 'Emma was so distressed when she called. She said he just packed a bag and walked out. He said he didn't want to go through with it anymore.'

'What a bastard, to leave her now.'

Liz shrugged. 'She said he'd been complaining about how much the wedding was costing . . . she reckoned he seized upon this as an excuse to get out of it.'

'What kind of a man would do that?' said Evie.

'You said he was upset when you called and told him about the melanoma?' said Ellen.

'He was,' Liz said. 'He was in shock. I can't explain it. Emma was so distraught, I couldn't really get much sense out of her, I had to give her something to get her to sleep. In the end I was just glad she agreed to come in for the tests. I wanted to focus on that.'

'Liz.'

She looked around as Rob McGrath strode into the waiting area.

'Hi Rob, how did it go?' said Liz, getting to her feet.

'It all went fine,' he said, glancing at Ellen and Evie as they drew closer.

'These are my sisters, and Emma's sisters,' said Liz. 'Ellen and Evie, this is Dr Rob McGrath.'

'All your names start with E?' he remarked with an amused smile.

'Take that up with our parents,' said Liz.

'Well, anyway, we've located the sentinel nodes under the arm, as expected. The tracer flowed nice and evenly, so it's all looking as good as we can hope at this stage. I've booked a theatre for Monday. I bumped her up the list so she'll be first cab off the rank at seven.'

'Thanks, Rob.'

'No worries,' he said. 'But now I have to head home. It's Madeleine's birthday party today.'

'Oh, Rob, why didn't you say?' said Liz. 'I feel terrible.'

He shook his head. 'She has one every year. It's a makeover thing this time, I was just in the way,' he added with a grin.

'That's so good of you,' said Evie.

'I'll be home before she blows out the candles,' he dismissed, glancing at his watch. 'Can I have a word, Liz? Maybe you can walk me out?'

'Sure.'

Soon after Liz had left with Rob, Emma was escorted into the waiting room by a nurse.

'Hi,' she said as they jumped up to greet her. 'You both came.'

'Of course we did,' said Ellen, giving her a kiss on the cheek.

'Where's Liz?'

'She's just seeing Dr McGrath out, she'll be back.'

'Hm,' said Emma, raising an eyebrow. 'They make a pretty cute couple, those two, don't you reckon?'

'He's going home to his daughter's birthday party,' Evie told her.

'Drats, foiled again.' Emma took a seat, wincing a little as she eased her back against the chair.

'Did it hurt?' asked Evie as she and Ellen sat down again.

Emma shrugged. 'It stung a little when they injected the stuff. After that it was just boring. It takes forever.' She looked at them.

'Thanks for coming all the way in,' she said. 'After the way I carried on last night . . .'

'Don't worry about it,' said Ellen. 'You were in shock.'

'I'm so sorry about Blake,' said Evie.

Emma blinked, her eyes glassy. 'Yeah well, so much for "in sickness and in health", eh? It's just as well this happened before we went through with the wedding,' she added, but then her face crumpled.

Ellen reached over to take her hand, while Evie jumped up to sit on the other side of Emma, putting her arm around her.

'It doesn't feel real,' Emma sniffed. 'None of this feels real. One day I'm running around with my whole life ahead of me . . . and the next . . .'

'You still have your whole life ahead of you,' Ellen said firmly. 'You've done the right thing, Em, getting on to this early. You are going to have a long, healthy life . . .'

'Without Blake,' she said sadly. 'He was my life.'

They didn't know what to say to that.

'Do you want something to eat?' was the best Evie could do.

Emma shook her head. 'I'm not hungry,' she sighed. 'God, there are so many calls I'm going to have to make.'

'You don't have to worry about that now,' said Ellen.

'But they will have to be made soon,' Emma insisted. 'Things have to be cancelled. People have to be informed.'

'I could do all that for you,' said Ellen. 'Maybe you could make a list?'

'There's a folder, at the apartment.' Emma paused. 'God, the apartment . . . what am I going to do about the apartment? I can't afford it on my own.'

'Emma,' said Ellen, 'you really don't have to worry about that now. Blake hasn't dropped off the edge of the earth.'

'Pity,' Emma muttered.

'What I was getting at,' Ellen explained, 'is that he's going to have to sort out all of that with you, but that doesn't have to happen today, or tomorrow, or this week or next. For now, tell me where I can find this folder, and I'll pick it up on my way home and start making the calls.'

'Or I could do all that?' Evie offered. 'You have to work next week, Len. I have more time.'

Ellen nodded. 'See, Em? We'll work it out.'

But she seemed deep in thought, staring out in front of her, a worried frown on her face.

'Emma, seriously, the only thing you should be worrying about is getting through this –'

'And getting well,' Evie added.

Emma stirred. 'Sure, I know. But I was just wandering, whether I'd prefer you to tell everyone that I've got cancer, or that Blake dumped me.' She glanced from one to the other. 'Which one sounds better, or worse, if you know what I mean?'

Evie looked faintly horrified, but Ellen detected a glint in Emma's eye.

'Well, cancer's always going to get you the sympathy vote, naturally,' said Ellen. 'And the dumping thing, that never spins well, does it?'

'You're right,' Emma agreed. 'Cancer's more noble, more heroic. Whereas being dumped is just pathetic.'

'You're not pathetic, Emma!' Evie declared. 'You mustn't say things like that about yourself.'

Emma and Ellen both broke into wide grins. Evie groaned.

'Why do I always let you guys suck me in?' she said. 'Every time!'

Liz came back into the waiting area and pulled up a chair. 'Hey, how are you doing?' she asked Emma.

'I'm okay,' she said. 'I hear that cute doctor is married.'

'All the cute ones are,' Liz sighed. 'Anyway, he's booked you in for surgery Monday morning.'

'He's waiting till Monday?'

'That's a good sign.'

Emma sighed. 'Well, at least I can go home in the meantime.'

'Yeah, you can, but you'll have to be back again in the morning,' said Liz. 'Rob's ordered more tests for tomorrow. He wants to get them out of the way so that you're ready to go first thing Monday.'

'More tests?' Emma frowned.

'It's routine to do a chest X-ray to check your fitness for surgery.' And to look for signs of spread to the lungs, but Liz decided to keep that part to herself. 'And Rob thinks it's worth doing a complete MRI, just so we have the full picture.'

'So they can see how far the cancer has spread?' Emma said bluntly.

'Emma, the chances of that are very small, and it's too early to detect anything on an MRI anyway.'

'So why are they doing it?' Ellen asked.

'To have a point of comparison for the future,' said Emma. 'Isn't that right, Liz?'

'What does she mean?' Evie was getting confused.

'Yes, okay,' Liz said. 'It will give us a map of your internal organs so if there are any concerns in the future we will have a point of comparison, as you put it. But Em, they're just being thorough. Please try not to worry, you're in good hands, the best.'

Emma sighed. 'Okay. So how early do I have to come in?'

'Earlier the better,' said Liz.

'I don't really want to stay in that apartment alone tonight.'

'You won't have to,' said Liz, covering her hand. 'You can come home with me if you like. Or I'll stay at the apartment with you.'

'Or I will.'

'Or I will.'

'I'll be the one staying with her.'

All four of them turned around and cried 'Mum!' in unison.

'What are you doing here?' said Emma, as Evelyn walked over to them. 'Aren't you supposed to be climbing Machu Picchu right about now?'

'It's not going anywhere,' Evelyn dismissed, leaning down to kiss her daughter on the cheek.

'Is Dad with you?'

'No ... or I should say yes,' she corrected herself. 'He's here in Sydney, but he's gone with Eddie to book us into one of those serviced apartments.'

'Why not just stay with me?' said Liz.

'Or me?'

'Or me?'

'You girls are like a gaggle of geese when you get together,' said Evelyn. 'We wanted to be nice and close to the hospital, and there are apartments just up the road. Dad and Eddie both send big kisses,' she said as Evie made room for her so she could sit next to Emma. 'They'll be here just as soon as they've checked in and dropped off the luggage. I had them bring me straight here from the airport.'

Emma frowned. 'Do you all think I'm about to croak it?'

'No!' the gaggle cried at once.

'But when did you find out about this?' Emma asked her mother. 'And how did you get home so quickly?'

'I called Mum and Dad when the initial results came through,' Liz broke in. It had been an instinctive reaction. She'd just needed to talk to her mum and dad. She hadn't expected them to jump on a plane and fly straight home though.

'Which was just as well,' Evelyn was saying, 'because she caught us barely hours before we were about to leave on the trek. After that, communication would have been patchy at best. So we went straight to the airport and waited on standby for the next available flight.'

'You didn't have to come all the way back,' said Emma.

'Nonsense,' said Evelyn. 'You think we would have gone ahead, happily marching up Machu Picchu with our daughter in the hospital?' She gave Emma's hand a quick squeeze, shaking her head. 'Wait till you have children of your own, then you'll understand.' She glanced around. 'Where is Blake anyway?'

*

The decision was finally made that Liz and Evelyn would take Emma home to her apartment so that she could pack up some things for her hospital stay. If she didn't feel like sleeping the night there, she could go back and stay with her parents. Ellen and Evie both left after their father and Eddie arrived. There were more than enough people to fuss over Emma, and they didn't want to overwhelm her. Ellen turned on her phone as she left the hospital building – there were several messages from Finn, both voicemail and text. The last one had been sent around midday. *I guess you had to keep your phone off. Call me when you can. Thinking of you.*

She stared at the phone for a while. This was really none of his business. Sure, she supposed he was being considerate, but at the same time he was being somewhat *in*considerate expecting Ellen to keep him updated. He didn't even know Emma. It would have been better if he'd just left it at 'Thinking of you'.

By the time Ellen got to her car she'd composed a text message in her head, which she typed into her phone once she'd unlocked the door and climbed into the driver's seat.

More tests tomorrow. Picking up kids now. Thanks for your concern.

After the message was sent, Ellen rang Tim.

'How are you?' he said when he answered.

'Oh, okay, we're getting through it.'

'So what's happening?'

Ellen didn't feel like 'sharing' with Tim either – it was really none of his business anymore, and she certainly wasn't going to get any comfort from going over it with him, so why should she?

'Look, I'm really beat, so I'd just like to come and get the kids.'

'Are you sure? I can keep them here if you want.'

'I think I'd like to be with them tonight,' said Ellen. 'And anyway, I should talk to them about what's going on . . .'

'Oh, that's okay, I've already told them.'

'What? Why did you do that?'

'Well, after you messaged this morning and said you were going to be at the hospital, I had to tell them something.'

'But you didn't know anything,' said Ellen. 'What did you say to them?'

'I explained Emma has skin cancer and that she'd been taken to hospital, and you wanted to be with her. But don't worry, when they asked if she was going to die, I told them no one knows yet.'

Jesus, it was like dealing with an adolescent.

'All right, I'm on my way now,' she said, trying to stay calm. 'Please ask the kids to get ready. And don't tell them anything else, Tim, because you don't actually know anything else, right?'

Sunday morning

'Mum, there's someone at the door to see you,' Sam called.

Ellen stepped into the hall and was immediately shocked to see Finn through the open doorway, standing on the front porch. What the hell was he doing here? She had to think quickly.

'Oh, hi there,' she said, walking slowly up the hall. 'Sam, this is the mechanic who fixed the car a little while ago, you remember?'

'Hey,' Sam said with a nod.

'Hey, Sam,' Finn returned.

'You must be here about that spare key, Mr Finlayson?' Ellen said as she came closer to the doorway.

'Ah . . . yeah,' he said warily.

'You didn't need to bring it over on a Sunday,' said Ellen, with an awkward glance sideways at Sam. He just shrugged and wandered back down the hall to the kitchen. Ellen watched him over her shoulder, and when he was out of sight she stepped quickly through the door, closing it behind her.

'What are you doing here?' she hissed.

'I just wanted to see how you were,' said Finn.

'My kids are here!' Ellen declared. 'You did get my message, didn't you?'

'Yes I did,' Finn said in a level voice.

'Well what were you thinking?'

'I was thinking about you.'

'Shh!' she exclaimed in a whisper. 'What if they hear you?'

'Ellen, why are you making such a big deal about this?' said Finn. 'What do you think I'm going to do? Start groping you or something?'

'Shh!'

He sighed. 'I just wanted to check if you were okay. See how your sister was doing.'

'You had no right to come here when you knew my kids were here,' she said. 'What am I supposed to tell them?'

He shook his head, meeting her gaze directly. 'Sounds like you've got that covered. I'm just the mechanic.'

'Mum!'

'That's Kate now!' Ellen whispered urgently. 'You have to go.'

The door opened suddenly and Kate peered out. 'Oh, sorry,' she said.

'Nothing to be sorry about, darling,' Ellen said in a strange high-pitched voice that didn't even sound like her. 'This is just the mechanic who fixed the car, you know, he's returning the spare key.'

He nodded. 'Hi, how are you doing?' he said to Kate.

'Good thanks.' She smiled at him. 'Hey Mum, you wanted me to check with you before I put that load of washing on.'

'Yep, coming right now,' she said. 'Well, thanks again, Mr Finlayson. See you next service.'

'Ms Cosgrove.' He gave a nod before turning away down the steps.

Ellen ducked inside and closed the door.

'So did he give you the key?' asked Kate.

Shit. Ellen closed her fist. 'Yeah, right here,' she said, snatching her keys off the hall table with her other hand and turning away slightly as she rattled them around. 'I'll put it back on this keyring while I remember.'

'You keep your spare key with all your other keys?' said Kate.

'Oh, no, I'll find a place for it later,' she said. 'I just don't want to lose it for now.'

Kate shrugged and started down the hallway. 'He's cute,' she said.

'What?' Ellen said, turning abruptly.

Kate looked back at her. 'Mr Finlayson, he's cute. Well, old-guy cute anyway.'

Ellen laughed nervously. 'I wouldn't know, he's just the mechanic, Kate.'

She frowned. 'Mum, you're such a snob!'

Ellen sighed.

Ward 6E

'You should go back to the apartment, Mum,' said Emma. 'You haven't even had a chance to unpack yet. You don't need to wait around, this is going to take a while.'

They were sitting in her room at the hospital, facing the window that looked out across the suburbs, while Emma waited to be taken down for her MRI. She was frightened. She was trying not to show it, but Emma had never been so frightened in her whole life. She realised now that she had been in denial – she had acted pretty crazy – but she'd just been told that a lousy little mole might end her life. And there wasn't a thing she could do about it, except wait and hope and pray they'd caught it in time.

But Emma could almost feel the cancer rushing in to fill the void that Blake had left inside her. If he loved her, if he had ever loved her, how could he have left her like this?

'Of course I'm going to wait,' Evelyn was saying. 'For as long as it takes. That's what a mother does.'

Emma raised an eyebrow. 'So it took getting cancer for me to find that out?'

Evelyn looked at her daughter with a bemused expression. 'It took you needing me,' she said.

'You think this is the first time I've ever needed you?'

'Maybe not, but it certainly hasn't happened very often,' said Evelyn. 'You've always been so independent, Emma.'

'I don't think I've had a choice,' she returned. 'You were never all that interested in what I was doing, so I had to make my own way.'

'Is that what you think?'

Emma shrugged. She might as well say it now. 'You haven't always been there for me, Mum, not like you were for the others.'

Her mother took a moment to respond. 'I guess I always felt that you were more than happy for us to stay out of your life.'

'Why do you say that?'

'Well, you seemed embarrassed by us,' she said. 'We were – what do the kids call it now? – nerds. I know you thought the same way about Ellen and Liz. We didn't wear the right clothes, keep up with the right TV shows, know all the celebrities. Dad and I were just boring old teachers who watched the ABC and read books, and your sisters were too serious about school.'

'That isn't true,' Emma said. 'I mean it is true, the whole last part, but that doesn't mean I was embarrassed by you. I wanted you to be involved. I used to beg you to help out at my dancing concerts.'

'Oh, sweetheart,' her mother shook her head, 'is that still bothering you after all these years? I tried to tell you back then I couldn't sew to save my life. And as for helping on the day with makeup and hair? I would only have embarrassed you even more.'

Emma shrugged. 'I just would have liked you to show an interest. Or even just to show up.'

'Your father and I never missed a single one of your concerts,' she insisted.

'But you never came to my classes.'

'Because after Eddie started walking you asked me to stop bringing him,' she said. 'He was a beggar, that kid, couldn't get him to sit still in his pram for two minutes. I used to bring Evie, do you remember? She was as good as gold, she loved to sit and watch the dancing. But Eddie, he'd run riot around the hall, across the dance floor, disrupting everyone. You seemed to think I could just park him with a neighbour or something, but I'd never done that with any of the rest of you, it didn't seem right to do it with Eddie.'

Emma was frowning as she listened to her mother.

'What?' said Evelyn.

'I don't remember that, I only remember that you stopped coming.'

Evelyn sighed. 'I'm sorry, Emma. It's difficult juggling the needs of five children, someone's bound to get lost in the rush. I often worried it was Evie who didn't get enough attention, I always thought you'd get along fine. And you did – you knew what you wanted and you went out and got it. Your dad and I are very impressed with what you've made of your life.'

'Come on, Mum, you can't say that you've exactly approved of the choices I've made,' said Emma.

'That isn't true, darling,' she said. 'We may not have always understood them – look at your brother, he hang-glides for a living.' She shook her head with a wry smile. 'You think that's been easy for us?'

'Why, because it isn't good enough?'

'No, because we live in constant fear he's going to kill himself one day,' she said frankly. 'But it makes him happy. And all your father and I have ever wanted is for you kids to be happy.'

'Is that why you always gave me such a hard time about Blake?' Emma said. 'Because you didn't think he'd make me happy?'

Evelyn looked at her.

'You must be dying to say I told you so right now,' she added.

'No, I'm not actually.'

'Sure you are, I know that's what everyone's thinking,' said Emma. 'They're just keeping it to themselves because I have cancer. They don't want to upset me.'

'Okay,' said Evelyn, turning to her, 'do you want to know what I honestly think? I was surprised, shocked in fact, when you told us he'd left. Because I believe Blake loves you, that's why I always wondered why he wouldn't marry you.'

Emma started to tear up.

'It's going to be okay, darling,' said Evelyn, patting her arm. 'You just have to give him a chance to cool down. He'll come around.'

'I'm in hospital having treatment for cancer,' Emma said squarely, wiping a tear away. 'He doesn't care. He hasn't called, he hasn't left any messages, nothing.'

'But he probably doesn't know,' her mother suggested.

'He knew I had the melanoma, that I was supposed to be getting it treated. Wouldn't you think he'd call someone to find out what was going on?'

'Maybe he will.'

Emma shook her head. 'It's too late, Mum.'

Monday

'Dr Beckett!'

Liz turned around to see Andrew striding up the corridor towards her. She was just about to head into theatre and scrub in for Emma's surgery.

'Liz,' he said once he was closer, and out of earshot of anyone. 'What's going on? I saw *E Beckett* on the surgery list for this morning, and it startled me for a minute until I realised it was Emma. Why didn't you tell me?'

'Andrew, don't you think I might have had other things on my mind?' she said with a raised eyebrow.

'Yeah, of course, I'm sorry,' he sighed. 'So she's having a wide excision and node biopsy?'

Liz nodded. 'She's at T3, we just have to hope we've got it in time.'

'Well, Rob McGrath's the best around.'

'That's why I asked him.'

'Are you assisting?'

Liz shook her head. 'Just observing. I want to be with her when they put her under.'

Andrew nodded thoughtfully, staring down at her.

'I should go in,' said Liz.

He stirred. 'Of course. Can I see you after, when it's over?'

'I don't know,' she said. 'Things are so crazy at the moment. Michelle is doing her best to move my appointments around, but I'll probably have to go into work later.'

He was still staring at her, she could almost see his mind ticking over.

'Andrew, I really have to go.'

'Of course, but Liz,' he said, 'we should find some time to talk.'

'I know,' she said. 'I'll be in touch.'

*

Ellen found a space in the hospital carpark and made her way up to the same room where she had waited with Evie and Liz only two days ago. But it felt like a lot longer. At times like these, everything seemed to take on momentous proportions, as though whole lifetimes were being played out in a single day. Her mother was standing over by the window, gazing out.

'Hi Mum,' Ellen said, coming towards her.

'Oh hello, darling,' she said, turning to give her a kiss and a hug. 'Liz said to look out for you. Shouldn't you be at work?'

'I decided to take special leave this week. What's happening with Emma?'

'She's in surgery. They're probably finished by now.' Evelyn looked up at the clock on the wall. 'Liz said she'd come up and tell us when they've taken her to recovery, but we still won't be able to see her until she's back in her room.'

They wandered over to the row of hospital-issue green vinyl chairs and took a seat next to each other.

'It was good of you and Dad to come back,' said Ellen. 'I know it must mean a lot to Emma.'

'We'd do it for any of you,' she dismissed. 'Though Emma seemed to think we wouldn't do it for her.'

Ellen looked at her mother, surprised. 'She said that to you?'

'Oh, she said a lot of things. But she's going through a difficult time. It's good for her to get things off her chest. It just breaks my heart that she felt I didn't love her as much . . . I love every one of my children equally, but differently, because you're all different people.'

'I think we're all a little guilty of making Emma feel sidelined,' said Ellen. 'We didn't really get her, so we tended to dismiss her.'

'But I'm her mother,' said Evelyn. 'I should never have let her feel that way.'

'Don't be too hard on yourself, Mum. You're here for her now, and that's what matters.'

Evelyn turned in her seat. 'What about you, darling? How are you coping with everything?'

'Well, I'm worried about her –'

'We're all worried about Emma,' she said. 'That's a given. I'm talking about you. How are things at home? Are you getting by all right? Are you and Tim sorting things out?'

Ellen frowned. 'What do you mean, Mum? You do realise we're not planning on getting back together?'

'I know that, darling. I meant are you sorting out . . . being separated?' She shook her head. 'I can't imagine how hard it must be. You were together for so long.'

'Were you very disappointed, Mum?' Ellen asked. 'You know, that we didn't find a way through?'

'Oh, you did your best, I'm sure,' she said, patting Ellen's arm. 'You were very young when you married, after all.'

'So were you and Dad,' Ellen pointed out. 'You were a lot like us, in fact. You met at uni, started having babies straightaway. But you're going stronger than ever.'

Evelyn was shaking her head. 'It's funny you say that, because I've never thought Dad and I were anything like you and Tim. Your father and I were absolutely besotted, we couldn't get enough of each other. Still can't.' She smiled wistfully. 'But I never got that impression with you and Tim. Oh, you seemed happy enough as boyfriend and girlfriend, but when you found out you were pregnant . . . Do you remember me saying you didn't have to marry him?'

Ellen shrugged. 'I remember you saying you'd be totally supportive of whatever we decided to do.'

'I probably should have been more straightforward,' she sighed. 'Truth is, I was desperately worried about you, Ellen. You hadn't had the chance to work out who you were and suddenly you were getting married with a baby on the way. You're right, Dad and I were young too, but somehow I knew that whoever I was going to be I'd find it with him by my side. But Tim . . .' She paused. 'Now don't get me wrong, he's a very nice man, and he's been a good father, but I couldn't help feeling that you weren't going to be really fulfilled in the marriage.'

'Wow,' Ellen said thoughtfully. 'Why didn't you ever say any of that to me?'

'You wouldn't have listened.' Her mother looked at her sideways. 'Think about it, could you imagine saying something like that to Kate now, if she was in a similar predicament?'

Ellen saw her point.

'Your dad and I would have loved to insist that you delay the wedding, have the baby, see how you felt then,' Evelyn continued. 'But that wasn't our style, and besides, you were very determined.'

'Was I?'

She grinned at her. 'Bull-headedness comes with being an eldest child.'

'I never realised you were so against the marriage,' Ellen mused.

'Oh, but we weren't, exactly. Like I said, Tim's a good man. Once you made your decision, we were one hundred per cent behind you, naturally. And you made it work. Those children are a credit to you, Ellen.'

'Thanks, Mum.'

'But I can't say I was altogether surprised that you decided to separate.'

'You were the only one then,' said Ellen. 'No one else saw it coming.'

'Maybe I didn't put that right,' Evelyn reconsidered. 'I should have said that I'm not surprised your marriage didn't work out, but I was surprised that you actually did something about it. And I have to say, just a little bit relieved. I'm glad that you didn't stick at it for the rest of your life out of some sense of duty. Now you might have a chance of finding happiness for yourself.'

Ellen glanced sideways at her. 'I am happy, Mum.'

Evelyn patted her arm. 'Oh, you know what I'm saying. I want you to find someone special.'

Not her mother as well. Ellen groaned. 'You know, everyone keeps pushing this on me, as though the only way I can be happy is on the arm of a man. It's a little insulting, you know, Mum.'

'I don't think it's the only way you can be happy,' said Evelyn. 'But I think the right man could bring you happiness you haven't experienced before, Ellen. That's all I want for you.'

She shrugged. 'I'm not thinking about that right now.'

'Why not?'

'The kids need me.'

'The "kids" are almost grown. What about your needs?' she said with a knowing wink.

Ellen frowned. 'Mum, you're not going to start talking about sex, are you?'

'I'm just saying, the best years of our sex life have been since you kids grew up.'

'Oh God, I don't want to know.'

The double doors swung open and Liz walked into the waiting room.

'Thank God you're here.' Ellen almost leapt off the chair towards her.

'Hey, settle down,' said Liz. 'It's a fairly routine procedure, you didn't have to get so worried.'

'No, Mum was starting to tell me about her and Dad's sex life.'

'Eew, Mum!' said Liz.

Evelyn shook her head, ignoring them. 'Will you tell me how my daughter is, please?'

'She's fine, she's in recovery,' said Liz. 'The biopsy was straightforward, as we thought, and she just has a tiny nick under her arm. As for the excision, Rob decided to go pretty aggressive, not take any chances.'

'That's good, isn't it?' said Ellen.

'Absolutely, but he took a pretty big chunk out of her back.'

'Oh,' Evelyn said, her face dropping.

'But, because of where the primary tumour was situated, he was able to follow the curve of her shoulder blade, and I reckon it should heal up quite naturally. However, plastic surgery is always an option down the track if Emma's not happy with it.'

'When can we see her?' asked Evelyn.

'You can go down and wait in her room right now if you like, she shouldn't be long.'

'Then let's do that,' Evelyn said to Ellen. 'Are you coming with us, Liz?'

'Sure, I'll follow you down soon, I just have a call to make.'

*

Emma was still groggy when she was brought back to her room, and she kept slipping in and out of consciousness. Their dad arrived at the hospital around noon, and as both parents insisted they were going to stay with her for the rest of the day, Ellen decided she might as well leave them to it.

'But Evie and I will be here for the whole day tomorrow,' she told them. 'You two really need to take some time out to get over your jet lag,' she insisted.

As she left the building, Ellen turned on her phone to check her messages. But there weren't any. She'd expected some word from Finn. She'd felt a bit uneasy about the way she'd shooed him off yesterday, though she was sure he would understand under the circumstances. So she'd sent him a text this morning, briefly outlining the procedure Emma was going through today, and thanking him again for his concern. But he hadn't replied. Maybe he was busy. Ellen looked at the time, it was getting close to lunch. She could drop around to the garage on her way home, see if he could take a break.

When she drove into the parking bay, Finn was outside the workshop, talking to a delivery man whose ute was pulled up at an angle right next to where they were standing. Finn glanced across at her briefly and went back to his conversation. Ellen cut the engine and climbed out of the car; she stood leaning against the boot until the man shook Finn's hand, jumped into the ute and drove past her and out onto the street. She expected Finn to wave her over then, but he was already walking off towards the office, without acknowledging her at all. That was odd, she was sure he'd seen her.

Ellen strolled up to the office and knocked lightly on the doorframe to announce herself as she stepped inside. Finn was sitting at his desk behind the counter.

'Hi,' she said, coming closer.

He glanced up briefly. 'What are you doing here?' He sounded a bit gruff.

'Did you get my message earlier?' she asked tentatively.

'I did.'

'Oh, okay then . . .' She pushed on. 'Well, Emma's out of surgery, and Mum and Dad were going to stay with her, so I didn't need to hang around. I thought I'd see if you were taking a break for lunch.'

She noticed his shoulders heave with a sigh. 'I don't have time today.'

'Oh.' Ellen just stood there at the counter, while he shuffled papers around on his desk. This was getting awkward. 'Are you angry with me, Finn?'

'What would I have to be angry about?' he said, not looking at her. 'I'm just your mechanic.'

Ellen sighed then. 'Don't you think this is a bit childish?'

He shook his head and swivelled his chair around to face her. 'That's rich.'

'All right, so you are angry about yesterday,' she said, keeping her voice level. 'I'm sorry, but the kids were right there, what did you expect me to do?'

'Oh, I dunno, maybe treat me in a civilised manner instead of brushing me off like the hired help.'

'But you know the kids don't know about you.'

'So it was the perfect opportunity, don't you reckon?' he said. 'You could have introduced me as a friend, invited me in for a chat, a cup of coffee maybe. All very innocent, non-threatening . . . normal.'

Ellen didn't know what to say.

'But you don't even know whether you want to introduce me to your kids, do you?' he said squarely.

'I just haven't thought that far . . .'

He shook his head. 'So what are we doing, Ellen?'

'I don't know.' She shrugged.

'Well, perhaps I can paraphrase it for you – you want me to be available for sex whenever it suits you, and to stay out of your life the rest of the time.'

'Finn!' she protested.

'That's the truth, isn't it?' he said, getting up off his chair and coming over to place his hands on the counter. 'Why don't you just go on the internet, Ellen. I'm sure you'd find plenty of blokes who would love that arrangement. Seriously.'

She dropped her voice. 'It's not only about the sex. I thought we were having a good time, that we enjoyed each other's company.'

'Hm,' he grunted. 'As long as no one else is around, and I don't get in the way, and I always come running whenever you click your fingers. You're calling all the shots here, Ellen.'

She was getting her back up now. 'Oh, okay, now I see what this is about. You're threatened by that. You think it should be the other way around, I suppose?'

'Oh don't start that crap with me.' He shook his head. 'This isn't about who has the power. I don't give a shit, Ellen, but it can't all be on your terms. I've gone along with it for a while because of your situation, but I have my limits.'

'So what exactly do you want from me?' she said, folding her arms.

'I don't know.' He sighed deeply. 'I just . . . I like you, Ellen, I like being with you . . . most of the time,' he muttered. 'I don't understand why it has to be so complicated. Why can't you just let things . . . unfold?'

'Because I have kids, I have responsibilities.'

'So? I have responsibilities too, and do you really think I'd do anything to impose on your relationship with your kids?'

'But you will,' she said plainly. 'Any relationship I have is going to impact on the kids, no matter what.'

'Have you ever thought that could be for the better?'

'I don't know, possibly, down the track. But they've made it pretty clear they're not that comfortable about their father dating. And knowing that, I don't feel right about exposing them to any more changes.'

Finn was just staring at her. 'Well, it sounds convincing. I think you may have even convinced yourself.'

'What's that supposed to mean?' Ellen frowned.

'You've made a pretty iron-clad excuse for yourself there. Everything's for the sake of the kids. And who can argue with that? I just wish I could understand what you're so afraid of.'

Ellen was sick and tired of being accused of that, and of everything else every man and his dog seemed to be throwing at her lately. Why had she suddenly been put under so much scrutiny? What gave people the right to think they understood her better than she did herself and, worse, to judge her.

'I'm not afraid of anything,' she said defiantly. 'It's just not the right time.'

He folded his arms in front of himself. 'And when do you think it will be?'

'I told you, I haven't thought that far.'

Finn nodded as though he was expecting that. 'Well, don't worry, you won't have to think about it anymore.'

Ellen felt her heart drop. 'What are you saying, are you breaking it off?'

'Breaking what off? What's there to break? You don't want me to be a part of your life, so fine, I'll stay out of it.'

'I didn't say that, Finn.'

'You didn't have to.' He turned around to the door that led to the garage. 'Don't worry, I'll still service your car, if that's what you want,' he said, glancing back at her. 'You seem happy enough to have me as your mechanic.' Then he walked out.

Tuesday

'Everyone loves you,' Evie exclaimed. 'Really, everyone loves her,' she repeated, looking around at Liz and Ellen.

'You don't have to say it like it's so remarkable,' Emma muttered out of the side of her mouth, her face pushed in against the pillow. She had yet to find a truly comfortable position, but lying on her stomach, her head at the foot of the bed, and propped up by pillows, meant at least she could join in the conversation with her sisters, who had arranged their chairs in a semicircle facing her.

Evie had spent the entire day yesterday going through Emma's files and making calls according to priority. It was no use worrying about the dresses, for example, they were all done, with only a final payment owing. But the venue, the cake, the flowers, the cars – the list went on and on – there was still time to cancel most of them, even if the deposit had to be forfeited. But Evie had been surprised, to say the least, by how accommodating every one had been.

'One man even started to cry,' she told Emma.

'Nigel, right?' she said. 'He's the florist. Cries like a girl at the drop of a hydrangea.'

'Anyhow, people have been waiving deposits altogether,' said Evie, 'or cutting them right back only to cover any costs they've run up so far, and this is despite very strict cancellation policies. They said you're not to worry about anything, just to get better.'

'We said cancer would get the best sympathy vote.' Emma winked at Ellen.

'Oh, don't you two start that again,' Evie scolded.

Emma tried to shift her position slightly, making her wince.

Liz jumped up. 'Are you okay? Let me take a look at that.'

'You've looked at my wound three times since you got here, Liz,' said Emma. 'And the nursing staff have looked at it as many times in between. Give it a rest.'

Liz sat down again. 'I really think it's going to heal up nicely though.'

'As long as I never attempt to move my shoulder again.'

'That's not true,' Liz said. 'It just feels like that for now. In fact, you'll probably have the physio up here tomorrow to start you on some exercises.'

'Already?'

'They'll only be very gentle, but you have to keep movement in your shoulder, or else you'll end up with more issues.'

'Great,' she said wryly. 'So how much longer do they expect me to stay in here?'

'Probably only another day or two,' said Liz. 'To make sure the wound is draining okay, and that you do get some movement back in your arm.'

Emma sighed. 'I don't know why I'm in such a rush to go home to an empty apartment.'

'Well, you shouldn't be left alone anyway,' said Ellen. 'One of us can always stay with you.'

'I can't expect you to disrupt your lives like that.'

'I have every second weekend free, remember?'

'What about the mechanic?'

'What about what mechanic?' Evie frowned.

'I wouldn't feel right taking your Tim Tam rations away,' added Emma with a wink in Liz's direction.

'Is this another one of your in-jokes?' said Evie, a little frustrated.

'Sorry, Evie,' said Ellen. 'I haven't said anything about this to you, because, well, mostly I haven't had the opportunity, but also there wasn't really much to tell, it's not like it was super-serious or anything . . . so –'

'Oh would you just tell her?' said Liz.

'Okay,' she relented. 'So Evie, I've been kind of seeing this guy, he's the mechanic where my car was towed that time it broke down, not my usual place. My usual mechanic,' she pulled a face, 'I wouldn't touch him with a barge pole.'

Emma grinned. 'That's such a Mum-ism.'

'And what exactly does it mean?' said Liz. 'That there are people you *would* touch with a barge pole? And who's carrying barge poles around anyway, to test the theory?'

Evie was shaking her head. 'Can you get on with the story about the mechanic, Ellen? And does he have a name?'

'Finn,' Emma and Liz said at once.

'Oh, that's unusual,' Evie remarked. 'Nice, though.'

'It's a shortening of his surname,' Emma explained. 'Did you ever find out what his real name is, Len?'

'I did, as a matter of fact,' said Ellen. 'It's Michael.'

'Well there's nothing wrong with Michael,' said Emma. 'I expected something hideous for him to go by his surname.'

'It's a long story,' said Ellen. 'He was named after his father, who was a real bastard apparently, abandoned the family. So he didn't want to go by that name anymore.'

'Oh,' said Evie. 'That's sad. So he's a nice guy?'

'Of course he is.'

'Is he hot?' asked Liz.

Ellen shrugged. 'Kate thought he was cute for an old guy.'

'So he's met the kids?' Liz sounded surprised. 'Ooh, it is getting serious then?'

'No, that's what I've been trying to get to,' said Ellen, 'if you'd all stop interrupting. So, Evie, we were kind of going out –'

'By that she means they've been having sex,' Emma broke in. 'Really great sex.'

'Emma!'

'You're blushing.'

'So it is quite serious, then?' Evie said.

'No, actually, it's not,' Ellen insisted. 'I know you probably think it should be, if I've been having sex with him –'

'And introducing him to the kids,' Liz added.

Ellen sighed, exasperated. 'Look, I'm not even seeing him anymore,' she said, cutting to the chase.

'You're not?' said Emma.

'You broke up?' added Liz.

'No, we didn't "break up",' she insisted. 'There wasn't anything to break up. It was only a casual thing anyway.'

'Okay, since when did you stop "casually" seeing him?' Liz persisted.

'Since he started making all these demands,' she said. 'In the middle of everything that's going on, he's ringing me, leaving messages – *How's your sister? Thinking of you*. He even came round to my house when the kids were there.' She turned to Evie. 'The kids didn't know about him, for obvious reasons.'

Evie was beginning to get confused.

'So anyway, I had to put on this whole charade that he was just the mechanic and he was returning the spare car key, and I got rid of him. And then he was all miffed.'

'I can't imagine why,' Emma said.

Ellen ignored that. 'He wanted to know what we were doing. He accused me of calling all the shots, not including him in my life, only wanting him for sex.'

'And he had a problem with that?' asked Emma. 'He is a guy, isn't he?'

'A guy who wants more out of a relationship than just sex.' Liz shook her head. 'Bastard.'

'Very funny,' Ellen said. 'Look, I have to think of the kids. I don't have the time or the energy for a relationship, having to worry about his needs and his feelings . . .'

'Wow, now you sound like a guy,' Emma said.

'Well, maybe I should be more like a man,' said Ellen. 'They seem to get everything their own way, and if they don't, they have little hissy fits. You know,' she went on, 'women lose power when they go into a relationship. They've done studies that show that single women are the happiest.'

'Who did that study?' Liz said, raising an eyebrow.

'It's true,' Ellen insisted. 'Single men are the least happy, and their happiness increases when they marry, whereas a woman's happiness decreases when she marries. What does that tell you?'

'That they can do a study to pretty much prove anything,' said Liz.

'Hear, hear,' said Emma.

Ellen rolled her eyes. 'I'm just saying that maybe women would be a lot better off if they stopped thinking that having a man is the be-all and end-all.'

Liz was thoughtful. 'Maybe she has a point.' She looked around at her sisters. 'I don't think Andrew's ever going to leave his wife.'

'You've just figured that out?' said Ellen.

'For someone so smart, you sure can be dumb,' Emma added.

'Fine, okay, I guess I deserve that,' said Liz. 'I've planned my whole life around an eventual future with Andrew, but I don't think he sees us as the future anymore. It's just time out, a way for him to escape.'

'I would suggest that's all it's ever been,' Emma said archly. 'Ah, but who am I to talk? I'm beginning to think Blake never really saw a future with me either.'

'Oh, that isn't true. He asked you to marry him, Emma,' said Evie.

'And then bailed at the first sign of trouble.'

'He might have had his reasons,' Liz offered.

'Yeah,' said Emma, 'it was all getting too hard.'

'Bloody men,' said Ellen. 'See, what was I telling you? More trouble than they're worth.'

Emma and Liz murmured in vague agreement.

'So, Evie,' Emma said, noticing she'd gone quiet, 'looks like you're the only one left standing.'

She stirred. 'Hm?'

'Out of all of us, you've ended up with the most successful relationship,' said Emma.

'Yeah,' said Ellen. 'What's your secret?'

Evie looked around at her sisters, her mouth opened as if to say something, but then, quite unexpectedly, and quite violently, she burst into tears.

'Oh, Evie,' said Liz, putting her arm around her. 'You take things to heart too much. Don't be sad for us.'

'I didn't mean to imply people who were married couldn't be happy,' said Ellen, reaching over to pat her shoulder. 'You're allowed to be happy.'

'But I'm not happy,' she sobbed. 'I'm not happy at all!'

'What's wrong?' said Liz. 'What's happened?'

'I can't tell you, it's too awful.'

They all looked warily at one another.

'Come on, Evie, you can tell us,' said Ellen. 'It's not as though any one of us is in a position to judge.'

'What is it?' Liz urged.

Evie was shaking her head. 'I don't know if I can say it, even though I've been dying to tell you all for so long.'

'Evie, just spit it out,' said Emma.

She sniffed, wiping her eyes with the tissue Ellen had passed her. 'Craig and I . . . well, it was Craig's idea, and I didn't want to go along with it, and I didn't, actually, in the end . . .'

They were all hanging on what she was going to say next, their expressions a mixture of anticipation and dread.

Evie took a deep breath. 'We went to a swingers' club.'

Six eyes widened and three mouths dropped. Then Liz made a snorting sound and started to laugh. She held up a hand to her mouth.

'I'm sorry, Evie, inappropriate laughter response,' she explained, composing herself. 'I'm not laughing at you. I think I'm in shock, actually.'

'You said it was Craig's idea?' said Ellen, trying to make sense of it. 'And that you didn't go along with it? Or you did? Sorry, I'm confused now.'

Evie sighed heavily, and the whole sorry tale poured out of her.

'I just can't believe it,' Ellen was shaking her head, 'I mean, I believe you, of course, Evie, but you are the last person . . .'

'I wasn't the one who suggested it.'

'Of course you weren't,' Ellen assured her, giving her arm a rub. 'As if you could ever . . .'

'What on earth was he thinking?' Liz grimaced.

Evie looked around. 'So you do think it's weird?'

'Absolutely,' they chorused.

'I could never even entertain the idea,' said Ellen. 'Not that I can imagine Tim would ever have suggested it.'

'If Blake had ever suggested something like that I'd have cut off his balls,' said Emma.

'I'm so relieved,' Evie sighed. 'I wondered if I was naive, or even frigid.'

'No way!' Liz exclaimed.

'You should have told us sooner,' said Ellen. 'You would have had a better perspective on this. You might have stood up to him with our support.'

'You poor thing,' said Liz. 'You even went to the place for his sake?'

'Was it totally disgusting?' asked Emma.

'Pretty much,' she said. 'But I kept well clear of the . . . action, so to speak. I met a nice man, though.'

'What?' said Liz.

'Nothing happened,' Evie assured her quickly. 'He was just a kindred spirit. His wife was into it but he wasn't, so I had someone to talk to.'

'This is so weird,' muttered Liz.

'What are you going to do about it, Evie?' said Ellen. 'I assume Craig has given up on the idea?'

She shrugged. 'I guess so, but we haven't talked about it. Things are at a stalemate.'

'What do you want to happen?'

'I'm not sure.' Evie looked around at her sisters. 'I don't know how I feel. My whole reason for being has always been to make sure *he* kept loving me, so I put up with anything for the sake of that.'

'That's not the way it's supposed to be, Ev,' said Emma.

'I look at my life now,' said Evie, staring at her hands, 'and who I've become . . . I don't like what I see. I've been a doormat as a wife, and I'm not even a very good mother.'

'Yes, you are!' Emma insisted.

'Of course you are!' Liz agreed.

'You're a wonderful mother,' said Ellen. 'You're incredibly devoted.'

'Then why are my kids so awful?' she said bluntly.

Ellen blinked. 'No they're not. They're just . . . spirited.'

'Cody's gorgeous,' said Liz.

Evie nodded. 'He is. He's a sweet boy, for some reason.'

'Takes after his mother,' said Emma.

'Thank you,' she said. 'But Tayla and Jayden, they're so naughty, and defiant, and rude, especially. I don't know what I've done wrong.'

'Who said it's you?'

'Like it or not, I'm the parent at home, I'm the one with them all the time,' she said. 'I can't blame it on Craig.' She took a breath. 'I think I lost myself somewhere along the way. I thought it was more important to please everyone than to stand up for myself. And look where it's got me.'

'Well, see, you've figured that much out for yourself,' said Ellen.

Evie turned to her. 'So what am I supposed to do about it? You're a wonderful mother, Ellen. Your kids are lovely. How did you do it?'

'Boundaries,' Ellen said automatically.

'What do you mean?'

She thought about it. 'You have to set clear boundaries and then stick by them. You can't let the kids dictate to you. They feel secure when they know what's what, and who's in charge.'

'Perhaps you should listen to your own advice,' Emma muttered.

'What?' said Ellen.

'She has a point,' said Liz. 'You keep saying that your needs come second to the kids.'

'That's entirely different,' Ellen argued. 'My kids aren't dictating to me, I'm the one setting the boundaries . . . about what I think is best for them . . . and for all of us,' she added uncertainly. 'Anyway, we're talking about Evie now.'

'Boundaries,' Evie murmured thoughtfully. 'I don't know, isn't it a bit late?'

'Of course not, they're ten and eight, they're not exactly hardened criminals,' said Liz.

That made Evie smile.

'Look!' Emma declared. 'She's smiling again.'

'Smiling at what?'

They all turned to see Eddie walk into the room.

'Eddie!' they chorused.

'Greetings, my adoring fans,' he replied, holding his arms out towards them.

'Oh, get over yourself,' said Emma as he came over to give her a kiss on the top of her head.

'How's the patient?' he asked.

Emma looked around at her sisters. 'All the better for the company I'm keeping.'

'Looks like you've formed a coven here,' he said. 'Is it safe for a man to break the circle?'

'No, but you're just a boy.' Liz grinned. 'You'll be all right.'

Eddie shook his head and smiled, perching on the arm of Liz's chair. 'So when are they going to let you out of here, Em?'

'In a day or two, apparently.'

'And then what? Will you have to have more treatment?'

Emma looked at Liz. 'Ask the doctor.'

'Well,' Liz began carefully, 'they might know something in a couple of days, but the full pathology report will take about a week.'

'And?' Eddie prompted her.

'Hopefully it'll show no spread to the lymph nodes and she won't need any further treatment right now. We'll just have to keep a close eye on her after that, regular follow-ups, that kind of thing.'

Eddie frowned. 'And if there is cancer in the lymph nodes?'

'They'll take them out,' Liz said, making it sound simple. 'And there's various options after that – they might prescribe ray treatment, for example.' She didn't want to say more now. Because if cancerous lymph nodes were found, that would be a fairly strong indication it had spread further, and Liz didn't even want to entertain that idea. It was better for everyone to stay positive.

'Okay, well I for one have got big plans for you, Emma, when this is all over,' said Eddie.

She looked at him, waiting.

'I am going to take you for a tandem glide.'

She groaned along with her sisters.

'I'm not going to take no for an answer,' he said. 'In fact, I'm determined to talk you all into it.'

'You can talk till you're blue in the face,' said Liz.

Evie was shaking her head. 'Not going to happen, Ed.'

'I already told you no way,' added Ellen.

'Oh, you're all such fraidy cats,' Eddie said. 'What do I keep telling you? You have to face your fears. It'll make you stronger.'

The girls exchanged a knowing smile between them.

'What's going on?' he said.

'You have no idea, little brother,' said Emma. She winced as she propped herself up on her elbows. 'In this room right now are four of the strongest women you're ever likely to come across.'

'Oh yeah?' he said dubiously.

'Oh yeah.' She nodded. 'Look around you. I'm not going to give away names, but between us, we're fighting cancer, saving lives, raising kids, dumping men and being dumped by men, visiting swingers' clubs, and having a great deal of very hot sex.'

Eddie was gobsmacked. And clearly uncomfortable.

'Whereas you, little brother,' Emma went on, 'are too frightened to even introduce us to your girlfriend. From where I sit, or should I say lie, I don't think this hang-gliding caper is making you very brave at all.'

Wednesday

Emma noticed Liz glance at her watch again.

'You know,' she said, 'if you have to be somewhere, Liz, it's fine. Same goes for all of you,' she added, looking at Evie and Ellen. 'Mum and Dad will be here soon anyway. You really don't have to keep up the constant vigil.'

She was sitting up today. With the pillows propped behind her in a particular arrangement, Emma found she could be quite comfortable, for short periods at least.

'I've got nowhere I have to be,' said Ellen, flipping through a magazine from the stack that had been brought over from Emma's place. 'I have to admit, I'm kind of enjoying taking a break from school,' she added. 'In fact, I'm thinking of making it more permanent.'

'What, you're going to quit?' Evie asked her.

'Hey, I never asked,' said Emma. 'Did you hear from the private school?'

Ellen nodded. 'I didn't get the job.'

'You applied for a job at a private school?' said Evie, wide-eyed. 'Did Mum and Dad know about that?'

'No, they didn't, and now they don't have to,' she warned. 'Anyway, I think it was for the best, I'm actually feeling a little burnt out. Maybe I need a break.'

'What will you do?' asked Liz.

'I have no idea. But I have some long service leave owing. I might take some time off to figure it out.'

'Hm,' Evie mused. 'I'm starting to think I need to get a job, but I don't know who would employ me.'

'Don't be so hard on yourself,' said Ellen. 'You might not have worked for a while, Evie, but your qualifications are still good.'

'Yeah, in childcare,' she said. 'But I think I've had enough of that. It might be time for a change.'

'I know how you feel,' Liz muttered.

There was a knock on the door. It was chocked halfway open, and they all looked around as Blake stepped out from behind the door.

Emma's heart dropped into her stomach. 'What are you doing here?' she managed to say.

He looked uncharacteristically nervous. Emma had rarely ever seen him nervous. He was one of the most unflappable people she knew.

'I . . . ah . . . I wanted to see you,' he said. 'I was hoping we could talk.'

Her heart was beating so hard it was throbbing in her ears, and her legs felt twitchy. Part of her wanted to hear what he had to say for himself, but the other part didn't want to give him the time of day. And she felt angry just looking at him. But on the other hand, she was so glad to see his face . . . Emma had so many conflicting emotions running through her she couldn't think straight.

'Okay,' she said finally. 'Go ahead, what do you want to say?'

Blake glanced across at her sisters, all lined up in a row on the other side of the bed, like a guard of honour.

'Um, do you think . . .?' he said. 'Well, do you think I could see you on your own?'

'No,' all four of them said as one.

'Anything you have to say to me,' said Emma, regaining at least some of her composure, 'you can say in front of my sisters.'

'Oh, okay then,' he said. He took a couple of tentative steps into the room. 'How are you feeling?' he began.

Emma sighed. 'It's a bit late in the day to be acting concerned, Blake.'

'I never stopped being concerned,' he said sincerely. 'I know you probably find that hard to understand.'

'To say the least.'

He took a breath, and another step closer. 'I'm so sorry, Em, so sorry for hurting you, but I'm not sorry that I did what I did. It was the only way.'

She frowned. 'What's that supposed to mean?'

'If I didn't walk out, you would never have gone ahead with the tests, or the treatment. You would have stuck to your guns about the wedding, kept making excuses. I know you too well.'

'Oh come on, Blake,' she said, 'be honest. You were looking for a way to get out of the wedding. And you got it. It's all off now, Evie's cancelled everything. But don't think for a minute you're going to get out of paying your share.'

'I don't care about that, I don't care what it costs.'

'That's all you cared about.'

'No, Emma, all I cared about was you getting well,' he said, his voice becoming more insistent. 'It's true, the wedding was getting out of hand, and no, it didn't matter to me the way it mattered to you.' He paused. 'But it paled into . . . into such utter insignificance compared to the thought of anything happening to you.'

Emma just stared at him.

'The only thing I could do was to walk out on you,' he went on. 'You should have heard yourself – you were being so stubborn, so irrational, you just weren't making any sense.'

She glanced at her sisters. They all looked sheepish, avoiding her gaze.

'I didn't know what else to do,' said Blake.

'Well, you didn't have to do that,' she said. 'Do you have any idea how much you hurt me?'

Blake sighed heavily. 'I do, and I'm sorry, but I was prepared to piss you off forever,' he said, 'even if you never wanted to have anything to do with me again. That was preferable to . . .' His voice faltered then. He cleared his throat. 'I just couldn't go through with the wedding, Emma, and I could never have gone away for weeks on a honeymoon, knowing that every day . . . So I left. It was the hardest thing I've ever done because I was so worried about you, but I knew it was the only way.'

Emma was trying to steel herself. She couldn't forget how she'd felt the night he walked out. Every doubt she'd ever had over all their years together had come to the surface, and for the first time in her life she'd understood why they called it being heartbroken. Her heart had broken. And she didn't know if she could get past that.

'If you cared so much,' she said eventually, 'if you were so worried, why didn't you call, or check how I was?'

He glanced at Liz. 'I've been in touch with Liz several times a day most days.'

They all looked at her, and she nodded.

'Why didn't you tell me, Liz?' Emma said.

'I asked her not to,' Blake answered for her. 'Not until you'd had whatever treatment you needed to have. So there was absolutely no chance you'd back out and not go through with it.'

Emma sat there, silent. She hadn't expected any of this, she didn't know what she was supposed to think.

'I asked Liz to let me know before you get the next round of results,' Blake went on, 'so I can be here for you, whatever happens.'

There was a knock on the door and a nurse stepped in wheeling a trolley.

'Excuse me, Ms Beckett,' she said. 'You have to take your meds.'

'Can we do this later?' said Emma. 'It's not a good time right now.'

'Well, sorry, but it's the right time.'

'Okay, just leave them here.'

'I'm supposed to stay to watch you take them.'

Emma groaned.

Blake turned to the nurse. 'What if you give them to me?' he said. 'I'll make sure she takes them.'

'Well, we're not supposed to . . .' She hesitated.

Liz raised her hand. 'I'm Dr Beckett. I'll supervise.'

The nurse nodded then. 'Okay, I guess that will be all right.' She made a tick on her clipboard and then handed the little paper cup to Blake and left the room. He turned back and picked up the jug on Emma's bedside cabinet, pouring her a glass of water. 'Here, you should take these now.'

She ignored that. 'Look, Blake, I don't know where we're supposed to go to from here.'

He held the little cup out to her.

'The wedding's been cancelled. The whole thing's off, you got your way.'

'Take your meds, Emma.'

'Are we supposed to go back to the way it was?' she demanded. 'Because I don't see how that's going to work.'

'Just take your meds,' he persisted, holding the cup out.

'Oh for crying out loud,' she said, snatching the cup from him and tossing it back into her mouth. She gagged. What was that? It wasn't a pill. She held her hand out in front of her and let it drop from her mouth into her palm. Emma's heart stopped. It was a ring. A simple platinum ring. She stared at it as tears sprang into her eyes.

'Remember?' Blake said quietly. 'It was my job to organise the wedding rings. I went to pick them up the other day. I want to marry you, Em. More than ever. We can have any kind of wedding you want, I don't care what it costs . . . just please say you'll still marry me.'

Emma looked up at him then, and the tears fell over her lashes and rolled down her cheeks. He brought his hand to her face and wiped a tear away with his thumb. 'Don't you know by now I couldn't live without you?' he said. 'I just wanted to make sure I didn't have to.'

Liz gave her sisters a pointed look, and all three of them stood up and quietly filed out of the room. She glanced back when she got to the door, Blake was leaning over Emma, and they were kissing.

'Oh my God!' Evie said once they were outside, tears streaming down her cheeks. 'That was so beautiful.'

Ellen brushed a tear away herself, and then gave Liz a gentle thump on the arm. 'Why didn't you tell us?'

'I couldn't,' said Liz. 'He actually made me swear on Emma's life. The poor guy was beside himself.'

'Well, what do you know?' said Ellen, shaking her head. 'He really does love her, doesn't he?'

Evie let out a sob.

'He really does,' Liz agreed.

'Girls!'

They turned to see their mother marching up the corridor towards them, their dad following in her wake.

'What are you all doing out here?' She stopped when she saw their tear-streaked faces. 'Oh my God, what's happened?' she said, aghast. 'There hasn't been bad news, has there?'

Liz took her arm. 'No, Mum, don't worry. No bad news, it's all good,' she assured her. 'In fact, it couldn't be better.'

Thursday

Evie knew she'd been avoiding dealing with Craig and the whole sorry mess of their marriage. But, like going to the dentist, she suspected the treatment was going to be almost as bad as the pain she was already experiencing. She really didn't want to dredge it all up, but she knew she had to – it was not going to go away by itself. Of course Emma's plight had taken precedence over everything else, but when Blake had walked into that hospital room yesterday, and said those things to Emma, Evie had realised she had a right to expect more for herself, even to demand it.

Emma had left the hospital today, and she and Blake were going home to wait for the results. She had someone to look after her now, and besides, the two of them needed time together alone. So Evie had no further excuse, she could not put off the inevitable any longer. She gave Craig notice when he got home that they were going to talk tonight, and she bathed and fed the kids early and put them to bed. He was sitting dutifully at the kitchen table when she came back downstairs, a beer in front of him.

'Did you want anything to drink, love?' he said when she walked around to sit on the chair opposite him.

Evie shook her head. 'So Craig, I suppose you realise that things can't keep going the way they are,' she began.

He shrugged. 'I get you don't want to go to the place anymore. I'm okay with that.'

She sighed inwardly. 'Well, that's big of you, but it's not enough.' She took a breath. 'You didn't value me, Craig. I'm the best thing in your life, and you didn't value me. And worse than that, I stopped valuing myself.'

He frowned, listening to her.

'I don't mean to blame it all on you,' she said. 'See, I thought my primary role in the family was to keep everyone else happy. But it turns out I wasn't even doing that right. Tayla's the unhappiest little girl I know, and I don't know why. Maybe she sees her future in me and that's what makes her so angry with me.'

'I think you might be reading a bit much into that, hun,' said Craig. 'She seems pretty typical to me. My sister was a real little bitch at that age.'

'I'm not so sure her behaviour is typical,' said Evie. 'And if it is, then I'm not so sure it's okay.'

'What's this got to do with us?' he asked.

'What I'm trying to say is that things aren't right in this family, Craig,' said Evie. 'And I do partly blame myself. Maybe I can even understand on some level why you were craving for something more, but it wasn't the solution to look outside for it.'

He was staring gloomily at his beer bottle. 'Okay, I said we didn't have to go there again. Can't we drop it now, just move on?'

'No, Craig, we can't move on that easily. We won't move on, we'll go back to all the same old habits, not really talking to each other, the television on all the time, while I run around doing everything.'

'So you want me to help out more? Fine, just tell me what I have to do.'

'It's not that simple, Craig.'

'Ah jeez, Ev, why do you have to make a federal case out of this? It's over, it's not going to happen again. And I'll give you a hand with the kids . . . What else do you want?'

So much more than this, but it was no use trying to discuss it any further. It wasn't up for discussion anyway.

'I think we need some time apart,' said Evie.

'And how are we going to manage that?' he retorted. 'I know, I'll go down to the Grand Prix next month, if you like,' he said with a chuckle. 'That'll give us some time apart.'

Evie glared at him. 'I was thinking of something longer term, Craig.'

He looked at her. 'What do you mean?'

'Well, you could go to a hotel,' said Evie, 'but that wouldn't be very nice for the kids when they stay, and it would get too expensive anyway. There's always caravan parks, but there aren't any around here, and again, I don't think that's the best environment for the kids. Realistically, I don't see how we could afford two places right now. But I am planning to go back to work, so once I'm established, and depending on how things go between us, well, we can look at our options then. So the only alternative at the moment is for you to go and stay at your mother's.'

While she spoke, Craig's face morphed from confused to perplexed to stunned. 'You're kidding me, aren't you?'

'I realise it's going to cramp your style. You won't be able to spend nights looking at porn, for one thing.'

Stunned didn't even begin to describe the expression on his face now.

'I don't look at porn,' he said.

'Don't lie, Craig. I saw it on the history on the computer.'

'You've been spying on me?'

'No,' Evie insisted. 'I looked up "swingers' clubs" when you first brought it up, and when I went to clear the history, that's when I found it.'

'So now you think I'm some kind of pervert?' said Craig. 'Okay, I admit it, I've looked, I was curious, but I'm not addicted or anything. The guys at work are always on it, I'm not like that.'

Evie was relieved to hear that, but it didn't change anything. It wasn't really the issue at heart here.

'What's this about anyway?' said Craig. 'It's got to do with that bloke, Steve, hasn't it? I know you've been in touch with him.'

'Yeah, I have,' she said. 'He was someone to talk to when I didn't have anyone else. But he's a friend, and that's all he is.'

'And you expect me to believe that?'

'It's the truth – whether you choose to believe it or not is your problem.' Evie was surprised at how confident she felt. 'Steve was interested in taking things further, but unfortunately I couldn't muster up any feeling for him more than friendship. I don't know why. He's kind and courteous, able to express his feelings . . . he's not like you at all.'

Craig looked sullen.

'Needing time apart has nothing to do with hooking up with other people,' said Evie. 'It's so that we can work on our relationship.'

'And how are we supposed to do that if we're not even living in the same house? It doesn't make sense.'

'We've lived in the same house since we were barely more than kids, and I've just become another piece of the furniture to you. I don't believe we're going to have any chance of a future unless we really confront this. I think we need to be apart for a while, and that we should get counselling to help us through this.'

'This is bullshit.' He pushed his chair back and stood up. 'I don't need some crazy shrink with hairy armpits to tell me what's wrong with my marriage or, more likely, what's wrong with me. And I'm not moving out of my own house. Why the fuck should I?'

'Okay, Craig, if that's the way you feel,' Evie said calmly. She'd prepared herself for this, because she knew this was more than likely the way he'd react. 'But the fact is, I can't stay in the same house as you right now. So, if you won't go, that forces me to move out with the kids, and if you put me in that position, everyone is going to know why. Your mother, and your father, the rest of your family, our friends. I'll tell everyone all the gory details, you can count on that.'

He looked crestfallen. 'Why are you doing this, Ev? Do you really hate me that much?'

She shook her head. 'If I hated you I could walk away. Or I could have taken up with Steve. But I didn't, so what does that tell you?'

He just shrugged in response. He really did look miserable.

'I want to work on our marriage and our family, Craig, but I can't do it on my own. I hope you'll decide to do your part.'

Friday

Liz burst through the double swing doors of the hospital's pathology lab clutching a piece of paper, and started down the corridor, virtually at a run. She glanced at the lift bay as she shot past, but the stairs would be quicker, it was only the next floor down anyway. She leapt down the stairs, taking two at a time, and darted around the corner and into the waiting room where she'd left Emma and Blake barely ten minutes ago.

They were sitting close together on a couch, their arms entwined and their hands clasped. They both looked up as Liz rushed in, catching her breath. She beamed at them.

Emma sat forward. 'All clear?' she said, her voice barely making it out of her throat.

'Clear as a bell,' said Liz. 'There is no evidence of cancer in the lymph nodes. *No further treatment is required,*' she added, quoting from the report.

Emma turned to Blake with tears in her eyes. They didn't speak. He took her face in his hands and kissed her soundly, and then folded his arms around her as they held each other close.

'Hey,' said Liz as she came over to them, still catching her breath, 'don't I get a bit of loving?'

Emma broke away from Blake and jumped to her feet with a broad smile, throwing her arms around her sister.

'So the lymph nodes are all clear,' she said over Liz's shoulder.

Liz nodded.

'The cancer hasn't spread at all?'

Liz shook her head, and then she couldn't contain it anymore, she burst into tears.

'Liz, Lizzie,' Emma consoled her, patting her back, 'it's okay, everything's going to be okay now.'

'I know.' She sniffed, pulling back to look at Emma. 'It's just such a relief. I've been so worried, ever since that day, knowing what could happen . . .'

Emma took her hands in hers. 'And I didn't listen to you. You must have been so angry with me. I've been on the internet at home, and it's terrifying. I came so close, I can't believe it. I was sure today we'd find out . . .' Her voice petered out, and Blake stood up and put his arm around her.

Emma took a breath. 'I dodged a bullet, I know that, and it's only because of you, Liz. If you hadn't pushed me to have that mole removed, and then called Blake . . . well, there's no question what would have happened. I don't know how to thank you, Liz, I owe you –'

'You owe me nothing,' she said. 'Except to stay away from solariums.'

'Don't worry,' said Blake. 'They're out of bounds from now on.'

'Like I need to be told that,' Emma assured them.

'And, look, you are going to have to have regular check-ups,' said Liz.

'Of course.'

'Seriously, every six to eight weeks at first. This is not me overreacting,' she insisted. 'I hate to put a dampener on things, but you do have a higher chance of recurrence. But now that we're aware of it, we can keep a close eye on you, and anything that crops up will be detected early and dealt with straightaway. We can keep it under control.'

'I promise I'll do whatever you tell me to from now on, Liz,' Emma said solemnly. 'I can't believe it's over,' she went on. 'I've got so much to do now.'

'For the wedding?'

'Oh, yes, of course, but I wasn't talking about that,' said Emma. 'I know it's only been a week or so, but that's a very long time to have your life flashing before your eyes.'

Blake gave her arm a squeeze.

'Everything changed. I had no idea what was ahead of me, my whole life was on hold.' She looked at them both. 'I have so many things buzzing around in my head that I want to do, and now I'm going to get the chance to do them.'

Liz pulled a face. 'You're not talking about hang-gliding, are you?'

'No way,' Emma assured her. 'I'm talking about getting out there and doing something really worthwhile.'

'Don't forget you only got out of the hospital a couple of days ago,' said Liz. 'You have to take it easy.'

'I'll make sure she does,' Blake said.

'So when are you going to tell Mum and Dad?' Liz asked them.

Emma hadn't wanted anyone to know when the results were going to be ready, she didn't need the pressure. So Liz had told everyone else Monday, so that Emma would have the entire weekend to come to terms with the news if she needed it.

She glanced at Blake. 'I think we might go see them right away. What are you doing now?' she said to Liz. 'Do you want to come with us, we could all go and have lunch afterwards?'

'To celebrate,' added Blake.

'I'd love to,' said Liz. 'But I'm meeting Andrew for lunch.'

Emma nodded. 'Do you know what you're going to do?'

'Yeah . . . but I better tell him first.'

'Wow,' she murmured, leaning forward to hug her again. 'Call me later, if you want, if you need to talk.'

'Thanks.'

*

Liz had arranged to meet Andrew in a café up the road from the hospital, giving them some privacy away from staff and people they might bump into, but not too much privacy. He had suggested meeting tonight instead, at her place, but Liz knew that wasn't a good idea. She still loved him, still found him just as attractive, none of that had changed . . . so if she was going to get through this, they needed to be in a public place.

After they ordered at the counter and found a table, Liz told Andrew about Emma's results.

'That's great news,' he said. 'Everyone must be so relieved.'

'Everyone doesn't know yet,' said Liz. 'She's off telling them now. You know, it was a horrible thing to go through, and I wouldn't wish it upon anyone, but life and death experiences change people. She's brimming over with all the things she wants to achieve, she and Blake are stronger than ever. The wedding's back on, they were just waiting till after she got the results to set a new date.' She paused. 'I'll let you know when they do, maybe you'll come?'

He looked uncomfortable. 'Lizzie, you know I'd love nothing more, but . . .'

'Yeah, I know.' She gave a resigned sigh.

'Is that why you wanted to meet,' said Andrew, 'to put me through some kind of a test?'

Liz shook her head. 'No. That's not why. I did want to let you know I've applied to join a surgical program.'

He nodded slowly. 'So you went ahead?'

'I did.'

'Where did you apply, here?'

'No. I put Westmead or St George as my preferences.'

'Why?'

'Because near either of those hospitals I can get a house with a yard. A proper yard, not a pocket handkerchief courtyard.'

'What do you want with a big yard?'

'It's for the dog.'

'You don't have a dog.'

'I will once I have a yard to put one in,' said Liz. 'Besides, it's time to move out of the area. Mum and Dad have moved now, and who knows where they're going to end up, they certainly don't. Ellen will have to move eventually, Emma and Eddie are both pretty central, and if I get Westmead I'll be closer to Evie.'

'But not to me.'

'This is not about you, Andrew,' Liz said plainly. 'But you know I wouldn't be able to work at the same hospital. I had to try this, I had to at least give it a go. If I am too old and they don't want me, well, I'll have to rethink my options.'

'You won't continue with dermatology?'

'I don't think so.'

'I'm surprised you're still so set against it after what's happened. Surely you see the worth in it now, given you probably just saved your sister's life.'

Liz nodded. 'That's the thing, that's why I can leave it now. All those years plugging away at something I wasn't really committed to, well, if that put me in the right place at the right time to help Emma, then it's all been worthwhile. And now I can walk away.'

Andrew was listening intently.

'You see,' she went on, 'when you invest so much of your life into something, you can get stuck. It doesn't matter if you're not happy or fulfilled anymore, it feels like a waste of all those years if you walk away.' She paused. 'But that's what you have to do if you don't want to waste the rest of your life.'

'You're not just talking about work, are you?' said Andrew. She could see the defeat in his eyes.

Liz reached over and covered his hand with her own, gazing steadily at him. 'I can't do it anymore, Andrew. I might have given you the best years of my life, but I hope not, I hope there's something better for me ahead. I've been more tied down than if I was married to you. It's time for me to get on with my own life.'

He was staring down at her hand on his, and gradually he lifted his head to look at her. His eyes were glassy. 'I know it hasn't been fair on you all this time. I hated that I couldn't give you more.' He shook his head. 'Funny thing is, now the end really is in sight, I reckon maybe only a couple more years.'

Liz sighed. 'Andrew, do you know how many times I've heard that?'

'I do, and I'm sorry. But I just couldn't do it to Jen,' he said. 'Do you know how hard it's been for her? What it would do to her if I . . . ?' He sighed heavily. 'She's a good person, she doesn't deserve it. I couldn't dump her with all this now.'

'I'm not asking you to,' said Liz. 'I wouldn't even want you to. What I want you to realise is that you still love her.'

He hadn't been expecting that. 'No . . . I mean, yes, in a way, but not the way I love you. I feel compassion for her, but I feel passion for you.'

'That's not enough,' she said. 'You need to realise what it means that you've hung in there for your family, and how much they really mean to you. See, I do know how much you love me, Andrew, and I'm sure you know I would have been there for you in a heartbeat. You could have walked away, you could have had it easier, but you stuck with your family. So it's time to give them their due. And their rightful place.'

*

'Where are you guys?' Liz covered her other ear, shouting into her phone as she walked along the street away from the café. Someone was tearing up the footpath with a jackhammer opposite, so she could hardly hear. 'Sorry, can you say that again?'

It turned out that Emma and the others were in a restaurant only about a block away up on King Street. Liz gave up trying to hear anything beyond the name of the place, hung up and hurried out of the street and away from the jackhammer.

When she arrived at the restaurant, only Ellen and Emma were sitting at a table towards the back, and they waved her over.

'I didn't know you'd be here,' Liz said, leaning down to give Ellen a kiss.

'I've put in for long service leave,' she said. 'The boss said I should just stay off. The approval is only a formality, and they already have a casual covering for me.'

'Where's everyone else?' Liz asked as she took a seat.

'Mum and Dad were about to leave for the bank when Blake and I showed up,' Emma explained. 'You know they were due to settle on the apartment next week, when they originally planned to be back from Peru? Anyway, they rang the bank to confirm, and they told them the papers were just sitting there, waiting for their signatures. As soon as they sign, they'll hand them the keys. So Blake drove them straight over to the bank, and I waited for Ellen to arrive, said we'd meet up back here.'

'How much longer do you think they'll be?' said Liz. 'I could really use a drink.'

'We're way ahead of you.' Ellen winked at her.

As if on cue, the waiter arrived at their table and popped the bottle for them.

'Champagne?' Liz remarked.

'Of course,' said Emma, 'what else? We are celebrating after all.'

The waiter filled their glasses and left them again.

Liz held up her glass. 'To you, Emma. What did I say last time we toasted? To a very long life.'

Emma smiled as they clinked glasses and drank.

'I want to propose a toast to my sisters, not forgetting Evie in her absence,' said Emma. 'I wouldn't be here without you all.'

'I think that toast goes to Liz,' said Ellen, clinking glasses with hers.

'So, tell us,' said Emma, 'before Mum and Dad get back, how was lunch with Andrew?'

'That was today?' said Ellen. 'No wonder you need a drink.'

Liz nodded. 'But it went all right,' she said. 'Andrew took it like a grown-up. I think he'd seen it coming for a while now.'

'What about you?' said Emma.

Liz thought about it. 'I feel strangely . . . free, I guess. I've been waiting for so long . . . God, I've spent almost a decade waiting. And now the waiting is over. Not the way I'd hoped, but there's definitely a sense of relief.' She took a sip of her champagne and gave her sisters a rueful smile. 'Okay, we all know I'll probably get drunk and cry into my wineglass later and wonder what on earth I've done . . . but for the moment I feel free.'

'Then here's to living in the moment,' said Emma, raising her glass again.

'I'll drink to that,' said Ellen, following suit. 'Which, I'll remind you, is what you told me I should do.'

Liz raised an eyebrow. 'No, that was a completely different context. We wanted you to live in the moment while you were with Finn, not to dump him.'

'He dumped me.'

'Because you treated him like crap.'

'Says who? Have you been talking to him?'

'No, we never even got to meet him.'

'Because you hid him away like he was some kind of dirty secret,' added Emma.

'Why are we talking about Finn again?' Ellen sighed. 'It's in the past.'

'Ooh, that's right,' Liz muttered. 'It was, like, a whole week ago.'

'Honestly, Ellen,' Emma leaned forward, 'if you'd been through what I've been through, you might see things differently, and you might not be discarding him so lightly.'

'Okay, once and for all, I didn't do the discarding, I was the discardee. And on top of that, I need to know, Em, are you going to become slightly unbearable now because you beat this thing?'

'Yes, I believe I am,' she said with a grin. 'It's just such an amazing feeling. I don't want to take anything for granted, ever again. And I will not put barriers up to stop myself from doing exactly what I want to do.'

'Did you ever?'

'I'm talking about you now, Ellen. Finn sounds like a really nice guy, why are you afraid to let him in?'

Ellen felt something snap inside her. 'Why does everyone keep saying I'm afraid? Look at Liz, we all think she's brave for finally ending things with Andrew. I think it's a lot braver to be on your own rather than hide behind the safety of a marriage or a relationship. I was with Tim forever, and most of that was so stifling I could hardly breathe. I want to find out who I am before I get sucked into the vortex of another relationship and lose myself.'

'It doesn't have to be like that, Ellen,' Emma said carefully. 'Didn't you discover something of yourself being with Finn?'

'I think it's called the G-spot,' Liz whispered.

Ellen groaned, reaching for the bottle.

'Oh, come on,' Liz cajoled. 'I'm only joking around.'

'Yeah, well, the jokes are beginning to wear thin.'

'Okay, we'll drop it now,' said Emma. 'We'll support you whatever you do, Ellen, won't we, Liz?'

'I suppose,' she said begrudgingly. 'At least you and I can start hitting the singles bars together.'

'Look out,' said Ellen, her face relaxing into a smile again.

'Now I have something I want to talk to you about before everyone gets back,' said Emma. 'I have a project in mind and it's going to involve all of us.'

'It is?' said Liz.

'I have to get an endorsement, but I've already been in touch with the Cancer Council, and that shouldn't be a problem. And the only other thing is funding, of course, but with my contacts in the fashion industry, that shouldn't be a problem either.'

'What is it?' asked Ellen.

'I'm going to mount a campaign to make tanning unfashionable.'

'Oh, is that all?' Liz said drolly. 'You realise dermatologists have been trying to do that for decades?'

'But they haven't had me on their side,' said Emma. 'And speaking of dermatologists, you'll be our medical advisor of course, Liz.'

'Okay, but I might not be a dermatologist for much longer,' she said. 'I've applied for a place in a surgical program.'

'You have?' said Ellen. 'That's fantastic.'

'I don't know if I'll get in –'

'Oh you will,' Emma dismissed. 'So you'll just have to be our interim advisor until you find us a replacement.'

Liz smiled. 'Whatever you say, Emma.'

'And I want to launch a program into schools, so that will give you something to do while you're on leave, Ellen.'

'Oh?'

'You don't have to say yes now,' Emma assured her. 'Think about it, and then say yes.'

'You said "all of us". What about Evie?' asked Liz.

'She's going to be my assistant in charge of administration. She showed a real knack when she took care of all the wedding business.'

'So, you've talked to her about this?' said Ellen.

'No, not yet,' said Emma. 'It's a pity she couldn't be here.'

'Where is she anyway?' Liz asked.

'Today's the day,' said Emma. 'Craig's moving to his mother's, but she doesn't want us to say anything to Mum and Dad yet. She's going to tell the kids this afternoon.'

*

'I can't believe you're making Daddy leave!' Tayla cried. 'I hate you, how could you?'

'Tayla, calm down.'

'Well, I'm going with him.'

'No, you're not.'

'Yes I am, you can't stop me,' she said, heading for the door of her bedroom.

'Yes, I can,' Evie said firmly, raising her voice. Tayla wasn't expecting that, and it stopped her in her tracks. 'Now come back here and sit down, shut up and listen to what I have to say.'

Tayla actually did as she was told without a word, obviously thrown by her mother's show of force. Though when she sat on the bed opposite Evie, Tayla set her face in its usual scowl, crossing her arms in front of herself like a shield.

But Evie was not going to be intimidated by her daughter. Ever again.

'Tayla, whatever you're thinking,' she began, 'you are much too young to understand what's going on with Daddy and me, so I'm not going to talk to you about that. What I do want you to understand is that it's very important that we do this, because we want to fix things so that we can stay together. This is just like time-out – remember, when you were little and I used to make you go to your room?'

'You still do it now sometimes,' she grumbled.

Not often enough. 'Sometimes people need a little time out from each other,' Evie went on, 'to calm down, and think about what they've done, and the way they should behave in the future. Sometimes adults need time out too, Tayla, so they can work things out.'

'Why can't *you* go? Why does it have to be Daddy?'

Evie sighed heavily. 'Tayla, all you do is complain when I leave you with your father for even one day,' she said, but she kept her tone level and calm. 'So I know you're saying that just to be mean to me.'

Tayla was caught unawares by that, glancing furtively at her mother, then looking away again, her eyes blinking furiously. Evie decided to use it to her advantage.

'You know what, Tayla, it makes me so sad to say this, because I love you very much, and you're such a beautiful, strong, capable little girl . . .' She paused. 'But you're not a very nice person.'

Now Tayla was clearly shocked. Her mouth dropped open as she stared straight at her mother.

'But that's my fault,' Evie went on. 'I made you this way, because I didn't expect more from you, or more for myself. You see, I've got a problem with trying to be too nice, wanting to make sure everybody likes me, and you know what, that's just as bad. It's a weakness. I let you speak to me very rudely. I let you become selfish, and sometimes even cruel.'

Tayla could not maintain eye contact with Evie any longer, and she dropped her head to stare at her lap.

'But I didn't stop you or correct you enough, or teach you another way. How are you to know any better if your own mother doesn't teach you? You're a child,' Evie said gently. 'So from now on, I'm going to be a better mother. Maybe we'll both have to work together – I need to stop being too nice, you need to be a little nicer. It's going to be hard at first, like learning a new instrument or something. You'll get frustrated, because you'll make mistakes, and sometimes we'll both feel like giving up. But I'm not going to. I love you too much to let you grow up into an unhappy person, Tayla. Because that's what you'll be if we don't do something about it now.'

Evie noticed a tear drop onto the back of Tayla's hand, which was clasped tightly in her lap. Evie got up and sat next to her on the bed.

'And now I'm going to hug you, and you're not going to want me to, but I'm going to anyway. You don't have to hug me back.'

Tayla didn't hug her back, but she didn't push her away either. And they sat that way, together on the bed, for quite some time.

Summer

'Hey, Mum?'

Ellen had started preparing dinner and Kate had wandered into the kitchen and, inevitably, over to the fridge.

'You know how I've been going out with Jordan?' she said, staring into the refrigerator.

'Did I?' said Ellen, looking up from the chopping board, her brain scrambling to remember mention of a Jordan.

'Yeah, I told you about him,' she said. 'You've been pretty preoccupied lately.'

That was true. But she was sure she would have remembered any announcement about a boy . . . Hmm, but it probably hadn't been an announcement as such. Kate had probably tossed his name in with a whole bunch of friends she was going out with. Now this was her way of telling her mother that he stood out from the bunch.

'Go on,' said Ellen as she resumed chopping the carrots.

'So, you know it's the end of semester and we're planning a big night on Thursday. It's going to be huge, and well, it'll probably carry on till, like, four or five in the morning, and Jordan, he lives over the north side, way up, near Hornsby, and anyway, so I was thinking, would it be all right if he just stayed over here?'

'Sure. On the fold-out couch.'

'Seriously, Mum?' she moaned, closing the fridge door and turning to look at her mother, finally. 'I thought you'd be a bit more open-minded.'

Now Ellen turned around to look at her. 'Kate, give me a break. I haven't even met the boy.'

'He's not a boy, Mum.'

'Okay, sorry, the "young man". I haven't met him, I haven't had any time to get used to the idea that there even is a boyfriend. And well, to be honest, I don't know how I feel about the whole sleeping-over thing. And there's also your brother to consider.'

'What's he got to do with it?'

'He lives here too,' Ellen pointed out. 'Look, I know it seems to be the done thing these days, boyfriends and girlfriends sleeping over, but in my day –'

'You were still having sex!' Kate said wide-eyed. 'God, Mum, I'm living proof of that.'

'Exactly,' said Ellen. 'And I don't want you to end up in my situation, not that I'd ever change it.'

'Yeah, yeah, I know the spiel, you wouldn't give me up for anything, blah, blah,' Kate dismissed. 'But Mum, think about it, you were having sex with Dad, it didn't make any difference that you couldn't have it in your bedroom at home. You're being hypocritical.'

'Well that goes both ways.'

Kate frowned. 'What do you mean?'

Ellen sighed, putting the knife down on the chopping board. 'You expect a lot from me when you weren't even prepared to entertain the idea of my seeing someone.'

'When did I ever say that?'

Ellen leaned back against the kitchen bench, crossing her arms. 'When your father started seeing Therése, you said you were glad that everything was out in the open and there were no more secrets.'

'Yeah, so? When did I say I was against you seeing someone?'

Ellen was getting a bit rattled now. She knew that's what Kate had meant at the time. 'It was the context,' she said. 'After your father made such a mess of things, it seemed pretty clear you and Sam didn't want to have to deal with any more changes.'

'Mum, you're reading things into whatever I said back then,' Kate insisted. 'I didn't like all the secrets, but I don't have a problem with you dating.'

'You don't?'

'Why should I?'

'Well, Sam definitely does.'

'And what did he supposedly say to make you think that?' said Kate, pulling out a chair and plonking down on it.

Ellen looked at her. 'He did actually say it would be weird if I started dating.'

'Yeah. He's sixteen, and you're his mother, and he's a boy, of course he's going to think it's weird, and it's going to freak him out probably, but why should you let that stop you?'

'It doesn't seem fair to him.'

'It doesn't seem fair to you either.'

'Well, be that as it may, as the parent, my needs have to come second.'

Kate pulled a face. 'Then remind me never to have kids.'

'It's not forever.'

'So how long are you going to wait? Till he finishes school? University? Moves out? You haven't got that much time, Mum.'

'Hey, it's not like I've got one foot in the grave,' Ellen protested.

Kate shrugged. 'I've heard it gets harder the other side of forty.'

Ellen rolled her eyes. 'Your Aunty Emma said the same thing.' She pulled out a chair for herself opposite Kate. 'I really am starting to feel like I've got one foot in the grave.' She sat down, resting her chin in her hands.

'So you've got to put yourself out there, Mum.'

Ellen groaned. 'Oh, not you too. Now you really sound like your aunties. They haven't let up ever since . . .' She stopped, glancing at her daughter.

Kate looked at her suspiciously. 'What?'

'Nothing . . . I didn't say anything.'

'But you were about to.'

'No I wasn't.'

'*Mu-um!*'

'What?'

'Did something happen?' Kate persisted.

'No . . . maybe . . . kind of.'

She squealed, leaning forward on the table. 'Spill. Who was it?'

Ellen sighed. 'Remember the "cute for an old guy" mechanic who came to the door that day?'

Kate's mouth dropped open. 'You're kidding?'

'You don't approve?'

'What are you talking about, I said he was cute, didn't I?'

Ellen shrugged. 'Anyway, it doesn't matter, it's over now.'

'So there was something?'

'Very briefly,' she admitted. 'I just didn't think it was a good idea to let it go any further, it would get too complicated with you kids.'

'So you used us as an excuse?'

'What? No, I made a decision about what was best for our family . . .'

Kate folded her arms, raising an eyebrow.

'Okay, actually I screwed it up really badly and he dumped me,' said Ellen. 'So that's that.'

'How long ago did this happen?'

'Oh, I don't know, a few weeks, I guess.' Ellen could tell her the exact date, but she wasn't going to.

'So there's still time to apologise.'

'Why do I have to apologise?'

'You just said you were the one who screwed it up,' Kate reminded her. 'Don't you think the least you should do is apologise? I know that's how you brought us up.'

Ellen gave her a look. 'So now you're lecturing me.'

'I'm just saying, Mum, how many decent guys are you going to come across at your age? You're not going to let one go without a fight, are you?'

'Oh, Kate . . . I don't know,' said Ellen. 'I don't think he'd even listen. He was pretty unimpressed with me when he dumped me.'

'Well, yeah, but he might have calmed down by now.'

'What are you suggesting? I can't just show up and . . . What would I even say to him?'

Kate seemed to be thinking about it. 'Start fresh. Ask him out. I know!' she said, her eyes lighting up. 'Tell him you need a partner for something.'

Ellen sat there, contemplating. Not a day had passed that she hadn't thought about Finn. If she actually thought there was a chance . . .

Kate was watching her. 'Do you still like him?'
Ellen looked across at her daughter and nodded slowly.
'So, go for it.'

Evie

'We're finished now, Mum,' Jayden said urgently. 'Can we go play?'

'Please, Mummy?' Cody added.

They had been meeting once a week for a family dinner, initially at home, but since Evie had become so busy she liked to have a night off from cooking. Tonight they'd chosen McDonald's. She and Craig needed to talk, so the kids needed to be occupied.

'Okay, boys,' said Evie. 'But, Jayden, you know the rules. You look after your little brother.'

'I will,' he said, coming around to help Cody as he climbed down out of his chair. 'Come on, Codes,' he said, walking off with his arm around his brother.

Tayla remained in her seat, shrinking a little, in the hope she wouldn't be noticed, Evie suspected.

'Tayla,' she said, 'Daddy and I need to talk. Can you go with the boys, please?'

'Do I have to?'

Evie leaned closer to her daughter. 'I would like you to, just for a while,' she said. 'I'd really appreciate if you'd do that for me without an argument.'

Tayla looked up at her. 'Okay then, Mummy,' she said, sliding off her seat. 'Will you come and get me as soon as you're finished?'

'It's a deal.'

'Wow,' Craig remarked in a low voice as Tayla walked away. 'She's like an actual little human being.'

'She's getting there,' said Evie, watching her go. She looked back at Craig. 'So, I want to go over the schedule with you.'

Emma was proving to be a wonderfully understanding boss. Evie worked entirely around school hours, or from home when she had Cody, though Emma didn't mind her bringing him into the office for a few hours. Evie was loving every minute of it, she felt like a new person – a new, capable, *interesting* person.

'Now that I'm working most days, I'm not getting a chance to fit in much exercise. I'd like to join a gym, so we have to work out what nights you're prepared to come over and cook dinner for the kids.'

'Can't they just come to Mum's?' he said.

Evie looked at him. 'If you want to prove to me why I should have you back, Craig, I want to make sure you can cook for the kids at least one night a week. Besides, you know the counsellor suggested this.'

'Yeah, I know,' he relented. 'What if I promise to cook every night? Can I come back then?'

'Baby steps, Craig, let's just start with this,' said Evie. 'Have you done the homework he suggested last week?'

Craig frowned, thinking.

'Remember, he said we have to think about whether we'd marry each other again if we met now.'

'Oh, yeah, that was easy. I'd marry you in a shot,' said Craig.

'Anything to get away from your mother's, right?' Evie said dryly.

'No,' he protested. 'Well yeah . . . but no, that's not why I'd marry you again.' He paused, looking awkward, and bashful, and kind of cute. 'I love you, Pud. I know I was a dickhead. I thought I was missing out on something, but it's nothing compared to the way I miss you now. I'll do anything, really. I'll cook dinner as many nights as you want. But just give me a little hope?'

Evie considered him. He had been trying really hard, he hadn't even baulked at going to counselling. He had finally managed to explain to the counsellor what had brought on the idea of going to a swingers' club in the first place. He'd been getting a little bored, he admitted, but he wasn't interested in the slightest in straying from Evie, or having an affair. So it seemed like a way they could liven things up together. Yes, it was weird, and it certainly showed a breathtaking lack of judgement. But hearing him tell it had softened Evie towards him.

Counselling had forced her to examine her own role in the decline of their marriage. Just like with the children, Evie had never established boundaries with Craig either. He wasn't a child, it wasn't her job to train him to behave, but she was responsible for how she expected people to treat her. And she hadn't expected much.

This break had been the best thing they could have done, because Evie was beginning to miss Craig, the best part of him, the part that made her laugh, that was dependable and steadfast, the man who had always made her feel safe.

So Evie had hope, but it was going to take time.

'I tell you what, Craig,' she said, 'things keep going the way they are and I might even invite you to Emma's wedding.'

'They've set a date?'

Evie nodded. 'They were waiting until she got the all-clear at her follow-up appointment. They've chosen New Year's Day, which is appropriate, because it's a new start for them.'

'Maybe for all of us?' Craig suggested hopefully.

Elizabeth

'. . . and so we extend a warm welcome to the surgical intake for the new year,' the chief registrar announced from the podium, followed by a polite round of clapping. 'Please take this opportunity to introduce yourselves to the other members of your group, and of course to your supervising senior surgical fellow. You will have noted you were all given colour-coded name tags on your way in, so it shouldn't be too difficult to find each other. Please mingle, have a drink, something to eat, avail yourselves of our hospitality. On behalf of all the surgical staff at the hospital, we are delighted to have you as our guests this evening, and excited that you will be part of our dynamic team.'

After a while, Liz began to think she should remove her name tag. One by one, she had been approached by bright young things, wearing the same purple name tag as she was, introducing themselves with wide-eyed eagerness, desperate to impress, presuming she had to be their supervisor. She was clearly the only one over thirty, and therefore obviously their senior. This was going to be worse than she thought. Eventually she sidled over to the drinks table and picked up a glass of wine. Maybe it was best if she just hid over here in the corner.

'Dr Beckett?'

Liz turned around to see another young, smiling, eager face. 'Hello, it's nice to meet you, but let me just say upfront, I'm not your supervising doctor.'

'No, but I'm yours,' he said with a grin.

Liz blinked, glancing down at his name tag. 'Oh my God, I'm so sorry, Dr Gannon.' She cleared her throat and thrust her hand at him. 'I just . . . it's that . . .'

'It's Nate,' he said, shaking her hand.

'Pardon?'

'You can call me Nate,' he said. 'At least when we're not around patients.'

'Oh, okay,' she replied.

'It is a huge pleasure to meet you finally,' he said. 'And an absolute coup to have you in my group. We fought over you, you know.'

'You did?' she said. 'I didn't think I'd even get in.'

'What are you talking about? Your application was . . . well, it was superior.'

Liz could feel herself blushing.

'It'll be great to have someone with experience in the group, I'm pretty new to this teaching gig.'

Liz nodded, starting to relax. He seemed so . . . *nice*. 'Hm, well, I feel like housemother,' she said.

He laughed at that.

'Oh, you needn't laugh. I feel like housemother to all of you.'

'What?' He frowned. 'No way. I have this stupid baby face. I'm actually thirty-two.'

She sighed. 'And you'd know from my application that still makes me older than you.'

'Barely,' he said. 'Certainly not old enough to be my mother.'

He was smiling at her. He had a lovely smile, and his eyes crinkled at the corners, eyes that were a bright blue . . .

'Your publishing record is impressive as well,' he was saying. 'Surgeons don't tend to think about research, but they're expecting it from everyone these days. Maybe we could collaborate on something down the track?'

Really bright blue. Oh, this could be dangerous.

'Can I ask you a personal question?' said Liz.

'Sure. I guess.'

'Are you married?'

He looked a little taken aback.

'I'm sorry,' she said. 'There's a history, I have to ask, it's a phobia . . . oh God, shoot me now.' She closed her eyes, wincing, but when she opened them again, he was smiling that lovely smile at her.

'I'm not married . . . Elizabeth,' he said. 'May I call you Elizabeth?'

'Oh sure, you can call me whatever you like,' she said. 'Though mostly I get Liz.'

'Okay, Liz. What do you say we go face the young 'uns?' He touched her elbow.

'Lead the way.'

As they made their way through the crowd, his hand still cupping her elbow, Liz turned to him. 'Hey, are you doing anything New Year's Day?'

Ellen

Ellen cut the engine, but then she just sat there, not moving. Well, she was moving a little – her legs were shaking. It was one thing to drive over here, quite another to get out and go speak to the man. She thought about driving away again, but what if he'd seen the car? She dared to turn her head and peer over towards the garage and the office. She couldn't see anyone, any movement. It was Friday afternoon, she'd left it late so there was unlikely to be anyone else around. She'd nearly left it too late, realising at the last minute that he might have closed up, then racing over here, barely keeping to the speed limit, cursing every red light and honking impatiently at cars that got in her way.

And now she was here, wishing she'd never come. But she had to do this, if only to get everyone off her back. She would finally be able to say to her sisters, and now Kate as well, that she had gone to talk to Finn and, as she suspected, it was well and truly over. The end. Of course, then she was going to have to put up with their exhortations to 'put herself out there' all over again. But one thing at a time.

What she hadn't admitted to them, and barely to herself, was that she wanted to see Finn again. She really did. She wanted to see if there was any chance, so she was using her sisters' goading to motivate her. She had missed him, more than she was prepared to admit to anyone.

So Ellen forced herself to open the car door and step unsteadily onto the tarmac. She closed the door again, took a deep breath and turned around. Her heart was thumping in her chest as she looked over towards the office and the garage, expecting Finn to appear at any minute. But he didn't. There was music blaring out from the garage, and as she walked, slowly, tentatively closer, she saw a pair of legs, well, half a body leaning over the engine of a car, the top half obscured by the bonnet.

It was probably Dave. Ellen didn't know what to do. The music was very loud, no one would have heard her approach. She should walk over to the office, check if Finn was in there. As she drew closer, she could see through the glass that it was empty. Maybe Finn wasn't even here? Ellen glanced over towards the garage and, from this vantage point, she could tell it was the top of Finn's head leaning over the engine. It wasn't Dave, Dave was blond. She quickly stepped back out of sight, blocked now by the body of the car. Ellen stood there, breathing hard. This was getting ridiculous. She had to go through with it. She walked, as though on eggshells, right up to the back of the car and cleared her throat.

'Excuse me . . . Finn,' she said, but her voice was drowned out by the music. Ellen contemplated her approach. She didn't want to come up behind him and risk startling him. She could imagine him jerking his head up suddenly, hitting it on the underside of the hood, like a scene from a bad slapstick comedy. So she walked tentatively along the opposite side of the car. That way he would see her at the same time that she got his attention.

'Finn?' she said in a loud voice.

He jerked his head up suddenly, hitting it on the underside of the hood.

'Ow,' he said, wincing and rubbing his head as he stepped back from the car and straightened up.

'I'm sorry,' Ellen said loudly over the music, 'I was trying not to startle you.'

'That was never going to happen,' he said. Or at least that's what she thought he said.

He walked over to a bench by the wall and flicked off a console. The music reverberated in her ears for a moment. And then there was silence. Finn strolled slowly back over to the car, and leaned one elbow on the roof. His expression was wary, perhaps suspicious. She'd go with wary.

'What are you doing here, Ellen?' he said finally. 'Car troubles?'

'No,' she replied.

He raised his eyebrows then, waiting.

Oh God. She felt stupid. 'Well, I, um, well, I came by, um, well, to ask you something.'

'Oh?' He seemed curious, at least. That was something.

'What did you want to ask me?' he prompted when she didn't say anything.

She really felt stupid now. This was a bad idea.

'Ellen?'

Just go ahead. Ask him. Make a fool of yourself.

'Well, I wanted to ask you . . . if you want to come to a wedding with me.'

'What?'

She took a breath. 'Emma, you know, my sister? Well, she's been cleared by the doctors, so the wedding's back on. It's New Year's Day.'

She couldn't decipher the expression on his face.

'And you want me to come with you?'

'I'd like you to come with me,' she said. 'If you want.'

He seemed to be thinking about that. 'Who's going to be there?' he asked eventually.

Interesting question. Ellen leaned against the car, looking at him directly over the roof. 'My kids, my parents, my sisters, my brother.'

He nodded. 'And how would you introduce me?'

'Oh, as my mechanic, of course,' she quipped, but his face was stony. 'Just trying to break the ice, make a joke.'

'Not a very funny one.'

Ellen sighed. 'No, it wasn't,' she said seriously. 'I'm sorry, Finn. I'm sorry for everything. I'm sorry for the way I treated you, it was inexcusable,' she blurted out all at once. 'Well, maybe not so much inexcusable, because what I want to say to you is that I . . . I didn't know what I was doing. I haven't dated for so long, since I was a teenager. I stuffed it up and I'm sorry. I took you for granted, and I was obnoxious, and rude, and inconsiderate of your feelings . . . and . . .' She paused, looking at him. 'You can jump in here any time.'

'No, you're doing great, don't let me interrupt.'

'What else do you want me to say?' she said plaintively. 'I said I was sorry, and I didn't know what I was doing. I mean, think about it from my perspective. I was going through such a hard time, and then my car breaks down, and it's towed here, and I meet you, and really, how weird is that? We never would have met otherwise, let alone . . . you know, and that was . . . overwhelming . . . and how was I supposed to deal with all that?'

His face finally cracked a smile.

'What?' she said in a small voice.

'I've told you before, you think too much.'

Ellen breathed out as Finn walked towards the back of the car. She followed on her side, watching him. Then they were standing, facing each other, at the back of the car. He shoved his hands in the pockets of his overalls and turned to lean back against the boot.

'So what happens after the wedding?' he said.

'Hm?'

'After your sister's wedding, what then?'

'They live happily ever after, I suppose.'

He looked at her. 'I'm not talking about them . . . I'm talking about us.'

He said 'us'. Ellen took a step closer and turned and leaned back against the boot, next to him.

'You know,' she said, 'you think about things too much, Finn. Why does everything have to be so complicated, why can't you let things just unfold?'

She looked sideways at him. He was shaking his head, but he was smiling.

'Do you want a beer?' he asked her.

She smiled back at him. 'Do you have any lemon?'

New Year's Day

Emma was waiting for her sisters. They better not take too much longer – a bride missing from her own wedding reception was a tad conspicuous.

Just then the door burst open and all three of them spilled into the room, talking over the top of each other.

'Sorry, Em.'

'I couldn't get away from –'

'Have you been waiting long?'

'No, it's fine,' she said. 'But I think I might be missed if I don't get back soon.'

Ellen was shaking her head in admiration. 'You're such a beautiful bride, Em.'

'Why, thank you.' She gave a little curtsy. 'And you three scrubbed up all right yourselves. I can't get over how the champagne suited everyone so well.'

'Are you enjoying yourself?' Liz asked her.

'I am.' She was beaming. 'It's better than even I imagined, and you know how long this has been cooking in my imagination.' She clapped her hands together. 'But listen, we don't have much time. So, what do we think? What's the consensus?'

They all drew closer in a huddle.

'She's very attractive,' said Evie.

'Looks aren't everything,' said Emma.

'I'm just glad he found someone sensible,' said Ellen.

'Being a lawyer doesn't necessarily make her sensible,' said Liz.

'She works for a charitable foundation!' said Evie.

'I had a good talk to her,' said Ellen. 'She's definitely got her head screwed on right.'

'And most importantly, Eddie seems happy,' said Liz.

Emma smiled. 'So we like her?'

They all nodded.

'Why'd he have to fall for an Eliza?' said Emma. 'Another E?'

'At least she fits in,' said Liz.

'They do make a handsome couple,' said Ellen.

'Speaking of handsome,' said Emma, 'your doctor's very easy on the eye, Liz.'

'He's not my doctor.'

'I should hope not, that'd be weird, and awkward, having your boyfriend as your doctor.'

'He's not my boyfriend either,' Liz insisted. 'It's not serious, I'm trying to keep my head here. I've only just got out of a very long-term relationship, let's not forget.'

'All right, all right,' said Emma.

'He does seem nice, though,' said Evie.

'Very nice,' Ellen agreed. 'How old is he?'

Liz winced. 'You can tell, can't you?'

Ellen frowned. 'Tell what?'

'That he's younger than me.'

'I thought he looked about the same age.'

'Then why did you ask?'

'Wow, Liz,' said Emma. 'How much younger is he?'

'A couple of years, well, not quite, it's about twenty months, almost.'

'That hardly makes you a cougar,' Emma said drily.

'But he's my boss as well.'

'At least he's not married . . . is he?'

'Of course not, do you think I'm going to make that mistake again?'

There was a knock at the door and they all jumped.

Emma cleared her throat. 'Come in.'

The door opened and Tayla popped her head around. 'Excuse me, Mummy, Uncle Blake asked if I could find his wife for him, please.'

'That's me!' Emma exclaimed happily. 'I'm Blake's wife. Oh I love the sound of that.'

Tayla grinned at her aunt.

'Would you please tell my *husband* we'll be along in a moment, thank you, Tayla.'

'Okay, Aunty Emma.'

'She has been an absolute delight, Evie,' Emma said as Tayla closed the door again. 'You should be very proud of her.'

Evie smiled. 'I am.'

'And what about you and Craig,' said Liz, giving her a nudge. 'You looked like a couple of teenagers out on the dance floor.'

'Things are going well,' she said.

'So you are getting back together?' asked Ellen.

'We will, but I'm not in any hurry. I'm having too much fun.' Evie dropped her voice. 'And the sex has never been better.'

They all laughed.

'Okay, that's the end of the briefing,' said Emma. 'I best be getting back to my husband.'

Evie and Liz linked arms with Emma and they headed for the door.

'Guys . . .' Ellen said plaintively.

They turned around.

'Oh, I suppose you want to know what we think of the mechanic?' said Emma.

'Don't call him that.'

'But he is a mechanic,' said Liz. 'He's going to service my car.'

'And mine,' said Emma.

Ellen's face dropped. 'You haven't been talking to him about cars the whole time, have you?'

'Stop teasing her, you two,' said Evie, coming to Ellen's side. 'Finn is gorgeous, Lenny, I really like him.'

'Second that.'

'Third that.'

'You do?' she said. 'Really?'

'Yes, really,' Liz insisted. 'What's not to like?'

'And the way he looks at you . . .' said Emma.

'Hm, I noticed that,' said Evie.

'I don't know . . .' Ellen stood wringing her hands, her forehead all creased. 'I'm falling so hard.'

'So, what's the problem?' asked Liz. 'Enjoy the ride.'

'Don't you think it's too soon?'

'It's nearly a year since you separated,' Evie reminded her.

'But he's the first man since . . . you know, maybe I should see what's out there . . .'

'First we couldn't get her out there,' Emma muttered.

'I'm just worried I'm rushing into this. I mean, Finn's wonderful, we get on so well, I've never felt this way . . . But maybe it's infatuation, and I'm not seeing things clearly. I can't be this lucky.'

'I thought you were working on that whole glass half-empty thing?' said Liz, raising an eyebrow.

Emma stepped forward and took Ellen's hands in hers. 'Ellen, I was lucky that Liz was at the fitting that day, when I think about what could have happened . . .' She paused. 'Yes, it was luck that your car was towed to Finn's garage, but that doesn't mean it shouldn't have happened, or that it wasn't meant to be. Quite the opposite. I know you're scared. I'm scared too, scared it will come back, that I won't be so lucky next time. But I'm not going to let that stop me now. You shouldn't either.'

Evie sniffed, and they looked at her as tears filled her eyes.

'Oh, Evie,' said Ellen, putting her arm around her. 'You're always so emotional.'

'There's only one thing for it,' said Emma. 'Cake. Let's all go have a nice big piece of my wedding cake.'

Evie gave her stomach a pat. 'Gosh, I don't really eat cake anymore.'

'Well, you're going to eat this – I had them do a whole layer of chocolate fudge cake just for you,' said Emma, linking her arm through Evie's. Liz opened the door, and the four of them walked out of the room.

Acknowledgements

I'm so glad this book has actually made it into your hands – it was touch and go for a while there. You see, I rather boldly booked a holiday a couple of months before my deadline, and no sooner was that confirmed than I was offered a spot as guest author on a Pacific cruise, due to leave six days after my return from the first holiday. But it was an offer I couldn't refuse, so I decided I would just have to write while I was on the cruise.

Therefore, I must acknowledge Gabbi, Anna, Andrew, Zac, Alicia, Sarah, Nathan and a host of others who made it impossible for me to spend any time at all working in peace in my cabin. It is certainly no thanks to them that this book is finally in print! (But thank you all for a great holiday!)

As you may imagine, a stressful few months followed, and so I'm grateful to my boys, Zac, Pat, Dane and Joel for their long-suffering love and support. And also sincere thanks to Diane, Desley and Elizabeth, who put up with more than their fair share of whingeing.

At times like these I'm lucky to have a phenomenal publisher, Cate Paterson, an exceptional editor, Julia Stiles, and the support of the most marvellous Louise Bourke, who takes such care pulling everything together and keeping it on track, despite my tardiness.

Finally I want to take this opportunity to specially thank the absolutely fabulous Jane Novak, who has been my publicist since the beginning, but has lately moved on to bigger and better things.

Jane has boundless energy and good humour in any situation, and never made me feel that traipsing around with me was just her job. I'm going to miss her.

Wishing you all the very best for a wonderful future, Jane.

More Titles from Dianne Blacklock

About Call Waiting

Of course Meg was a success: she planned, she set goals, she made lists. Ally never made lists.

Ally Tasker is trapped in a dead-end teaching job and a relationship that's going nowhere. Her college friend Meg has a fabulous job in advertising, a doting husband and a gorgeous baby boy. Why did Ally's life seem to be permanently on hold?

When her grandfather and sole relative dies, Ally has to return to the Southern Highlands. As she sets to restoring the rundown home of her childhood, the past unravels, and Ally realises the choice to be happy has been in her hands all along.

Meanwhile Meg's life is not as idyllic as Ally imagines. She longs to inject more passion and spontaneity into her life, but at what cost to her career, and more importantly, to the people she loves most in the world?

Sometimes you have to risk all you have to realise what is worth saving.

Find out more at: books2read.com/callwaiting

About Wife for Hire

When she was a little girl, all Samantha Driscoll ever wanted was to be somebody's wife. She would marry a man called Tod or Brad and she would have two perfect children. But instead she married a Jeff and he's just confessed to having an affair.

Desperate times indeed. Sam has to find a way to support her kids and keep her dream house, but she has no qualifications, having given up any career aspirations she might have had to become the consummate wife. So much for that. Then she finds the job she was born for: Wife for Hire - a service offering everything from domestic help to personal shopping to planning social events for people who don't have the time - people who need a wife.

Surrounded by a gaggle of girlfriends, an eccentric sister, a mother who brings whole new meaning to the word 'demanding', and two teenagers discovering their dad has hormones too, Sam successfully manages a cast of clients from the sublime to the ridiculous, including American businessman Hal Buchanan, who insists he doesn't need her services even if they are part of his executive package. If that's the case, why does he keep hanging around?

Sam may be a born organiser, but there are some things in life that do not go to schedule.

Find out more at: books2read.com/wifeforhire

About Almost Perfect

It's no big deal to love someone who's perfect ... The trick is to love someone despite the fact they're not.

With a beautiful house in an upscale Sydney suburb and two successful careers, anyone would think that Mac and Anna have the perfect life. But their marriage is cracking under the strain of infertility. Consumed by her dream of having a child, Anna cannot see how her pain and disappointment are driving Mac away.

Close by, in a beachside suburb, Georgie Reading and her sister-in-law have made their bookstore, The Reading Rooms, an unqualified success - unlike Georgie's love life. In her thirties, with a deadbeat roommate and no romantic prospects in sight, her beloved brother Nick suggests that maybe she's waiting for someone she was never going to find - the mythical perfect man.

Then Liam walks into the bookstore, and Georgie thinks she has finally found just that. Well, he's perfect for her, anyway. ... At the same time Mac and Anna reach breaking point, putting Mac on a path that will have unforeseen consequences for them all.

Find out more at: books2read.com/almostperfectblacklock

About False Advertising

Helen and Gemma, two women who couldn't be more different, are thrown together when their lives take an unexpected turn.

Helen always tries to be a good person - she recycles, she is even polite to telemarketers. As a mother, wife, daughter and nurse, Helen is used to putting everyone's needs before her own. But it only takes one momentary lapse of concentration to shatter her life forever.

There was no such momentary lapse for Gemma, she had never done anything by halves, and she had certainly never been quiet about it. So when she barges unceremoniously into Helen's life - pregnant, alone, estranged from her family, with a once-promising career in advertising in tatters - things will never be the same again for either of them.

FALSE ADVERTISING is about loss and grief and second chances, it's about knowing when to hang on, and knowing when to move on. And it's about realising that when life falls short of our expectations, it was all just false advertising anyway.

Find out more at: books2read.com/falseadvertising

About Crossing Paths

Jo had learned the hard way that life was not mystical, or magical; it was hard and grey and cold most of the time. Much better to see it for what it is than to be perennially disappointed.

It's not as though Jo Liddell never had dreams. She was going to be a journalist and travel the world, but life had a way of stealing her dreams right out from under her. Okay, she had her column, but heaven forbid she had an opinion about anything that mattered. And now that she's saddled herself with a hefty mortgage, Jo has resigned herself to living a less-than-perfect life.

That is, until she crosses paths with Joe Bannister - a celebrated foreign correspondent, returning home to care for his dying father, take the pressure off his long-suffering sister and maybe pull his recalcitrant brother into line. He did not expect to find himself falling for a headstrong woman who seems to resent him.

But after devastating news, Joe is forced to make an impossible choice, and Jo must fight hard for everything she never believed in - success, self-acceptance, and above all, real love.

Find out more at: books2read.com/crossingpaths

About Three's a Crowd

'Well, we're different, we lead such different lives. I'm not sure how we'll go now without Annie. She was like Carrie, you know, in Sex and the City. Annie was our Carrie.'

Without Annie, friends Catherine, Lexie and Rachel are lost. How will they fill the void? Will their friendship survive?

Catherine is characteristically unfazed, forging ahead in her high-flying career while struggling to connect to her unfathomable teenage daughter. But secrets from the past emerge to shatter her carefully constructed image, and threaten all the relationships she holds dear.

Meanwhile Lexie is juggling the demands of her young family and the ego of her hardworking husband, while taking the first tentative steps to achieving her own dreams. She just wished Annie was around to talk to - Catherine is so bossy, and Rachel ... well, her head seems be more in the clouds now than ever.

Rachel knows what her friends think of her - but what they don't know is that she's currently in the thrall of a new relationship. And she doesn't want them to know, because when the truth comes out, fragile friendships will be put to the test all over again ...

Find out more at: books2read.com/threesacrowd

About The Secret Ingredient

'Taste was such an evocative sense; Andie had closed her eyes, with the scone melting in her mouth, and been transported back to her grandmother's kitchen …'

Nourishment is nurture. That's what Andie learned from her grandmother and what she's always believed, but somehow, since marrying Ross, she's allowed her love of cooking to take a back seat and given up her dream of becoming a chef.

Lately she's been craving more. And as her marriage implodes, deception, betrayal and tragedy lead Andie all the way back to what really matters to her. The new Andie is ready for anything, even a bad-tempered chef who makes it clear he won't tolerate mistakes.

With help from the unlikeliest of allies, Andie uncovers the secret ingredient for a new life, and shows that no matter how many false starts, if you hold on to your passion and your dreams, anything is possible.

Find out more at: books2read.com/thesecretingredient

About The Best Man

Is the best man always the right man?

With American fiancé, Henry Darrow, publicist Madeleine has at last found the yin to her yang - or whichever way round it is. The calm to her storm, the stillness to her constant motion. Balance.

Her boss, Liv, had to be talked into marriage, which predictably ended in divorce. Liv knows that she and her twins are better off on their own anyway. She just wished everyone would stop telling her to 'put herself out there', whatever that's supposed to mean.

However, when Henry's best man arrives from the US to meet Madeleine for the first time, and Liv has a spontaneous chat with a stranger, the settled lives these women thought they had finally achieved are thrown into chaos. Secrets are unravelled and new doors are opened.

May the best man win.

Find out more at: books2read.com/thebestman